House Witness

Praise for Mike Lawson and the Joe DeMarco Thrillers

"M   e Lawson . . . should be a fixture on the bestseller lists, if not a
   :hold name . . . [he] is the only writer I know who comes close
atching the stories of the great Ross Thomas, the finest thriller
r to ever roll a blank page into an Underwood."
—*Strand Magazine*

vson's] work is a potent combination of high good humor, deft
:, and insider smarts." —*Seattle Times*

: nice thing about Mike Lawson's Washington thrillers is that
dy is high-minded. Certainly not John Fitzpatrick Mahoney,
ker of the House ('and God help the country') and as unscrupu-
a politician as you'd hope to find outside a federal prison cell.
could you pin that high-and-holy tag on Mahoney's go-to guy,
DeMarco, who holes up in a subbasement office of the Capitol
ling and surfaces only when the speaker has some dirty business
needs to be done." —*New York Times*

/son has a true insider's insight about real-world spinelessness,
lity, and corruption that have taken the place of moral courage
true leadership on Capitol Hill . . . a fine ear for dialogue . . .
¡ a good eye for irony." —*Washington Times*

ke Lawson shows every understanding of the skill required of a
!er writer to keep a reader fully engaged and utterly thrilled."
—*Guardian* (UK)

DeMarco, 'fixer' for Speaker of the House John Fitzpatrick Ma-
ey, is shrewd, tough, discreet, and resourceful . . . Lawson creates
.tifaceted characters . . . [and] the pacing is relentless."
—*Booklist*

"Lawson wr   lumor that
hurts."   ndent (UK)

000000003011071

House Witness

Mike Lawson

Grove Press
New York

Published simultaneously in Canada
Printed in the United States of America

First Grove Atlantic hardcover edition: February 2018
First Grove Atlantic paperback edition: February 2019

This book was set in 12 pt Garamond Premier Pro
by Alpha Design & Composition of Pittsfield, NH

Library of Congress Cataloging-in-Publication data available for this title.

ISBN 978-0-8021-2931-4
eISBN 978-0-8021-6560-2

Grove Press
an imprint of Grove Atlantic
154 West 14th Street
New York, NY 10011

Distributed by Publishers Group West

groveatlantic.com

19 20 21 22   10 9 8 7 6 5 4 3 2 1

For all the caretakers. My wife, Gail, took care of an elderly neighbor, Betty Ash, for about the last twenty years until Betty died at the age of ninety-eight. I know that there are a lot of people out there like my wife who simply always do the right thing when it comes to others—they just can't help themselves—and my hat is off to all of them.

House Witness

Prologue

Mahoney disconnected the call, then just stood there staring out the window.

From his apartment in the Watergate complex, he could see a portion of the Kennedy Center, the broad black ribbon that was the Potomac River, and the lights of Northern Virginia. Had it been daylight, he would have been able to see some of the white headstones in Arlington National Cemetery, a view, that when he was in his cups, often brought tears to his eyes.

Tonight there were tears in his eyes, but not because he'd been contemplating the final resting place of so many valiant Americans. The tears had welled up after the call he'd received.

His wife said, "John, is something wrong? Who was that?"

Mary Pat could tell the call had stunned him, but he couldn't tell her why. No way could he tell her why.

He wiped a big hand across his face to brush away the tears, and finally turned to face her. She was standing in the living room doorway, in a robe. She'd been about to go to bed when he'd received the call. Her face was scrubbed free of makeup, and he thought: Geez, she looks old. But then, if Mary Pat—who, unlike himself, didn't drink or smoke and exercised daily—looked old, he knew he must look like the walking dead. He supposed it was the call that had made him think about what little time they both had left on this capricious planet.

He said, "I gotta . . . I gotta go out for a bit."

"At this time of night?"

It was almost midnight.

"Yeah, I need to . . ."

He didn't finish the sentence. He couldn't tell her that it felt as if the walls were closing in on him. He needed air. He couldn't breathe. And he was afraid he might burst into tears—and then he wouldn't be able to explain to her why.

He headed for the door, and Mary Pat said, "I hope you're not planning to drive anywhere. You're in no shape to be driving."

That was probably true. He'd been drinking since he got home from work, but he always drank when he got home from work—and usually drank while he was at work. He was an alcoholic. But he wasn't planning to drive. He just needed to be alone.

He said, "I'm not driving. I just need some fresh air."

"John, what's wrong?"

"I'll tell you tomorrow. Go to bed."

Now he was going to have to make up something to tell her. He didn't know what; he'd figure it out later. He opened the door, and she said, "John! Put on a coat. You'll freeze out there."

She was right. It was March. It wasn't raining at the moment, but the temperature was in the low forties, and he was wearing only the suit pants he'd worn to work and a white dress shirt. He grabbed a trench coat off a hook near the door and shrugged it on. Mary Pat was saying something as he closed the door, but the words couldn't penetrate the fog surrounding his brain.

John Mahoney had just been told that his son had been killed—and his wife didn't know that he had a son.

Mahoney stepped outside the building and started walking in the direction of the Lincoln Memorial, a couple of miles away. The wind whipped the trench coat around his legs and stung his cheeks, but he didn't notice.

Mahoney was a handsome, heavyset man, broad across the back and butt. His most distinctive features were sky blue eyes and a full head of snow white hair. When he appeared on camera, he had the makeup lady cover the broken veins in his nose.

He was currently the minority leader of the United States House of Representatives. He'd been the Speaker of the House for more than a dozen years, then lost the position when the Republicans took control, but he was still the most powerful Democrat on Capitol Hill. When he'd had the affair with Connie DiNunzio, he'd been in Congress for only three years.

Connie, like him, grew fat as the years passed, but when he met her she was . . . hell, she'd looked like Sophia Loren: thick dark hair, a long straight nose, full lips, heavy breasts, shapely legs. She'd been an absolute knockout—and Mahoney was a man who rarely met a temptation he was able to resist. Connie was neither the first nor the last affair he'd had—he'd had a lot of affairs over the years—but she was the only one to bear him a child. Connie DiNunzio wasn't too Catholic to sleep with a married man, but she was too Catholic to get an abortion.

When she'd told him she was pregnant and that he was the father, he'd had no doubt she was telling the truth. He also figured that if she had the kid it could be the end of his fledgling political career. But Connie never told anyone. She'd been an aide to a New York congressman when they met and she quit the job, went back to New York, and had the child. And she never asked anything of Mahoney—at least not for herself or her son. She did ask for a favor later—and Mahoney was still paying back that favor.

Anyway, time went on. Connie married a guy she later divorced and ended up becoming a career bureaucrat in Albany and a major player in the backstabbing, bare-knuckles world of New York state politics. As for the kid, he went on to college, got married, had three kids, and started his own accounting firm in Manhattan. Mahoney had kept tabs on his illegitimate son—but he'd never met him.

The call he'd gotten had been from Connie. She'd told him that her boy—*their* boy—had been shot and killed in a bar in Manhattan. She wasn't crying when she called. She didn't intend to share her grief; she'd called because she wanted vengeance. She told him that the man who'd killed her son was the son of a rich guy, a guy rich enough to buy his way out of anything. She said, her voice as cold and hard as ice, "You make sure this little prick gets what's coming to him, John. Dominic was the father of the grandkids you never met, and you damn well better do everything in your power to make sure that the man who killed him pays for what he did."

Mahoney had three daughters, but none of them were currently married and none of them had given him and Mary Pat grandkids. As Connie had said, the only grandchildren he had were as much strangers to him as their father had been.

Mahoney sat down on a bench and thought for a time about all the mistakes he'd made in his long life. He thought about his son's wife and his grandchildren, and made a promise to do whatever it took to make sure they were financially okay. Regarding what Connie had told him—how he'd better make sure the killer went to prison—he could think of only one thing to do immediately.

He took out his cell phone. The face of the iPhone informed him that it was now one a.m.—and Mahoney didn't give a shit. He called a man who worked for him. A guy named DeMarco.

He woke DeMarco up. After DeMarco said a sleepy hello, Mahoney said, "Dominic DiNunzio was killed this evening in Manhattan. Get your ass up there and find out what's happening with the case."

DeMarco said, "What? Dominic? Dominic was killed?"

DeMarco knew Dominic DiNunzio. He just didn't know he was Mahoney's bastard.

———————◆◆◆———————

Connie DiNunzio happened to be Joe DeMarco's godmother because Connie was DeMarco's mother's best friend. Connie DiNunzio was also the only reason that DeMarco had a job working for John Mahoney.

The way it all came about was that DeMarco's Irish mother had had the misfortune to fall in love with a man who worked for the old Italian mob in Queens. DeMarco's dad had been a mob enforcer. A killer.

When Gino DeMarco was killed, young Joe DeMarco—who was a few years younger than Connie's son—had just graduated from law school and couldn't find a job, as no law firm on the eastern seaboard wanted the son of a Mafia hit man on its payroll. And that's when Connie had called Mahoney and asked for the only favor she'd ever asked. And actually she didn't *ask* for the favor—she demanded it. She told Mahoney, who at that time was the Speaker, to give young Joe a job. If he didn't give young Joe a job, well then, Connie might . . . Mahoney hired young Joe.

Over the years, DeMarco had become Mahoney's go-to guy when Mahoney had problems he couldn't or didn't want to solve by going through normal channels. He was also Mahoney's bagman—the one he sent to collect contributions some nitpickers might construe as bribes. DeMarco was smart enough—and ethically bent enough—to do the job well, but he was also lazy. He was a guy who would rather play golf than work, and Mahoney knew he was just marking time, doing as little as he could until he could collect a federal pension. That is, he'd collect one if he didn't get indicted and go to jail first. One thing about

DeMarco, though, and even Mahoney had to admit this, was that if he had a personal stake in an assignment he could be as determined and devious as he had to be to get results. And this time Mahoney knew it would be personal for DeMarco, because he loved Connie DiNunzio and had known her son.

DeMarco called Mahoney from New York the next day and said, "There's no doubt whatsoever that the guy who killed Dominic is going to be convicted of second-degree murder. The case is a slam dunk for the prosecutor."

DeMarco was dead wrong.

Part I

1

Manhattan—March 15, 2016
The night Dominic DiNunzio died

Toby Rosenthal couldn't remember killing Dominic DiNunzio.

He remembered what happened before he killed him, and he knew what he did afterward, but the killing itself . . .

He'd been drinking all afternoon. Actually, he'd been drinking for the last three days, ever since Lauren dumped him. He'd also been snorting coke—he'd bought an 8 ball off a guy he knew—which was why he'd hardly slept in three days, too. He stopped by McGill's because it was close to Lauren's office and she often went there with some of the girls she worked with. Since she wouldn't answer her doorbell or her phone, he didn't know what else to do.

He ordered a scotch, slammed it down like a tequila shooter, then ordered another that he drank more slowly. He never saw Dominic DiNunzio lumber into the bar and take a seat. Fifteen minutes later Lauren hadn't shown up, and Toby was trying to decide if he should check out some of the other bars near her office, or go to her apartment and ring the bell again. He decided to wait a bit longer—and have one more scotch. He waved at the bartender, but the guy just stood there, looking at him, scowling. Finally, reluctantly, he walked over like he was doing Toby a fuckin' favor.

"Another Glenfi . . ." It was hard to say Glenfiddich sober, let alone drunk. "Another one, same thing."

"You don't think maybe you've had enough," the bartender said.

"Hey, what are you? My mother?"

As soon as the words left his mouth, Toby knew he shouldn't have said them. The bartender was a tall guy, skinny but with a paunch, like a martini olive in the middle of a swizzle stick. He was in his sixties, maybe seventies, but his hair was jet black. The hair had to be dyed, and it looked ridiculous with his seamed old face. But Toby could tell, the way the bartender's mouth was set, that he was going to eighty-six him from the bar.

Toby pulled a hundred off his money clip—money was the least of his worries—and slapped it on the bar. "That's for the drinks I've already had and the one more I'm gonna have. The rest is for you."

"Yes, sir, another Glen," the bartender said. He didn't say "Thank you"; it was like he thought he *deserved* a forty-buck tip.

Toby caught sight of his reflection in the mirror behind the bar and realized he looked like shit: unshaven, his eyes like glowing embers in his pale face, his hair all wet and matted down from the rain outside. The last thing he needed was Lauren seeing him like this. He could at least go comb his hair, splash some water on his face; he wished he had some Visine to squirt into his eyes. He stepped off the bar stool, stumbled, and almost fell—and noticed the bartender, who was now pouring his scotch, give him a look. Fuck him.

He walked back toward the restrooms, bumping into a table where two old ladies were sitting. One of the women lost half her drink and let out a little shriek. "Shit, sorry," he muttered.

The restrooms were down a long, narrow hallway, and he could feel himself lurching from side to side, like he was walking along the passageway of a rolling ship. Maybe he should just call it a day and go home. He pulled open the men's room door, and at the same time a guy came through the opening, and they collided.

The guy was a whale. Toby was only five foot seven, so most men were taller than he was—but this guy had to be at least six four and with a gut on him like a potbellied stove. He was wearing a tan trench coat and one of those flat skimmer hats, and his coat was dripping water as if he'd walked miles in the rain. Before Toby could apologize for bumping into him, the guy said, "Watch where the hell you're going."

"Hey! Who the fuck you think you're talking to?" Toby said, taking an aggressive step toward the man as he spoke. Not something he normally would have done with a guy this size, but he'd had a lot to drink and his life sucked and he wasn't in the mood for taking shit off anyone.

It should have ended right there: two New Yorkers trading *fuck yous*, two urban gorillas pounding their chests, then going harmlessly on their way. But it didn't end there.

The man put a hand the size of a catcher's mitt on Toby's chest and pushed.

He actually didn't push that hard—he was mainly moving Toby out of his way—but Toby was having a hard time maintaining his balance as it was, and he bounced off the wall opposite the restroom door and fell to the floor. Then Dominic DiNunzio sealed his fate. Looking down at Toby, he said, "Today's not the day to screw with me, you little shit."

Dominic DiNunzio wasn't a bad guy. All his friends would later tell this to the media and the cops. He looked big enough to have played for the Jets, but he wasn't a violent man. He hadn't been in a fistfight since he was eight. The problem was, as he'd told Toby, today was the wrong day to screw with him.

Dominic was an accountant, and he used a program that had cost him ten grand to prepare his clients' tax returns. That morning he found out that the program had an error in it, and that the *program*—not Dominic—had incorrectly calculated the taxes his clients owed. Fifty of his clients now owed the government money. Three of them fired him the moment he told them about the problem, and a dozen more were thinking about firing him.

When Dominic left his office and started walking toward the subway, the rain started coming down in buckets, the wind blowing it into his face—the perfect end to a perfect fuckin' day. Normally, Dominic didn't stop for a drink on his way home, but he decided as he was passing by McGill's to have one and unwind a bit before facing the wife and kids. The last thing he was in the mood for was some little prick mouthing off to him.

But this was the wrong day to screw with Toby, too.

Toby was twenty-six but still got carded in bars. He had wavy dark hair, long eyelashes, and perfect features: a short straight nose, small flat ears, cupid-bow lips, dimples in both cheeks when he smiled. He was so handsome, he was almost pretty. In fact, Lauren's girlfriends—the ones he'd thought would be the bridesmaids at their wedding—were always saying he was prettier than Lauren. It was a joke—but only sort of.

When Lauren broke up with him three days ago, she said it was because they were "incompatible," whatever the hell that meant—but he couldn't get her to tell him what he had to do for them to *be* compatible. When she wouldn't return his calls, he hung around her apartment, hoping to catch her alone outside so he could talk to her, and that's when he learned that "incompatible" meant she was seeing another man.

Toby saw this man and Lauren step out of a cab the night before last. He saw the guy put his arm around her shoulders as he walked her into her brownstone, then stay the night—while Toby sat outside in his car, snorting coke, sipping from a pint of scotch, sometimes crying. Whoever the guy was, he wasn't all that good-looking—at least Toby didn't think so—but he was over six feet tall and built like Superman.

So Toby was feeling the sting of losing the woman he'd planned to marry, and he'd lost her to a man who was arguably more manly-looking—and then this fat fuck knocks him down and calls him a little shit. It was like igniting a half-inch fuse on a stick of dynamite—and from that moment forward Toby couldn't really remember what he did. It was as if a bloody red curtain had dropped down over his mind.

But what he did was walk out to his car, which was parked directly in front of McGill's. That was the only luck he'd had in the last three days: finding that parking spot. He jerked open the passenger-side door, opened the glove compartment, and pulled out the gun—a Smith & Wesson .357 revolver with a walnut grip and a three-inch barrel. He slammed the car door shut and walked back into McGill's—and immediately saw the whale at a table, sitting by himself, still wearing his trench coat and his stupid hat. Toby walked over to him and, without hesitating, shot him three times. "That'll teach you to fuck with me," he muttered.

It was as if the sound of the gunshots woke him from a nightmare, and he suddenly realized what he'd done. He stood for no more than a second looking at the fat man—whose white shirt was turning crimson—then he ran. He almost hit a busboy carrying a tray of glasses before he got to the door, banged it open, jumped into his car, and took off. He was driving away less than a minute after he killed Dominic DiNunzio.

As he was driving he kept saying, "What did you do? What did you do?" The short-barreled .357 was on the passenger seat, but it was no longer an inanimate object. To Toby it was alive, like a malignant machine in a Stephen King novel, giving off heat, possessing a dark, throbbing heart. It was as if the gun had somehow taken possession of his soul and made him do what he did. He couldn't help thinking that if he hadn't bought the damn gun he never would have shot that asshole.

Six blocks from McGill's, he pulled into a parking garage. The killing had shocked him almost sober, and he knew he shouldn't be driving. He wouldn't have been driving in the first place if it hadn't been for Lauren. When she wouldn't answer his calls on her cell phone, he'd called her office, but some girl told him Lauren had taken the day off. He suspected the bitch was lying—that she was screening Lauren's calls—but maybe she was telling the truth and Lauren had gone to her mom's place in

Jersey. So he'd driven to Jersey, but when her mom said Lauren wasn't there—and that Toby needed to let her daughter alone—he drove back to Lauren's office, hoping to spot her leaving work, but the traffic screwed him and he got there too late, which was when he drove to McGill's. But if he hadn't taken the car, he wouldn't have had the gun with him. And if he hadn't bought the gun . . .

It was as if some playful god had put everything in perfect alignment so Toby would do exactly what he did: kill Dominic DiNunzio.

He hit the button for a ticket to enter the parking garage; it took forever for the gate to go up. He found a space on the second floor, grabbed the .357, and got out of the car. He shoved the gun into the front of his pants, pulled the tails of his shirt over the weapon to conceal it, and left the garage.

He walked two blocks—the same mantra going through his head every step of the way: *What did you do? What did you do?* He stopped when he saw a garbage can overflowing with trash and a big McDonald's bag sticking out the top of the can. He grabbed the McDonald's bag and kept walking, and at the next trash can he came to, he looked around to see if anyone was watching, pulled the gun out of his pants, stuck it in the McDonald's bag, and shoved the bag deep into the trash can.

Now what? He could hear sirens—but in New York you could always hear sirens. What was he going to do?

He did the only thing he could think of: started walking to his parents' apartment.

His dad would know what to do.

2

Two uniformed cops arrived at McGill's two minutes after the shooting. They had been only a block away, on a break, getting a slice, when they got the call. They arrived at McGill's so fast that the customers who'd been in the bar when the shooting occurred were still there, most of them standing, freaked out by what they'd seen. One of the cops was a bright Irish kid named Murphy—son of a cop, grandson of a cop.

Murphy walked over to the victim and checked for a pulse, knowing before he checked that he was wasting his time.

He called out, "What did the shooter look like? Anyone. Tell me quick."

A woman near the door said, "He was white, not very tall, maybe five six, dark hair, clean-shaven, dark sport jacket, probably blue."

Murphy said to his partner, "Get that description to dispatch. The guy might be out there walking, maybe toward the subway or looking for a cab. Tell them to get cars patrolling a three-, four-block radius around this place to see if they can spot him. And to be careful—he's armed. Then call back to the precinct and get someone started on calling cab companies to see if they picked up a short white guy in a dark sport jacket near this bar. Go!" His partner, who was older than Murphy but used to taking orders from him, did what he was told.

Murphy looked at the customers, who were all potential witnesses, and said, "Okay. Now I want all of you to sit down exactly where you were when the shooting happened." Nobody moved. "Go on," Murphy said. "Sit down. Nobody's leaving until the detectives get here, and they'll be here in just a few minutes to take statements from you."

The detectives showed up fifteen minutes later, a couple of hefty old warhorses named Coghill and Dent, both two years from retirement. The first thing they did was stand in the doorway and take in the room, which was larger than expected from the outside. They noticed that the place was dimly lit, but bright enough for them to make out people's faces. Along one wall was a bar with twenty or so high-backed leather stools, and to the right of the bar was a small stage containing a baby grand and an acoustic guitar on a stand. They'd seen a poster near the entrance that said a pianist would start playing at eight and that at nine some singer they'd never heard of would be performing.

The entertainment probably explained why the place was so dark, with most of the illumination coming from small lights set into the bottom of the stage. There were maybe thirty tables in the room, but most were unoccupied. The place probably got busy after ten p.m., but at a few minutes before eight there were only about a dozen customers.

The dead guy was sitting at a table at the back of the room, near a hallway that led to the restrooms. Coghill and Dent walked slowly over to the corpse. The victim was a heavyset man with a five o'clock shadow, sitting upright behind a small round table, his chair against the wall. Dent thought he looked Italian and wondered if this could have been a mob hit.

The victim, whoever he was, was wearing a trench coat over a blue suit, a white shirt, and a blue and red striped tie loose at the collar. On his head was a flat hat, the type cabbies and newsboys used to wear. The guy's trench coat was still damp from the rain and his white shirt had turned dark red from three apparent shots to the chest.

"No shell casings," Coghill said.

"I noticed," Dent said, which meant the shooter had most likely used a revolver.

Dent figured the man had come into the bar to get out of the rain and have an after-work belt and, without bothering to remove his coat or hat, had sat down at the table. The drink he'd ordered—a martini with two olives—was sitting in front of him, but it didn't look as if the guy had taken more than a sip or two.

Dent took two photos of the victim with his cell phone. He and Coghill would now have to wait for the ME to declare the obviously dead man dead and remove the body, and for the crime scene weenies to gather whatever evidence there was to gather, and while all that was going on he and Coghill would question the witnesses while the killing was still fresh in their minds. Not knowing how long it was going to take to remove the corpse, Dent pulled a tablecloth off a nearby table and draped it over the victim's face and upper torso so the civilians wouldn't have to look at the man's half-open dead eyes.

"That's going to piss off the CSIs," Coghill said.

"Fuck 'em," Dent said. The CSIs, thanks to television, all thought they were rock stars these days.

They took a seat at a table near the bar and started with the bartender. They wanted to get his statement out of the way so he could bring them coffee. Coghill took out a small digital tape recorder and placed it on the table. He would also make notes during the interview, his impressions of the interviewee or something to follow up on later. Dent would ask the questions. They were like an old married couple: They had a routine and didn't deviate from it.

They began each interview exactly the same way: Tell us your full name, your date of birth, your address, and your phone number. Now show us some ID (so we know you didn't lie when you told us your name). Now tell us what you saw.

The first thing Jack Morris did was lie to the cops.

He'd been a bartender for twenty-five years, the last ten at McGill's. No way in hell was he going to say that the shooter was drunk when he arrived at the bar—and that then he served him two *more* drinks before he killed the fat guy. He knew if he admitted that he'd served a drunk, some slimeball lawyer would find a way to sue the bar, saying it was *his* fault the guy was killed. So Morris said: "I served him a drink. An eighteen-year-old Glenfiddich that goes for twenty bucks a pop. He finished it, ordered another one, then went back to the restroom before I could serve him the second drink. But I didn't see him come back from the restroom because I was making a margarita for those two old ladies over there—one of them had spilled her drink. I'd just put the margarita on the end of the bar for Kathy to pick up, when he walks back in through the main door and shoots the guy."

"Wait a minute," Dent said. "He walked back into the bar from the *street*? I thought you said he went to the can."

"He did. I saw him go toward the restrooms, but the next time I saw him he was coming through the door, like he went outside for a minute and then came back in. Then he shot the guy."

"That's weird," Dent said. "Did he say anything to him before he shot him?"

"Not that I saw. Just walked up, blam, blam, blam, then ran out."

"Had he spoken to the victim before he went to the restroom?"

"No. He was sitting at the bar the whole time he was here, until he got up to go to the can."

"When did the shooter get here?" Dent asked.

"It must have been close to seven-thirty, because Jerry had just finished setting up."

"Jerry?"

"The piano guy. He gets here about an hour before he starts playing, makes sure all the equipment is working, then goes back into the kitchen and has something to eat before he plays. Anyway, the killer must have got here around seven-thirty."

"When did the victim arrive? Was he in the bar already, or did he come in after the shooter?" Dent was wondering if the shooter had followed the victim into the bar, then had a couple of drinks to screw up his courage before he shot him.

"I don't know," Morris said. "Kathy takes care of the tables. Maybe she knows."

"Do you know the shooter's name?" Dent asked, realizing he should have asked that earlier.

"No, and I can't remember ever seeing him before. He's not a regular. I don't know the dead guy, either."

"How did the shooter pay for his drink? Did he use a credit card?"

"No, he gave me cash. It's in the register."

"How 'bout the glass he used?" Dent asked. "Did you pour the second drink into the same glass as the first one?"

"Yeah, it's sitting there on the bar."

"Don't touch it; the CSIs will get it. Anything else you can remember?"

"No, nothing. He just had a drink, went to the can, and plugged the guy."

"But you got a good look at him, sitting at the bar, and when he shot him?"

Morris hesitated. He didn't want to get caught up in this whole thing. But then he said, "Yeah, well, I guess I got a good look at him."

Esther Behrman was eighty-six years old, but sharp as a tack as far as Dent could tell. She was wearing a floral-print dress with a pearl necklace and clunky black grandma shoes. She had one of those wrinkly old turkey necks as though she'd once weighed more than she did now, and glasses with bifocal lenses.

"Leah and I were just sitting there having a drink," Esther said. "We come here sometimes to see Jerry."

"The piano player?" Dent said.

"Yes. He's Leah's cousin's grandson. We come early because we don't like to sit too close to the stage because they play the music too loud. Anyway, we were just sitting there and we didn't notice the . . . the *killer* until he went to the restroom. He bumped into the table where we were sitting, spilled half of Leah's drink, so she had to order another one. He said he was sorry, but you could tell he didn't mean it. And I think he was drunk, the way he walked."

"Okay," Dent said. "What happened next?"

Esther looked over at the tablecloth covering the corpse. She may have been shocked by what had happened but Dent could tell she was thrilled, talking to a detective like the ones on TV.

"Esther, what happened next?" Dent asked again.

"Oh, well, the one who got shot, he came out of the hall where the restrooms are and sat down. Then a couple minutes later the killer, he came back and—"

"Hold it," Dent said. "Are you saying the victim and the shooter were both together down the hall at the same time, maybe in the restroom together?"

"I don't know. I told you what I saw. I never saw the man who got shot go down the hall to the restrooms but I saw him come back and sit down, then, like I said, a couple minutes later the killer came back from the restroom, I guess."

"Okay, what happened next?"

"The killer walked out of the bar—I was keeping my eye on him since he'd spilled Leah's drink—and—"

"Wait a minute. The killer came back from the restroom and just walked out of the bar? He didn't say anything to the victim?"

"No, he just walked outside. Then a minute later—maybe not even a minute—he walks back in and shoots him."

"Did he say anything to the victim before he shot him?"

"I didn't hear him say anything. He just shot him and ran."

"But you got a good look at him when he shot the man."

"Oh, yes. I'll be able to pick him out of a lineup. You're going to have a lineup, aren't you, after you catch him?"

Dent almost laughed. "Yes, ma'am, we most likely will. Now could you send your friend Leah over so we can talk to her?"

"Oh, Leah didn't see anything. Her back was to the table where the, the *victim* was sitting." Dent saw a little shiver pass through Esther when she said "victim."

"Send her over anyway," Dent said.

While waiting for the other old woman, Coghill said, "We find this guy, it's gonna be a slam dunk."

———◆◆◆———

Dent thought that Rachel Quinn was an attractive young woman: trim build, short auburn hair, smart brown eyes. She was thirty-five, and based on her address and the suit she was wearing, he figured she had money. She wasn't beautiful but she was certainly pretty, especially when she smiled. She also struck Dent as being very bright. She was the one who'd immediately given Murphy the description of the shooter when he'd asked for it.

Quinn had been on an eHarmony date with some guy she was meeting in person for the first time. Her back had been to the door of the bar and she'd been facing the table where the victim was sitting. She never saw the shooter sitting at the bar, she didn't see either the shooter or the victim go down the hall to the restroom, nor did she see the shooter leave the bar and come back inside. She said she'd been busy talking to her date, and that at one point he'd started showing her photos of his dog on his smartphone. Dent wondered why in hell the guy would do that, but didn't ask.

"The only thing I saw," Quinn said, "was the killer walk up to the table where that man was sitting, hold his arm out, and shoot him. I didn't even realize he was holding a gun. Then he turned and ran out of the bar. He ran right past the table where I was sitting."

"Did you get a good look at his face?" Dent asked.

"A *good* look? Well, it's rather dark in here and he went by me pretty fast, but I think I'd recognize him if I saw him again."

"How many drinks did you have before the shooting occurred?"

"One. A glass of Chablis, and I hadn't even finished it."

Then, just because he was curious, Dent asked, "Why was your date showing you pictures of his dog?"

"Because I have a dog, too. It's one of the things we have in common." Then she paused and said, "It may be the only thing we have in common."

Dent had no idea at the time that Rachel Quinn's owning a dog would turn out to be important.

◆━━◆◆◆━━◆

Kathy Tolliver was a stunner.

Rachel Quinn, the eHarmony lady, was a pretty young woman but not what Dent would call a head-turner. But the barmaid . . . She was in her early twenties, tall—maybe five ten; she'd be six feet in heels—and had a mass of swirling dark hair and gray bedroom eyes. She was wearing a tank top that showed off a nice firm pair and a tight, short black skirt that stopped about four inches above her knees. If Dent hadn't been old and fat, he would have gotten down on his knees and begged her to go out with him.

"We noticed the victim was drinking a martini," Dent said. "Did you serve him?"

"Yeah. He walked into the bar and took a seat over there," Kathy said, pointing at the corpse, which the medical examiner's guys were, thank God, finally getting into a body bag. "He sat down, didn't even take off his coat or his hat, and I asked him what he wanted. He said a Stoli martini with olives. Jack made his drink, but when I took it to his table he was gone. I figured he must have gone to the restroom."

"Talk to me about the shooter," Dent said.

"Well, he was sitting at the bar for maybe ten, fifteen minutes before it happened," Kathy said. "I'm not sure how long exactly but he had a couple of drinks, looking all mopey, like somebody had killed his puppy or something. You know, staring down into his drink, lips moving like he was talking to himself, but not out loud. If I had to guess, I'd say his girlfriend just dumped him or he lost his job."

"Okay, then what did you see?"

"I was serving drinks, so I wasn't paying attention to him, but I saw him get up from the bar stool and walk back to the restrooms. A minute later, he comes back out, but before he did, the guy who was killed came back out, too. I mean, the dead guy went to the restroom, too, like I told you, and he came back into the bar before the little, cute guy did."

"The shooter was little and cute?" Dent said.

"Yeah. He was short—too short to interest me, anyway—but he was cute."

"Then what happened?" Dent asked.

Kathy Tolliver shrugged. "The guy who got shot sat down . . . I was over there at the end of the bar waiting for a margarita for one of those old ladies, and when I looked over, I saw the shooter, the killer, standing in front of him. Then he shoots him."

"Where did the killer come from before he shot him?"

"I don't know what you mean."

"I mean, you said the shooter went to the restroom. Did he come back from the restroom and shoot him or did he maybe come from the front door of the bar?"

"I don't know. When I saw him, he was just standing in front of the guy and he shot him. Then he ran out the door."

Coghill spoke for the first time, but to Dent. "Who got here first?"

"Oh, yeah," Dent said, then directed his question to Kathy. "Your bartender said the shooter got here around seven-thirty. Is that right?"

"Yeah, I guess. I wasn't looking at my watch, but that sounds right."

"And when did the victim arrive? Was he already here when the shooter got to the bar?"

"No, he came in maybe five, ten minutes after him."

This was important: It meant the shooter hadn't followed the victim into the bar. But for all Dent knew, the shooter could have known the victim was going to be in the bar and was waiting for him. At any rate, it was good to know who arrived first.

"How long do I have to stay here?" Kathy asked. "I was supposed to pick up my kid from the sitter's early tonight, so if this is going to take much longer, I need to let my sitter know."

<hr />

The last person Dent interviewed was Edmundo Ortiz, a busboy, a short man about five five, fifty years old, heavy Hispanic accent. And Dent thought: fifty and working as a busboy. That had to suck.

Dent's next thought was: illegal immigrant—which was the last fuckin' thing they needed. If Edmundo was an illegal he was going to lie and say he didn't see anything because he wouldn't want to come to the attention of the immigration boys.

"Where are you from, Edmundo?" Dent asked.

"Queens," Edmundo said.

Dent smiled. "No, I mean originally, like before you came to New York."

"Oh," Edmundo said. "Honduras." Now it was Edmundo's turn to smile—this big, wide smile showing off a bunch of stubby teeth. "But I'm a citizen. Two years now."

"Well, congratulations," Dent said.

"Gracias," Edmundo said.

"So what did you see?" Dent asked.

All Edmundo had seen was the shooter running out of the bar. He didn't see the shooter sitting in the bar before he shot the man, nor did he see the shooting itself. He was bringing a trayful of clean glasses from the kitchen to the bar, heard the shots, and then a man went sprinting past him and out the door. "He almost ran into me," Edmundo said.

"But you saw his face?"

"He went by fast," Edmundo said.

"But you think you might recognize him if you saw him again?"

"Maybe," Edmundo said. Then he added, "Probably."

———◆———

Dent told all the customer/witnesses that they could leave, but that they'd be contacted later to sign statements. They had five eyewitnesses who saw the shooting or could at least place the shooter in the bar: Jack Morris, the bartender; old Esther Behrman; Rachel Quinn, the eHarmony lady; the gorgeous barmaid, Kathy Tolliver; and U.S. citizen Edmundo Ortiz. There were four other people who'd been sitting in the bar when the killing occurred, but they hadn't seen anything because they'd been facing in the wrong direction or not paying attention, and all they saw, after the shots were fired, was the shooter's back as he ran from the bar. The piano player had been in the kitchen eating when everything occurred, so he was no help.

Seeing that Coghill and Dent were done questioning the witnesses, one of the crime scene techs walked over and said they'd ID'd the victim from the driver's license in his wallet. His name was Dominic Anthony DiNunzio. According to a business card in his wallet, DiNunzio was a CPA and had an office three blocks from McGill's.

So DiNunzio was a wop, as Dent had thought when he first saw the corpse, which made him wonder again if this could have been a mob hit. But he rejected the idea. He couldn't remember the last time the Italian mob whacked a guy in a restaurant filled with a dozen people.

Coghill called the precinct, asked a cop to do a quick records check, and was told Dominic DiNunzio had no criminal history, no prior arrests, no outstanding warrants.

The same crime scene tech who ID'd the victim came back to the detectives' table just as they were getting ready to leave.

"We got two perfect sets of prints off the glass the shooter used," the tech said. "One is probably the bartender's, and the other set has to belong to the shooter."

Dent said to Coghill: "If there's a God in Heaven, this mutt's prints will be in the system."

That evening, God was at home, relaxing in Paradise.

3

Henry Rosenthal and his wife, Miriam, had just finished dinner when their son walked into their apartment. Henry's first reaction was anger, followed by disgust. It was obvious Toby had been on a bender—he looked like hell, and Henry could smell the booze on his breath.

Henry knew that Toby had been dumped by his girlfriend—a pretty little thing, but a complete airhead as far as Henry was concerned—but that was no excuse for this sort of behavior. To make matters worse, his son was an associate at his law firm—a clear, undisguised case of nepotism—and Henry had been forced to lie to his partners and say that Toby had the flu when he didn't show up for work three days in a row.

Henry Rosenthal was the senior partner at Rosenthal, Canton, White, and Brown. RCW&B specialized in corporate law, primarily figuring out ways to merge gigantic companies while avoiding the antitrust laws. Henry billed his time at eight hundred dollars an hour and had billed enough hours over the thirty years he'd been practicing law to have an apartment on Park Avenue. You could see Central Park from one of his balconies.

Toby hadn't yet passed the bar exam. He'd failed once and would try again in six months. In fact, most of Toby's time at work was spent studying for the bar. Henry loved his son but didn't particularly like him and certainly had no respect for him. Toby was spoiled—that was Miriam's fault—unmotivated, lazy, and, frankly, not all that bright. Even with all of Henry's money and connections, he hadn't been able to get Toby into a top law school like Stanford or Harvard. Toby's law degree was from the University of Miami, the university selected by his son primarily for its proximity to beaches filled with bikini-clad coeds.

"What are you doing here?" Henry said. "And how dare you not show up for work and not return my calls."

"Dad, I just shot someone. I think I killed him."

Following Toby's pronouncement, Miriam rose to her feet, clamping her hands over her mouth, like someone trying to hold back a scream.

"What did you say?" Henry said.

"I just shot a man," Toby said again. "I don't know what to do."

"Oh, my God," Miriam said, and collapsed onto the couch as if her legs could no longer support her.

"Where did you get a gun?" Henry said.

Toby didn't answer, just started sobbing.

Twenty minutes later, Henry let David Slade into the apartment.

***

David Slade was the best criminal defense lawyer Henry Rosenthal knew. He'd defended Wall Street crooks, politicians caught taking bribes, and a bishop accused of molesting altar boys. His most famous case was a Tony-winning actress who'd killed her lover, and somehow Slade had been able to convince a jury that the woman had been temporarily insane at the time. Three years later, the actress was back on Broadway.

Slade was tall—about six two—and slim. He had a hawkish nose, thin lips, and thick dark hair he wore long, swept back over his ears and touching his collar. Had he been dressed in a dusty black suit, a white shirt, and a string tie, he would have looked like an Old West gunfighter. But he wasn't dressed that way. He was wearing a brown leather bomber jacket, a black T-shirt, jeans, and Top-Siders, because when Henry called Slade had been at home.

Henry had told Slade on the phone that his son had just admitted to shooting a man in a bar—and Slade immediately told Henry not to say another word and that he was on his way. The Rosenthals lived only ten blocks from Slade, and he'd grabbed the bomber jacket, sprinted out of his apartment, then got lucky—considering the rain was coming down in buckets—and caught a passing cab less than two minutes after he stepped outside.

Miriam and Toby Rosenthal were seated in the living room when Slade arrived. Toby was slumped in a chair near the fireplace, staring down into his lap. Miriam was still on the couch, where she'd landed after Toby's announcement. Her eyes were red from weeping and she was shedding Kleenex, little white flecks dropping onto her robe.

Miriam was only five foot one. She'd probably been as pretty as a porcelain doll when Henry married her forty years ago, but she'd turned into a gray-haired butterball. Slade had spoken to her only a couple of times, at social occasions, and had gotten the impression she wasn't very smart.

Henry was standing, having just let Slade into the apartment. He looked completely helpless, which was surprising considering that he was such a powerful and successful attorney—but then maybe not so surprising, given that he'd just learned his son had shot a man. Henry was wearing a blue jogging suit with white stripes down the legs. This wasn't because he'd been exercising; the jogging suit was just what he'd put on after work because it was comfortable. Like his son, Henry was short, but he was stouter than Toby. He'd lost most of his hair; all that remained was a white horseshoe band over his ears. Slade wondered if handsome Toby knew that one day he'd probably look just like his father.

The first thing Slade said was, "Henry, I need to speak with Toby alone."

"But . . ."

"No buts, Henry. You and Miriam need to leave the room. This is for your own protection as well as Toby's. And Miriam, I'd suggest you lie down; your color isn't good at all. And do not, under any circumstances, call anyone and talk about what Toby said." He could just see Miriam calling a sister or a friend.

Henry took one of Miriam's pudgy hands, pulled her up from the couch, and led her from the room.

"Toby, let's go sit over at the dining room table," Slade said.

Toby got to his feet slowly and walked over to the table. Slade couldn't help noticing that he reeked of booze.

"Okay, Toby, tell me what happened."

"I shot a guy."

"I know. Your father told me. But why."

"I, I was drunk. I'm still drunk. I've been drunk for three days because my fiancée dumped me and I guess I went, I don't know, crazy. I was in this bar and I go to the bathroom and I bump into this fat fuck coming out of the men's room. I mean, it was an accident. But he pushed me and knocked me down and called me a little shit."

"I see," Slade said. Slade knew this sort of thing happened all the time—murders committed for no good reason—but not usually with the class of people he represented. *Why did you kill your wife, Leon? . . . She just wouldn't shut the fuck up, so I stabbed the bitch.*

"Toby, did anyone see this man push you or hear what he said to you?"

"I don't think so," Toby said. "There wasn't anyone else in the restroom or in the hall outside."

"Did he threaten you after he pushed you?"

"No. He just went back into the bar."

"Okay, then what happened?"

"I don't know. I just went nuts. Him knocking me down, all the shit with Lauren, I just . . . I walked out to my car, got my gun, and went back into the bar and shot him. Jesus, I still can't believe I did it."

"What happened after you shot him?"

"I ran out of the bar and started driving, then realized as drunk as I was, a cop was liable to pull me over. So I pulled into a parking garage and walked over here to my dad's place."

"Where's the gun? Did you leave it in your car?"

"No. I stuck it in a bag and threw it in a trash can."

"How far is the trash can from the bar where the shooting happened?"

"I don't know. Maybe six, seven blocks."

"And you say you put the gun inside a bag."

"Yeah. A McDonald's bag."

"Is the gun registered to you?"

"No."

"Where did you get it?"

"I can't believe I—"

"Toby! Focus! Answer my question: Where did you get the gun?"

"Brooklyn."

"I mean, *how* did you get it? Did you buy it from a gun dealer, from a friend?"

"No. I was in a bar, this was like three years ago, and I ran into a guy I went to high school with. The guy was a complete loser"—Slade restrained himself from rolling his eyes—"but we had a drink together and on TV they were talking about some carjacking in Manhattan and I said I wished I had a gun. I was thinking I'm not a big guy, so it might be good to have one. This guy from high school . . ."

"What's his name?"

"Jim Turner."

"And he sold you the gun?"

"No. He said he knew a guy. He gave me the guy's number and I called him the next day. I met him at a park in Brooklyn and he had a bunch of guns in the trunk of his car, and I bought one."

"What was the man's name?"

"I don't remember. It was three years ago, when I first started dating Lauren."

"Do you still have the phone number?"

"No."

"Did you ever register the gun or get a license for it?"

"No. Why would I?"

"How many people know that you own a gun?"

"Shit, I don't know. I know I've told a few people about it."

"Okay, we'll get back to the gun later." But Slade was really thinking that if the gun wasn't registered in Toby's name and if they never found it in the trash can . . .

"What was the name of the bar where the shooting occurred?" Slade asked.

"McGill's, here in Manhattan, over on—"

"Did you know anyone in this bar? Did anyone know you? Had you been there before?"

"I've been there a couple times, but like seven, eight months ago. And I didn't know anyone there tonight, and as far as I know, no one knew me."

"Were there witnesses to the shooting?"

"I guess. There were probably a dozen people in the bar."

"A *dozen*?"

"Yeah, maybe. Jesus, I don't know why I—"

"Be quiet a minute, Toby. I need to think."

Slade could see only one possible defense for Toby Rosenthal, and that would take a miracle. Actually, several miracles. But it was too early to worry about that.

"Toby, go get your father."

Toby left the room and came back a minute later, following Henry like a whipped pup.

"Toby, I want you to go take a shower, a very hot shower. Scrub your hands and face very hard. Do you understand?"

"Uh, yeah, I guess."

"And Henry, I want you to wash Toby's clothes. All of them." Then it occurred to Slade that Henry might not know how to operate a washing machine; he had a maid for that sort of thing.

Henry said, "Is that legal?"

Henry was bright enough to understand what Slade was doing. Slade was worried about gunshot residue and blood splatter on Toby's clothes. But it was a stupid question to ask, especially for a lawyer.

"Of course it's legal, Henry. They're your son's clothes. He's been walking around in the rain, his clothes are wet and dirty, and if they need to be washed, he can wash them. Now, please, both of you, move quickly."

Five minutes later—Slade assumed that Toby's clothes were now in the washing machine and Toby was in the shower—Henry came back into the living room.

"Should Toby turn himself in?" Henry asked.

"Henry, if Toby turns himself in, and if the man he shot is dead, he'll be convicted of aggravated manslaughter and probably spend at least ten years in jail. To complicate matters, your son disposed of the weapon he used."

"Where the hell did he get a gun? He wouldn't tell me."

"It doesn't matter. What matters is that Toby had the presence of mind to get rid of evidence, which will make it harder for me to argue that he had a mental breakdown and was in some state of diminished capacity."

"But he was drunk. He's still drunk."

"Henry, half the people convicted of murder were drunk at the time they committed the crime. Being drunk is not a defense."

"So what does he do?"

"Right now, I need to find out about the status of the investigation. I'm going to make a call and then we'll talk some more."

One reason David Slade was such a good defense lawyer was that he had numerous contacts in the NYPD as well as in the district attorneys' offices in all five boroughs. He punched a number into his phone.

"Captain, it's David Slade. I need some information and I need it right away. A man was shot this evening in a Manhattan bar called McGill's. I need to know if the man is alive, his name, and what the police know about the person who shot him."

As Slade was waiting for a call back, Toby came into the room, dressed in gray sweatpants, a Vampire Weekend T-shirt, and scuffed tennis shoes. He wasn't wearing socks.

Slade said, "No, Toby. I want you to put on clothes that are similar to the ones you were wearing when I first saw you."

"I don't have anything like that here. I just keep a few things here in case I sleep over."

"Toby, your father is about the same size as you. Go look in his closet. Henry, please help him. And hurry, Toby."

Toby came back a few minutes later wearing a dark blue sport jacket, a blue shirt, and gray pants. The shirt was a lighter blue than the one he'd been wearing in McGill's, but close enough. The pants were the correct length, but because Henry was twenty pounds heavier than his son, Toby had to tighten his belt to hold them up.

"That's better," Slade said.

"My dad's shoes are kinda tight on me."

Slade shook his head—the kid was a moron. "Just sit down, Toby. I'm waiting for a phone call, then we'll talk some more."

Slade walked over to a window and looked out at the city lights, thinking back on a conversation he'd had with his best friend, Scott Barclay, in Aspen two years ago. It was a good thing that Henry Rosenthal was incredibly rich. If he hadn't been, there would have been no hope for Toby.

Slade's phone rang. He glanced at the caller ID.

"Yes, Captain," he said.

"The guy shot in McGill's was Dominic Anthony DiNunzio. He was shot three times with a large-caliber weapon and he's dead. About fifteen minutes ago, we identified the shooter. His name is Tobias Rosenthal."

"How did you identify him?"

"He left his fingerprints on the glass he was drinking from, and his prints were on record because he got a DUI when he was eighteen. A SWAT team is on its way to Rosenthal's apartment as we speak."

"Thank you, Captain. You know, one of my partners has two season tickets for the Knicks and he hardly ever uses them. Would you like to use them sometime in the near future?"

"Courtside seats?"

"Almost courtside. Just two rows up, right behind the Knicks bench. I'll send the tickets over in the next day or two. And thank you again, Captain."

Slade turned to Toby and Henry. "Where's Miriam?" he asked Henry.

"Lying down. She took a pill."

"That's good," Slade said. He didn't want to deal with any hysterics from Miriam. He was also relieved to see that Toby appeared to be a little more sober as a result of the shower.

"Henry, if you wouldn't mind, please make a pot of coffee. And don't forget to put Toby's clothes in the dryer. Toby, I want you to drink the coffee and try to get some food into your stomach before the police get here."

"The police are on their way here?" Henry said.

"They'll be here soon," Slade said. "Right now a SWAT team is breaking down the door to Toby's apartment, and when they find out he isn't there, they'll start searching for him, asking his neighbors where he might be and so forth. But one of the things they'll most certainly do is call here and ask if you've seen him."

"They'll call?" Henry said.

"Yes. And the reason they'll call is they'll be worried that if Toby is here and has a gun, he might be using you and Miriam as hostages. Or they might be concerned that he could be suicidal. At any rate, they'll call. But when they call, there will be policemen out in the hallway waiting to apprehend Toby if he tries to run."

"What do I say when they call?"

"As I said, they'll ask if Toby is here, and you'll say yes. And that's all you'll say. Then they'll ask if he's armed or if you're in danger, and you'll say no. If they ask anything else or ask to speak to Toby, give the phone to me."

"But how do we explain Toby being here?" Henry asked. "And how do we explain *you* being here?"—and for a moment David Slade found it hard to believe that Henry Rosenthal was a lawyer.

"Henry, you say nothing. Nothing at all. And Toby, this is the most important legal advice I'm going to give you tonight: You say nothing to the police after they arrest you. The next time you speak will be at your arraignment, and the only thing you'll say then is, 'Not guilty, Your Honor.' Is that clear?"

Toby nodded, but Slade wasn't sure the message was getting through.

"The police are going to handcuff you, Toby, and read you your rights. You're going to be scared. And as soon as they get you alone in the back of their car, they're going to start asking you questions, questions like 'Why did you shoot him?' and 'What did you do with the gun?' They're going to tell you that things will go better for you if you cooperate and confess to what you did. They'll tell you that they'll put in a good word for you with the prosecutor if you're honest. They'll be lying to you, Toby. If you say one word to anyone—to the cops, to the people in a cell with you, to the nice lady cop who brings you a Coke—you will go to jail for many, many years. Do you understand?"

"Yeah, I understand," Toby said, and tears began to well up in his bloodshot eyes.

"I hope so, Toby. You and I are about to embark on a long, painful journey, and I am going to be with you every step of the way. But the journey will end before it even starts if you speak one word to the police without me present.

"And Henry, you need to get Toby's clothes out of the dryer as soon as possible and hang them up in your closet. Wipe off his shoes very carefully with a wet cloth and put them with your shoes. When the police get here they are going to search your apartment."

"They'd need a warrant," Henry said, clearly unable to imagine the police searching his home.

"They'll get a warrant, Henry. If they apprehend Toby here, they'll get a warrant to see if the gun he used is here."

For the next forty minutes, the three men sat in near silence, Slade thinking again about the conversation he'd had with Scott Barclay in Aspen, Henry most likely wondering how he'd sired an idiot. Toby, in spite of the coffee he drank, began to nod off, not having slept in days. When the phone rang, all three men jerked as if a firecracker had exploded.

Henry walked slowly over to the phone—as though he was approaching a dog that might bite him—and picked it up. Slade heard him say, "Yes", then, "No, he's not armed. And we're not in any danger." Then he handed the phone to Slade. Slade said, "This is David Slade, the Rosenthal family attorney." Slade listened for a moment, then said, "Toby and I will be leaving the Rosenthals' apartment in one minute, Detective. I need to have a few words with my client before we leave, but we'll be right out." There was a brief pause, and Slade said, "Not unless you have a warrant, Detective. But I can tell you that Toby isn't armed and wasn't armed when he came to his parents' apartment. Like I said, we'll be right out."

Slade put down the phone and said to Henry, "As I expected, the police want to search your apartment to see if the weapon Toby allegedly used is here. I told them that you won't allow them to search without a warrant, but they'll obtain one in less than an hour. And while they're waiting for the warrant, they'll leave an officer outside to make sure you or Miriam don't remove anything from the apartment. Do you understand, Henry?"

"Yes," Henry said, "but—"

"There's no time to talk, Henry. Keep in mind that in this matter, I'm not only Toby's lawyer, I'm also your lawyer. Yours and Miriam's. If the police attempt to question you, refuse to speak to them unless I'm present. When they conduct the search, make note of anything they take with them. We'll meet again tomorrow, after the arraignment."

"Will Toby be granted bail?" Henry said.

"I'll do my best to see that he is, but you'd better put a lot of money in your checking account. Like two or three hundred thousand. Let's go, Toby."

Toby was visibly trembling. Slade hoped the idiot wouldn't vomit.

Slade opened the door and shouted, "We're coming out," then he and Toby left the apartment. Down the long hallway, Slade could see two big men, partially out of sight in the alcove where the elevator was. They were wearing body armor and helmets with face shields, and holding automatic rifles. One of them screamed at Toby to lie down on the floor.

Slade said, "No. My client is unarmed. He's going to raise his hands and walk down the hall toward you and you can place him under arrest."

"Get down on the goddamn ground," the SWAT behemoth yelled, but Slade told Toby to raise his hands and they walked down the hall together. As soon as they reached the elevator, one of the SWAT guys pushed Toby against the wall—not that hard, because Slade was watching—and frisked and handcuffed him. Then two heavyset men dressed in cheap suits—detectives, Slade assumed—stepped out of the elevator, which had been sitting stationary on the Rosenthals' floor.

One of the detectives said they were arresting Toby for the murder of Dominic DiNunzio and read him his rights. David Slade introduced himself as Toby's lawyer and asked to see the detectives' identification. Their names were Coghill and Dent, a couple of NYPD dinosaurs.

Dent asked, "How did you happen to be here at the Rosenthals' apartment when we called, Counselor?"

Slade said, "Seriously, Detective? And, Detective, I'm telling you now, in the presence of witnesses, that no one is to speak to my client without my being present. I'll meet you at the precinct and will be there while you process Mr. Rosenthal."

"No problem," Dent said, and smiled—and Slade could see that the detective was supremely confident Toby Rosenthal was going to be convicted of murder.

4

Fifteen hours after Dominic DiNunzio was killed, David Slade attended a lineup in which five witnesses were separately asked to identify the man who shot him. Each witness identified Toby Rosenthal. Three of them did so without hesitation: old Esther Behrman; the barmaid, Kathy Tolliver; and the lady on the eHarmony date, Rachel Quinn.

When the bartender, Jack Morris, was asked to identify the shooter, he paused, then said, "I think it's number four." "You think?" Detective Dent said. "No, it's him, number four," Morris responded.

When Edmundo Ortiz was asked to make an ID, he said the same thing he said when Dent interviewed him at McGill's: "He went by me pretty fast." "But do you see the man?" Dent asked. "I only saw him from the side," Edmundo said. Dent told the men in the lineup to all turn to the left; Edmundo would have seen the shooter's right profile as he ran out the door. "I think number four," Edmundo said. "You think?" Dent said, just as he'd done with Morris. Edmundo frowned and squinted at Toby Rosenthal's face. "Si. Number four. He's the one."

As David Slade knew the lineup was being videoed, he didn't bother to make notes regarding the exchanges between Dent and Morris and Ortiz.

The lineup was a joke, as far as Slade was concerned. There were five men in it in addition to Toby Rosenthal, and they were all Caucasians with short, dark hair. However, three of the men were several inches taller than Toby, two were several years older, and none of them really looked much at all like Toby. It had apparently been difficult to find short, handsome, young cops that day to participate in the lineup. But Slade didn't complain; he did ask for a copy of the lineup video.

Following the lineup, Slade met briefly with Assistant District Attorney Justine Porter. Slade figured it was just simple bad luck that he'd ended up with Porter as the prosecutor; he really would have preferred someone else. He'd been up against her only once before—he won, she lost—but he knew ADA Porter was bright and competent, and considering the salaries ADAs were paid, competent was better than average.

Porter was in her early fifties—and she looked her age. She was about five seven, and thin, because she worked about fourteen hours a day and often forgot to eat. Her dark hair was streaked with gray, long and straight, not styled in any way; Porter didn't have time to waste in beauty salons. She'd been married once, years ago, but was now single and had no kids. Slade suspected she didn't even have a cat; her work was her life.

As far as ADA Porter was concerned, the case against Toby Rosenthal was, as Detective Coghill had said, "a slam dunk." Four eyewitnesses saw him shoot Dominic DiNunzio, his fingerprints on a glass proved that he'd been in the bar, and all four had picked him out of a lineup. A fifth witness, Edmundo Ortiz, didn't see him shoot DiNunzio, but did see him run from the bar with a gun in his hand, and he'd also picked Toby out of the lineup. There was no reason, Porter said, to waste the state's time and money on a trial. More important, from ADA Porter's perspective, there was no reason to waste *her* time. She already had a workload that would have broken the back of a Clydesdale.

"He's been charged with second-degree murder," Porter told Slade. "If he pleads guilty, I'll agree to voluntary manslaughter. And I'd call that incredibly generous considering that Dominic DiNunzio was an outstanding citizen with no criminal record and the father of three, his youngest only eight."

Slade waited for the other shoe to drop. "If he refuses to plead guilty at the arraignment, I'll stick with the murder two charge, and if he's found guilty at trial, which you know he will be, he'll get fifteen to twenty years. He'll be eligible for parole in maybe twelve, assuming he survives that long." The implication being that a cute little guy like Toby was going to suffer miserably in prison.

Slade knew that when it came to charging his client, Porter had a dilemma. She couldn't charge Toby with first-degree murder and expect to win at trial. By definition, first-degree murder requires "malice aforethought"—which basically meant that when Toby killed DiNunzio he'd committed a cold-blooded, calculated, premeditated crime. The eyewitness statements, however, didn't support this definition. All agreed that Toby rushed out of the bar, then rushed back in and shot DiNunzio. Furthermore, and more important, Porter had not been able to find any motive for the killing, nor any prior connection between Toby and DiNunzio. Other than Toby Rosenthal and David Slade, no one knew what had happened in the hall outside the restroom door when DiNunzio shoved Toby and called him names. The bottom line, unless the state could find a motive, was that it would be impossible to prove Toby had premeditated or calculated in any way with regard to the death of Dominic DiNunzio. Consequently, the state had two choices: voluntary manslaughter or second-degree murder.

Although legal scholars will tell you otherwise, there really isn't much difference between second-degree murder and voluntary manslaughter. Second-degree murder is an *intentional* murder, but is not premeditated or planned in advance. Voluntary manslaughter—often called a "heat-of-passion murder"—is also an intentional killing involving no prior intent to kill, but it's committed under circumstances that would "cause a reasonable person to become emotionally or mentally disturbed."

For example, say Bob finds his wife in bed with Tom and he pulls out his gun and shoots Tom. The law is willing to concede that Bob had cause to become emotionally disturbed, as Tom was boinking his wife. On the other hand, if Tom just pisses Bob off in a bar, and Bob pulls out his gun and shoots him, the law is less inclined to think that Bob had reasonable cause to shoot Tom.

So there was always a lot of hairsplitting when it came to the difference between voluntary manslaughter and second-degree murder, but the important thing was that voluntary manslaughter was considered to be the lesser of the two crimes and therefore the penalties were less. And that was the bone that ADA Porter was tossing Slade if his client agreed to plead guilty: ten years max for voluntary manslaughter versus fifteen or more for second-degree murder.

Slade's response to the bone was: "I'll think about it, Justine, and get back to you."

"Well, you'd better get back to me before the arraignment," ADA Porter said. "I won't make the offer again."

He believed Porter when she said she'd stick to the charge of second-degree murder and take the case to trial if Toby didn't plead guilty immediately—Porter didn't make idle threats—but as David Slade had no intention at this point of taking any deal short of dismissal of all charges, he didn't respond.

———— ◆◆◆ ————

As promised, at the arraignment that afternoon ADA Porter said that Tobias Rosenthal was being charged with murder in the second degree—to wit, the intentional killing of Dominic DiNunzio. Judge Albert Martinez—a heavyset, perpetually scowling man who reminded

Slade of the late Supreme Court Justice Antonin Scalia—asked how the defendant pled. Slade wished they hadn't drawn Martinez for a judge; he was fair, but extremely impatient, constantly prodding attorneys to speed things up, as if a trial were a race against the clock.

In answer to Martinez's question, Toby softly said, "Not guilty, Your Honor."

"Speak up!" Martinez snapped.

Toby cleared his throat and again said, "Not guilty, Your Honor."

Toby was completely sober, for the first time in days, and so frightened he was trembling as he stood next to his lawyer.

"Now as to the matter of bail," Judge Martinez said.

"Remand, Your Honor," Porter said. "Mr. Rosenthal comes from a very wealthy family, and since five witnesses identified him as the man who killed Mr. DiNunzio, there is no doubt he will be found guilty at trial. The people, therefore, consider there to be a significant risk that Mr. Rosenthal, aided by his family, will flee before his trial, and most likely to a country with which the United States has no extradition treaty."

"Your Honor," David Slade said, "I almost don't know where to begin in responding to such an absurd statement. First, it should be noted that Mr. Rosenthal's father is one of the most respected attorneys in this city, and no way would he aid his son in fleeing. Henry Rosenthal, in fact, wants a trial to clear his son of these false charges."

ADA Porter made an unattractive snorting sound, and Judge Martinez gave her an appropriately admonishing look.

"More important, Your Honor, the state has offered no motive for my client having murdered Mr. DiNunzio. There is no motive because my client never met or spoke to Mr. DiNunzio. Nor does the state have any physical evidence that my client committed this crime, such as the gun that was used to kill Mr. DiNunzio. And the police, with my client's consent, performed a gunshot residue test and there was no evidence that he had fired a gun."

ADA Porter opened her mouth to object, but Judge Martinez silenced her with a raised hand.

"As for these so-called eyewitnesses," Slade said, "four times in the last three years in the state of New York, men incarcerated as a result of eyewitness testimony have been released from prison when DNA evidence proved them innocent. Four times, Your Honor. As Ms. Porter surely knows, there is no testimony less reliable than eyewitness testimony. And in this case, and as will be demonstrated at trial, the police contaminated the witnesses. The witnesses were allowed to remain in the bar where the murder occurred for approximately half an hour before they were questioned by detectives, giving them plenty of time to talk with each other and reach some sort of consensus regarding what occurred. As for the so-called lineup in which these same contaminated witnesses identified my client, I would call it laughable were it not such a serious case of police incompetence.

"In summary, Your Honor, the state has a weak case, in spite of Ms. Porter's statements to the contrary. My client has no intention of fleeing, his respected family has no intention of helping him flee, and he's willing to give up his passport, wear a GPS device, or take any other action the court considers appropriate to ensure he remains within this jurisdiction. And one final point, Your Honor. The state has charged my client with murder two when, if he'd actually committed this crime, the more appropriate charge would be voluntary manslaughter, and, as you know, it's extremely rare that manslaughter defendants are not given the opportunity to post bail. We all know how full the court's calendar is, and it would be a miscarriage of justice for my client to have to spend months in jail prior to his trial."

Porter again started to object, but Martinez raised a hand, signaling that he'd heard enough, then looked down as if he might be consulting a document. He was actually looking at a text message he'd just received from his wife, reminding him not to be late for a dinner party.

"Bail is set at one million dollars," Martinez said.

As Slade was leaving the courtroom, he stopped to speak to Henry and Miriam. Henry immediately said, "When can we get together and talk about Toby's defense?"

"Not for a couple of days. I need to—"

"If you have higher priorities than Toby's case, David, I need to know right now."

"I don't have a higher priority, Henry. Toby's my only priority. But there's a man I need to speak to about the case, and I may have to travel to talk to him."

"Who?"

"I'm not going to tell you that—I can't tell you. But as soon as I've spoken to this person, we'll get together. I promise." Then, looking directly at Miriam Rosenthal, he said, "Before I leave, there's something I need to make sure you both understand. You cannot, under any circumstances, talk to anyone about what Toby told you the night he was arrested." They both nodded, Henry looking grim, tears welling up in Miriam's eyes.

Slade was particularly worried about Miriam—and he made it clear that he was. "This is important, Miriam: I know you're in pain right now and would probably like to talk to someone—a friend, your sister, your rabbi. But you can't. You absolutely cannot do that. If you do, you'll destroy Toby's life."

That was unfair—Toby had destroyed his own life—but he had to make sure she got the message. "Do you understand, Miriam?"

She started to say something, but then started sobbing, so Slade said to her husband, "You need to make sure she understands, Henry."

5

———◆———

Justine Porter crammed the case folder on Toby Rosenthal into her briefcase. Actually, it was more like an airplane carry-on bag—a small suitcase with wheels—because she was always working on a dozen cases simultaneously, running from courtroom to courtroom. She'd just zipped the bag closed when a man said, "Can I speak to you for a moment?"

She looked over and saw a broad-shouldered, muscular guy. He was younger than she was and good-looking: thick dark hair, blue eyes, a prominent nose, a big square chin with a dimple in it. He was on crutches, but she didn't see a cast on a foot or anything else, and she wondered what the crutches were for.

"Who are you?" she said.

"My name's Joe DeMarco. Dominic DiNunzio was my cousin. Well, not exactly a cousin, but sort of."

"What's that mean, 'sort of'?"

"Dominic's mother is my godmother. I always called her Aunt Connie. And Dominic, being her son, I always thought of him as a cousin."

Aw shit, Justine thought. She had already spoken to Connie DiNunzio—when Connie called to threaten her. If you'd been around New York politics for any length of time, you knew that Connie

DiNunzio was a major player up in Albany. As for the threat, Connie had said that if her son's killer wasn't sentenced to the maximum time in prison, she would do her best to get Justine fired. Normally, Justine would have lost her temper, but she restrained herself, as she knew she was dealing with a grieving mother. And now here was Dominic's sort of cousin, and she assumed he was here for the same reason: to tell her she'd better make sure that rich, white Toby Rosenthal didn't slip through some crack in the judicial system.

"Look," Justine said, "I have to get to another courtroom. I'm sorry about your cousin, and like I told your aunt, I'm going to make sure he goes to jail. The case is strong, and I'm going to get him. That's a promise."

"That's good to hear," DeMarco said, "but you need to know something. I represent John Mahoney."

"John Mahoney?" Porter said. "Which John Mahoney?"

"The one who's the minority leader of the U.S. House of Representatives. Mahoney is a close friend of Connie DiNunzio, and I wanted you to know—"

Now this was starting to piss her off, this guy telling her that a DC heavyweight was going to bust her balls. She interrupted him and said, "What did you say your name was again?"

"DeMarco. Joe DeMarco." Then he did a little balancing act on the crutches, pulled out his wallet, and handed her a business card. It read "Joseph DeMarco," and there was a phone number with a 202 area code, but no job title or anything else.

DeMarco said, "What I was starting to say was that John Mahoney is a man with a lot of influence and he has a very deep, personal interest in this case. So all I wanted to tell you was that if you need anything, anything at all, call me. Okay?"

Justine said, "Well, I appreciate that, but you can tell Congressman Mahoney that I have this one under control. Now I gotta run."

DeMarco started back up the courtroom aisle, and one of his crutches hit a leg on the defense table. He wobbled a bit but didn't fall. Fucking crutches. He'd be glad to be shed of them, which wouldn't be for a couple of months.

He wondered how good Porter was. He hadn't had a chance to do much research on her before the arraignment—basically he'd just looked her up on his cell phone, and seen that she'd been an ADA for more than twenty years. And she looked over fifty, which made her older than most New York ADAs he knew, and this was worrisome. Landing a job as an ADA out of law school was a good deal, but the job didn't pay that much, particularly considering the cost of living in New York, and most ADAs moved on if they were any good. On the other hand, with five eyewitnesses, the case against Rosenthal looked like a no-brainer, and Porter could probably handle it easily.

What he'd told Porter about Mahoney having a deep personal interest in the case was true, but he didn't really understand Mahoney's relationship to his aunt Connie. All he knew was that Connie had something on Mahoney—which wasn't necessarily surprising, considering Mahoney's character. Connie had known him back in the early days of his congressional career, and when DeMarco was looking for a job after he graduated from law school and couldn't find one, she called Mahoney and forced Mahoney to hire him. When he'd asked Connie why Mahoney had agreed to hire him, all Connie would say was, "Honey, I've got his big balls in the palm of my hand. He'll do anything I want."

After having worked for Mahoney for years, and knowing him the way he now did, DeMarco assumed that his boss had done some sneaky, underhanded thing and Connie had found out about it. Whatever the case, she had some hold over Mahoney, and DeMarco was grateful that she'd been able to get him a job. However, the longer he worked for the man, the less grateful he was.

As for Dominic DiNunzio, DeMarco hadn't really known him all that well. Dominic was five years older than him, and DeMarco only saw him when Connie came down from Albany to visit his mom in Queens. Nonetheless, DeMarco had always liked him and felt terrible that he'd been killed. Mostly, however, he felt sorry for Connie and for Dominic's wife—whom he'd met only a couple of times—and their three kids.

DeMarco walked out of the courtroom, took a seat in the hall, and called Mahoney. He told him that the case against Dominic's killer was a sure thing, based on what he'd heard at the arraignment. He also said that a date hadn't been set for the funeral because the ME hadn't released Dominic's body.

Mahoney said, "Tell Connie . . . Aw, never mind."

DeMarco walked outside the courthouse, gingerly descended the courthouse steps, and tried to wave down a cab to take him to his mom's place in Queens. But it's hard to wave gripping crutches. In fact, it's hard to do almost anything on crutches.

How he'd ended up on crutches—and he still couldn't believe it— was playing golf, which nobody would ever call a contact sport. He'd gone to a public course in Arlington, planning to play a round by himself, because the men he normally played with were all working. He was actually supposed to be working too, but since Mahoney had been visiting his congressional district in Boston at the time, who would know if he played hooky? Anyway, he got to the course and was paired up with this old guy, who'd also shown up alone.

The guy was in his sixties, potbellied, bandy-legged, and only about five six. DeMarco's first reaction was: *Shit*. He was a decent golfer and he didn't like playing with guys who were terrible, guys who would take a dozen shots on a par 5 hole, because then the game would go too slow. And the way this guy looked, and considering his age, DeMarco figured it was going to be a *long* eighteen holes.

It turned out he was right—but not for the reason he thought.

He'd let the old guy drive first, and he'd hit the ball only about 150 yards, confirming what DeMarco had feared. But DeMarco also noticed that the guy's drive was straight as an arrow and landed in the middle of the fairway. DeMarco's drive, by comparison, went maybe 240, but sliced into the high grass on the right side of the fairway. The guy's next shot didn't reach the green, but again was as straight as a laser-guided missile. DeMarco's second shot sailed over the green. Then the old guy's pitch landed three feet from the hole, and he made the putt: par for the old guy; bogey for DeMarco. And that's the way it went for the next sixteen fuckin' holes. The old fart kicked his ass.

On the seventeenth hole, DeMarco's ball landed in a sand trap that was deeper than a coal mine. Okay, it wasn't that deep, but it was deep. Already pissed that he was losing, and then doubly pissed that his ball had landed in the trap, he jumped down into it—maybe only a three-foot drop—and landed weird. His ankle twisted, he slammed into the edge of the trap, his hip hit the head of a rake that was there for smoothing out the sand—and a pain shot through his leg as if he'd been shot with a musket ball.

The humiliation continued. He tried to stand and couldn't, and they had to call an ambulance. At the hospital he learned that he had a hairline crack in a bone in the hip socket called the acetabulum. The doctor said the injury was a total fluke, one he usually saw only in car accidents or in old people with brittle bones. They couldn't put his hip in a cast, and the only cure was for him to stay off the leg for a couple of months, not put any pressure on it at all, and eventually the bone would heal. Hence the crutches.

The only good news about the whole thing was that the leg injury gave him an excuse to avoid a job that Mahoney had tried to give him. Mahoney had wanted him to fly up to Boston and help out with his campaign there, which meant that he'd have to run around and lean on people who owed Mahoney favors and ask for money. So he'd told Mahoney that the doctor had told him to rest as much as possible, that the crutches were only so he could make it to the toilet and microwave his dinners, and if he didn't . . . Well, who knows what awful things could happen. Like what if his leg got infected and they had to amputate. Mahoney, being Mahoney, wasn't the least bit sympathetic, but he gave in when DeMarco whined hard enough.

But when Mahoney had told him that Dominic had been killed, he didn't try to dodge the assignment. He owed Connie too much.

6

What David Slade hadn't told Henry Rosenthal was that he needed to talk to a man about a magician.

Two years ago Slade had gone to a legal conference in Aspen. In other words, he'd taken a tax-deductible ski vacation, but the main reason he'd gone was that his best friend, Scott Barclay, was attending the conference.

David Slade and Scott Barclay had both attended the University of Virginia and then gone to law school there. They roomed together, got drunk together, and took spring breaks together in Florida. After law school they went their separate ways, Slade returning to New York and Barclay to San Diego. But like David Slade, Scott Barclay specialized in defending criminals, almost all of them absolutely guilty. In the twenty years since law school they'd kept in touch, talking frequently on the phone. They emailed jokes to each other. Their wives got along, and their families had taken three vacations together.

The last time Slade had seen Scott was at the Aspen conference, and truth be told Scott had annoyed him. He didn't know exactly how much Scott made, but based on his California home and his lifestyle, Slade figured that they were in about the same income bracket. With the cost of living in Manhattan, however, Slade couldn't afford property in Aspen, whereas Scott had spent part of his time there looking at chalets in the one- to two-million-dollar range. (You actually don't get all that much of a chalet for a million in Aspen.)

In addition to hunting for a chalet, Scott had mentioned several times—actually, *crowed* about—how he'd made a killing off one client, winning a case that had been virtually impossible to win. In fact, according to Scott, a prosecutor in San Diego had been fired because of the way Scott had snatched victory out of the jaws of defeat.

Even though he kept bragging about the case—and how it was providing the down payment on his soon-to-be Aspen chalet—Scott wouldn't share the details with Slade. The final night they were there they got roaring drunk, and Scott finally told him what had happened, but even then he didn't share everything.

He said the case involved a woman in her fifties, an heiress who was arrested for killing her husband, a handsome young man in his thirties. The husband played tennis at almost the professional level, could sail a boat and golf with the best of them, but had never had a real job in his life. All agreed he was basically a gigolo who had married the homely heiress for the several hundred million she was worth.

The night of the murder, the heiress and the gigolo had dinner at their county club—and got into a terrible row. Two people in the restaurant heard the heiress accuse her husband of cheating on her with a cocktail waitress in La Jolla. They also heard the heiress say that she was going to kill him. Then the heiress stormed out of the restaurant, leaving her embarrassed young husband behind, and he was forced to take a cab home.

At eleven that same night, the heiress called the police, crying hysterically, and said that a burglar had broken into her house and shot her husband. She claimed not to have been home when the shooting occurred. She did admit that she'd had an argument with her husband during dinner, after which she drove around in her cute little Mercedes convertible to clear her head. The police found a broken windowpane in the front door, which explained how the thief/killer had gotten into the house, but nothing had been stolen. The heiress assumed that her husband had confronted the thief when he broke in, and that the thief had then shot him and fled.

The cops suspected she was lying right from the get-go. They asked her to account for her time that evening, and she told them when she arrived at and departed the country club and when she got home. No, she hadn't stopped for gas. No, she hadn't seen anyone she knew. She had no way to prove that she'd spent two hours driving around—but then neither could the cops *disprove* that she had. Unfortunately—for the cops, that is—the heiress didn't have live-in help who might have contradicted her statement. Her housekeeper/cook showed up at six every morning to prepare her breakfast and returned to Tijuana at seven each night.

When the cops asked if she would agree to a gunshot residue test and give them permission to search her house, she became shrill and indignant, outraged that they would think a person like her would lie, much less shoot her spouse. And that's when she called her lawyer, a guy who primarily took care of her money, and he dispatched Scott Barclay.

A gunshot residue test was eventually administered to the heiress, but the results were negative. The technician who administered the test noted the woman's hands and wrists were a startling red, as if she might have scrubbed them with a bristle brush. She had no weapon registered to her, and after a search that went on for days, no gun or bloodstained clothes were found.

On the other hand, the woman had a large estate with numerous outbuildings—toolsheds, a gazebo, a four-car garage, a greenhouse for her orchids—and, most important, she wasn't stupid. They knew there were plenty of places on the property for her to ingeniously hide the weapon, but they never did find it. The diligent cops did, however, find two witnesses at the country club—a waiter and another diner—who heard the heiress accuse her husband of infidelity and threaten to kill him.

Lawyer Scott Barclay, at this point, was feeling fairly confident. With no murder weapon and no proof that his client had been home at the time of the murder, a conviction seemed unlikely. So what if a couple of witnesses heard her arguing with her husband? Husbands and wives argued, and the threat she'd made about killing him . . . Well, that was simple hyperbole.

Then Scott Barclay's confidence in keeping the heiress out of prison dropped to zero.

The heiress stayed in her San Diego home about half the time. The other half she spent in Europe or Hawaii or wherever her fancy took her. Unbeknownst to her, a neighbor's teenage son would sneak over to her place and go skinny-dipping with his girlfriend in her pool when she was gone. The night her husband was murdered, the kid came over to see if she was home, planning to call his girlfriend if she wasn't. He saw the heiress walk out her door carrying something in a white plastic garbage bag at exactly nine forty-two p.m. The kid knew the exact time because he'd immediately called his girlfriend to tell her no skinny-dipping tonight, sweetie pie, and the time of the call was recorded on his cell phone. When the kid's mom saw in the paper that the heiress claimed to have been taking a scenic drive the night her husband was killed, the kid said, "No way, Mom. I saw her." And Mom, who had always despised the woman, called the police.

The heiress had now been caught in a go-straight-to-jail lie, since she'd told the cops she'd been tooling around in her convertible from nine until eleven p.m. The cops had two witnesses who provided a motive—the gigolo husband diddling a cocktail waitress—and a third witness who established that she was home at the time the murder occurred.

"Jesus," Slade said to Scott that drunken night in Aspen. "How did you get her off?"

"With the help of a magician and his lovely lady assistant," Scott said.

"What the hell does that mean?" Slade asked.

"Sorry, buddy, I can't say more. But if you ever need a magician, give me a call."

———◆◆◆———

After David Slade returned from Aspen to New York, he took the time to research the heiress's case—and found out that magic had indeed been involved.

The waiter who overheard the heiress accuse her husband of infidelity and threaten to kill him was Mexican. Before the trial, he scooted across the border, never to be heard from again. Slade concluded that this was fortunate but not all that surprising.

The second witness was a county club member who knew the heiress, and had been seated at the table next to her and her late husband that fatal night. She had been adamant before the trial about what the heiress had said—then, during the trial, developed amnesia. At the trial, she said she didn't think the woman had said anything about killing her husband. It was very noisy in the restaurant. Yes, she may have heard some discussion about a woman in La Jolla but really couldn't place the discussion in context. The San Diego papers quoted the frustrated prosecutor, in open court, screaming, "Are you shitting me!"

The prosecutor had a right to be frustrated. The most important witness was the teenage skinny-dipper. He was the one who could prove the heiress had lied about where she was the night her husband died. And if she hadn't killed him, why would she lie? But like the Mexican waiter, the skinny-dipper disappeared before the trial. The boy's mother was frantic, convinced that the vile heiress had paid someone to execute her randy young son.

A month after the trial, after the heiress had been acquitted—thank God for no double jeopardy—the skinny-dipper returned home, looking tanned, relaxed, and sexually sated. For the last month, he'd been having the time of his young life. He'd traveled to Thailand with a stunning young woman who was twenty-five years old and who worked for an escort service before falling madly in love with the pimply dipper. There was no record that the kid and his hooker girlfriend had left the United States using valid passports, and when the cops tried to make the boy tell them who had funded his journey to beaches in paradise, the kid—upon the advice of his lawyer—refused to tell them.

It was obvious what had happened, or at least it was obvious to David Slade. Someone had paid a gorgeous hooker to seduce a horny teenager, giving him the option of testifying at a trial or seeing the world and learning every position in the Kama Sutra. Slade supposed there were some young men who would have turned down the offer, although he doubted that he would have been one of them. The other thing that occurred to Slade was that it would have been much cheaper to put a bullet in the back of the kid's head and drop him into a shallow grave than pay for his vacation. He couldn't help wondering what might have happened if the kid had declined the hooker's offer.

———◆◆◆———

Following Toby's arraignment, Slade called Scott Barclay in San Diego. After five minutes of how have you been, how are the wife and kids, Slade got to the point.

"Scott, when I saw you in Aspen a couple of years ago you told me that if I ever needed a magician I should give you a call. I need one now."

This statement was greeted with silence.

"Scott," Slade said.

"I was pretty drunk that night, David, and shouldn't have said anything."

"Scott," Slade said again, the single word reminding Scott of their quarter-century friendship.

"Okay, but this is not a subject I'm willing to talk about on a telephone," Scott finally said.

"You could email me," Slade said. Before Scott could respond, Slade said, "That was a joke, Scott. Lighten up. I'll see you tomorrow."

The next day Slade flew to San Diego and took his good friend to dinner at Morton's. Slade waited until they finished a meal that included two bottles of wine and center-cut filets mignons, at a cost of five hundred dollars. Over brandy, he finally said, "So, Scott. Tell me about the magician."

"There's a lawyer in Minneapolis named John Bronson," Scott said. "I've known John almost as long as I've known you. He practiced in San Diego for years before he moved to Minnesota. He'd read about my case—it was all over the tabloids—and suggested I come see him. He said he knew some people who might be able to help, but he wouldn't say more than that over the phone. So I flew to Minneapolis.

"John told me he'd had a case similar to mine. He wouldn't share the details, but he said the prosecution's case was based primarily on a witness, and that he'd used a team, referred to him by another attorney, to turn things around."

" 'Turn things around'?" Slade said.

"Those were the words he used. John said this team only took on cases where the client had a lot of money, and where the prosecution was relying mostly on witnesses as opposed to hard evidence like ballistics or DNA. They charged John's client two million."

"Whoa!" Slade said.

"Yeah, whoa," Scott said. "Can your client afford them?"

"No, but his daddy can. And I take it that after you talked to Bronson, you bought this team in to help with your case, with all those witnesses you had."

"I'm not going to talk about my case," Scott said. "And that's final. But if you want to consult with them, call a lawyer named George Chavez in San Antonio."

"Chavez," Slade repeated.

"Yes. Tell him you need to hire an exceptional jury consultant. Use those exact words: 'exceptional jury consultant.' He'll ask who referred you to him and you can give him my name, just like I gave him John Bronson's name. These people apparently work on a referral basis. Chavez will ask you what the case is so they can do some research and decide if they want to get involved. Then you might hear from them or you might not."

Scott finished his cognac and said, "David, I love you like a brother, and that's the only reason I'm helping you. And unlike John Bronson, I'm not going to stick you with a referral fee. But, buddy, if you ever claim we had this conversation I'll deny it, and then I'll spend the rest of my life trying to find some way to fuck you."

7

David Slade flew back to New York the next day and asked Henry Rosenthal to come to his office at five. He told Henry not to bring his son or his wife, that it wasn't in their best interest to hear what he and Henry needed to discuss. He didn't say that he didn't trust Toby or Miriam, or that he didn't want to listen to Miriam's hysterics, but those were two more reasons why Slade wanted Henry to come alone.

Henry arrived promptly at five and Slade's fifty-something secretary ushered him into Slade's office. Slade understood his own nature well enough to know that hiring a pretty young secretary would not be good for his marriage. Slade had no way to know then that in the end, everything would almost unravel thanks to a middle-aged secretary.

Slade asked Henry if he'd like a drink. "I don't know about you, but I could use one," he said. He almost added, *And after we talk, you're going to need one.*

Henry said, sure, a scotch would be good, and Slade poured them two Macallans.

"You did a good job at the arraignment," Henry said. "I was terri-fied they weren't going to grant Toby bail. And was it true what you said about the lineup being flawed and the witnesses' statements being contaminated?"

"The part about the bad lineup was true. I have no idea, however, if the witnesses were allowed to talk to each other before they gave their statements to the police. It doesn't really matter."

"It doesn't matter?" Henry said.

"Henry, as things stand right now your son is going to jail. He'll be convicted of manslaughter as opposed to murder two, and spend at least seven years behind bars. And that, I'm afraid, is a best-case scenario. The state has four reliable witnesses who saw Toby shoot DiNunzio, and a fifth one who saw him running from the bar holding a gun."

Henry seemed to deflate. "I see," he said. "So what did you want to discuss? Whether Toby should plead guilty and take a deal? Or did you call me here to discuss your fee, which you haven't mentioned yet?"

"No, Henry, I did not ask to see you to discuss my fee; I trust you'll pay me when I send you a bill. But since you brought the subject up, I imagine with a case this simple, my fee will be only about a hundred."

He meant only one hundred *thousand,* which Henry understood.

"I mean," Slade continued, "there really isn't anything I can do other than argue that the charge should be reduced from murder two to manslaughter and then do my best to ensure they don't give Toby an outrageous sentence. If Toby is sentenced to six or seven years in jail, and eligible for parole in four or five, I will consider that I've done an outstanding job on your son's behalf. One problem we'll have with sentencing is that the court will be inclined to demonstrate that a rich white kid like Toby is treated just as harshly as poor, minority kids. The other problem is that Dominic DiNunzio had three children. His oldest is fifteen and his youngest is eight. The court is not going to be inclined toward leniency."

"Jesus," Henry said. "Can you imagine what's going to happen to Toby if he has to spend seven years with the animals in a state prison?"

"Yes, Henry, unfortunately I can imagine."

For a moment, Slade was afraid that Henry Rosenthal was going to cry. But he didn't. "So you're saying that there really isn't anything that can be done for my boy." Then, looking defiant, he added, "Maybe I need to consult another attorney."

"No, Henry, that's not what I'm saying. At least not yet. You see, there is a defense I could mount. It means going to trial and not accepting a plea, and it will be risky. But if I'm successful, Toby will be found innocent."

"What defense? I don't understand."

"My argument will be that Toby didn't shoot Dominic DiNunzio. Toby was in the bar, there's no debating that. Not only do the witnesses place him there, but his fingerprints on a glass prove he was there. But what the witnesses *really* saw was Toby leave the bar and another man, one who bears a strong resemblance to Toby, enter the bar immediately after Toby left and shoot Mr. DiNunzio."

"Are you joking?" Henry said.

"No, Henry, I'm not. Maybe DiNunzio had a client who committed embezzlement and felt it necessary to silence Mr. DiNunzio. Maybe this Italian-American accountant worked for the Mafia. Who knows? But the point is, Toby didn't know DiNunzio and therefore had no reason to shoot him. The only logical explanation is that somebody else shot DiNunzio, some person who *did* have a motive."

"But the witnesses."

"Yes, Henry, that's the rub. The witnesses. If there were only *one* witness, and that witness was unreliable—say, for example, an old woman with poor eyesight or a bartender who drank on the job. But *five* witnesses . . . Five are going to pose a very knotty problem."

"I don't understand. What are you saying, David?"

"Let me freshen your drink before we proceed."

Rosenthal looked understandably confused, but Slade ignored his confusion and poured him a second scotch.

"Henry, what I'm about to say next must be said in hypothetical terms. If I don't speak hypothetically, you and I could be accused of engaging in a criminal conspiracy. Or worse."

"A conspiracy?"

"Yes, Henry, a conspiracy. You need to decide if you want me to proceed or not."

"Yes, I want you to proceed! He's my only son. So quit . . . *tantalizing* me. Spit it out!"

"All right, as long as you understand." Slade paused, then said, "Hypothetically, if a team could be hired that could make all or some of these witnesses not testify against Toby, would you be willing to engage such a team?"

Henry immediately said, "Of course I would."

"No, Henry, I will not allow you to do that. I will not allow you to say yes without really thinking about what I just said. This is no longer about Toby. This is now about you and me. If I proceed down this path, you and I could, hypothetically, go to jail ourselves."

"When you say this team could make these witnesses not testify, are you saying . . ."

"I'm only saying what I just said, Henry. But think about it. There are many reasons why a witness might not testify. He might simply have a change of heart and decide the original statement he made to the police was incorrect. He might not appear in court to testify for some reason having nothing to do with Toby's case. For example, a witness might flee the county because of a crime he'd committed, and thus not be available to testify. But that's all I'm going to say. If we go down this path, I will have no control over the actions this team takes to assist Toby."

Henry nodded. He understood. Henry Rosenthal hadn't become an enormously wealthy man because he was stupid.

"The other thing you need to understand, Henry, is this defense will cost a considerable amount of money—much, much more than a hundred thousand."

"How much?"

"I don't know for sure, but at least three million. I was told that this team charged one client two million—but the client was exonerated. I do know that my fee will become one million."

Henry raised an eyebrow to convey his shock.

"Henry, the reason I'm charging that amount is that A, I'm taking a significant personal risk, and B, I'm now going to have to work considerably harder to ensure Toby is found not guilty.

"The first thing I'm going to have to do is delay Toby's trial as long as possible. If I can delay the start of the trial by one or two years, I will do so, because a lot can happen in one or two years; for instance, one of the witnesses is eighty-six years old, and she might die before the trial starts. The other reason I have to delay is to give this team time to do their job.

"In addition to delaying the trial, I also have to present an alternative suspect for Dominic DiNunzio's murder. I'm going to have to tear DiNunzio's life apart to show he had enemies and that one of those enemies killed him.

"Last, I have to convince this team to do the job, which is not a sure thing. They don't take every case, and they charge so much they can choose not to work if they're so inclined. So, before I proceed further, I need to know if you want to do this and agree to pay whatever is asked."

Henry didn't hesitate. "Yes, I agree. Toby's a spoiled brat and he got drunk and killed a man, but I won't have my son brutalized for years."

"That's all I needed to know," Slade said.

The next morning, David Slade called the law office of attorney George Chavez in San Antonio, Texas. He told Chavez he needed an exceptional jury consultant to assist on the case of *Tobias Rosenthal versus the State of New York.* He said he'd been referred to Chavez by Scott Barclay. Chavez said he'd pass on the message and if Slade didn't hear back from anyone in a couple of weeks, he could assume the people he represented had declined.

"A couple of weeks?" Slade said.

But Chavez had already hung up.

8

Dominic's funeral was held the second week in April at Holy Family Church in Queens and he was buried at Mount St. Mary Cemetery. It was one of those days when you felt lucky to be alive: the temperature in the mid-seventies, not a cloud in an azure sky, spring flowers in bloom. It was a day to be at the ballpark, walking through Central Park, having a picnic—doing anything but watching a man get buried as his mother, wife, and children cried.

The funeral was well attended. There were probably more than two hundred people in the church, and DeMarco suspected that a lot of the attendees were friends and associates of Connie's from Albany. Connie, in spite of her age, was still a major force in the state capital, and these people wanted her to know that they were there for her.

After the burial, there was a reception at the church; DeMarco's mother had been in charge of organizing it. Connie took a seat in a chair at the back of the hall and people came up to her and tried to console her, knowing nothing they could say would do so. Connie was wearing a black dress that came down to the middle of her calves and a small black hat with a short veil. DeMarco knew she was the same age as his mother, but she looked a decade older. She was also heavier than the last time DeMarco had seen her, her ankles were swollen, and there were coffee-colored half-circles under her eyes from lack of sleep. DeMarco had seen pictures of Connie DiNunzio holding him the day he was baptized. That beautiful young woman had disappeared, altered by age and grief.

Dominic's wife was a plump, pretty, dark-haired woman, and her three children, all boys, were on the heavy side, reminding DeMarco of the way Dominic had looked as a kid. He hadn't known Dominic well, but he had no doubt he was a good father and that his sons had loved him. Toby Rosenthal had shattered their lives.

DeMarco waited until the line of people talking to Connie had almost come to an end before he walked up to her. He took one of her hands, and said, "Aunt Connie—"

"I don't want hear it, Joe. You and John just make sure that son of a bitch pays for what he did."

DeMarco had dinner with his mother that night in Queens, at an Italian restaurant she and his dad always used to go to.

Maureen DeMarco had been a beautiful, lively girl when she married his dad, but as she'd aged she became grim and bitter, and the sadness never seemed to leave her eyes—which was somewhat understandable. She fell in love with a man who became a Mafia hit man, and spent half her life worrying that he might be arrested or killed. Then, after he was killed, she never got over his death or remarried.

She said, "Connie's worried that the guy who killed Dominic will get off because his dad is so rich. Do you think he will, Joe?"

"No. The prosecutor's got an airtight case. Plus she knows Mahoney will destroy her career if he gets off."

"Well, we'll see," his perpetually pessimistic mother said.

"I'm curious about something, Mom," DeMarco said. "Do you have any idea what Connie has on Mahoney? I know she's got something on him; he wouldn't have hired me if she didn't."

His mother looked at him for a long moment, then said, "No. I just know she knew him from the time she worked in Washington."

His dear old mother was lying to him. She and Connie had been friends forever, and DeMarco could tell, by the way she'd hesitated, that she knew the truth. But there was one thing he knew about his mother: No one was more loyal, and no one could keep a secret better. Like all the secrets she'd kept about his father.

Part II

9

Fifteen years earlier
Calhoun Falls, South Carolina—May 2001

Ella Sue Fieldman was eighteen years old the day she looked into a mirror and decided to change her life.

Ella realized that she'd never really had a chance. Her parents, Bob and Shirley, were devoid of ambition; they hadn't graduated from high school, they didn't read, not even the newspaper, and they watched nothing but mindless crap on television. Bob was a janitor at a nursing home; he started the job when he was seventeen and was still working there twenty-two years later. Her mother worked off and on, usually as a waitress. Most often Shirley lost the job because she rarely made it to work on time and when she was there, she moved so slowly she barely stirred the air.

When Bob and Shirley got home from work, after one of Shirley's pathetic dinners they'd start drinking beer and watching television, sitting side by side on a couch that hadn't been vacuumed since the day Shirley bought it at a Goodwill store. If something broke around the house, it would remain broken for weeks before Bob got around to fixing it—and then he usually couldn't fix it. As for Shirley, she didn't do home improvement projects, she didn't garden, she had no hobbies. If it weren't for the miracle of television, Ella was convinced, her mother would have just sat on the couch and stared at the wall.

If a single word were used to describe her parents, the word would be "indifferent." They were indifferent when it came to their jobs, the home they owned, the world they lived in. And they were indifferent toward their only child. Thinking back on it, Ella wondered how she had survived infancy; she was amazed that her mother had been able to work up the energy to change her diapers and feed her.

Ella did horribly in school, and the main reason was that she didn't learn to read until she was almost seven. Most kids she went to school with were reading in kindergarten. Later in life, she would learn that children whose parents didn't read to them when they were little—or for that matter, barely spoke to them when they were little—struggled their entire lives with reading and vocabulary. As for math, forget it. There was no one Ella could turn to to explain the mysteries of long division.

But Ella didn't inherit her parents' apathy. From an early age, as young as six, she was *embarrassed*—embarrassed by her grades and the way she dressed and spoke. So she tried—she *really* tried—to keep up with the kids around her. Ella was also competitive—another trait she hadn't inherited from mom and dad—and although she hardly ever won at anything, at least she made the attempt.

Life changed for Ella when she was fourteen—about the time she began to get noticeable breasts and hips—because there was one area where she could compete with her classmates: her looks. Ella was a beautiful girl. Her mother had gotten fat over the years, but was only passable-looking before that, and her father was downright homely. But Ella—with her blond hair and her cornflower blue eyes and her perfect long-legged, high-breasted body . . . Well, it didn't take long for her to realize that the boys wanted her—and, for a while, she gave in to their desires.

The other thing that Ella had going for her, in addition to her beauty, was a quality rarely found in one so young, and that quality was *objectivity*. She didn't know how she came to be this way, but she was able to shine a harsh light on herself and dispassionately evaluate what she saw. And that's what she did the day she graduated from high school.

The day she graduated—a graduation that her parents hadn't bothered to attend—she looked around at her female classmates. Most of them were going off to college, even if it was only a community college. They would become teachers or nurses, maybe even doctors or lawyers. Those girls had sat at the graduation ceremony just *glowing,* looking forward to whatever came next. Then there were those girls like Ella, the ones who were dumb and poor. They would become waitresses or hairdressers or clerks at Winn-Dixie, marry a mechanic or a salesman at the tire store, have two or three snot-nosed kids, buy a shitty home and a shitty car—and basically become Ella's parents.

It was after they played *Pomp and Circumstance* for the graduates that Ella had her epiphany. She looked at her image in the streaked bedroom mirror, dressed in her dark blue graduation gown, the mortarboard with the silly little tassel on her blond head, the tear tracks on her cheeks. And that's when she said to the pretty girl in the mirror, "So what the hell are you gonna do now, Ella Sue?"

Well, what she did was sit down, still dressed in her graduation gown, and make up her list. It was a things-to-do list and a things-*not*-to-do list. When she finished there were twelve items on it.

Item number one was: *Leave Calhoun Falls.*

Item number two was: *Marry a rich guy.*

Ella knew that this was the only way she was going to escape the drudgery that would certainly become her life. She couldn't stay in Calhoun Falls. All the rich men there were already taken, and those who would become rich all knew Ella Sue Fieldman as the dumb, easy lay in high school.

She decided that in order to snag a wealthy mate, she needed to make herself over in every way possible. She would study the way sophisticated women dressed and spoke and acted. (That was item number nine on her list: *Learn how not to be a hick.*)

She would also stop calling herself Ella Sue Fieldman—item number five. Ella had always hated her name. "Ella Sue" was a hick's name and, as stated, she was not going to be a hick. As for "Fieldman," it made you think of sharecroppers and tenant farmers.

———◆———

That summer Ella got a job at the truck stop on Highway 72. She worked as many hours as she could get and put only about half her tips into the tip jar so she wouldn't have to share so much with the other servers. And she didn't spend a dime on herself that summer, not for clothes or entertainment or even a recreational joint. By September she'd saved twenty-eight hundred bucks, enough to pay the first and last months' rent on a cheap apartment in Charleston and buy some of the items she would need.

She'd selected Charleston, South Carolina, for the simple reason that she needed a town with a decent-sized population—a population large enough to have a lot of rich, single men but not so large that she would be just one of a million pretty girls. She sure as hell wasn't going to LA, where there was a potential starlet on every corner. But item number four on her list was: *Do not get hooked up with a married man no matter how rich he is.* She was *not* going to become some married guy's bimbo girlfriend.

Ella left for Charleston driving her father's car. She stole the car. There were many times in the past when she'd stayed out all night, so she figured it might be a couple of days before her folks decided that she wasn't sleeping at some guy's house and had taken the car. And she doubted the cops in Charleston would hunt relentlessly for a stolen Corolla from Calhoun Falls.

The reason she stole the car was not to get to Charleston—she could have taken a bus—but because she needed a car to go job hunting.

Which was item number three on her start-a-new-life list: the kind of job she was going to get. She knew she could get a job at a titty bar in a heartbeat, and it would pay better than waitressing, but no way was she going to do that. A rich man meets a woman in a strip joint, he's most likely not thinking she's the ideal candidate for a wife. And she wasn't going to waitress in any place like the truck stop in Calhoun Falls where she'd worked that summer. Truck stops and diners and family restaurants weren't places where rich guys tended to dine. Her plan was to get employment in one of those restaurants that had four dollar signs behind the name in magazines. If there was a place in Charleston that had *five* dollar signs, she'd apply there.

Two weeks after arriving in town she became a waitress at Charleston's most exclusive yacht club.

———◆◆◆———

Ella studied the women at the yacht club and got catalogs from Macy's and Sears and Target—the kind of places where she could afford to shop if the clothes were on sale. After careful consideration, she bought three outfits she could wear to expensive restaurants and bars. All the clothes showed off her legs and her figure, but none of them screamed *I'm a cheap hussy*. She also bought two pairs of panties and two bras—marked down 40 percent—from Victoria's Secret. If the right man came along and she allowed him to take off her dress, she wanted to look just as good in her underwear.

The other thing she did after she arrived in Charleston was legally change her name, and it was surprisingly easy to do. She was no longer Ella Sue Fieldman. She was now Ella Fields. She thought that sounded classy.

Years later, when she looked back on what she had done, she realized it had really been quite remarkable. She had always known that she wasn't stupid; she'd just had no one to guide her. But she hadn't allowed herself to become a victim. She hadn't allowed her circumstances to dictate who she would be. As young as she was, Ella Fields had developed a plan, and then relentlessly executed it.

After two months Ella was pretty much settled in Charleston—she had a job, an apartment, new clothes, and a stolen car—and she was ready to begin . . . well, "hunting" was the only word she could think of. After work, three or four times a week, she'd go to the nicest bars in Charleston, the kind of places that charged ten or twelve bucks for a drink. She hardly ever had to pay for more than one drink, as some man would almost always offer to buy the second one.

She quickly became brutally efficient at weeding out the undesirables. There were the obvious signs: a wedding ring, cheap clothes, unshined shoes, tattoos, dirty fingernails, and so forth. And the first question she usually asked a man was what he did for a living. Everyone tried to sound more important than they really were—teachers became professors, salesmen became marketing vice presidents, engineers became project managers—but she'd expected that. And teachers, salesmen, and engineers—almost anyone paid by the hour—weren't what she was looking for.

Occasionally, a man would appear to meet all her criteria—but item number seven on her list was to never leave a bar with a man she'd just met. For that matter, she had no intention of going to bed with a man until at least the third date; she wanted him absolutely *panting* for her. When a man asked her out, she would ask for a card and say I'll call you tomorrow to let you know if I'm free on Saturday. She wanted the card for two reasons: Married guys would lie about their names, and a card would tend to confirm that a man really had the kind of job he said he had. As for guys who didn't have business cards . . .

In her first six months in Charleston she slept with no one and had only two second dates.

The seventh month, a week before her nineteenth birthday, Ella Fields met Bill Cantwell.

10

It had been twelve days since David Slade had called George Chavez in San Antonio to put him in touch with the team that was going to save Toby Rosenthal's life—and the waiting was driving him insane. He knew it would take some time for the team to research Toby and the case, but almost two weeks should have been long enough. He was beginning to think they had decided to give Toby's case a pass—which meant he was going to lose a million-dollar fee and have to tell Henry Rosenthal that his punk kid was going to prison. He was thinking about calling Chavez again when his secretary told him there was a woman on the phone who refused to give her name but said she'd been referred to him by a lawyer in Texas.

Slade snatched up the phone. "This is David Slade," he said. "I'd about given up on you."

"Meet me in the MObar at the Mandarin Oriental at seven," a woman said in a voice that was low and calm.

Then she hung up. She hadn't even told him her name.

The MObar in the Mandarin Oriental hotel is on the thirty-fifth floor and offers a view of Central Park and the city's lights. It's a small, intimate place with a hammered-nickel bar and high-backed booths. There were only five people in the bar when Slade arrived, and four of those people were coupled up. The only single woman was a gorgeous blonde with short hair who appeared to be in her early thirties. She sat at the bar, drinking a glass of white wine. She was wearing a black suit over a white blouse, the skirt short enough to display two outstanding legs. On her feet were black stilettos with three-inch heels. Had David Slade known anything about women's shoes he would have known they were Manolo Blahniks and sold for about six hundred bucks.

She gave him a little wave and got off the bar stool as he walked toward her. He wasn't surprised she recognized him; all she had to do was google him to find his picture. Close up, he could see her eyes were blue and her complexion was fair and flawless.

"Let's take a booth," she said.

Watching her walk ahead of him to the booth was one of life's small, but extraordinary pleasures.

David Slade had cheated on his wife, but only three times, and the last time had been ten years ago. He had a beautiful wife, she was the mother of his two children, and he didn't want to lose her. But he knew if he ever had the opportunity to sleep with this woman, he would do so without hesitation.

Slade ordered a martini, and while waiting for it to arrive, he said, "I was told you were part of a team."

"I am," she said, "I work with a partner. But you'll never meet him or speak to him. That's for his protection. He's the one who handles the, shall we say, more complex tasks."

By "complex," he assumed she meant illegal.

"We need to talk about the money first," she said. "Our price is two million. And that's not negotiable."

Slade nodded. "That's what I was told to expect."

"Good. You have a week to deposit a million into our account. We know it takes a little time to arrange for that kind of money. But if you take more than a week, we'll walk."

"I don't think so," Slade said. "How do I know you won't take the money and I never hear from you again? I certainly can't go to the police."

"David, we don't advertise. We work on a referral basis. If we went around cheating our clients and failing to perform, you never would have heard of us in the first place." Before Slade could object again, she continued.

"We'll expect the other million a week before the trial starts. By then we'll have done our job. That is, we'll have provided you with a viable defense. Whether you win or lose at trial will depend on you. We don't expect you to pay us if we haven't done our job, but if we have, and if you fail to pay us, then I can assure you that we will use our considerable talents to come after you and Henry Rosenthal. And I'm not talking about a lawsuit, David."

Slade nodded. He could see there was no point in arguing with her. He had no doubt that if he didn't agree to her terms she would walk. And it wasn't like it was his money anyway.

"The other thing is, your client will be expected to pay any expenses related to dealing with the witnesses."

He assumed she was talking about bribes. "Understood," Slade said. "So what's your plan?"

"Our plan is to make sure that all, or at least the most important, witnesses don't testify against Toby. Those who do testify will support your defense. And I can't be more specific at this point, as we haven't started looking at the witnesses in detail. And I have to be honest with you here: We've never had a case where we've had to deal with five witnesses; this is not going to be easy. We will also assist you in providing a plausible suspect for who killed Dominic DiNunzio. We're assuming that's your defense: that Toby left the bar, never returned, and someone else entered and killed DiNunzio."

"Are you a lawyer?" Slade asked.

"No, but my partner is."

"So what do you need from me?"

"Everything you have on the witnesses and DiNunzio. Make copies of your files and I'll send a messenger to your office tomorrow to pick them up. But the files aren't the main thing we need from you."

"So what is?"

"Time. We need you to be prepared to delay the trial if we need more time; with five witnesses, that's imperative. So get ready to ask for a delay, and after you've gotten one, get ready to ask for another. When's the trial scheduled to start?"

"June seventeenth. For a felony case in the state of New York, the prosecution has to be prepared to go to trial ninety days after the arraignment. But nobody expects that to happen. The judge and the ADA both know I'll ask for a delay, and I won't have a problem getting one. How much time do you need?"

"We won't know until we've had time to review everything: the witnesses, their statements, the victim, et cetera. But don't ask for a delay yet, because as soon as we have everything in place, it will be to our advantage to have the trial as soon as possible. So, for now, figure out how to get a delay if we need one, then after that, figure out how to get another. That's your primary job at this point: Delay the trial until everything is in place."

She removed a folded piece of paper and a cell phone from her purse. "Use that phone to communicate with me, but only if necessary. My number is in the contacts list."

"What's your name?"

"David, do you seriously think I'm going to give you my real name? Anyway, don't call me. Send text messages. You can never tell who might be listening in on phone calls these days. So if we need to talk, send a text and we'll arrange a meeting. But we won't be meeting very often. It's not in your best interest or ours for us to be seen together.

"On that piece of paper are instructions for the best way to transfer the money. We have a lot of experience at this and suggest you follow the instructions. It'll be safer for you and Henry Rosenthal if you do it our way. But the main thing is, wire the money to the account specified. After we have it, we'll make it vanish."

She rose from the table. "I think that's all for now. I'll be in touch, but like I said, not very often. Don't pester me for status reports."

She rose from the table and walked away, and he watched her until she was out of sight.

He wondered if she slept with her partner. Whoever he was, even if she wasn't sleeping with him, he was a lucky man.

11

Fourteen years earlier
Charleston, South Carolina—May 2002

Ella Fields met Bill Cantwell at the yacht club.

He was at a table with a woman about his age and an older couple. The couple were their sixties, married, and members of the club. Ella had served them before; the woman was a bit of a snob but her husband was nice.

The woman with Bill was in her mid-thirties. She was slender and attractive, although not a beauty queen. As for Bill, well, he was a hunk in Ella's opinion. Tall, maybe six two, and well built, with muscular forearms and strong wrists. He had thick dark hair, a perfect straight nose, warm brown eyes, and a cleft in his chin. He reminded her of that old actor James Garner.

They all ordered margaritas and Bill pulled out his wallet and handed Ella a Visa. She noticed he was wearing a Rolex. "Start us a tab, please," he said.

The other man objected, saying, "Hell, Bill, you don't need to do that. You've paid for everything today. And it's my club, for crying out loud."

"No, no, it's on me," Bill said. "I appreciate you showing me around and helping me out."

Ella went back to the bar to place their order, but before she handed the bartender the credit card she looked at it. The name on it was William S. Cantwell.

—◆◆◆—

Ella served the foursome their drinks and a plate of appetizers, and about twenty minutes later Bill left the table and walked toward her. She was standing at the end of the bar where the bartender placed the drink orders.

He smiled at her—fantastic smile, perfect white teeth—and said, "They think I'm over here ordering another round, which I am, but would you mind doing me a favor?"

She raised an eyebrow instead of answering.

"Serve the drinks, but about five minutes after you do, come back to the table and say, 'Are you Bill Cantwell? Your secretary is on the phone at the hostess desk, and needs to speak to you urgently.' Can you remember all that?"

"Gee, I don't know," Ella said, like: *How dumb do you think I am?*

Bill got it, and smiled. "Sorry. But will you do this for me?"

"Sure," she said. She noticed he wasn't wearing a wedding ring and that his shoes were Mephistos—about the most expensive casual shoes you can buy.

She served the drinks and five minutes later, as he'd asked, she walked up to his table. "Are you Bill Cantwell?" she said.

"Yes," he said, pretending to be puzzled.

"Your secretary is on the phone and said she needs to speak to you urgently."

Bill pulled out his cell phone and looked at the screen. "Damn, I didn't hear the phone ring."

The young woman with him asked Ella, "How did you know who Bill was?" She sounded suspicious.

Bill started to answer but before he did, Ella said, "His secretary told the hostess that he was very handsome and had dark hair and a cleft in his chin."

"Well, he certainly is handsome," the older woman said, patting Bill's forearm, but the younger one, Bill's date, just frowned.

"Let me see what she wants," Bill said, and left the table.

Ella went back to the bar and picked up an order for another table. She saw Bill return to his table, and it appeared as if he was making apologies for having to leave. He walked over to Ella. "Thanks. Let me have my credit card back, but keep the tab open, and give yourself a twenty percent tip. And this is also for you," he said, and placed a fifty-dollar bill on the bar next to her hand. "You don't need to share that with the other servers."

Ella was impressed. This guy was not a penny-pincher.

He turned to walk away, then turned back and said, "I have to tell you that you're one of loveliest young women I've ever seen." Then he left without saying anything more.

Ella didn't know how to articulate it, but men were always telling her how pretty she was, and when they did, it was always a prelude to a come-on. With Bill Cantwell, somehow it hadn't been like that. He was simply stating a fact, making an observation; he hadn't been trying to seduce her. It was as if he simply appreciated her beauty and wanted her to know it. Whatever the case, she liked him, and hoped like crazy she'd see him again.

Her wish came true.

———◆◆◆———

Bill Cantwell stopped by the yacht club bar the following night. This time he was wearing a suit—a lightweight gray one with a blue shirt and a tie that was a combination of colors but a perfect match for the

jacket and shirt. The way the suit hung on him, Ella was willing to
bet it had cost a bundle, and she was pretty sure the tie was Armani.
She'd become quite the connoisseur of men's clothing since she'd left
Calhoun Falls.

"There you are," he said. She liked the way the skin around his eyes
crinkled when he smiled. "I would have been heartbroken if you hadn't
been working tonight."

"'Heartbroken'?" she said, trying to make it sound as though she
doubted that.

"Are you working Saturday?" he asked.

"No," she said. She was, but if she had to, she'd call in sick. She hadn't
missed a day since she started working at the club.

"Good. Another couple and I are going to take a cruise over to Isle
of Palms. We're planning to make a day of it: leave about ten, have
mimosas on the way over, have lunch on the isle, do a little shopping,
then be back by seven or eight in the evening. I have a boat moored
down at City Marina." He smiled again. "Fantastic boat—forty-five
feet long, all the bells and whistles."

She wanted to go, she really did, but she had her rules, and she wasn't
going to break them just because the guy intrigued her. "I'd like to go,
but I don't really know you. You could be married."

He laughed. "Not anymore. I was once, back when I was about twenty-
two and didn't really know what I was getting into. No kids, either."

She wasn't sure she liked that answer, the part about not knowing
what he was getting into when he got married. What did he *think* he
was getting into? She also wanted to ask how old he was. She was guess-
ing thirty-four or -five, but instead of asking his age, she said, "Do you
mind telling me what you do?"

"Well, I have a law degree, but I don't practice law. I'm not trying to
be mysterious, but basically I fix things for other lawyers."

"You fix things?"

"Yeah, and unfortunately I don't carry three reference letters with me. So would you like to go on a little boat ride? I'm not going to kidnap you and sell you to white slavers."

She could tell he was becoming a tad impatient with her, and she didn't want to blow this.

"Sure," she said. "It sounds like fun. I'll meet you at the marina at ten." She didn't want him to pick her up; she wanted to have her car available so she could split as soon as the boat docked, if she wanted to. "What's the name of the boat?"

"*House Odds*. It's docked at Pier B in the marina."

"*House Odds*?"

"Yeah, you know. The odds are always in the house's favor."

She didn't know. She'd never been to a casino in her life.

"The weather should be great, according to the forecast," Bill said. "So bring a swimsuit if you feel like it, but dress casual for shopping and lunch. If it gets chilly or rains, there's rain gear and windbreakers on the boat, so you don't need to bring anything like that. See you Saturday." He smiled again—and she felt her heart do a backflip.

After he left, she almost had a panic attack. She was nineteen years old and had never been on a boat before, not a rowboat or a canoe or a ferry. She wondered if she might get seasick. Wouldn't that be perfect, her puking over the side of his fancy boat.

She also needed to go shopping. She had a bikini, one she'd worn the last two years of high school, and she had no doubt it would still fit. The problem was that it looked cheap—because it was. So before Saturday she needed to buy a new bikini, and she needed an outfit to wear on a boat. Shorts, a nice top, a lightweight sweater, some cute tennis shoes. Maybe a baseball cap. This little boat ride was going to cost her at least two hundred bucks. She hoped like hell that this guy was worth it.

She arrived at the marina early, about nine-thirty, and found the pier where the boat was docked, but didn't walk down to it. She didn't want to seem overeager. At five before ten, she strolled down the pier and saw it: *House Odds*. As Bill had said, it was magnificent: a sleek, gleaming white hull, shining brass rails, polished hardwood decks. There was a flying bridge, so you could steer from the outside or inside depending on the weather, and a bunch of antennas and other things she thought might possibly be sonar or radar devices. An awning covered a sundeck.

She didn't see anyone on the boat, however. She called, "Hello?" A moment later Bill stuck his head out of a door that she discovered later was called a "hatch" and led to the galley. "Hey, you're here," he said. "Come aboard."

He was wearing white shorts—he had nice muscular legs—a faded red polo shirt, and Top-Siders without socks. "Patty and Bryan should be here in just a minute. Would you like a mimosa?"

"Uh, sure," she said, but she planned to just sip it. She didn't know if she was going to get seasick but figured that alcohol at ten in the morning wouldn't help.

He started to hand her the drink, then pulled it back and said, "You are old enough to drink, aren't you?"

She thought about lying. She figured she could pass for twenty-one, as she wasn't usually asked to show her ID when she went to bars. She supposed one reason bartenders didn't card her was that they liked having nice-looking young women present. Plus Charleston was a wink-and-look-the-other-way sort of town. When she did have to show ID, she had a poorly made fake that she'd been given by a guy during her senior year in high school, and it worked 99 percent of the time.

But she decided not to lie. If there was any future with this guy, she didn't want to start off with that particular lie.

"I'm nineteen," she said.

"Oh, God," he said. "I'm robbing the cradle." But she could tell he didn't feel too bad about it.

To change the subject, she said, "This is a beautiful boat. Do you own it?"

"Hell, no. I'd never buy a boat. Something's always breaking on the damn things, and most of the people who own them only use them three or four times a year. I just rented this one to impress you."

"Well, I'm impressed," she said—and she was. "Where's your house in Charleston?"

"I don't have a home here. I live—" Then he stopped and yelled to a couple standing on the pier, "Hey there. You're late for drinks. Come aboard."

But Ella was still thinking about the fact that he didn't live in Charleston, and her reaction was: *That's not good.*

"Look," he said to her, "we'll talk later. But I have to warn you, I need to spend some time on this trip talking to Bryan. I'm trying to convince him to do something for me. So just have a good time and we'll talk a lot more—I *want* to talk to you a lot more—but it'll probably be on the way back. You can help me drive the boat."

Bryan and Patty were a handsome couple. Bryan was about Bill's age, maybe thirty-five. Patty was a long-legged redhead with eyes so green they had to be contacts. She was older than Ella, maybe twenty-five. They all had mimosas—Ella was still on the first one Bill had given her—and made small talk about the weather and how much fun Isle of Palms was going to be and about Bill's fabulous boat.

They got under way, Bill and Bryan going up to the flying bridge while Ella and Patty pulled out lounge chairs and sat on the sundeck at the rear of the boat. A few minutes later, Patty stripped off her shorts and T-shirt to reveal a tiny, neon blue bikini. Ella did the same, pleased that she was built better than Patty.

She found out that Patty worked as a secretary for a judge and Bryan was a homicide cop. Bill had told her he was a lawyer but didn't practice law, and she wondered what he was trying to convince Bryan to do.

She heard Bill, on the bridge, say to Bryan, "Try not to run into anyone," then he brought both Ella and Patty another mimosa. He took in Ella in her bikini, making no attempt to act as if he wasn't examining her body, and said, "Wow."

It turned out to be a marvelous day. Not only was the weather perfect, but Ella didn't get seasick. They had a pricey lunch at a place with umbrellas and outdoor tables—Bill paid for everything—then Ella and Patty went shopping while Bill and Bryan sat in a local brewpub trying out the beers. Patty bought a couple of things: sandals that looked likely to fall apart in a month and some beads that Ella thought looked tacky. Ella didn't buy anything. She was a girl who bought things on sale, and she wasn't going to pay the prices they charged gullible tourists.

On the cruise back to Charleston, Bryan and Patty sat on the sundeck and were soon asleep. They were both a little drunk, especially Bryan. Ella was glad that Bill didn't seem drunk at all and had obviously paced himself. She wanted to marry a rich guy and preferred not to marry a drunk, although she hadn't written that down on her list of don'ts.

She stood next to Bill on the bridge as he steered the boat, and after they'd cleared the marina, he said, "Okay, let the grilling begin."

"Grilling?" she said. "I wasn't grilling you." But she had been, and she was irritated that she'd been so unsubtle that he'd noticed. "I'm just curious about you."

"So what do you want to know?"

"Well, you said you didn't live in Charleston. Where do you live?"

"I said I didn't have a *home* in Charleston. But right now this is where I'm living—I've rented a place down on the beach; you'll like it—and I expect to be here for about a year."

"A year? I don't understand. What exactly do you do, and where do you go from here?"

"As for what I do, it's complicated. Like I told you, I'm a lawyer but don't practice law anymore. The truth is, I was disbarred, which was probably the best thing that ever happened to me."

Uh-oh, Ella thought again. "Disbarred" didn't sound good.

"What I do now is I help out other lawyers who have difficult cases."

"Help them out how?"

"It depends on the case. Like I said, it's complicated, but if a lawyer needs some help to win, he might call me, if he can afford me. What I do now pays a hell of a lot better than practicing law."

"You keep saying it's complicated, like I'm too dumb and blond to understand." She tried to keep her voice light, but she was actually getting a little pissed.

"I don't think you're dumb at all. It's just that I can't give you specifics. I'm sure you've heard of lawyer-client privilege, and how what lawyers say to their clients is confidential. Well, that applies to what I do, too."

She found out later that the reason he couldn't be more specific didn't have anything to do with lawyer-client privilege. He just wasn't willing to admit to a girl he'd just met that he was a criminal.

Three months after their first date, Ella was living with Bill Cantwell.

One of her rules was not to fall in love—love was not a prerequisite to marriage—but she'd broken her own rule. She loved the damn guy, she couldn't help it, and she could tell he loved her, too.

In so many ways, he was the ideal mate. He was rich. He was fun to be with. He was great in bed. And she learned *so* much from him. In spite of all the effort she'd made to improve herself, she knew she wasn't sophisticated or well educated, and since Bill was older than she was and had been to college and seen the world, he was always teaching her—and he did it in a way that didn't make her feel stupid.

She had no idea how much money he made, but whatever the amount was, it had to be a lot. Bill Cantwell didn't scrimp. On anything. The beach house rented for eight thousand a month. He leased a Mercedes convertible for the nice days and a Cadillac SUV for the not-so-nice ones. His suits were tailored. She was shocked to learn he ordered some of his shoes from a shoemaker in Italy. He spent money on spas and massages and manicures when he was in the mood. Twice they flew up to New York because he liked the city and wanted to take in a couple of Broadway shows.

When it came to her, he was extraordinarily generous. Once she moved in with him, he couldn't help noticing her wardrobe: how few clothes she had and how cheap most of them were. Without making her feel embarrassed about it, he said she deserved an early Christmas present and that he was buying her a new wardrobe. They shopped that day from ten in the morning until nine at night, and Ella figured he easily spent five thousand dollars. Ella didn't know what was going to happen with him, but if they separated she'd have the clothes she needed to find another man.

After a month of living together, he convinced her to quit her job, not that he had to try that hard. His schedule was erratic, he often didn't leave the house for days at a time, and he wanted her to be there with him when he wasn't working. She asked him, "What am I going to do all day?"

"Think of this as a sabbatical," he said. She knew what a sabbatical was; she'd just never heard of a waitress taking one. "Use the time to educate yourself. Read. Go to art galleries and museums. Sit in on a couple of classes that interest you over at the university. And one thing you're definitely going to do is learn how to play golf."

He was a big golfer, and wanted her to learn so they could play together. He bought her a set of expensive Ping clubs fitted to her measurements, and for a month she took lessons every day with a pro at a nearby course. She was surprised to find out that she was quite good—the pro said she was a natural—and in a couple of months she was able to play with Bill without slowing him down too much.

As for what he did, she still didn't really know, and she had decided, for the time being, not to push him on the subject. As he'd done that day on the boat trip to Isle of Palms, he maintained that he was assisting a lawyer with a difficult case. But exactly *how* he was assisting wasn't clear to her. He'd spend days doing nothing that appeared to be business-related. Other days, he'd sit on the deck at the beach house making calls for hours or he'd be online, studying things on the Internet.

There were several times when he was gone for two or three days, and a number of nights when he left after dark and didn't come home until early in the morning. She wasn't at all worried that he was cheating on her—she was absolutely confident he was still mesmerized by her—but she had no idea what he did those nights he wasn't home. One morning, she found him sitting on the deck, staring at the ocean. He'd been gone for two days and must have come home while she was sleeping. He looked terrible: tired, unshaven—but more than that, he looked *shaken,* as if something had happened that scared him. Whatever it was, it was a couple of days before he was his old self again.

———◆———

Finally, as Ella knew it eventually would, things came to a head between them.

"My work here in Charleston is done," Bill said one day.

It was December, but clear and warm, more like fall than winter. They were sitting on the deck of the beach house, side by side in Adirondack chairs, both looking out at the ocean. There was the slightest breeze coming off the water, just enough to ruffle Bill's hair, and he looked tanned and, well . . . "gorgeous" was the only word she could think of.

"Really?" Ella said, not knowing what that was going to mean in terms of their relationship, and felt her stomach tighten.

"Yeah," he said. "I was able to wrap things up sooner than I expected. I don't know when the next job will come along, but it won't be here. I'm thinking about going to Hawaii for a couple of months, and I want you to come with me."

Ella didn't even hesitate. "No," she said. "Not until you tell me what you really do. And for that matter, who you really are."

For such a gregarious guy, Bill was amazingly adept at saying hardly anything about himself. In the time they'd lived together, she'd learned that he was raised in Colorado, attended the University of Colorado at Boulder, became a lawyer, moved to San Antonio, and then was disbarred. But he wouldn't tell her why he was disbarred; a misunderstanding, he said. He'd told her that he'd been married for a short time and had no children, and she believed him. His father was dead but his mother was alive and lived in Santa Barbara. He seemed fond of his mother, and called her fairly often. But as for his job, all she knew was the paper-thin story that he assisted lawyers with difficult trials.

She didn't want to lose him, however. She was living her dream. She was with a wonderful man who had money to burn and who had introduced her to a world that she'd never had a chance to be a part of until now. She wanted to marry him, but she wasn't about to marry a man whose life was a total mystery. She was fine with leaving Charleston, but she wasn't going to leave with him unless she understood what lay on the road ahead.

Finally he said, "Okay. I'll tell you what I do."

12

As Ella knew she'd be staying in New York for at least six months, she'd taken a lease on a one-bedroom apartment in Chelsea. Actually, she was subleasing. The apartment was owned by a doctor who was on some save-the-children mission in Africa, and he had marvelous taste; his place wasn't some leather-recliner, wide-screen-TV man cave. She wondered if the doctor might be gay. The artwork on the walls was subtle but stunning, he had two Iranian rugs that cost as much as midsize sedans, and the kitchen—which Ella couldn't have cared less about—was designed for a master chef. The place rented for seven thousand a month—which meant it was nowhere near as grand as the places she and Bill had lived in in the past; but it would do.

Two days after she met David Slade at the Mandarin Oriental, Ella spent the day in her apartment reviewing the files he'd given her, which included the witness statements, transcripts of everything said at Toby's lineup, a ballistics report on the bullets that killed DiNunzio, and the results of DiNunzio's autopsy.

The prosecution's case, as she already knew, boiled down to five eye-witnesses and the fact that the state could prove, with Toby's finger-prints, that he'd been in the bar—but that's really all the prosecution had. It had no motive, no murder weapon, and no physical evidence linking Toby directly to the accountant's death. But five witnesses . . .

As she'd told Slade, she and Bill had never had a case that involved five witnesses; the most they'd ever dealt with was three. She couldn't help wondering if she'd bitten off more than she could chew.

Her next step was to have background checks performed on all the witnesses. There are online sites that for a modest fee of $39.95 will provide you all the information supposedly available on a person that is a matter of public record: criminal history, addresses where the person has lived in the past, bankruptcy records, etc. But Ella wanted much more than what a generic online people search engine could provide, and it was going to cost a whole lot more than $39.95.

Five years ago, Bill had come across a company in Dallas that mined the Internet for data and had access to all the right databases. Somehow, and in spite of all those privacy protection guarantees that people are given, this company had relationships with banks and credit card companies, and could get information that a law enforcement agency would have needed a warrant to obtain. For a very hefty fee, Ella could get not only material that was a matter of public record but also an in-depth financial profile of an individual. And unlike the data provided by the companies that charged $39.95, the Dallas firm's information was accurate. She called the people in Dallas, gave them all she had on the five witnesses, and told them to start digging. It would take them a week to provide what she wanted, after which they would FedEx a report to her—Ella didn't want them sending her an email.

While waiting for the background checks to be completed, Ella visited the witnesses' residences. Jack Morris, the bartender, lived in a five-story walk-up in Brooklyn that was a complete dump. The barmaid, Kathy Tolliver, also lived in Brooklyn, in a similar dump. Ella, being an ex-waitress, couldn't imagine how bartenders and barmaids could afford to live in New York, even in the hovels Jack and Kathy lived in. Edmundo Ortiz, the busboy, lived in a public housing project in Queens called the Astoria Houses. Not a place Ella would want to visit alone after dark.

The other two witnesses appeared to have money. The old lady, Esther Behrman, lived in an upscale assisted living facility in Manhattan, on the Upper West Side off Riverside Drive, within a short walk of the Hudson River. Rachel Quinn, Ms. eHarmony, lived in a high-rise with a doorman on the Upper East Side, not far from the Guggenheim Museum.

A week after she requested the information, a thick FedEx envelope from Dallas arrived—and Ella could immediately see how she was going to take care of the bartender, Jack Morris. He was going to be a walk in the park. She could also see a viable approach for dealing with the barmaid and the busboy. The fact that none of these three people had much money gave her options. Rachel Quinn, however, turned out to be loaded, as was the old lady, Esther Behrman. Esther had a net worth of about two million and Rachel made almost four hundred grand a year working as a lawyer for a hedge fund.

Ella didn't see anything in the data about Rachel Quinn that she could use, making her think that Ms. eHarmony was going to be a challenge. In regard to the old lady, she could see a possible way forward, but it was going to be risky. Really risky. On the other hand, you couldn't expect to make two million on a case without taking some chances—something Bill didn't always seem to understand.

That night, Ella went to McGill's—the scene of the crime—and took a seat at the bar. She was wearing a black wig over her short blond hair and a pair of glasses with large black frames. Her dress was the fashion equivalent of a gunnysack, and on her feet were clunky black Doc Martens. On her ring finger was a wedding ring, but not the one Bill had given her, just a plain gold band. She dumped a purse the size of a small duffel bag on the bar stool next to her, then spread out the financial section of *The New York Times*. In other words, she did everything she could think of to keep men from hitting on her.

Jack Morris was behind the bar making someone a blue martini and was wearing black tuxedo pants, a white dress shirt, and a black bow tie. He was close to seventy and had the wrinkles of a longtime smoker. Ella could see that he was a competent bartender. He chatted with the customers if they were in the mood, but left them alone if they weren't. He made drinks fast and never overpoured, which the owner of McGill's certainly must have appreciated. And he caged tips.

Ella used to do the same thing when she worked in restaurants so that she wouldn't have to share all her tips with coworkers. Morris was careful and didn't get too greedy. If a customer left three ones on the bar, he'd deftly palm one, place the other two in the tip jar, and, when he was certain the barmaid wasn't watching, slip the one he'd palmed into his pocket. Once a drunk, probably by accident, left a twenty for a tip—and the twenty magically turned into a five. Ella liked the fact that Jack Morris was a sneaky thief.

Ella watched as Edmundo Ortiz lugged a couple of bags of ice into the bar and poured them into a cooler where bottles of beer were kept. Ortiz moved fast and efficiently, and Ella bet that he was a hell of a worker, and probably an honest one, unlike Jack Morris. She didn't see Kathy Tolliver. There was a short, chunky blonde in her forties who was serving drinks to the tables—definitely not Kathy—and Ella wondered if it was Kathy's night off or if she had called in sick.

While sitting at the bar, Ella took in the lighting and dimensions of the room. Included with the information provided by David Slade had been a sketch that showed where all the witnesses had been seated when the killing took place, and Ella had memorized it before coming to the bar.

Rachel Quinn had been sitting near the door that customers used to enter the bar from the street, and her table was about seventy feet from where Dominic DiNunzio had been sitting when he was shot. The problem—for the defense—was that Toby ran right past Quinn's table when he fled the bar. The entrance to the kitchen was about four feet from Quinn's table, and that's where Edmundo Ortiz had been standing, holding a tray of glasses, when Toby ran past him holding a gun in his hand. What all this meant was that Toby Rosenthal had been only a couple of feet away from Quinn and the busboy as he ran from the bar—which was not good at all. Ella wasn't too worried about the busboy, but again Rachel Quinn was looking like a major problem.

The bar, where Jack Morris and Kathy Tolliver had been standing when DiNunzio was shot, was also about seventy feet from DiNunzio's table. Toby's face would have been recognizable from this distance, but because of the dim lighting in the room, Jack and Kathy could claim to be less sure about what they saw—and when Ella was done with them, that's exactly what they'd claim.

The old lady, Esther Behrman, was a different story. Esther, in fact, had had the catbird seat. She'd been sitting only about ten feet from DiNunzio's table and she'd clearly seen Toby when he shot the accountant—that's what she'd told the detectives who interviewed her, and she'd had no problem at all picking Toby out of the lineup.

It was really a shame, but Esther . . . Well, Esther just had to go.

13

Fourteen years earlier
Charleston, South Carolina—December 2002

"Okay," Bill said as they sat there on the deck of the rented beach house in Charleston, "I'll tell you what I do."

"Good," Ella said, but she was as nervous as she'd been three years ago when she was sixteen and missed her period—an occasion that turned out to be a false alarm.

"Like I told you, I assist lawyers, defense lawyers," Bill said.

"But I don't know what that means," Ella said.

"If you'll stop talking, I'll tell you." Then he smiled to take the edge off his words. "Let's say a man runs over another man with his car and flees the scene and is later caught by the police."

"You mean a hit-and-run," Ella said.

"Exactly. And in this particular case, let's say three witnesses saw the man commit the crime. They got his license plate number, or maybe he stepped out of the car and they were able to identify him. You with me?"

It *really* irritated her when he did that, like she was too slow to keep up, but all she did was nod.

"Well, the man's lawyer might ask me to help out. In this case, that means I need to make sure the three witnesses don't testify, or that if they do testify, they say they were mistaken and can't identify the driver."

"So what did you do?" Ella said. "And stop pretending this is all hypothetical."

Bill gave her a little, rueful okay-you-got-me smile. "This was actually the first job I had, and it turned out to be fairly simple. One of the witnesses, a guy who was about one step from being evicted from his house, I just paid to lie when he testified, and that's what he did. He got on the stand and said he'd had quite a bit to drink that night and really didn't see the driver all that well."

"Okay," Ella said.

"The second witness was a kid. He was eighteen years old, living on his own, just like you when I met you. He had a shitty job at a Home Depot stocking shelves from midnight till six and was taking about one class a quarter at some community college to get a degree. He was renting a room in this old lady's house, and to keep the rent low, he mowed the lawn and fixed shit and was basically the old lady's slave.

"Well, I found out he wanted to be a writer and was always talking about going to Europe, so I sat down with him one day and handed him an airline ticket—a one-way ticket to Paris that departed the day the trial started. I picked Paris because I figured he'd probably read stories about Hemingway and F. Scott Fitzgerald writing in some little café on the Left Bank."

"Left bank of what?" Ella said.

"The Seine River; we'll see it together one day. Anyway, I explained to him that I didn't want him to appear at the trial and that in addition to the ticket, I'd give him enough cash so he could bum around Europe for six months.

"He wasn't a terrorist, his name wasn't on any sort of watch list, and the prosecutor wouldn't even know he'd left the country until it was too late. I told him once the trial was over, he could go wherever he wanted. He was a bright kid and his life sucked and he knew an opportunity like this might never come along again. He took the deal."

"Huh," Ella said. "And the third witness?"

"The third witness was a problem. He was an upstanding citizen—married, had a decent job and a kid. He wasn't rich but he didn't have much debt, so I wasn't sure I could buy him off. I followed him for two months to see if he had any vices, like seeing hookers or visiting gay bars on the down low—something I could use to blackmail him—but he was squeaky clean."

"So did you kill him?" Ella said.

"No," Bill said—but he didn't say it like: *My God, of course not. I'd never do that.* He just said, "No."

"What I did was kidnap his little girl."

"Jesus, Bill!" Ella said.

"Well, 'kidnap' is maybe a little strong. I picked up his daughter from her day care place, told the idiot day care lady I was little Susie's uncle, and took her to a petting zoo. I bought her an ice cream cone and a balloon, and we actually had a pretty good time. Four hours later, when her parents were frantic, I dropped her off at a store near her house and called the dad and told him where his daughter was. But I told him that if he testified against the driver, his kid would disappear and he'd never see her again. It helped that the driver was rumored to have connections to a Mexican drug cartel—this was in Texas—but the truth was he wasn't connected to them in any way."

"And I take it the dad didn't testify," Ella said.

"Nope. Got amnesia on the stand, and the defendant walked."

"Huh," Ella said. "Would you have done it?"

"Done what?"

"Disappeared the little girl if he testified?"

"Of course not. Not only was she a little girl, but if the guy had testified against the driver at the trial, the game would have been over. I took a stupid risk as it was taking her, and I've never done anything that dumb again, but I bluffed the guy and it worked. If it hadn't, there was no way I would have hurt a kid."

He paused and said, "Now you understand what I do, Ella. So are you going to come with me when I leave Charleston?"

Ella's mind was spinning.

She'd fallen in love with a criminal.

"Judging by where we're living right now," she said, "what you do pays pretty well."

"I don't work cheap, and I only take cases where the defendant is very rich. I'm not going to risk going to prison for a few thousand bucks."

"So how much do you charge?"

Bill hesitated. They'd never talked about money before. "A million per case," he finally said.

"Jesus," Ella said. Now, that was impressive.

"So what are you going to do, Ella? Are you going to come with me or not?"

"Bill, I'm going for a walk. I need to think."

———— ◆ ————

Ella stepped off the deck, walked through the dunes, and went down to the beach. She took off her sandals and strolled along the edge of the water, where every once in a while a cold wave would come in and tickle her feet.

"Well, Ella Sue," she said out loud, "what are you gonna do?"

She called herself Ella Sue only when she felt particularly stupid.

Falling in love with a disbarred lawyer and self-confessed criminal was definitely *not* on her things-to-do list. Her plan had always been to marry a rich man, figuring if things didn't turn out the way she wanted, she would divorce him—and she'd divorce him while she still looked good enough to snag another man. If the man insisted she sign a prenup, she'd make him see what he'd be missing if he didn't marry her, then walk away—and he'd tear up the prenup and beg her to come back. And when she divorced him, she'd end up with a big house, a fancy car, and a pile of cash. Maybe not enough cash to live on for the rest of her life, but enough to let her live in style until she could marry another rich man.

Yep, that had been her plan—and that plan had just flown out the window like a big-ass bird.

She loved Bill Cantwell, no doubt about it, but more important than love was that he was just about perfect in so many ways. Not only was he fun to be around, but he'd broadened her horizons; she was growing in so many ways because of him. Best of all, he seemed to have money to burn, which you'd expect if he made a million on each job—unless, of course, he was lying about that.

But what would happen to her if they arrested him—which was certainly a possibility. If she were living with him, they'd probably think she was his accomplice, and she might get arrested, too. She was not going to end up in prison, and she wasn't going to wait around for him if *he* ended up in prison. And although he'd never brought up the subject of marriage—and she hadn't pressed him on it—what if they got married? He'd already told her he didn't own a home—he just lived wherever his work took him—so she wouldn't end up with a house if they divorced. For that matter, she might not end up with half his money in a divorce, either. She didn't know for sure, but she figured that if he made his money illegally, the government might be able to take whatever he had. Or that, because he made his money illegally, he hid it somewhere, like in an offshore account or buried under a damn rock. Whatever the case, she might not see a dime of his money as his ex-wife.

"So what are you gonna do, Ella Sue?" she said again. This was not a time to get emotional. This was a time for cold-blooded, dispassionate logic. This was her *life* she was talking about.

The smart thing would be to walk away. She was only nineteen years old. She had plenty of time to find another man. But would another one like Bill—minus the criminal history, that is—ever come along? Then there was Bill's age. He was a virile thirty-five right now, but still sixteen years older than her. His being sixteen years older didn't make much difference now, when she was nineteen and he was thirty-five, but it could make a lot of difference when he was old and sick and senile; she did *not* intend to become some old man's nursemaid.

Yeah, no doubt about it, it was time to walk away.

Hell, it was time to *run* away.

Ella returned to the beach house. Bill was still sitting on the deck, drinking a beer, looking out at the waves slapping the beach.

"Looks like the wind's picking up," he said. "I wonder if it's going to rain tonight." When she didn't answer—could he possibly think she wanted to talk about the fucking weather?—he turned to face her. "Well?" he said.

"I'll go with you on two conditions," Ella said.

"Okay."

"First, we're going to get married."

To hell with cold-blooded logic.

Bill smiled at her. "Darling, nothing on this earth would make me happier. What's the second condition?"

"We're going to have a serious—and I mean *serious*—talk about money."

14

Ella knew three important things about Esther Behrman. First, she was eighty-six years old. Second, her short-term memory and her eyes worked just fine; she'd had no problem at all picking Toby Rosenthal out of a lineup and would make an excellent witness. And third, as Ella had concluded after visiting the crime scene, Esther was the *best* witness against Toby, since she'd been seated closest to the table where Dominic DiNunzio had been shot. Considering Esther's age, the longer David Slade could delay the trial, the better the chances were that she might croak from natural causes. Unfortunately, however, Ella had no way to ensure that Mother Nature would cooperate.

No one stopped Ella when she walked into the assisted living facility where Esther lived. Off to the right of the entrance was a hotel-like reception desk. A sign said that visitors were required to check in, and a woman was at the desk, looking down at some paperwork as she talked on the phone. The lobby had a number of sofas and chairs where people could sit, coffee tables stacked with magazines like those in a dentist's waiting room, potted plants next to the sofas. There were about a dozen people in the lobby: a couple of old ladies sitting and chatting, wearing coats, probably waiting for someone to pick them up; a few more old women in wheelchairs, sitting alone as if someone had parked them where they were and forgotten them; and two middle-aged couples hovering over an old woman. It was a busy place, and from what Ella had read online, there were at least three hundred residents.

Ella walked briskly past the reception desk, expecting the woman there might call out to her, but she didn't—so Ella walked to the stairs and started up. She found Esther's apartment on the fourth floor. The only other person in sight was an ancient crone who had her back to Ella and who was bent into the shape of a question mark from scoliosis or something. Ella examined the lock on Esther's door. She had no intention of breaking in today; she just wanted to see what she'd be up against. She'd been hoping Esther would have a cheap lock, one she could open by slipping a knife blade between the latch and the doorframe—but no such luck. Esther had a good lock.

Ella went back down to the lobby and strolled around the facility. She saw a few people dressed like housekeepers or nurse's aides, but again no one asked her who she was or what she was doing. If she'd had a relative living there, she would have complained about the lack of security. Near the dining room she found a poster board that took up an entire wall, and on the board were photos of the residents. Under each photo was the person's name—Ella was surprised at how few men lived there—and a short phrase saying something about the person.

The Dallas data miners had provided Ella with a photo of Esther taken from a driver's license that was long expired, and Ella was hoping the poster board would have a more recent photo. It did. Under Esther Behrman's smiling picture—Ella had to admit the old girl looked as though she still had a lot of life left in her—the label said: *Esther can play bridge with the best of them. And poker, too.* Ella used her phone to take a photo of Esther's photo.

As Ella was leaving, she noticed a security guard standing near the reception desk. He was an overweight black man in his fifties, wearing a white shirt with a gold patch resembling a badge. On his belt he had a radio, a flashlight, and a big ring of keys, but no weapon. He was your basic useless rent-a-cop, and Ella imagined his only job was to chase away any bums who might try to enter the facility. Since Ella didn't look like a bum, she wasn't worried about the security guard.

Ella had an idea for how to deal with Esther. It occurred to her when she looked at Esther's credit card charges and saw that every three months, regular as clockwork, she paid a pharmacy bill. What Ella needed to do was break into Esther's apartment when she wasn't there and take a look at her medications—but she hadn't figured out how she was going to do that.

Ella hated driving in New York, but she decided to rent a car in case she had to follow Esther. She left the car in the parking lot behind the facility in one of the spots marked for visitors. There were a lot of empty visitors' spots, and she thought it pretty unlikely that her car would be towed. The first morning she waited outside the front entrance, hoping Esther might venture out. She didn't. At lunchtime, Ella went inside, took a seat in the lobby, picked up a magazine, and pretended to read, as if she was waiting for one of the residents. No one said a word to her.

At noon Ella saw Esther and another old lady get out of the elevator. Esther was five foot six, a bit stout, but moved well for her age; she didn't use a walker or a cane. The woman with her was short and slim, and chatting like a magpie as she and Esther walked to the dining room.

Ella left the lobby, walked up the stairs to Esther's apartment, and checked to see if the door was locked. It was. Rats. Esther hadn't been carrying a purse when she went to lunch, so she probably had her apartment key in a pocket. The next two days, Ella did the same thing, going out of her mind with boredom, hanging around the assisted living facility, hoping Esther would leave. She wore a different-colored wig each day, sometimes a hat, and sunglasses.

On the fourth day, a Tuesday, at ten a.m., a short bus that would hold about twenty people pulled up in front of the main entrance to Esther's building and a gaggle of old women came shuffling out and boarded the bus. One of the women was Esther, and with her was the little lady that Esther had had lunch with the other day. It seemed as if she and Esther were best friends.

Today Esther was wearing a navy blue Yankees baseball cap, a white sweatshirt, blue jeans, and neon blue running shoes. Ella couldn't help smiling when she saw Esther's shoes. Her pal was also wearing a baseball cap—a pink one, probably a breast cancer cap—jeans, and tennis shoes so white they looked as if they'd never touched dirt. Esther's friend had a fanny pack—and Ella thanked God that Esther wasn't wearing one. Esther was carrying a large purse.

Ella followed the bus to the Manhattan Mall on Broadway off Thirty-third Street. It appeared the residents were going on a shopping trip, where they'd most likely have lunch and maybe get their hair done, and Ella wondered if this was a weekly excursion. But now Ella had to scramble: She had to park the damn car, then get back in time to follow Esther, because the mall didn't have its own parking lot.

A sign near the mall told her that there was a parking lot a block away. Ella's tires squealed on the asphalt as she raced to the lot, then she sprinted back to the shopping mall. By the time she got back, all the old ladies had gotten off the bus and a young woman, most likely a member of the facility's staff, was giving a lecture to the group, probably telling them what time they needed to get back to the bus. Ella wondered if they had GPS devices strapped to the old women so they could find them if they got lost. If they didn't, they should have.

The group broke up and Esther and her friend took off, looking ready to shop until they dropped. Ella followed them, and when they entered a women's clothing store, she took a seat outside the store and pulled out her cell phone and searched Google Maps. Thank God for smartphones and the Internet. She found what she needed only two blocks from the mall.

Moving quickly, Ella went into a sporting goods store across from the women's clothing store that Esther had entered. She paid cash for a cheap New York Knicks blue nylon jacket with orange sleeves and an orange baseball cap with a Nike swoosh on the front. She asked the clerk for a large shopping bag to hold her purchases, but once outside the store, she put on the jacket and the cap, keeping the empty shopping bag. Ella had a plan—now all she needed was some luck.

Esther and her buddy came out of the women's clothing store and continued down the mall, Ella following. Ella couldn't help noticing that Esther moved at a pretty good clip. In fact, for an eighty-six-year-old, Esther was amazingly fast on her feet.

Ella noticed that Esther had her purse slung over her shoulder and kept one hand on it. She'd most likely heard stories about young thieves running by, snipping purse straps with a switchblade, and running like Jesse Owens. Ella needed to snatch that purse—and she had an idea for how she was going to do it—but an hour later Esther and her friend were *still* wandering around the mall. They didn't buy a damn thing—but, man, did they have stamina.

Finally, Esther gave Ella the opportunity she'd been waiting for. Esther's friend went into a store called Perfume Heaven, which made Ella smile. Who was the old gal wearing perfume for? Did she have a young seventy-year-old stud back at the assisted living place? Esther, however, didn't go into Perfume Heaven with her. Instead, Esther headed toward the ladies' room.

Ella allowed Esther enough time to take a seat in a stall, then walked into the restroom, praying it wouldn't be crowded. It wasn't. Only one other stall was being used; Ella could see a woman's calf-high boots beneath the door. Esther's bright blue running shoes were visible in the other occupied stall. Ella peeked under the door of the stall Esther was using, and there was Esther's purse, on the floor, near her feet. Ella dropped to her knees, and quick as a striking cobra, she grabbed the purse. She heard Esther shriek as she ran toward the bathroom door.

Ella threw Esther's purse into her shopping bag and walked quickly to the nearest large store, a JCPenney. As she walked toward one of the fitting rooms, she dropped her orange baseball cap on the floor near a rack full of puffy ski jackets. In the dressing room, she removed Esther's purse from the shopping bag, opened it, and found what she wanted: Esther's key ring.

There were only two keys on the ring, and one looked as if it might open a safe-deposit box at a bank. The other key was certainly for Esther's apartment door. Ella put the keys and the cash she found in Esther's purse—a grand total of forty-two bucks—in her jeans and dropped the purse back into the shopping bag, where she also deposited the black wig she was wearing and her new Knicks jacket. The reason Ella had bought the jacket and the orange baseball cap in the first place was so that if a witness spotted her when she stole Esther's purse, the witness would most likely identify those two distinctive items—items Ella was no longer wearing.

Ella left JCPenney and walked rapidly to the nearest mall exit. The information she'd looked up on her smartphone was the location of hardware stores near the Manhattan Mall, and she'd found a place called Elm Electric & Hardware between West Thirty-first and Thirty-second, less than two blocks from the mall. She wouldn't even have to use her car to get there.

Outside the mall, Ella jogged to the hardware store and had a copy of Esther's door key made. It took only fifteen minutes. Now she had to return Esther's purse to Esther, because the last thing she wanted was Esther changing her lock. Back at the mall, she stopped the first security guard she saw, and said, "I saw this purse on a bench. Someone must have forgotten it."

By now Esther would have reported to mall security that someone had stolen her purse, and Ella figured that before long an announcement would be made over the public address system telling lucky Esther where she could reclaim her property. And when Esther saw that the only thing missing was her cash, but that her credit cards and keys were still there, she'd thank the Lord—and certainly wouldn't change her lock.

15

Ella returned to the assisted living facility the following day, arriving there just before lunchtime. Ten minutes later she saw Esther get off the elevator and walk toward the dining room. As soon as Esther disappeared into the dining room, Ella headed to her apartment on the fourth floor and, using the key she'd had made, opened the door.

She noticed that Esther's furniture was simple and sleek, not the old floral-patterned, heavy stuffed chairs and couches she'd expected. She had a beautiful Persian rug in her small living room and a secretary's desk painted in black lacquered enamel with a gold foil design that Ella thought was really quite lovely. But Ella didn't have time to spend admiring Esther's furniture.

She went to the bathroom and opened the medicine cabinet above the sink—and was surprised to see how few items were in it. There was a toothbrush, toothpaste, and dental floss; it appeared as if Esther still had her own teeth. There was deodorant, a box of laxatives, a big bottle of Tylenol for arthritis pain, and a blue bottle of Mylanta. There were also three amber-colored prescription vials with white "easy open" tops that are harder than shit to open—exactly what Ella had been hoping to find.

Reading the labels, Ella saw that the first prescription vial contained omeprazole, the second Coumadin, and the third digoxin. Ella knew that omeprazole was for acid reflux, because Bill had to take it at one time. Ella couldn't help smiling when she thought about Bill and the omeprazole. One day while they'd been playing golf, Bill had thought he was having a heart attack—he'd scared the hell out of her—but it had turned out to be acid reflux and the doctor had given him a prescription for omeprazole. Bill, instead of changing his eating and drinking habits, started taking the omeprazole in advance on nights when he was planning to overindulge.

But Ella didn't know what the other two prescription meds were for. It also appeared that Esther wasn't going to need a refill anytime soon. There were about sixty pills in both the Coumadin and the digoxin vials; the labels on the vials said that Esther had to take one pill a day and that she'd started out with ninety pills in each vial. Ella went to the cute desk in Esther's living room and found two small envelopes, the type used for birthday or sympathy cards. She wrote *Coumadin* on one envelope and *digoxin* on the other, returned to Esther's bathroom, and placed the proper pill in the proper envelope. She was certain Esther wouldn't notice a single pill missing.

Then, because she was curious and wondered what else she might learn about the state of Esther's health, Ella opened the linen closet in the bathroom. There were towels and washcloths neatly folded on the top shelf, but the other two shelves were a mess. There were hand mirrors, brushes, combs, and a hair dryer; there were a dozen squeeze tubes containing sunscreen lotions, creams for itches and bug bites, and antibiotic ointments; there were Band-Aids in every size imaginable. It appeared as if the linen closet was where Esther dumped all the crap she rarely used and the medicine cabinet was where she kept the things she used frequently, like her prescription meds.

Ella then walked quickly through the apartment looking for one other thing she was sure she would find, but that she hadn't seen in Esther's bathroom. Nor was it in Esther's bedroom on a nightstand, as she thought it might be. She hoped Esther didn't keep it in her purse, but didn't think she did because Ella hadn't seen it in there when she'd stolen it. She finally found it on the small table in Esther's kitchen, next to a napkin holder: one of those pill organizer boxes, the type that have little compartments marked with each day of the week. Ella opened the box and saw that the slots for Sunday, Monday, Tuesday, and Wednesday were empty but that Thursday, Friday, and Saturday each contained two pills: one Coumadin, and one digoxin. It appeared that Esther didn't take the omeprazole on a daily basis.

Ella glanced at her watch; only twenty minutes had elapsed since Esther had gone to lunch. She took one last look around the apartment to make sure she hadn't left any telltale signs that she'd broken in. She poked her head out the door and glanced down the hallway. It was empty; not an old person in sight. She closed the door behind her, made sure it was locked, and left.

Ella returned to her apartment in Chelsea, made a pot of coffee, then got on the Internet to learn about Coumadin and digoxin.

She discovered that Coumadin was an anticoagulant used to prevent thrombosis, basically a blood thinner to prevent blood clots that could lead to strokes. Digoxin, Ella was surprised to learn, was essentially a poison made from the foxglove plant but used for treating various heart conditions like atrial fibrillation and atrial flutter. After studying a dozen websites, Ella concluded that Esther had some sort of serious heart condition and that if she failed to take her medication she could have a heart attack or a stroke.

Perfect.

Ella noted that Esther's Coumadin was a little blue pill. It had the word "Coumadin" and the number 4 on one side; nothing was written on the other. The digoxin pill was eggshell white and had the letters

JSP and the number 545 on one side; as with the Coumadin pill, the other side was blank.

Now knowing everything she needed to know, Ella went shopping. She visited two drugstores and one of those places that sold vitamins and diet supplements and all sorts of homeopathic crap. In each store, she bought two or three different medications that looked as though they might do. Then she went back to her apartment and examined the medications in detail and found one blue pill that was an over-the-counter antihistamine and a little white pill that was an appetite suppressant, a diet pill. The pills were identical in size and color to Esther's Coumadin and digoxin pills, but had different markings on them. Ella doubted, however, that Esther studied the pills before she popped them into her mouth.

———◆———

Now Ella needed Esther to leave her apartment again, and she wanted her to be gone for more than an hour. The trip Esther had taken to the Manhattan Mall had been at ten a.m. on a Tuesday, and Ella was hoping that Tuesday was the regular weekly field trip day for the old folks. Ella arrived at the assisted living facility at nine thirty a.m.— and sure enough, the little bus pulled up at ten. Esther and her short pal were the first people to board, Esther again wearing her Yankees baseball cap.

The bus took off, and Ella, this time wearing a wig with short auburn curls, entered the lobby carrying a large bouquet of flowers to partially obscure her face—not that anyone was watching—and took the stairs up to Esther's floor. She placed the flowers outside a randomly selected door, thinking some old person would get a nice surprise today. She entered Esther's apartment using the key she'd had made, and walked straight to the medicine cabinet. She opened the Coumadin vial and started to dump the pills into the toilet—then stopped. No, dumping the pills wouldn't be smart.

She walked into Esther's kitchen and got two plastic sandwich bags and returned to the bathroom. She poured the Coumadin pills into one of the plastic bags and the digoxin pills into the other. She filled up the prescription vials in the medicine cabinet with blue antihistamine pills and white diet pills, then did the same with Esther's pill organizer, which was still sitting on the kitchen table. The next thing she did was put the half-empty bottles of antihistamine and diet pills in the linen closet where Esther kept the lotions and bandages and all the other medications she didn't use very often.

There had been approximately sixty Coumadin and digoxin pills in each of the prescription vials before Ella refilled them with antihistamine and diet pills, which meant that if Esther didn't have some sort of cardiac event in sixty days, Ella would have to refill them. Ella knew that if Esther didn't take her prescription meds it wouldn't be good for her heart, but she wondered if the antihistamine and diet pills might actually speed her decline along. Oh, well, all she could do was hope for the best.

Ella figured that if an eighty-six-year-old woman had a stroke and died there wouldn't be an autopsy, and she doubted that anyone would examine her pills to see if they were the correct type. If, however, for some strange reason, someone did check and saw that the pills in Esther's pillbox were diet and antihistamine pills rather than Coumadin and digoxin, then saw the appetite suppressant and antihistamine bottles in Esther's linen closet, they'd conclude that a muddleheaded eighty-six year-old had just put the wrong pills in the pillbox.

On the other hand, if someone saw that the prescription vials contained the wrong pills, that could be a problem. No way would Esther have filled up the prescription vials with the wrong pills; those vials would have been filled by a pharmacist. So Ella was going to have to find a way to deal with the unlikely but potential problem that someone might discover that Esther's prescription vials contained the wrong meds.

Ella returned to the assisted living facility the next day. She needed to find a way to keep tabs on Esther's medical condition. In other words, she needed a spy. Ella had read enough spy novels to know there were basically three ways you recruited a spy: You paid him, you blackmailed him, or you appealed to his ideology. Ideology didn't seem to apply to this situation, and she figured a combination of bribery and blackmail would be best.

Ella spent two incredibly boring days watching the assisted living facility. Every day she arrived at six in the morning and parked in the lot behind the building in one of the visitors' spots. The parking lot was good, because she could see the back of the building from there as well as the entrance on one side. She arrived early, figuring the staff—the nurse's aides, the cooks, the maintenance guys—would arrive early.

Ella was looking for a drunk. In the restaurants where she'd worked before meeting Bill, there was always a boozer, one of those guys who would periodically take little nips from a bottle he stashed in his car or out by the Dumpsters, then spend the day in cruise control: mellow but not falling-down, slur-his-words drunk. On the first day she found one candidate, and on the second day she found another.

The first was a white man who was maybe sixty, and dressed as if he might be part of the kitchen crew. He had a white jacket and those checkered black-and-white pants cooks sometimes wear. He'd go out for a cigarette, then walk over to a beat-up Ford with Jersey plates parked at the far end of the parking lot. He'd look around to see if anyone was watching him, slip into the car, look around again, and pull a pint bottle out of the glove compartment. He'd take a couple of swigs from the bottle, return it to the glove compartment, and, as he walked back to the building, eat about a dozen Altoids.

The second candidate wasn't a boozer; he liked a little Mary Jane a couple times a day. He was a young black guy with dreadlocks that hung to his shoulders and dressed in blue coveralls like a maintenance man. He was well built and moved like an athlete, and Ella thought he was kind of cute.

The facility had grounds with walkways that wound through a garden filled with ferns and trees and flowering plants, and there were a number of benches where the old folks could sit. One of the benches was behind a big rhododendron that was in full bloom and more secluded than the others, and the pot smoker would take a seat there and light up a joint. For whatever reason—stupidity or maybe because he was always half-stoned—he didn't seem concerned that another staff member might catch him.

So. The old drunk or the young doper? She decided to go with the doper.

She watched the next day when he walked out of the building and headed toward his smoking bench. She gave him enough time to light up, then sneaked up on him. When she popped into view, he was startled, trying to figure out what to do with the joint.

"It's okay," she said. "Finish your smoke. In fact, be polite and let me have a hit."

He smiled then and offered her the joint, and she took a puff, holding the smoke in her lungs, the way she used to do when she was a kid. She hadn't smoked pot since she'd left Calhoun Falls.

"Nice," she said as she handed the joint back to him. "What's your name?"

"Curtis," he said. "You, uh, visiting someone here?"

"Yeah, Curtis, I'm visiting you. You're going to do me a favor. It's not a big deal, it's nothing illegal, and in return for this favor I'm going to give you five hundred bucks today and two hundred bucks a week, as long as you continue to do me the favor."

"What's the favor?" he said, now suspicious. At the same time, Ella could tell Curtis was already spending the money in his head.

"Before we get to the favor, let me tell you what's going to happen if you don't do what I want. I'm going to march into the building and tell whoever's in charge that you come out here every day to smoke dope and I don't want my dear old aunt around people like you."

Curtis shook his head, like a guy that life had shit on before. "So what's the favor?" he asked.

"It's simple. There's a resident here named Esther Behrman."

"Yeah, I know Esther. She's a good tipper."

That surprised Ella. "Anyway, what I want you to do is call me every day and tell me how Esther's doing. Just leave a message if I don't answer."

"How she's doing?"

"Yep, that's all. I'm concerned about her health. It's a family thing, a legal thing—you don't need to know exactly what—but once a day you call and tell me if everything's okay with her. If she gets hauled off to the hospital, I need to know."

"That's it?"

"That's it."

"But how would I know how she's doing? I'm not on the medical staff."

"Esther eats lunch and dinner in the dining room every day. So you find a way to hang around the dining room before meals and see if she shows up. If she doesn't show up, you find out why. Can you do that?"

"Yeah, I guess."

"I'm sure you can do this, Curtis. You're a smart guy. You're also a good-looking guy, and I'll bet the nurses and the kitchen ladies like you."

"But I'm off on Sundays unless there's some kind of emergency, like a toilet backs up or something," Curtis said.

"I figured that. So I won't expect a call from you on Sunday."

"I don't know," Curtis said. "Are you sure this isn't illegal?"

"How could it be illegal, you giving me a call and saying you saw Esther eating her lunch?" She pulled a roll of bills out of a pocket—twenty-five twenty-dollar bills, which made for a very fat roll—and held out the money to Curtis. He hesitated, just for a second, then took the money. "Now give me your address so I can mail you the two hundred every week." Curtis gave her his address in Queens, which Ella put into her phone. Then she handed Curtis a yellow Post-it note. "That's my phone number. Don't lose it."

Phone security was one thing that Ella paid a lot of attention to. Cell phones were marvelous devices, computers that fit in the palm of your hand. You could look things up on the Internet—like where to get a key made—get directions, take pictures, read a book. On the other hand they were incredibly dangerous, because people—meaning cops—could locate you using your phone and listen in when you talked. So one of the first things Ella did at the beginning of a case was buy half a dozen prepaid cell phones.

She'd given one of the phones she'd purchased to David Slade and she used another phone, one marked with Slade's name, to communicate with him. The phone number she had just given to Curtis was the number of a third prepaid phone, and she'd mark his name on it with a piece of tape later. She didn't like the idea of talking to Curtis on a phone, even a phone that couldn't be traced to her, but it was going to be necessary in order to make sure things went right with Esther.

Ella stood up. "Finish your joint, Curtis, but I expect to hear from you once a day until I tell you otherwise. And if I don't hear from you . . . Well, I hear it's hard to find jobs these days, but I wouldn't know."

As Ella walked back to her car, she couldn't help thinking that Bill would never have done what she was doing with Esther. That had been one of the problems working with Bill. She'd loved the man dearly, but he didn't always have the . . . well, the *heart* to do the hard things that sometimes had to be done.

16

Thirteen years earlier
Hawaii—January 2003

Bill and Ella were married on the island of Kauai.

Bill asked if she wanted her parents to attend the ceremony, and Ella said no. She hadn't spoken to her parents since she had left Calhoun Falls—and never intended to speak to them again. Bill flew his mother over from Santa Barbara.

The first thing Bill's mother said when Bill introduced her to Ella was: "Well, aren't you just lovely. You're as pretty as the granddaughter I've always wanted."

Bill said, "Gimme a break, Mom."

But it turned out that Ella actually grew to like Bill's mother, whose name was Janet Kerns, her last name coming from her fourth husband. She was very attractive and well preserved, although Ella could tell that she'd had a little work done. Her first husband, Bill's dad, had died not long after Bill was born; the next two husbands she divorced—and the fact that husband number four didn't come to the wedding made Ella wonder if he was about to become *ex*-number four. Janet was witty and rather cynical and reminded Ella of herself in many ways, and judging by the way she dressed and the stones on her fingers, she certainly had money. Ella concluded that Bill's mom had done exactly what Ella had planned to do when she left Calhoun

Falls: She'd married a bunch of rich guys, and now lived well because she had.

For their honeymoon, they took a cruise that started in Honolulu and would cross the Pacific, go through the Panama Canal, and eventually end up in Fort Lauderdale. Bill wanted to see the Panama Canal, although Ella couldn't imagine why he'd want to see a ditch filled with water. She was, however, excited about the trip, never having been on a cruise ship before, much less traveled first class on one. Bill said that after they got to Lauderdale, they'd bum around the Florida Keys for a while—he particularly liked Key West—then maybe they'd rent a yacht and see the Caribbean Islands. Ella was in seventh heaven; it appeared as if marrying Bill hadn't been a mistake at all.

One day, as the cruise ship was crossing the Pacific—Ella couldn't believe how big the Pacific was; there was nothing in sight of the ship as far as she could see: not another ship, not land, not even a fucking seagull—she said to Bill, "So tell me how you got started doing what you do."

"By getting disbarred," he said.

"I know, but how'd that happen?"

He shrugged. "Jury tampering. I was young and stupid and it was only the second case I ever had, and I could see I was going to lose. Well, I didn't want to lose, so I tried to suborn one of the jurors to end up with a hung jury, and I got caught. I was an idiot."

"But that doesn't explain how you went from being a bad jury tamperer—if that's even a word—to what you do now."

"I was working for a lawyer named George Chavez in San Antonio, who eventually became, I guess you'd say, my agent. George is a bit of a sleazeball. He didn't care that I tried to fix the jury; he was just upset that I got caught. So he fired me. I mean, he didn't really want to, he liked me, but a disbarred lawyer wasn't going to do him much good.

"A couple months later, I'm working at a place making cold calls trying to sell some bullshit insurance annuity to suckers, and George calls. He says he's got a case where there are three witnesses—this was the hit-and-run case I told you about—and the only way George was going to win was if the witnesses disappeared or changed their testimony. The client was rich and willing to pay a hundred grand to make that happen, and George had no intention of doing anything illegal himself. So I took the job and the witnesses never testified and George won the case.

"Six months later—and by then the hundred grand was gone . . ."

Ella laughed, "Yeah, I'll bet." Even that early in their marriage, she could see how Bill and money parted ways in a hurry.

"Anyway, George called again and said there was a lawyer in Dallas who had a similar problem to the one George had had in San Antonio, and asked if I was interested. I said maybe, but only if the price was right. I'd decided after the first time that there was no way I was going to risk going to jail for a lousy hundred grand, that if I was going to do this sort of thing, the payoff had to be huge. Without realizing it at the time, I made up some rules, rule number one being I was only going to work cases where the client could afford to pay at least a million."

"What were the other rules?"

"I wasn't going to do anything involving kids. You know, child molesters, child pornography, any slimy, nasty shit like that. I wasn't going to do anything where a witness was in any sort of protection program; that was just too risky. If the case involved physical evidence like DNA, fingerprints, ballistics results, or someone caught on a surveillance camera, I'd tell the client's lawyer up front that I might not be able to help him—but that he'd still have to pay my fee. There've been times when I've been able to make evidence disappear or make it look like test results have been corrupted, but that's tough to do. And you need to keep in mind that a lot of times witnesses and evidence don't have to disappear. The defense just needs enough to create reasonable doubt." Bill smiled. "I guess you might say that's who I am: the Creator of Reasonable Doubt."

"Have you ever failed?" Ella asked.

"Sure. Who doesn't fail? But I've succeeded enough that George keeps finding me work."

"And how does that happen?"

"George keeps his eyes open for the right kind of cases, and like I said, the first thing he's looking for is a client who can afford my fee, and there aren't many who can. Then he'll take a look at the client's lawyer, and see if he or she is the kind of person who will be inclined to hire someone like me. Keep in mind, too, that defense lawyers represent people they *know* are criminals, and over time they tend to slide over the line themselves, or at least that's been my experience. And as time's gone on, like in any business, word gets around. A lawyer I've worked with in the past will refer me to a lawyer he knows, and that lawyer will contact George."

"How much does George make?"

"Ten percent, which is a hundred thousand tax-free dollars on a million-dollar fee. Not a bad paycheck for basically being an answering service."

"So, how do you do it? How do you get all these witnesses not to testify?"

"Think about it, Ella. There are only so many ways."

She knew she was young and still had a lot to learn, but it continued to irritate her when he tried to turn a discussion into some sort of Socratic teaching session. "Just tell me," she said.

Bill shrugged. "Sometimes I make a witness go away before the trial. I get him to take a trip or hide so he's not available. Or I just pay him to change his testimony, or I find some way to blackmail him or scare him so he's afraid to tell the truth. Or maybe I find something that makes him a shitty witness, someone whose credibility the defense can attack. I mean, it's really not that complicated. I just make sure that a witness doesn't show up for the trial or that if he does show up, he says what the defense wants him to say."

"But what do you do when bribery or blackmail doesn't work?"

"Hey, look! Dolphins," Bill said, pointing out at the bright blue sea.

Time passed, and Ella discovered that marriage to Bill wasn't perfect. But it was *almost* perfect.

When Bill wasn't working they had a marvelous time. Bill particularly liked taking cruises, and the honeymoon cruise was the first of many they took in the years they were married. They cruised the planet: the great cities in Europe along the shores of the Mediterranean; Scandinavia, Alaska, Antarctica, the Orient; the rivers of Europe, China, and Russia. Ella Sue Fieldman had never left the state of South Carolina; Ella Fields saw the whole wide world.

When they traveled, it was always first class—or whatever the category is that's a step *above* first class. And Bill loved showing off his hot young wife, who was always dressed to the nines. She had so many clothes that she always had to give some away when they moved to the next city where Bill was working; she'd usually take the clothes she no longer wanted to some battered women's shelter.

After they got married, and in between vacations, they lived in Seattle, Phoenix, Minneapolis, Houston, San Diego, and Las Vegas—and in each city they lived in a luxurious apartment or a house, and always a place with a spectacular view. As for his work, Bill took a job every eighteen to twenty-four months. For one thing, he liked to play and had no interest in working more often than that. But the other thing was that there were a limited number of cases in which the ultrarich had committed a crime, and in some cases Bill couldn't do anything to help the defendant. Like this one dot.com billionaire in San Francisco who killed his lover. The people in the adjacent suite heard the billionaire and his paramour screaming and breaking furniture, and when the police showed up Mr. Dot.com was standing with a butcher knife in his hand and his clothes soaked with blood. There was nothing even Bill could do for an idiot like that.

But the marriage wasn't perfect, and the reason it wasn't—as far as Ella was concerned—was that Bill wasn't perfect. He was a slob, leaving clothes strewn all over the house; she didn't think he'd ever put a dish in the dishwasher the whole time they were married. And he was always late; the man owned a ten-thousand-dollar Rolex but it was as if he never bothered to look at it. He was also a sore loser when it came to golf. Ella, after taking the lessons he'd paid for, eventually became a better golfer than he was, and he'd pout for hours when she beat him, so much so that after a while she just let him win. He didn't get drunk often, but when he did, he'd become belligerent and jealous and might start chest-bumping with some young stud he thought was hitting on Ella.

But that was just normal married-couple stuff. All the magazines said that married couples fought most often over sex and money. Well, sex wasn't a problem she and Bill had; they had a great sex life, and Ella made sure it stayed that way. The big problem, the really big problem, was money.

During the premarriage "serious talk" she'd insisted they have, Ella had found out, as she'd suspected, that when Bill was paid, the money went into offshore accounts, in a complicated enough way to make it hard for the IRS or the cops to trace. And that was okay by Ella, except for the fact that if something happened to Bill, his money would remain in those accounts until the end of time.

After they were married, Bill, with no argument whatsoever, put her down as a joint holder on all of his accounts—which was good, but which also posed a problem for Ella: If Bill was ever caught, she'd become an accomplice to his crimes just because of the money. But that was a secondary issue, and a risk she was willing to take. The major issue was that Bill drained money out of the accounts as fast as it went in—which, considering the amount he made on each job, was actually a hard thing to do.

As far as Bill was concerned, another job would always come along, and he was determined to live life to the hilt. He spent money on clothes, cars, restaurants, apartments, and vacations. He was always paying for everyone's drinks and dinner. And he spent money on her, buying her things she didn't want or need. He spent fifty thousand dollars once on a necklace that she was afraid to wear and a hundred thousand on a full-length Siberian sable coat. Where the hell would someone wear a full-length Siberian fur coat if she didn't live in Siberia?

Then there were the bad investments, essentially get-rich-quick schemes. He invested two million with a Florida developer they met on a cruise. It was a can't-fail, sure thing, bound to make him twenty or thirty million. Except that he made this investment in 2007 and then the real estate bubble burst, the bottom dropped out of the economy, and the developer couldn't *give* away the land in Florida. In 2011, he met a kid in San Diego who convinced Bill that he was going to be the next Steve Jobs—and another million went down the drain.

Bill was smart enough to know that he couldn't keep doing what he did forever. He knew that one day he was going to be old and maybe infirm, and that he needed some sort of retirement plan. He also knew that the longer he kept doing what he did, the more likely it was that one day he might get caught and go to jail. He knew, therefore, that it was in his best interest to acquire as much as he could as fast as he could, and then get out of the game for good. Yep, Bill *knew* all this—but it never changed the way he behaved, no matter how much Ella nagged at him.

The year after they were married—after the world's longest honeymoon—Bill took a job in Seattle. The case involved a retired

Microsoft executive worth several billion who'd been arrested for sexually assaulting a woman. It was basically a he-said, she-said case. The problem was that there was a witness, a wheelchair-bound woman who lived in the building across the street from the victim's apartment and spent virtually every waking hour staring into the windows across from her own. The invalid could swear that Mr. Microsoft had torn the victim's blouse—and disprove that she had torn it herself, as the billionaire claimed she had in an effort to scream rape and extort money from him.

Bill refused to allow Ella to help him and wouldn't tell her what he planned to do to get the witness to change her testimony—which she eventually did. It wasn't that he didn't trust Ella; he was simply trying to protect her. But Ella *wanted* to be involved, and she was convinced that she could help him. And she was bored. She didn't have a job and didn't have anything to do but shop and read and go to spas and the gym. Being practically a newlywed, however, she didn't assert herself and insist that he include her.

Everything changed in 2006; they'd been married three years by then. After an extended vacation where they spent eight months in the Bordeaux region of France—Bill briefly considered buying into a winery there, but fortunately Ella was able to talk him out of that—Bill took a job in Phoenix. The first thing Ella did was convince him to increase the amount he charged from one million to two million. Partly she did this because she figured they needed to increase their income, considering the lifestyle that Bill insisted on. The other thing was that, as she pointed out to Bill, his clients could easily afford two million. The ex–Microsoft executive in Seattle had been worth billions, and the guy in Phoenix was a developer and was worth hundreds of millions. So Bill raised his fee and was surprised—although Ella wasn't—that his new client and the client's lawyer didn't have a problem with the higher amount at all.

The other thing that happened in Phoenix was that Ella started helping him. They'd been married long enough by then that Bill shared everything with her, and so he told her how he intended to deal with the Phoenix case. There were three witnesses to deal with: a single man—a Mexican—and a married couple. Taking care of the Mexican was a piece of cake, but the couple turned out to be a challenge. It was Ella who finally came up with the solution, and although it was elaborate and time-consuming, and took a lot of money, it worked. At the time she couldn't help thinking it would have been a lot simpler to just burn down the couple's house with them sleeping in it, but when she mentioned this to Bill, he said, "No way. Two million bucks isn't worth the price we'll pay if we get caught, and there's no statute of limitations on murder." And that's when she began to have some doubts about Bill. But she still loved him.

After Phoenix, she and Bill did the grand tour of the Orient: China, Japan, Thailand, Cambodia, and Vietnam. They were treated like royalty everyplace they stayed—which wasn't surprising, considering the rates they paid and the way Bill overtipped. Then Bill reluctantly accepted a job in Minneapolis in 2008, though he wasn't really ready to go back to work; and besides, Ella thought, who in his right mind would want to spend a winter in Minnesota? It was in Minneapolis that she concluded that Bill, as successful as he'd been in the past, might not really be cut out for the business he was in.

The case in Minneapolis involved a rich guy, obviously—a direct descendant of a nineteenth-century robber baron—who'd tried to make his wife's murder look like suicide. What she and Bill needed to do was make one witness disappear or change his testimony, and destroy some evidence sitting in a holding cage in a police station—and both these problems turned out to be really tough.

Regarding the evidence, there were three cops who had access to the place where it was stored, and it took Bill almost six weeks to figure out which of the three could be bribed and then convince him to cooperate.

But it was the witness who turned out to be the bigger problem: He couldn't be bribed, because he was even richer than the defendant. Nor did he have any nasty, disgusting habits that could be used to blackmail him. On top of that, the witness knew the defendant personally and detested the man and was just dying to testify against him—which would result in Bill's client spending thirty years in Stillwater.

Bill and Ella looked at a number of options. The witness had a niece, his sister's daughter, and the niece had a drug problem and wouldn't be hard to set up to be arrested. They decided in the end, however, that this plan wouldn't work, because the witness was a prick, wasn't close to his sister, and wasn't likely to do anything to help his niece. The next idea Ella had—and it was *her* idea, not Bill's—involved the witness's maid, a good-looking Hispanic girl who resided in the witness's house and did all the domestic crap for the witness and his spoiled wife. Ella had the idea of paying the girl to testify that the witness had raped her, and then giving the witness a choice: Don't testify at the trial or go to jail yourself. But when Ella met the maid she concluded that she was dumber than a dust mop, and decided to drop that idea, too.

Finally, one night, she said to Bill, "Maybe we're just going to have to disappear this guy."

"What do you mean?" Bill said.

"What do you think I mean, Bill?"

"No way. I'm not going to end up doing life in fucking Minnesota if we get caught."

"Bill," Ella said, "we're looking at losing a million bucks if this guy testifies."

That was the deal they'd made with the defendant's lawyer: They'd been paid a million up front, but wouldn't be paid the other million until the evidence disappeared and they could guarantee that the witness wouldn't testify.

"I don't care," Bill said.

Well, Ella sure as hell cared. A million was a million—it wasn't chicken feed—and the way Bill spent money, they would need it. But she didn't say anything to him. So while he spent more time trying to find an angle he could use to blackmail the witness, Ella decided to deal with the problem on her own.

The witness was a health nut, and every day at six a.m. he went for a four-mile run. Since Bill and Ella had been watching him for months, Ella knew the exact route he took. The first thing she did was steal a car. A swanky restaurant she and Bill often went to provided valet service for customers' cars, and the valet put the keys in a little box outside the restaurant. When a car would drive up, the valet would park the car in a garage across the street from the restaurant, but he didn't lock the box where the keys were stored.

So Ella stood outside the restaurant one cold night wearing a wig and a ski jacket with a hood, and when the valet left to park a car, she took the keys for a car he'd already parked. The next morning, driving her stolen car at sixty miles an hour, she simply ran the witness down; it was still dark outside, and there wasn't a soul around. She then dumped the car in the parking lot of a large hotel—and that was that.

Bill was furious. He ranted and raved, and after he stopped ranting, he didn't talk to her for almost two weeks. But eventually he got over it and they made their entire two-million-dollar fee—which Bill invested and lost in the Florida land deal.

There were times when she just felt like strangling Bill.

17

Now all Ella could do was wait and see what happened with Esther; if nothing did after a month or two, she'd have to come up with a Plan B. But since the trial was scheduled to start in a month and a half, she needed more time.

She texted David Slade: *Get a 3 month delay.*

Slade responded immediately, as if he'd been holding the phone in his hand. *We need to meet!!* Ella smiled at the double exclamation points. She imagined by now that Slade must be feeling anxious, not knowing what she was doing, and with the trial so close.

She texted: *There's no need to meet. Things are going well. Just get me 3 months. We'll meet soon.*

We need to meet now!

No. Not yet.

She didn't even like texting Slade, much less meeting with him. She wanted as little contact as possible to minimize the chance that anyone would discover they were working together.

Ella texted: *Be patient. And trust me. I know what I'm doing.* Then she turned off the phone.

David Slade met with His Honor Albert Martinez and ADA Justine Porter and requested that the trial be moved three months to the right. Justine had been anticipating this and was not the least bit surprised. In fact, she'd been expecting Slade to ask for a much longer delay. She felt compelled, however, to play her part in the drama of the American legal system, and pretended to be outraged that Slade had waited until now to ask the court to change its calendar. "I strenuously object, Your Honor," she said.

Before Justine had a chance to explain why she objected—strenuously or otherwise—Slade said, "Your Honor, I need this time in order for my client to be able to participate in his own defense, which, as you know, is his constitutional right. You see, Your Honor—and I certainly hope that this information doesn't leave this room—Toby Rosenthal has been drinking quite heavily, which is somewhat understandable considering the stress he's under. He hasn't been coping well at all, Judge, and his father and I have convinced him he needs to admit himself to Glendon Hills for treatment. In the condition he's in right now, Your Honor, there's simply no way he'll be able to participate at trial, and I certainly can't ask him to testify, which I was planning to do."

Glendon Hills was a rehab facility that catered to upper-crust drunks and dopers. And what Slade had told the judge was mostly true. He had no intention of allowing Toby to testify at his trial—that was just something he'd tossed out to confuse Justine Porter—but Toby really had been drinking like a fish. He'd stopped going to work—which was fine with Henry Rosenthal, as he didn't want his son hanging around his law office while wearing a GPS anklet. All Toby did all day was drink and mope. He was supposed to be preparing for his second try at the bar exam, but all he could think about was what was going to happen to him in prison. The kid was a wreck. So Slade convinced Henry to force Toby to go into rehab. He did this primarily so he could delay the trial, but he also did it so there would be less chance of Toby doing something stupid before the trial.

Slade didn't expect Martinez to have any objection to his request, and a three-month delay was hardly excessive. What Slade didn't realize was that Martinez—like a number of his black-robed brethren—was tired of defense attorneys delaying trials. Sometimes trials were delayed for years, not months, and delaying a murder trial two or three years was not at all uncommon. In fact, it had become the norm. But Martinez had had enough. When you delay a trial for months or years, all sorts of things can happen, and most of them aren't good: Witnesses die or get ill or they move and can't be located. Cops, prosecutors, and public defenders retire or resign. Evidence gets lost or destroyed. And two or three years after an event occurs, how well can anyone really remember what happened?

"How long will Mr. Rosenthal be in the clinic for treatment?" Martinez asked.

"What?" Slade said. He knew the answer; he just hadn't been expecting the question.

"I asked, how long will Mr. Rosenthal be required to remain at Glendon Hills? And before you answer, Mr. Slade, I want you to know that a niece of mine was admitted there when she became addicted to painkillers a few years ago."

"The normal inpatient stay at the clinic is twenty-five days, Your Honor," Slade said. "But it could take longer in Toby's case. Each patient is different, and you never can tell. And then there are follow-up sessions, meetings with counselors, those sorts of thing. So I believe that a three-month delay—"

"I'll give you two months," Martinez said, "which means the trial starts three and a half months from today. If your client isn't sober by then, he probably never will be."

Slade couldn't believe it. This was terrible. He could have used a dozen other reasons for delaying the trial, and if he had known that Martinez was going to pull this bullshit, he would have used one of them.

Ella saw that she had a text message from Slade. More exclamation points.

The judge wouldn't grant a 3 month delay! He only granted 60 days! The trial is set for September 17th.

Ella texted back: *This is unacceptable. Do your damn job!*

She'd never expected this. From everything she'd read about him, she'd thought that Slade was a better-than-average lawyer. But there was no point in stewing over his incompetence. She needed to keep moving forward.

While waiting for Esther's new medications to do *their* job, Ella began working on the next witness: the busboy, Edmundo Ortiz. Ella had been hoping to learn that Edmundo was an illegal immigrant, which would have made things simple: She would have threatened to call ICE if he didn't decide to take a long vacation, one that would last until after Toby Rosenthal's trial. She was unhappy to learn from the Dallas data miners that Edmundo, after spending eleven years in the United States, was a newly minted U.S. citizen.

The data miners told her one other thing that was important. Edmundo's wife was dead—she'd died five years ago; some lymph cancer thing—and based on the records they'd obtained, Edmundo now lived alone. But his credit card statements showed that Edmundo purchased Pampers and baby formula and shopped at places that sold clothes for toddlers. Ella needed to take a closer look at Edmundo's living situation.

Since Edmundo lived in a public housing project—one in which white, blond Ella would tend to stand out if she started asking questions—and because she didn't speak Spanish, as many of the tenants in the project did, Ella hired a Spanish-speaking private detective.

Two days later, the detective informed her that Edmundo lived with his daughter and her two kids, who'd somehow made it from Honduras to New York. The daughter's husband—Edmundo's son-in-law—had come to the United States with his wife and kids, but one day he was grabbed in an immigration roundup and shipped back to Honduras. Ella imagined that Edmundo was now doing whatever he could to reunite his son-in-law with his family—not that she really cared. What she cared about was that Edmundo was most likely fearful that his daughter and grandkids could be deported just like his son-in-law.

Ella thought about using this information to force Edmundo to leave—telling him that if he didn't catch the next Greyhound out of town, she was going to make sure that his wetback daughter and her babies were deported. But she decided that this tactic could backfire on her if Edmundo got an immigration lawyer involved—which was why she decided to call an old friend in Seattle.

When she and Bill had lived in Seattle after they first got married—because of the case involving the Microsoft rapist—they'd rented a penthouse apartment with a view of the Olympic Mountains and Elliott Bay, and became good friends with the couple who owned the only other penthouse apartment in their building. Anyway, the man—his name was Shearson—was involved in the maritime business in a major way. He had a fleet of tugboats that pushed cargo ships around Puget Sound and a dozen oceangoing boats that fished for crab in the Bering Sea. He'd also just acquired a couple of drilling platforms that sucked oil from the ocean floor when they weren't being harassed by environmentalist nuts. After they left Seattle, Bill and Ella had kept in touch with the Shearsons—Christmas cards, a phone call now and then—and once when they took an Alaska cruise that departed from Seattle, they spent a few days with the couple, rekindling their friendship.

So Ella called Shearson. She didn't tell him she was no longer with Bill; she said that Bill was working out in New York and doing fine and that if he hadn't been so busy he would have called himself. Shearson knew that Bill was some kind of legal consultant, but that's about all he knew because Bill was such a master at talking a lot while never really saying much about what he did. After Ella chatted with Shearson for a while, asking him how the wife and kids were doing, she told him that she and Bill had met this absolutely *marvelous* man in New York named Edmundo Ortiz.

She told Shearson that Edmundo was a busboy at a restaurant they frequented, and that she and Bill came to know him because one time Ella lost a diamond earring at the restaurant and Edmundo found it. He could have pawned the earring—Lord knows he could have used the money—but being as honest as the day is long, he returned it to Ella. After that, she and Bill talked to Edmundo every time they went to the restaurant, learned about his family, his background, that sort of thing. Well, a couple of days ago, Ella noticed that Edmundo looked depressed, not at all his normal, cheerful self. When she asked him if something was wrong, he said that he'd witnessed a drug dealer who lived in his housing project kill a man. Edmundo, being a good citizen, told the cops and the drug dealer was arrested, but now Edmundo had a serious problem: The drug dealer's pals were going to kill him before the trial.

"Geez, that's awful," Shearson said.

"Yes, it really is," Ella said. "He's such a lovely man, and he's the sole source of support for his widowed daughter and her two little kids."

Ella had decided that making the daughter a widow might provide an extra tug on Shearson's heartstrings.

"Bill did a little research on the drug dealer, and he's convinced that Edmundo's right, that the guy will have him killed before he's able to testify."

"Geez," Shearson said again.

"What Bill and I were wondering was if you could give Edmundo a job on one of your ships. He's a hell of a cook—he was trained as a chef."

This was actually true. The Dallas data miners had learned about Edmundo's culinary education because Edmundo had filled out dozens of online applications trying to find work as a cook before he'd settled for busing tables.

Ella said, "We were wondering if you could give him a job on one of your fishing boats where he'd be gone for six months or so. In other words, Edmundo would disappear before the trial started, and these drug dealers would never find him if he was at sea. Then, after the trial's over, you could either keep him on or let him go, though I think you'll want to keep him because he's such a hard worker. But the thing is, if you hire him, you have to pay him in cash and make sure there aren't any records the drug dealers can trace. Bill said these people are connected to a big Mexican cartel and they're really sophisticated."

Shearson, with hardly any hesitation, agreed to help poor Edmundo. He liked being part of a drama, hiding a witness from an evil drug cartel. And he liked Ella. Now Ella just had to tell Edmundo that he was about to become a seafaring man.

Ella waited until Edmundo left McGill's one night; the poor guy worked until two in the morning. As he was dragging his weary brown ass toward the subway station, she walked up beside him. She wore a trench coat with the collar turned up, an auburn wig, and dark-framed glasses—although she wasn't particularly worried about him identifying her.

"Edmundo, we're going over to that coffee shop and have a chat," she said.

"What?" he said. "Who are you?"

"I'm your fairy godmother. Or the wicked witch. It all depends on you."

"What?" he said again.

The guy could barely speak English; she needed to stop trying to be cute. "Edmundo, if you don't do what I want, your daughter and your grandkids are going to be sent back to Honduras."

"I'm an American citizen," he said.

"So what? All that means is that you can be sent to jail for harboring illegal aliens. Let's go have a cup of coffee. I'm buying."

He followed Ella to an open-all-night restaurant, head down, looking like a sheep being led to an abattoir.

"Ed," Ella said, "in two days—two days should be plenty of time for you to pack—you, your daughter, and your grandkids are going to get on a bus for Seattle, Washington. You're not going to tell anyone you're leaving. You are not going to fly or take a train."

"What are you talking about?" Edmundo said.

Ella ignored his confusion and from her trench coat pulled out an envelope bulging with cash. The bills stuffed in the envelope were plainly visible, and she doubted the busboy had ever seen that much money all in one place before. "In that envelope are two things, Ed. First, there's ten thousand dollars in cash. Relocation expenses." Ella figured that Henry Rosenthal could afford to be generous. "The other thing is the name of a man and a phone number. You'll call that man when you arrive in Seattle—he's expecting your call—and he'll help you find a place for your daughter and your grandkids to live. Then you're going to get on a ship and disappear until after the Rosenthal trial.

"You see, we've gotten you a *great* job, Ed. You're going to be a cook on a fishing boat, which pays a hell of a lot better than being a busboy, and as I understand it, you get a bonus depending on how much fish they catch.

"So if you do what we want, you get a great job, you can provide better for your family, and you can stop doing shitty work like busing tables. But if you don't get on a bus to Seattle, your daughter and her babies are going to be tossed into a detention center and shipped back to that hellhole called Honduras."

"Why are you doing this to me?" Edmundo asked.

"Because we don't want you to testify at the Rosenthal trial. And listen carefully, Ed: We'll know if you talk to anybody about the conversation we've had tonight. We'll know if you don't arrive in Seattle. We'll know if you try to hide your daughter and your grandkids."

She kept saying "we" because she wanted Edmundo to imagine an army of people in trench coats, watching and eavesdropping.

"And think about this, Ed: You're only one of five witnesses, and all you saw was a guy run past you. There are four other people who can testify who saw much more than you did, so your testimony isn't really needed anyway."

This was something she'd learned from Bill: Give a witness a chance to rationalize that his testimony isn't important.

"So if you do what we want, you get ten grand and a great job. But I'm telling you—I'm not bullshitting you, Ed—that if you don't disappear from New York in two days and if you show up for the Rosenthal trial, we're going to destroy your fucking family."

Ella laid a small white hand on one of Edmundo's hard brown ones. "This is a *good* thing, Ed. Don't look so glum."

After Ella was sure Edmundo knew everything he needed to know and what to do—like ditching his cell phone and not using his credit cards—she rose to leave, then stopped, pulled a twenty out of a pocket, and handed it to him.

"Treat yourself, Ed. Take a cab home instead of the subway."

18

Thirty-one days after Ella swapped out Esther's pills, she got her daily phone call from her dope-smoking spy, Curtis. The thirty previous calls had normally been about ten seconds long, Curtis saying, "Everything's fine here. She's doing okay." To which Ella would say, "That's good. Talk to you tomorrow."

But on the thirty-first day, Curtis called and said, "Jesus. Esther had a stroke last night. They took her to the hospital."

"Oh, my God!" Ella said—and she meant it. Because now she really had to hustle.

Ella put on a wig and rushed over to the assisted living place. She went up to Esther's apartment, knocked on the door, and when she didn't get an answer, let herself in—and swapped out Esther's pills again. She took the diet and antihistamine pills out of the Coumadin and digoxin prescription vials in Esther's medicine cabinet and put those pills back in the diet and antihistamine pill bottles she'd placed in Esther's bathroom closet. Then she took the Coumadin and digoxin pills that she'd taken from Esther's prescription bottles—the ones she'd placed in plastic sandwich bags—and put those pills back in the prescription vials. Now if someone, for whatever reason, looked at Esther's pills, the right pills would be in the right bottles.

The only thing she had left to do was swap out the pills in Esther's daily pill organizer box—but then she couldn't find the damn box! It should have been on Esther's kitchen table but it wasn't. Where the hell was it? Well, it wasn't anywhere in the apartment that she could find after a thorough search.

She told herself: *Don't panic. It's okay.* If anyone—again for reasons she couldn't imagine—looked at the pills in Esther's pillbox and saw that they weren't Coumadin or digoxin, this person might then discover the antihistamine and diet pills in the bathroom closet and conclude that Esther had just mixed up her medications. Ditto if Esther died and an autopsy was performed and the pathologist discovered that Esther didn't have Coumadin or digoxin in her body. But why would anyone perform an autopsy on an eighty-six-year-old woman who'd had a stroke? There was no reason to panic. With the bottles of diet and antihistamine pills in Esther's closet, there was a logical explanation for why Esther had the wrong pills—pills that looked just like her prescription medications—in her pillbox.

Ella left Esther's apartment and called Curtis and told him to meet her back out behind the big rhododendron where Ella met him the first time.

Curtis looked flustered when he arrived, not his usual, mellow, dope-smoking self. "Man, this doesn't feel right to me."

"What doesn't feel right to you?" Ella said.

"What happened to Esther? I mean, did you . . ."

"Did I what?" Ella said.

"I don't know. You asked me to let you know how she's doing every day, and then this happens to her. So did you . . ."

"Curtis, I told you this was a family thing, a legal thing. Esther's got a lot of money and her will is a mess and she doesn't have any close family, just a bunch of distant relatives who are going to squabble over her estate. Well, I'm one of those relatives, and I needed to know right away if something happened to her so I could get my lawyer moving on things. That's all this is about."

Ella pulled a wad of bills out of her pocket. "That's a thousand bucks. Call it a bonus. But, Curtis, let me explain something to you. If you were to tell anyone that you were spying on Esther for me . . ."

"Spying?"

"That's right. Spying. That's what you were doing, spying on Esther for me, keeping me informed of her condition. So like I said, if anyone learned that you'd been spying on her, you could be in deep trouble. You'd lose your job for sure, and if, hypothetically, a crime was committed, you'd be an accomplice to the crime. Do you understand?"

"Yeah," Curtis said.

"Good. Now you sit here and have a joint and think about what you can buy with the money I just gave you. And forget you ever met me."

Ella went to a deli and ordered a pastrami sandwich for lunch; they made the best pastrami sandwiches in New York, New York. While she ate, she used her iPhone to see which hospitals were close to Esther's place, and the second one she called informed her that yes, an Esther Behrman was a patient, up in intensive care.

Ella, still wearing the wig she'd worn when she put Esther's pills back in the correct containers, went to the hospital. She stopped at the nurses' station in intensive care, said she was Esther's niece—well, actually her *grand*niece—and wanted to know how dear Aunt Esther was doing. Not good, a nurse told her. "The prognosis isn't . . . hopeful."

Ella said, "Oh, no, that's just horrible," and tried to squeeze out a tear, but couldn't make that happen. When she asked if she could see Esther, the nurse said there wasn't any point, Esther was completely unresponsive.

"This is just so horrible," Ella said again.

And it really was horrible. It would have been better for everyone—including Esther—if the stroke had killed her immediately. Ella certainly hadn't been trying to turn her into a vegetable. She wasn't a cruel person.

———————◆◆◆———————

Ella texted David Slade.

Two down, three to go. Everything proceeding well.

We need to meet!

No. Just make sure you can get another delay if needed. But the way things are going now, we might not need one.

And that was true: Ella really felt good about the way things currently stood.

Part III

19

DeMarco was glad he'd finally been able to ditch the crutches.

The last two months, they'd about driven him insane. It was a hassle to move around any room where the furniture was close together, like almost any bar or restaurant. It would take him three times longer to get anyplace he had to go on foot. He couldn't drive, even a car with an automatic transmission, because the bone he'd cracked was in his right leg; and getting into and out of cabs was a feat of acrobatics. He'd also developed a real appreciation for wheelchair ramps, as steps were a bitch, particularly when it was icy or raining and he was afraid he'd slip.

Finally, after he had stumped around for ten weeks, the X-rays showed the crack in his hip bone had mended itself. The bad news was that the doctor wanted him to use a cane for the next couple of months, just to keep him from putting too much weight on his bad leg too soon. Meaning no golf.

They gave him an aluminum cane at the hospital, one that could be adjusted to match his height, but he thought it looked like something an old codger on Medicaid would use. So he bought an ebony cane with a brass derby handle from a pawnshop, wondering briefly about the poor bastard who'd been forced to pawn it. Anyway, he felt better using the cane, mainly because he figured he *looked* better. Like an

RAF pilot you see in old movies, a guy with an Errol Flynn mustache whose Spitfire had been shot down by the Luftwaffe over the English Channel. Well, okay, maybe it wasn't that romantic, but the cane was definitely better than hobbling along on crutches.

He was taking his new cane for a test spin around the block when he got the call. It was from the 212 area code, and he didn't recognize the number.

"DeMarco?" the caller said.

"Yeah."

"This is Justine Porter."

"Who?"

"The ADA prosecuting the man who killed Dominic DiNunzio."

"Oh, yeah," DeMarco said. "Sorry, I forgot your name for a moment there." He hadn't thought about Porter since they arraigned Dominic's killer two months ago. He was glad she'd called, because he'd been wondering when they were ever going to hold the trial.

"What can I do for you?" DeMarco asked.

Porter began, "There might be a problem with the case against Toby Rosenthal."

Five hours later, DeMarco was in New York.

Porter worked out of the Manhattan Criminal Courthouse, located at One Hogan Place in Lower Manhattan, near Foley Square and within an easy walk of the Brooklyn Bridge, the Manhattan Bridge, and One World Trade Center. It was also just a few blocks from the Financial District, where some of the greatest American criminals plied their trade. From the upper floors of the courthouse, you could get a peek at the Hudson River to the west and the East River to the east.

Justine Porter's office was on the sixth floor and didn't have a view of anything because it didn't have a window. When DeMarco rapped on the doorframe, Porter was on the phone. She looked haggard, DeMarco thought, and judging by the smudges under her eyes, she wasn't getting much sleep.

She waved DeMarco into her office but kept talking on the phone: "I'm telling you, Morrie, I'm not going to plea-bargain this case down to a misdemeanor. We got your asshole of a client on video punching a seventy-two-year-old grandmother in the face after he stole her purse." Pause. "I don't give a shit how much a trial will cost. That little prick you represent is going to jail. So either plead him guilty or I'll see you in court." Porter slammed the phone down and said to DeMarco, "Everything in this city is a fucking negotiation."

She pointed DeMarco to a chair in front of her desk; the surface of the chair was the only horizontal space in her office that was unoccupied. There were brown accordion file folders stacked in towers on her desk, on the floor surrounding her desk, and on top of three olive green metal file cabinets along one wall. Some of the drawers in the file cabinets couldn't close because they were overstuffed. DeMarco knew that in New York trials were delayed for months and sometimes years because there weren't enough prosecutors and public defenders, and Porter's cluttered office seemed to confirm this.

DeMarco sat and said, "So what's going on? You told me on the phone that—"

The phone on Porter's desk started ringing at the same time her cell phone chimed an incoming call. She tapped her cell phone to send the call to voice mail, and while the other phone was still ringing, she looked at her watch. It was five p.m. "Let's get out of here," she said. "If we stay here I'm going to get interrupted every two minutes. And anyway, I need a drink."

"Sounds good to me," DeMarco said.

They left the courthouse and began walking down Baxter Street, along the perimeter of Columbus Park, DeMarco limping beside Porter on his cane. Not having put any weight on his bad leg for two months, he was aching even with the cane.

Porter said, "So what's with the cane? The first time I saw you, you were on crutches, but I never asked why."

DeMarco told her how'd he'd cracked a bone in his hip in a fluke golfing accident. Porter said, "My dad was a big golfer. Said it was a great way for an older guy to get some exercise, which in his case meant he'd ride around in a golf cart for three hours chasing a little white ball, then spend three more hours in the clubhouse drinking beer with his buddies. He died on a golf course."

"He did?" DeMarco said.

"Yeah. He and my mom decided to celebrate their fiftieth wedding anniversary by taking a trip to England, Scotland, Ireland—the whole grand tour. Well, my dad got a tee time at St. Andrews a year in advance, paid almost two hundred dollars to play a round, and dropped dead of a heart attack on the third fairway."

"Gee, that's a shame," DeMarco said, but he was really thinking: What a *perfect* way to go.

They ended up a couple of blocks from Porter's office at a place called Forlini's, an Italian restaurant that had been around since the 1940s. The bar was packed with lawyers, judges, and cops, and probably more than a few criminals, so Porter asked for a booth in the restaurant. The booth had red leather seats, and on the walls were faded oil paintings in gilded frames depicting bowls of fruit and rural Italian settings and photos of old Italian guys whose names nobody could remember.

Porter ordered a bourbon. DeMarco asked for a bottle of Birra Moretti, an Italian beer. When in Rome.

"So," DeMarco said. "What's going on? You said on the phone you lost two witnesses and were concerned about the case."

"Yeah. The busboy and the old lady. The busboy was a brand-new citizen and he was just dying to testify to show how American he is. But then he split, and we can't find him. As for the old lady, she had a stroke and the doctors say she'll probably be dead before the trial, and if she isn't, she won't be able to testify anyway."

"But you still have three witnesses," DeMarco said.

"Actually, I've really got two. The bartender—his testimony has always been a little shaky, him saying things at the lineup like 'I *think* it was Toby Rosenthal who did it.' He's not a strong witness. I also don't have any physical evidence that Rosenthal did the shooting, like a weapon or gunpowder residue on his clothes. Nor do I have a motive, which makes it even harder to convince a jury that Rosenthal did the crime. The case was strong when I had five witnesses, but with two of them out of the picture I'm worried, and I *really* got worried after what happened to the old lady. She was the main reason I called you."

"So what happened with her?" DeMarco asked.

"I think somebody might have caused her to have the stroke."

"What! How?"

"Never mind how, for now. Just listen. I wanna tell you a story." Porter took a sip of her drink and muttered, "Man, this hits the spot.

"This job doesn't have a lot of perks," she said, "but I got to attend this conference in Miami a couple of years ago. The conference was about all the crime-busting shit that prosecutors were doing, and DAs and ADAs came from all over the country. It was a total boondoggle, of course, but I went because I figured I *deserved* a week in the sun in January.

"Anyway, I'm sitting in the hotel bar with four, five other lawyers one night, and this one guy tells how he lost this case because a cop gets on the stand and steps on his crank with both flat feet. So we start playing I-can-top-that, about losing cases because of techs spilling coffee on evidence samples and witnesses flubbing their testimony and judges doing bonehead things.

"But this one guy from Phoenix said he had a big case that went south on him one time, and it wasn't because of bad luck or incompetence. He said he lost it because somebody tampered with all his witnesses."

"All of them?" DeMarco said.

"Yeah. He had three witnesses, but one disappeared and the other two, a guy and his wife, changed their testimony, and he was positive that somebody got to them."

"Okay," DeMarco said, but he was wondering what the Phoenix case had to do with Toby Rosenthal.

"Then one of the gals there says that never happened to her, but it did to a buddy of hers in Houston. He had a case he couldn't possibly lose, but witnesses disappeared or lied on the stand, and her buddy was absolutely convinced that somebody had orchestrated the whole thing." Porter polished off the bourbon and held up her glass to get the attention of a passing server.

She continued, "It turns out the two cases had only one thing in common: The defendants were both rich. And I'm not talking a couple million rich. I'm talking forty, fifty, a hundred million rich."

"Is the Rosenthal kid that rich?"

"No, but his old man is, and when two of the witnesses against his dipshit kid suddenly became unavailable, I couldn't stop thinking about what I heard in Miami. So just for the hell of it, I had my intern—this kid's really sharp—do a search for cases where the defendant had megabucks and was found not guilty at trial or the case was dismissed because witnesses vanished or changed their testimony. I told her to go back fifteen years, and it took her a week, but she found six cases. Actually she found nine, but I disregarded three of those for various reasons."

Porter's second drink arrived, and she took a long swallow. DeMarco was afraid that, as exhausted as she appeared to be, if she had one more drink she might fall asleep right there in Forlini's.

Porter said, "I called the prosecutors who tried the six cases, and after talking to them I think it's possible that there's a guy out there who makes it his job to get rid of witnesses in cases with superrich defendants."

"A guy?" DeMarco said. "What did these prosecutors say that made you come to that conclusion?" He was really thinking: *jump* to that conclusion.

"A couple of them said they got a whiff of a man who might have tampered with their witnesses, and based on the guy's description, it might have been the same man."

"A whiff?"

"Yeah, but that's all they got. Which is why I want somebody to independently investigate the six cases and see if it's possible that anyone involved in them could be messing with Rosenthal."

DeMarco shook his head. "Just because a couple of witnesses in these cases disappeared . . ."

"They didn't all disappear. It's more complicated than that. Some changed their testimony. In one case, evidence was tainted. But the main thing is that the cases against these six rich defendants were so strong that *none* of them should have been acquitted, but they all were."

"But still, you're saying you don't have anything solid showing that whatever happened has any bearing on Rosenthal."

"That's right, I don't," Porter said. "But I'm too old and battle-scarred to ignore my gut. And my gut's telling me if I don't do something, I'm going to lose."

"Well, I can tell you right now that that's not going to make Mahoney happy. And you *really* don't want to make him unhappy."

"Which is the reason I called you, DeMarco. You told me if I needed help, I was to give you a ring. Well, I need help. I want you to look into the six cases and see if there's a connection to Rosenthal."

"Me!" DeMarco said. "Why me? You got thirty thousand cops in New York."

"And normally I would use them, but I got another problem. I've told my boss the same thing I'm telling you, and he doesn't believe me. You see, my boss and I, we don't get along too well. He thinks I should accept more pleas and take fewer cases to trial. He thinks I spend too much on lab testing and paying experts to testify and all the rest of the things you have to do to win. And, of course, he's got budget shortfalls, which he blames on everyone but himself. The bottom line is, he's told me that I've got a strong enough case with three witnesses and to make do with what I've got."

"Does your boss know that John Mahoney has a personal interest in making sure Toby Rosenthal goes to prison?"

"Yeah, I've told him that, and he doesn't give a shit. My boss has been the Manhattan DA for twelve years, he's sixty-six years old, and he has no desire for another job, meaning he has no intention of running for another office. Frankly, he doesn't think John Mahoney can do anything to upset his applecart."

"You need to tell him he's wrong about that," DeMarco said, a little steel in his voice this time. "There was this developer up in Boston a year ago, and he thought the same thing, and now he's—" DeMarco suddenly realized he should stop running his mouth about what happened in Boston. He said, "Anyway, I'm not an investigator. When I said you should call if you needed help, I meant that I'd get Mahoney to lean on someone. Hire a PI or some retired cop if you want something investigated."

Porter, whose eyes were becoming a little unfocused with the second bourbon, raised a finger and wagged it in DeMarco's face. "I did some research on you, too, buddy-boy. Actually, my intern did. I know you're John Mahoney's troubleshooter and he's used you a few times to dig into things, like that thing you got involved in out there in North Dakota a couple years ago."

"What do you know about that?"

"Enough to know that you're bullshitting me when you say you don't do investigations for Mahoney. As for hiring a PI, that would be my preference, too, particularly if the PI was ex-NYPD. But like I told you, I don't have the budget for that. The only reason I have an intern is that she's free."

"Well, if you don't have the budget, who's going to pay for an investigation?"

"You work for John Mahoney, so don't bullshit me. He'll get you whatever you need."

DeMarco shook his head. "Look, I'd like to help you but—"

"DeMarco, don't act like I'm asking you to do me a fuckin' favor here. You're the guy who came to me, and basically threatened me, and said your boss wanted Rosenthal convicted. So if you want to make sure that happens . . ."

"Hey! It's your goddamn job to convict the guy, not mine. I'll have Mahoney call the DA and lean on him, but if that doesn't work . . ."

"Look, just do one thing for me," Potter said. "Okay?

"What's that?"

"Go talk to the two detectives who arrested Rosenthal and hear the story about what happened to the old lady. After you do, we'll talk some more. Okay?"

DeMarco hesitated, then said, "Fine. As long as I'm up here anyway, I can do that. But that's all I'm going to do."

"We'll see," Potter said—and DeMarco was beginning to understand why her boss didn't like her so much.

20

DeMarco met Coghill and Dent at a deli in Tribeca on Vesey Street. When he arrived, they were sitting at a table near the window, making crude comments about women walking by on the sidewalk outside. *Can you believe the gazooms on that one?* DeMarco thought they looked like bookends: both in their fifties, gray-haired, and overweight. They had small cynical eyes and faces best suited for displaying skepticism. They wore tight-fitting sports jackets, wrinkled white shirts, cheap striped ties, and thick-soled black lace-up shoes. New York's finest on display.

DeMarco told them Porter's theory: that she'd found six cases involving rich defendants and that someone had tampered with the witnesses in all six. Porter, he said, had reason to believe it could be the same person— she'd gotten a "whiff" of the guy, whatever the hell that meant—and she was afraid he might be screwing with the Rosenthal case.

Dent said, "I wouldn't be totally surprised if somebody got to the witnesses if the defendants were superrich. Fuckin' rich people can get away with anything. But it's hard to believe it's the same guy. I gotta admit, though, Justine's one of the sharper ADAs in Manhattan, and if she thinks it's possible . . . well, who knows."

"Anyway," DeMarco said, "Porter said she was suspicious about what happened to the old lady and said you could enlighten me."

Dent said, "When we first heard about Esther having a stroke, frankly we didn't think too much of it. I mean, shit, she was almost ninety years old. But Justine told us to go see if anything funny happened because she didn't like the coincidence of losing two witnesses."

"So we go to the hospital to see her," Coghill said, "but she couldn't talk. You know how folks look sometimes when they have a stroke? One side of her face all twisted down, drool coming out of her mouth? It was a shame."

"Esther doesn't have any family," Dent said, "except some cousin who lives out West she never sees. But her friend Leah was there at the hospital. Leah's the same lady who was with Esther in the bar when DiNunzio was shot, and she asks if we're there to investigate who poisoned Esther."

"We go, whoa!" Coghill said. "'Poisoned' her? What are you talking about? So Leah says after Esther had her stroke she went back to Esther's apartment to bring her things she might need in the hospital. You know—toothbrush, nightgown, slippers, whatever. Well, Leah can't find Esther's pillbox, one of those little boxes marked with each day of the week. Leah said it should have been sitting on the kitchen table because that's where Esther always kept it, but it's not there. Leah hunts for it for a bit, finally gives up, and starts packing up the stuff she's going to bring to Esther. And that's when she finds the pillbox. It was in the pocket of the robe Esther would wear in the morning after she got out of bed. It looked like Esther had taken her morning pills, then stuck the pillbox into the pocket of her robe instead of putting it back on the table."

"Okay," DeMarco said, but he wondered why Coghill was droning on about the pillbox. The old lady just misplaced it, the way he sometimes did with his keys, putting them someplace other than on the table beside the door.

"So Leah looks to see how many pills are in the pillbox," Coghill said, "and she sees there are only three. One blue one in the Saturday space and two pills for Sunday, one blue and one white. The blue one is supposed to be Coumadin and the white one digoxin."

"Leah, of course, knows what Esther takes," Dent said. "All these old people do is talk about their medical problems, and Esther and Leah are closer than sisters. Anyway, Leah goes to the medicine cabinet, planning to fill up Esther's pillbox. She opens the digoxin and Coumadin bottles and shakes a few out, and that's when she notices that the pills don't match the ones in Esther's pillbox."

Coghill picked up the story again. "The pills are the same color, blue and white, and the same size as the ones in the prescription bottle, but they don't have the numbers on them that Coumadin and digoxin do."

"Leah goes bananas," Coghill said. "She calls the nurse in the assisted leaving place and tells her someone switched out Esther's medicine. The nurse says, 'Oh, bullshit,' and comes up and starts pawing through the closet in the bathroom which is just full of crap and, sure as shit, the nurse finds pills that look just like the ones in Esther's pillbox. One pill is a diet pill and the other is an antihistamine. The nurse says it's obvious that Esther mixed up her pills.

"Now it's Leah who says, 'Bullshit.' No way would Esther have made that kind of mistake. Plus, she tells the nurse, Esther never took a diet pill in her life. And this is the story Leah told us when we went to see Esther in the hospital."

Dent leaned back in his chair. "So what do you think, DeMarco? Do you think an old lady mixed up her pills or that someone sneaked into her apartment and switched out the pills knowing if she didn't take her medication she might have a stroke? And why would this person have switched out just the pills in the pillbox and not the pills in the prescription bottles in the medicine cabinet?"

"I don't know," DeMarco said, but it seemed a lot more likely that old Esther had just mixed up her meds.

"What about this busboy who split?" DeMarco asked.

"Now that was weird," Dent said. "I mean, weirder than Esther having a stroke, because Ortiz seemed to us like a solid guy. But when Justine called him to check on something in the statement he'd made, she got a message that his phone had been disconnected. So we went looking for him, and found out that he'd moved out of his apartment. We asked the building super where he'd gone, and he said that Ortiz split in the middle of the night and didn't say anything to anyone about why or where he was going. He didn't even get back the damage deposit he put down, and left all his furniture. I mean, it's like he got scared and ran."

"Did you try to find him?" DeMarco asked.

"Yeah, sure," Coghill said. "Well, not us personally, but one of the missing persons gals who's good with computers. She searched to see if he had used his credit cards or bought an airline ticket or if his social security number had shown up on a tax document, but she couldn't find the guy. But, to tell you the truth, we didn't try to track him down like he was a serial killer. At the time, we still had four good witnesses who could testify against that little shit Rosenthal."

21

DeMarco ordered another beer after Coghill and Dent left—sticking him with the check, by the way. He mulled over what they'd said for a few minutes more, then called Porter. She didn't answer, but a couple of minutes later he got a text message that said: *I'm in court. Call you back in 20.*

So DeMarco sat there for twenty minutes, mostly just watching the girls walk by the deli as Coghill and Dent had done. New York, New York. If there was a better city for girl-watching, he couldn't imagine where it could be. Paris maybe? But then he'd never been to Paris, so he really didn't know. His mind ricocheted to Porter's father, who died on the links at St. Andrews. If he had a choice between seeing the Eiffel Tower or playing St. Andrews . . .

His phone rang.

"I've only got five minutes before I have to be back in court. Did you talk to Coghill and Dent?" Porter asked.

"Yeah, and I have to admit the story about the old lady is interesting, but it seems a lot more likely that she just had a stroke and wasn't poisoned."

"You never met Esther. I did. She was healthy as a horse."

"If you say so, Dr. Porter, but let me ask you something. If you're worried about somebody getting to your witnesses, why don't you just throw a net around them? You know, watch to see if anyone approaches them."

"Are you dense, DeMarco?"

"Dense?" he said. The woman really pissed him off.

"Yeah. How would I justify assigning about twenty cops, which is what it would take, to watch three witnesses full-time? This isn't a mob case. It's not even a murder one case. And frankly, although John Mahoney may have cared about Dominic DiNunzio, nobody else cares."

"Yeah, but this theory of yours . . ."

"My boss doesn't buy the theory. I already told you that. And I can see you don't buy it either. But I'm telling you right now that if you don't do something, Toby Rosenthal might literally get away with murder."

"Hey, Justine, quit trying to pin this fucking thing on me. This is *your* case, not mine."

"Yeah, well, if I lose I'm gonna let your boss know that I asked for your help and you refused. Now I gotta go."

The damn woman was incredible, having the nerve to threaten him. On the other hand, if Toby Rosenthal was acquitted, Mahoney was going to be pissed, and a pissed-off John Mahoney was not a pleasant person to be around.

DeMarco decided the best thing to do to cover his ass was tell Mahoney what Porter wanted, and then convince Mahoney to lean on the powers that be in New York to get her the manpower she needed. That way, he'd be off the hook, having put the ball back in the court of the people actually responsible for prosecuting Rosenthal.

He called Mahoney's office, knowing Mahoney most likely wouldn't be available and would be off doing whatever it is he did all day to keep the ship of democracy on its errant course. He told Mavis, Mahoney's secretary, to have the big man call him as soon as possible, and that the subject was Dominic DiNunzio.

Mahoney called him back five minutes later, which surprised him. Mahoney rarely interrupted his schedule to talk to DeMarco, which meant that the fate of Toby Rosenthal was a major priority—and this in itself should have told DeMarco what was likely to happen next.

DeMarco hadn't told Mahoney about the call he'd received from Justine Porter telling him she'd lost two witnesses. Nor did he tell Mahoney he'd gone to New York to talk to Porter. The reason he didn't do so was that he'd known, without having to be told, that Mahoney would expect him to go to New York.

So he told Mahoney about the two witnesses, and Mahoney began swearing before he was halfway through the story. Then he told him about Porter's cockamamy theory, that there was some phantom out there who went around tampering with witnesses in cases involving rich defendants.

"How does she know this?" Mahoney said.

"She doesn't," DeMarco said. "She came to this conclusion based on some research she had an intern do and from talking to the prosecutors involved in these other cases. She's going totally on her gut."

Before Mahoney could interrupt him, DeMarco said, "She wants me to investigate these other cases and see if I can find the phantom and stop him before he screws up the Rosenthal case. I've told her what she *really* needs to do is get NYPD to do the investigation and to throw a net around the other witnesses, but she says her boss won't support her, doesn't have the budget, yada yada yada. What I was hoping you could do is call—"

Mahoney said, "I know her boss. He's an arrogant prick and he's been the DA so long up there he thinks he's invincible." Mahoney paused and muttered, "And maybe he is."

"The other problem," DeMarco said, "and I hate to say this, is that Dominic wasn't a celebrity and whatever happens to his killer isn't going to make the front page. By now, nobody probably even remembers that this father of three got shot. But if you were to lean on the mayor up here . . ."

The mayor was a Democrat.

". . . and the police commissioner . . ."

A guy DeMarco knew had political ambitions.

". . . maybe you could get Porter the help she needs."

Mahoney didn't say anything for a moment, probably thinking about how much pressure he could bring to bear on the mayor of New York and its top cop, both of whom were celebrities in their own right—and in their own minds.

Finally, Mahoney said, "So do it."

DeMarco didn't understand. "Do what?" he said.

"Do what Porter wants. It's not like I got anything more important for you to do. Nothing's more important to me than convicting the guy who murdered Dominic."

"Wait a minute!" DeMarco said. "To do what she wants could involve traveling all over the country, talking to these other prosecutors, and—"

"I don't give a shit. Do it."

Although he knew it was hopeless, DeMarco said, "Who's going to pay for the travel and everything else involved? Porter says she doesn't have the budget."

"Just put it all on your credit card. I'll make sure you're reimbursed later."

Before DeMarco could raise another futile objection, Mahoney said, "Joe, that little prick Rosenthal is not getting off. And you damn well better make sure he doesn't."

Mahoney hung up—and DeMarco thought: How in the hell did this become *my* fucking problem?

DeMarco called Porter, the call went to voice mail, and DeMarco said, "I've decided to help you, like you asked. Call me."

Less than ten minutes later, Porter called him back, and the first words out of her mouth were: "You called Mahoney and tried to get him to lean on my boss, and he told you to do the job. Isn't that right?"

"No, that's not right. I discussed the whole thing with him and told him, after thinking everything over, that helping you might be prudent."

Porter made a raspberry sound.

DeMarco said, "Anyway, I want this intern of yours for the duration. I want to see the research she did and want her available to make reservations for me, do more research, whatever I need."

"She's yours," Porter said.

22

The intern's name was Sarah. She was a tiny thing—maybe five foot one on tiptoes—had a mop of short, unruly black hair, and wore big black-framed glasses perched on a nose that seemed too short to support them. DeMarco figured she had to be in her twenties, though she looked about sixteen.

She had a cubicle in the bowels of the Criminal Courthouse in a room she shared with about twenty other low-ranking paralegals and clerks. She said the place was so noisy, with people yelling, the phones constantly ringing, that she did most of her work at a Starbucks three blocks from the courthouse. She suggested that DeMarco meet her there.

When DeMarco arrived, Sarah waved at him as soon as he walked through the door, which made him wonder how she knew what he looked like. Then he remembered Porter saying the girl had done some research on him. He wondered what she'd found. Most of the things he did for Mahoney you wouldn't find online. He hoped.

He sat down at her table and she pushed a two-inch-thick three-ring binder over to him and said, "That contains the research I did on the six cases Justine told you about. Also contact information for the prosecutors involved. I'd suggest you flip through that and we can go from there. While you're doing that, I'm going back to the courthouse; there's a trial in progress I want to see. Just call me when you're ready to talk and I'll come back here."

"Yeah, okay," DeMarco said, and opened the binder.

In Seattle, in 2004, a former Microsoft executive, not worth as much as Bill Gates or Paul Allen but still loaded, was accused of rape. There was a single witness who could corroborate the victim's story, but the witness changed her testimony during the trial. Case dismissed.

In Phoenix, in 2006, it was a road-rage case, the one that Porter had heard about at the conference in Miami. A multi-multi-multimillionaire developer killed a Mexican driving the pickup he used for his lawn-mowing business. In spite of three witnesses, the developer walked.

In Minneapolis, in 2008, the wife of a billionaire supposedly committed suicide by hermetically sealing the garage with masking tape, then taking a seat in her Jaguar and running the engine until the gas tank was empty. The case was mostly circumstantial—the absence of the wife's fingerprints on the tape, the husband's shaky alibi, and the discovery of the husband's hot young mistress—but there was enough there that the Minneapolis cops decided that maybe it wasn't suicide. The one witness who could place the husband near the scene of the crime was killed in a hit-and-run a month before the trial. Case dismissed.

In Houston, in 2009, a former Miss Texas was arrested for hiring a man to kill her extraordinarily rich but abusive husband. The reason she was arrested was that the killer was arrested for another killing, and he gave up the not-so-grieving widow to avoid the death penalty in a state where they execute more people than anywhere else in the country. There was also a witness who could testify that he saw Miss Texas meeting with the killer. Then, lo and behold, the witness who saw the killer and Miss Texas together says he made a horrible mistake, and a man facing lethal injection changed his mind about testifying against the widow. Not guilty, twelve Texans said.

In San Diego, in 2011, a fifty-something heiress was accused of shooting her thirty-something playboy husband. The woman claimed she wasn't home when a robber tried to break into her house and that it was the robber who shot her young hubby. The cops, however, found a teenage boy who could testify that the woman was home, as well as two witnesses who heard the woman threaten to kill her husband for cheating on her with a cocktail waitress. Then, voilà, the teenage witness takes off before the trial, another witness disappears, and the third witness changes her testimony.

In 2013, in Las Vegas, a man's wife disappeared and her body was never found. The guy figured: no body, no evidence of murder, no conviction—just like that guy Powell in Utah. Unfortunately for him, a neighbor with insomnia saw him putting a shovel in his car around the time his wife disappeared—and the suspect couldn't explain what happened to the shovel. Then a park ranger saw the guy's Range Rover in the Lake Mead National Recreation Area. The ranger even got a partial license plate number. The man should have gone to jail for life. He didn't.

As Porter had said, in all six cases the defendants were richer than God. The other thing the cases had in common was that the defense lawyers involved were all top-of-the-line and all had well-deserved reputations for being sneaky and underhanded. But this didn't mean anything, DeMarco knew, as most high-priced defense attorneys were sneaky and underhanded. DeMarco also noted that in each case there was a lengthy period between the arrest and the trial. This also wasn't unusual—the wheels of justice in the United States grind slowly—but the thought occurred to him that a lengthy period between arrest and trial worked to the advantage of someone whose job it was to get rid of witnesses.

DeMarco also noticed that there was generally a gap of about two years between the cases—but he didn't know what that meant. If the same person had tampered with the witnesses in all six cases, maybe he—or she; or they—didn't need to work more than every other year. The other possibility was that cases involving superrich criminals just didn't come along very often.

He saw nothing in the summary, however, that showed that the cases were linked in any way. The defense lawyers were different. The cases occurred in different cities, although four of them had occurred in the Southwest. There was nothing that gave any indication of a wizard behind the curtain. Porter had said that she'd learned about the wizard after speaking to the prosecutors, but whatever came out of those discussions wasn't documented in the intern's file. Porter apparently wanted him to come to his own conclusions.

DeMarco closed the notebook, thought about the whole mess for a few minutes, then called Sarah. He gave the kid his credit card and driver's license information and told her to book him a flight to Las Vegas.

Next he called Porter, got her voice mail, and left a message saying: "I need you to call the prosecutors involved in these cases and let them know I'm working for you; I don't want them to blow me off when I try to meet with them. I also want a letter or credentials saying I'm an authorized investigator for the Manhattan DA. Something that makes me sound like a cop. I need that today. I'm flying to Las Vegas tomorrow."

23

DeMarco had decided he was going to work on the cases in order, starting with the most recent. He figured there was a chance of somebody remembering something that happened in 2013 than of someone recalling an event from 2004. He hoped. So he planned to visit the cities in the following order: Las Vegas, San Diego, Houston, Minneapolis, Phoenix, and Seattle.

The prosecutor who'd handled the Las Vegas case—the case of the guy whose wife disappeared—was named Albright, but he was no longer working in the DA's office, having retired the year before. His home was on the eighth fairway of the Painted Desert Golf Club and the fairway was as green as Ireland in spite of the region being in the fifth or sixth year of a drought. Albright was living DeMarco's dream.

Albright, a tanned, silver-haired guy in his sixties, was dressed in shorts and a polo shirt and appeared to be in excellent shape. He said, "It seems unlikely to me that one guy would be involved in all six cases, but I know for a fact that somebody got to the witnesses in the Otterman case. I mean, I know that son of a bitch killed his wife and buried her near Lake Mead. And I *know* the park ranger saw Otterman's car near Lake Mead when Otterman was supposedly in California visiting his sister."

"So what happened?" DeMarco asked, even though he knew the answer from the file Sarah had put together.

"First," Albright said, "we had a neighbor who saw Otterman putting a shovel in his Range Rover. This was at one in the morning and the neighbor, who has insomnia, couldn't sleep and she saw the light go on over Otterman's garage. You know, he had one of those motion detector lights, and when he backed his car out, the light went on. Then the neighbor sees Otterman stop his car in the driveway, and he goes back into the garage and gets a shovel. Most likely the wife's body was in the car when this happened, but all the neighbor saw was him getting the shovel, like the dumb shit had forgotten he'd need it to bury his wife.

"That same day, about five a.m., a park ranger sees a Range Rover in the Lake Mead Recreational Area, which covers about a million square miles. The ranger was . . . Never mind what he was doing; it doesn't matter. The point is, he saw a car, noticed it was a Range Rover, which is a pretty distinctive vehicle, and happened to get three letters of the license plate. The only reason he got the three letters was they spelled TUB. Otterman's license number was 216-TUB—I can still remember it—and the ranger noticed the TUB part. It just stuck in his mind.

"About a week later, Otterman reports his wife missing. He said he waited so long because he was visiting his sister in California and didn't realize his wife was gone until he got back. We start to investigate and learn from the wife's relatives that she was planning to divorce Otterman and take half his money and a house the size of the Bellagio. We also thought it kind of odd that the wife didn't take her car when she left and her closet was full of clothes and her makeup was still in her bathroom. Then we talked to the neighbor and learned about the shovel.

"We asked Otterman how come he put a shovel in his car. He says he was afraid it might snow on his way to visit his sister in California—and it was winter, so that sort of made sense—but he claimed someone stole the shovel from his car.

"The next month, I got a PR nightmare on my hands. The wife's relatives know Otterman killed her, and they and all their rich friends are hounding me. So I hold a press conference basically asking if anyone can remember seeing Otterman and his white Range Rover the day his wife disappeared and I give out the license plate number—and I can't believe it when I get a call from fuckin' Ranger Dave. He tells me he remembered seeing a white Range Rover near Lake Mead and the reason he remembers it is TUB, the letters on the license plate."

Albright laughed. "Ranger Dave was a beautiful witness. Deacon in his church, a veteran who helps out at the VA hospital, doesn't drink, has better than twenty-twenty vision. God couldn't have created a better witness. So we spend the next three months scouring the Lake Mead area with volunteers and cadaver dogs but can't find a grave. Finally I say, Fuck it, and arrest Otterman. I got a witness who can prove his sister was lying about him staying with her in California—plus the sister's an alcoholic skank who's totally unbelievable—and then I got Otterman's outrageous story that someone stole his shovel.

"We go to trial, and from out of nowhere comes this homeless guy who lives in California where Otterman's sister lives. He said he heard about the case on the news—like fucking bums actually watch the news—and that Otterman was in trouble because nobody believed someone stole his shovel. Well, the bum said he couldn't bear to see a man go to jail for something he didn't do, and admitted he stole the shovel out of Otterman's car when it was parked in front of the sister's house. And, don't you know, he still had the shovel attached to a shopping cart he stole from Safeway, and it was identical to the one Otterman bought from Home Depot.

"But I don't care," Albright said. "I figured no way is a jury going to buy the bum's story. They're going to have enough common sense to know that someone paid him to lie. And I've still got Ranger Dave. I put Dave on the stand and he says he made a mistake. He says he lied about seeing the TUB license plate. He doesn't know why he lied, maybe for the publicity, but he did. After I pick myself up off the floor, I start grilling him about why he changed his testimony and he starts crying, and anyone with half a brain can see that somebody got to him and did something to make him change his story. But I can't budge him, and Otterman walks, and that was that."

DeMarco asked, "Did you try to find whoever got to the ranger?"

"Of course I did," Albright said. "I was pissed. We looked into Dave's finances to see if he'd come into money. He hadn't. We looked at his phone records to see if anyone connected to Otterman had been calling him. No one had. We talked to his neighbors to see if they'd seen any strange guys hanging out around his house, maybe threatening him; nobody saw anything. We got one thing from this other ranger who worked with Dave, and it wasn't much."

"What was that?" DeMarco asked.

"One day, a handsome, dark-haired guy came to the Ranger Station—"

"Handsome?"

"That's what she said. Anyway, the guy was talking to Dave out in the parking lot as Dave was going home for the day. This lady ranger was looking through the window and said they talked for about fifteen minutes and then the guy drove away. She didn't think anything of it, but then she leaves the station half an hour later, and Dave's just sitting in his car. She goes up to ask him if something's wrong, and she could tell he'd been crying."

"Huh," DeMarco said.

"Yeah," Albright said. "I'll tell you what I think happened, even though I don't have one shred of evidence to prove it. Dave's wife used to work on the strip here in Vegas. Cocktail waitress, hostess, that sort of thing, and I wouldn't be surprised if maybe she hooked a little, even though she was never arrested. Then one day she gets religion, moves to Dave's hometown, marries Dave, and has two kids. I think—and like I said, this is coming totally from my gut—that the guy talking to Dave in the parking lot found something out about Dave's wife, something she did when she worked here. I think that's why Dave changed his testimony: to protect his wife and kids."

"But the only thing you got on the guy who talked to him," DeMarco said, "is that he had dark hair and was good-looking."

"That's it. One of these days we're going to find Arlene Otterman's bones near Lake Mead, and somewhere close by will be a shovel with a yellow handle. But it won't matter, thanks to double fucking jeopardy."

DeMarco wasted a day on Ranger Dave. He drove to the ranger station near Lake Mead, only to discover that Dave was out and about, doing whatever rangers do. So for three hours, instead of taking in the scenery, DeMarco sat on a bench until he could no longer stand the hundred-degree-plus temperature, and then sat in his car with the air conditioner blasting away as he waited for Dave to return to his home base.

What DeMarco planned to say was: *Hey, I can understand what happened at the trial. Somebody threatened your wife or your kids and you didn't have a choice. So no one's blaming you, Dave, and certainly not me. And if you'll tell me what happened, no one—not the Las Vegas DA or anyone else—will hear it from me. I'm just trying to get a lead on the devious, heartless bastard who forced you to change your testimony.*

Yep, that was DeMarco's plan: to convince Dave that DeMarco held him blameless and that everything they talked about would remain confidential. On top of that, Dave would have the opportunity to make things right.

DeMarco barely got two sentences out of his mouth.

Dave was sitting behind his desk, sipping a Coke, wearing his uniform: gray shirt, dark green shorts, and hiking boots. He was a good-looking man with sandy brown hair and a wide, open, honest face; if

DeMarco had been in charge of the National Park Service he would have used Dave for a model on recruiting posters. When DeMarco said he wanted to talk to him, Dave gave him a big smile. Dave was a friendly guy, and DeMarco could tell he genuinely liked people. He was the kind who, if he saw your car had broken down alongside the road, would stop to help.

DeMarco introduced himself and said he worked for the Manhattan DA, and showed his credentials. Justine had given him a letter on the DA's letterhead saying he worked for her and he had a badge case containing a card with his name on it and the DA's seal. DeMarco suspected that Sarah had made the card on her computer, but it looked official.

Dave looked puzzled when DeMarco said he wanted to talk to him, but was still friendly. When he said he wanted to talk about the Otterman case, before he could even launch into his spiel, it was as if a sheet-metal gate slammed down over Dave's face.

Dave said he had nothing to say about Otterman and that, by the way, he had things to do. He picked up his Smokey Bear hat and walked out of the station with DeMarco trailing along behind him, trying to say that he wasn't going to cause Dave a problem, honest to God, and that he understood why . . .

Dave got into his Jeep and drove away.

Shit. DeMarco could tell that what Dave had done—lying on the witness stand—would eat at the man for the rest of his life; it was probably the only crime he had ever committed. DeMarco didn't know what religion Dave practiced, but DeMarco was a Catholic—a severely lapsed Catholic—and he'd been taught that if you went to confession, told the priest your sins, and truly repented those sins, God would forgive you. Well, DeMarco knew from his own experience that God might forgive you, but there were some sins where the one who wouldn't ever forgive you was yourself. And that's the way it appeared to be with Dave: He was never going to forgive himself for his part in helping acquit a man who'd murdered his wife, but neither was he going to talk to anyone about what he'd done.

DeMarco called Sarah and told her to make him reservations for San Diego.

———————◆◆◆———————

DeMarco struck out in San Diego. San Diego was the 2011 case where the heiress was accused of shooting her gigolo husband. Like Albright in Las Vegas, the San Diego prosecutor was a bitter man who knew somebody had tampered with his witnesses but after a year of trying to find the culprit, he found nothing. All he knew was that the defense attorney, a sleazebag named Scott Barclay, made a fortune on the case, but he couldn't prove that Barclay had hired people to suborn perjury and make witnesses disappear.

DeMarco called Sarah. "Goddamnit, get me a flight to Houston."

24

———◆◆◆———

Ella thought that watching Jack Morris play blackjack was like watching a boxer taking a beating in a prizefight. After a while you just wanted the fighter's corner man to throw in the towel and stop the slaughter.

When Bill gambled, win or lose, he always had fun. He joked with the dealers and the players next to him. If he won, he'd buy the other players a drink, and win or lose, he always tipped the dealers. But then Bill wasn't a gambling addict, didn't have thirty grand in debt hanging over his head, wondering how he was going to pay next month's rent—which is what Ella had learned from the Dallas data miners about Jack Morris, the McGill's bartender.

Jack declared an income of approximately twenty-five thousand a year, although Ella was certain he declared only a portion of the tips he made. He also received social security and a $430-a-month disability check from the VA. He was sixty-seven years old and had served in the army from 1970 to 1972, so he might have been in Vietnam. Ella didn't know—and it didn't really matter—if the disability check was for a combat injury or something else, but Jack didn't move like a man with a disability. Ella wouldn't have been surprised if tip-stealing Jack

Morris had one of those impossible-to-diagnose back problems that might not be real.

Based on his credit card statements, Ella saw that every Sunday and Monday—Jack's days off—he took a bus to Atlantic City. On rare occasions he would stay in a cheap motel in AC on Sunday nights—those rare occasions almost certainly coinciding with some unexpected luck at the tables—but most often he came home Sunday night and then took the bus back to Atlantic City the following day. Jack had a serious, serious gambling jones—which was why, as soon as she'd seen his file, Ella knew that Jack would be a walk in the park.

Ella had been on Jack's bus when he left New York on a warm Sunday morning, a bus filled mostly with badly dressed old folks who didn't look as though they could afford the bus ticket, much less a place at a poker table. Jack got off the bus at the terminal in AC and walked—eagerly, it seemed to Ella—to the Resorts Casino, one of the oldest casinos on the Boardwalk. There was a spring in his step, as if he just *knew* that today was going to be different, that today he was going to be a winner.

He sat down at a blackjack table, pushed a hundred dollars toward the dealer, and collected his chips—and twenty minutes later, he'd lost a hundred bucks. And as he played, he was absolutely *grim*. Men probably had more fun visiting a proctologist than Jack had playing blackjack. And when he lost—and as near as Ella could tell, he lost every hand—he swore out loud, smacked his hand on the table, and the dealer would admonish him. After he lost the first hundred, he took out five more twenties, and this time the money lasted a bit longer, maybe forty minutes. Then it, too, was gone.

Jack walked away from the table and over to the bar. Ella wondered if he was through gambling for the day and planned to head back to New York. She suspected not. Most likely he'd wait a while for his luck to change—as if there was any connection between time and luck—and then go to an ATM and get more cash from one of his overloaded credit cards. Ella walked up to him, took a seat on the stool next to his, and said, "Jack, let me buy you a drink."

"What?" Jack said. Even the offer of a drink from a pretty woman wasn't enough to wipe the sour expression off his face.

Ella wore a red wig, the hair touching her shoulders, and bright green contact lenses. She was dressed in tight-fitting designer jeans and a tank top she'd bought at Neiman Marcus. She'd dressed casually to better fit in with the losers who'd been on the bus with Jack, but as soon as she'd dealt with him, she'd hire a car to take her back to New York. She hated Atlantic City. Other than the towering casinos on the Boardwalk, it was a shabby, depressing place, growing shabbier each year as state after state authorized casino-style gambling.

"Who are you?" Jack said. "And why would you want to buy me a drink?"

"Jack, I'm your salvation," Ella said. "I'm going to give you five grand today so you can keep on playing. And next month, provided you behave, I'm going to give you another five grand. Today is indeed your lucky day."

"What in the hell are you talking about?" Jack said, but the possibility of someone giving him five thousand dollars made him noticeably less belligerent.

"I'm talking about Toby Rosenthal, the man you mistakenly identified as the man who shot Dominic DiNunzio."

"Mistakenly?"

At that moment, the bartender came over, a heavily made up woman about Jack's age, and asked if Jack and Ella wanted a drink. Ella didn't even want to think about what the bartender would look like without her makeup. "I'll have a Black Jack on the rocks," Jack said. "A double. And it's on her." Ella had a Coke.

In the next thirty minutes, Ella went over Jack's original statement to the cops, what he'd said at Toby's lineup, and what he would say at Toby's trial. Jack may have been a lousy gambler, but he wasn't stupid and understood what was expected of him. Jack had no problem with what Ella wanted him to do. She figured Jack could rationalize his actions, as he was only one of five witnesses, and it wasn't his fault that he couldn't be sure that he saw Toby shoot DiNunzio.

Ella could tell that Jack, with this newfound money, was eager to get back to the blackjack table, so she concluded by saying, "I'm going to go over all this again before Toby's trial. In fact, I'll probably go over your testimony with you several times. And like I said, next month I'll mail you another five grand. I have your address. So are we good here, Jack?"

"Yeah, we're good. Now, can I have the money?"

He looked over at the blackjack table as if it was an oasis in a desert and he was dying of thirst. What a loser—but he was *her* loser.

Ella took an envelope from her purse—but didn't hand it to Jack. "There's one more thing," she said. "Now me, I've never hurt anyone in my life; I'm just not that kind of girl. But the people I work for . . . Jack, can you imagine what it would be like tending bar in a wheelchair? Because that's what you'll be doing if you take our money and don't do what you've agreed to do."

Ella handed Jack the envelope and started toward the exit of the noisy, depressing, smoke-filled casino. She noticed she had a quarter in her pocket and stuck it in a slot machine on her way to the door. She pulled the handle and three red 7s lined up across the face of the machine. The machine started making a god-awful racket as it spit out eighty quarters. She couldn't believe it: She'd just won twenty bucks. She laughed and kept on walking, not bothering to take the quarters out of the tray.

25

DeMarco was in a bar, having a beer, feeling disgruntled as he mulled over the five days he'd pretty much wasted in Texas. His cane was hooked over the back of his chair. His right leg throbbed, making him wonder if he'd gotten rid of the crutches too early.

The bar was less than a mile from the massive redbrick prison in Huntsville where the state of Texas executed folks. From 1819, when the prison was built, until 1923 they hanged murderers and rapists in Huntsville, but in 1924, thanks to the modern miracle of electricity, Old Sparky came into use. Sparky was used over three hundred times. In 1982, however, the state concluded that lethal injection was a less cruel and unusual form of punishment—at least no one's head caught on fire—and since then Texas has executed over five hundred people in this manner.

DeMarco had just come from seeing a man on death row in Huntsville who was waiting for his appointment with the needle, and he felt very much in need of a drink. The bar was called Humphrey's, and DeMarco stopped there only because it was the first drinking establishment he saw after leaving the prison. The irony was that the man DeMarco suspected he was chasing had used the name Humphry—spelled without an *e*— and he used it because he had a sick sense of humor.

Oh yeah, he'd gotten a whiff of the guy.

While sipping his beer, DeMarco called Sarah and told her to get him reservations tomorrow for Minneapolis, saying that between Las Vegas, Houston, and Huntsville, he'd seen enough of the American Southwest to last him a lifetime. He said this knowing that he might be flying to Arizona if he struck out in Minneapolis.

"What are you doing in Huntsville?" Sarah asked.

"I went to see a guy on death row who met with me only because they gave him a bucket of Kentucky Fried Chicken. And then he told me to go fu . . . to go screw myself."

"What?" Sarah said.

"Aw, never mind. I'll tell you about it later. Just get me a flight to Minneapolis."

<hr />

DeMarco had arrived in Houston five days earlier to talk to the Houston DA about the Miss Texas case. In 2009, a former Miss Texas—whose name was Stella Harrington—hired a killer to whack her abusive, cheating, wealthy husband. Then the killer, a bottom-feeder named Randy White, was arrested for another murder: Randy, drunk and higher than a kite on meth, had shot a pregnant convenience store clerk three times because she was slow to open a cash register—and a surveillance camera captured every gruesome detail.

Randy knew he was going to get the death penalty—there was no doubt about it, not in Texas—so he told the prosecutor that he was also the guy who'd killed Stella Harrington's husband, because Stella had paid him to do the deed. In exchange for his testimony against Stella, Randy White wanted life in prison for killing the pregnant clerk instead of the death penalty—and the Houston DA reluctantly agreed to the deal. At Stella's trial, however, Randy got on the stand, swore to tell the truth, and lied. He said that he'd never met Miss Texas, and she was acquitted—but since Randy had reneged on his deal with the DA, off to death row in Huntsville he went.

It took DeMarco two days to get a meeting with the Houston DA, a guy named Coogan, because Coogan had better things to do than talk about a seven-year-old case that he'd lost. After DeMarco finally got into see him, Coogan said, "Randy White killed two people that we know about and probably a few more we don't know about. I believe there are one-cell parasites that have a bigger conscience than Randy does, and I figured that he didn't care about one person on this planet, other than his own useless self. Well, it turned out I was wrong."

DeMarco—prejudiced by too many movies—had expected Coogan to look and sound like Boss Hogg from *The Dukes of Hazzard*, complete with a Stetson, cowboy boots, and a Texas twang. He turned out to be a soft-spoken man with no regional accent, short gray hair, and bifocals, and reminded DeMarco of a history teacher he'd once had.

"Randy had two sisters," Coogan said, "and the older one basically raised him, because his mother died when he was ten. Well, his older sister had ALS, you know, Lou Gehrig's disease, like Stephen Hawking has. She didn't have any money, was living in a shitty state nursing home, and was probably going to live another five or ten years, suffering the whole time, then die a horrible death."

"Okay," DeMarco said, having no idea what this had to do with Randy not testifying against Stella Harrington.

"Two days after Stella was acquitted," Coogan said, "someone helped the sister commit suicide. She went peacefully and painlessly, and that was the deal I'm sure Randy made with the Devil: He agreed not to testify that Stella had hired him to kill her husband, and in return the Devil ended his big sister's misery, which she'd been begging the doctors to do for years."

"But I take it you couldn't find the Devil," DeMarco said.

"No, but God knows I tried. I knew I couldn't get Stella, because she was found not guilty at trial, but I thought I might be able to get her dirtbag attorney for suborning a witness. And because Randy was in the county jail before the Harrington trial for murdering that poor pregnant woman, I knew somebody had to have visited him there and convinced him not to testify. I found out Randy's sisters visited him— even the one with ALS—and his public defender, of course, and a couple of his low-life, white-trash friends. Plus one other person: A man named Derek Humphry met with him four times. Do you know who Derek Humphry is?"

"No," DeMarco said.

"Well, I didn't either until I tried to find the Derek Humphry who visited Randy. Derek Humphry is the man who back in 1980 founded the Hemlock Society, an organization pushing to get laws changed for assisted suicide. Whoever the guy really was, he was just rubbing my nose in what he did."

"But I take it you couldn't identify him."

"No. We looked at video footage at the jail and interviewed guards, and the best we got was a guy about six two with a dark beard who wore glasses and a baseball cap. And Randy, of course, told me to go fuck myself when I tried to get him to tell me who the guy was, although I doubt Randy knew his real name."

"Did the same person visit Randy's sister before her death?"

"I don't know. The nursing home where she was living doesn't have any real security; it's amazing the old folks who live there still have their wedding rings. At any rate, no one saw a man visit the sister the night she died or at any time in the weeks before she died. The only one who normally visited her was Randy's other sister. We did find one aide, a girl who could barely speak English. She said she saw a woman with Randy's sister a couple of times before her death, but she couldn't describe her at all. Just said she was a white woman who had long dark hair. You have to realize that this place is so understaffed the aides run around like squirrels all day."

"Are you saying that this woman may have been working with Humphry, and that she may have helped the sister commit suicide?" DeMarco said.

"Maybe," Coogan said, "although no one saw a woman visiting the sister the night she died. But you wouldn't have to be a cat burglar to sneak into this facility, so it's possible a woman—or maybe Derek Humphry himself—sneaked into the place, helped the sister with her suicide note, then put the needle into her and helped her push down the plunger. Somebody had to have helped her with all that—she could barely do a thing for herself."

"Have you talked to Randy recently to see if he'll give you more information on Derek Humphry? I mean, since his sister's dead and Stella Harrington can't be tried again, maybe he'll talk. He's got no reason to protect whoever he made the deal with."

"After Stella's trial, I talked to Randy till I was blue in the face, and he wouldn't tell me a thing. But I haven't talked to him in five years. The problem is, Randy's sitting on death row and knows he's going to die eventually, and he knows I don't have one single thing to offer him to convince him to talk. Plus, Randy is the type that if he can screw you over in some way, he'll do it just for the fun of it."

"Well, I have to try to get him to talk," DeMarco said. "Can you get me a meeting with him?"

It took Coogan three days to convince Randy to agree to meet with DeMarco, and all DeMarco could do in the meantime was wait in Huntsville, bored out of his mind, wilting in the heat and humidity.

—◆◆◆—

Randy was led into a small room about the size of a standard closet, hands cuffed in front, legs manacled so he was forced to take short, choppy steps. The room contained a single chair and a phone sitting on a plastic shelf, and had a wire mesh screen in the back wall so the guard could see his prisoner at all times. DeMarco and Randy were separated by a thick sheet of Plexiglas.

Randy was wearing a plain white T-shirt, jeans, and flip-flops. He was a slender man of medium height with a pockmarked complexion, lifeless blue eyes, and dishwater blond hair hanging to his narrow shoulders. He didn't look dangerous. He didn't look like a killer. He just looked pathetic. For a moment he sat there, staring at DeMarco, then finally he picked up the phone.

DeMarco knew he had two significant problems when it came to Randy. First, as had been the case with Coogan, there wasn't anything he could offer him. Randy was going to die and he knew it, and there was nothing anyone could do about that. The second problem was that Randy was most likely grateful to the man who had helped his sister escape her pain and end her life with some dignity. Certainly, he'd feel no animus toward the man who had called himself Derek Humphry. The only card DeMarco might have to play was that Randy might want to meet his Maker with a clear conscience. Not surprisingly, people on death row tended to find religion as their time grew near.

DeMarco said, "I know that a man who called himself Derek Humphry made you a deal to help your poor sister die a peaceful death." DeMarco didn't *really* know this, but like Coogan, he couldn't think of any other reason why Randy would trade life in prison for lethal injection. "And I have to tell you, Randy, that I admire you for what you did."

This earned DeMarco a smirk.

"No, seriously, Randy, I do," DeMarco said. "You could have avoided the death penalty, but you cared enough about your sister that you were willing to give up your life to spare her years of misery. So I'm not bullshitting you when I say I admire what you did. It took courage, a lot of courage. I also know you're probably grateful to the man who helped your sister, and that there's nothing I can do to make you tell me what you know about him."

Randy still didn't say anything, but he seemed amused.

Then DeMarco played the only card he had: "Randy, the man who helped your sister might have done the right thing by her, but he's an evil man. For years, he's been helping rich people avoid paying for their crimes, just like Stella Harrington avoided punishment, even though you didn't. And I know *you* know that's not right. This man's a sinner, in spite of what he did for your sister."

Now Randy smiled—and DeMarco was willing to bet that he was providing him with the most entertainment he'd had in years. But he plowed ahead, already knowing he was wasting his breath.

"Do you believe in God, Randy? Do you believe that you'll be rewarded in Heaven if you leave this earth with a clear conscience?"

"You mean the God who made my sister sick?" Randy said. "The God who made me an orphan when I was ten? The God who let me kill that pregnant bitch? Well, I gotta tell you, buddy, when you ask if I believe in God, I gotta say not so much."

Well, shit.

"You know the reason I agreed to meet with you?" Randy said.

"No," DeMarco said, not that he cared at this point.

"A bucket of Kentucky Fried Chicken. You know how sometimes you get a craving for something and you just can't stop thinking about it? Well, I've had this craving for the Colonel's chicken for the last two months. I told Coogan I'd talk to you if they brought me a ten-piece bucket of Extra Crispy. That bucket's sitting in my cell right now, because I wouldn't talk to you until they brought it to me. But I'm not going to tell you shit about the guy who helped my big sis."

While still holding the phone and looking at DeMarco, Randy yelled to the guard, "All done here, boss." Then he smiled at DeMarco again, and when the guard opened the door he walked away without a backward glance.

It was after his encounter with Randy that DeMarco went to the first bar he saw, hoping a beer would help get the stench of Huntsville prison out of his nose.

A waitress bounced over to his table and cheerfully asked if he wanted another beer. He had to admit that Texas had some of the best-looking servers he'd ever seen, and they were definitely the friendliest he'd ever encountered. He said, "Sure, and some of those chicken wings, too." Then he thought of Randy back in his cell eating fried chicken, licking the grease off his fingers, and said, "Wait. Forget the chicken wings. Just bring me another beer."

He'd been thinking that he'd wasted five days in Texas, but on reflection he really hadn't. Based on what he learned from the Las Vegas DA and from Coogan in Houston, he knew the man he was chasing was about six foot two, had dark hair, and was good-looking. He'd also learned that a woman might be helping him. And there was something else he'd learned.

The man who called himself Derek Humphry had discovered the *only* thing about Randy White that he could use to make him change his testimony: Randy's love for his sister. Then he was able to convince a man like Randy to give up his own life so his sister could end her suffering. Derek Humphry had to be one hell of a salesman. Last, he—or maybe a woman he worked with—had been willing to take the risk of sneaking into an assisted living facility to essentially murder a person, and that had taken balls.

Whoever the hell he was chasing, the guy was impressive.

26

Although things were going well, Ella was a bit worried.

Three of the witnesses were in the bag: Edmundo Ortiz was on a fishing boat off Alaska cooking for a hungry crew; old Esther Behrman was now a bedridden turnip as a result of her unfortunate stroke; and the gambling bartender, Jack Morris, would testify that he wasn't sure Toby was the guy who'd shot Dominic DiNunzio. This left two witnesses: the hot young barmaid, Kathy Tolliver; and Rachel Quinn.

Rachel Quinn was the one who concerned Ella. According to the information provided by the Dallas data miners, Quinn was as pure as the driven snow. She had no criminal record, hadn't ever been busted for anything in her lily-white life—not for smoking a joint in college or getting a DUI. She was a lawyer—did Wall Street financial crap, not criminal law—and made so much money that it wasn't likely Ella was going to be able to buy her off. Ella was certain that if she approached Quinn and even *insinuated* that she wanted her to change her testimony, the woman would immediately whistle for a cop.

The other problem Ella had—and it might be a tougher one than the remaining witnesses—was that she hadn't even started looking for an alternative suspect for DiNunzio's murder. And that was Toby's defense: Toby didn't kill Dominic—some other dude did it—and Ella had yet to identify the dude.

But when it came to the barmaid, Kathy Tolliver, Ella knew exactly what to do.

———◆◆◆———

Kathy was twenty-four years old and had a four-year-old daughter. She had been busted half a dozen times for taking drugs, usually coke, then going a bit nuts and breaking things and assaulting folks. The father of her child was an abusive alcoholic and Kathy had divorced him about a year after her baby was born.

The interesting thing about Kathy was that she was engaged in a vicious custody battle with her ex—although according to the Dallas data miners, the battle was really between Kathy and her ex-husband's parents. The *grandparents*—not the father—wanted the kid and they were determined to prove that Kathy was an unfit mother, in which case the child would be given to her ex-husband and then raised by grandma and grandpa, who doted on the little girl.

Kathy, to her credit, was doing her best to be a good mom. She'd stopped taking drugs, attended Narcotics Anonymous meetings three times a week, and worked her lovely tail off to support her child. Raising a child had to be a financial struggle; she was a single woman with a minimum-wage job whose primary source of income was the tips a looker like her could generate. So Kathy was vulnerable, and Ella figured the best strategy when it came to her was to use both the carrot and the stick. She'd start with the stick.

———◆◆◆———

Ella spent a few days following Kathy Tolliver. She worked at McGill's from four p.m. until midnight, five days a week. Mondays, Wednesdays, and Fridays she attended a noon NA meeting near her crummy apartment in Brooklyn. A lady who lived in her building and appeared to have about a dozen kids of her own took care of Kathy's little girl when Kathy was working.

Ella soon learned that the first thing Kathy did when she got off work was to go to a bar near McGill's and have a single glass of white wine before catching the subway home. While she was in the bar, some drunken ass would inevitably try to hit on her, but Kathy would blow the guy off, and sometimes wasn't very nice about the way she did it. The girl just wanted a half hour to herself to decompress before she went home to her kid.

The other thing about pretty Kathy was that she was a smoker, and since you can't smoke in any bar in New York anymore, what she'd do was sip half her white wine, step outside for a cigarette, and then go back inside to finish her wine before trudging to the subway station.

Ella decided that she needed a drug dealer, but she didn't know any dealers in New York. However, Curtis—the maintenance man at Esther Behrman's rest home—was a pot smoker, and he might know a few guys who dealt in commodities other than pot. She called Curtis—she hadn't spoken to him since Esther's tragedy—and offered to mail him five hundred bucks. Curtis hooked her up with a dealer, who steered her to another dealer, and she bought what she needed.

———◆◆◆———

Kathy left McGill's at midnight and went to her favorite after-work watering hole. She chatted briefly with the bartender, a mannish-looking woman about Ella's age, and ordered her glass of Chablis. Ella thought Kathy looked tired and noticed she had a run in the black fishnets she was wearing. Ella had been sitting in the bar, at a table, for half an hour before Kathy arrived.

A guy with a ridiculous pompadour immediately went up to Kathy, hoping to chat her into the sack, but whatever Kathy said to him caused him to back away, holding his hands up in a don't-shoot-me gesture. She finished half her wine, and then, as was her custom, asked the bartender to watch her purse and went outside to have her pre-subway smoke.

As soon as Kathy stepped outside, Ella walked up to the bar and asked the bartender for another drink, and when the bartender turned her back to reach for the bottle of Stoli, Ella dropped the tablet into Kathy's Chablis. Kathy came back into the bar five minutes later, chatted a bit more with the bartender, and then began her weary schlep to the subway. Ella again thought that the poor girl looked frazzled, and actually felt sorry for her.

Kathy walked about a block before she began to stagger, and as she was about to collapse facedown on the sidewalk, Ella walked up to her and said, "Are you all right, honey?"

"No," Kathy said, then slumped to the ground, with Ella grabbing her arm to make sure she didn't fall too hard.

Ella called 911. "A woman just collapsed. You need to send an ambulance right away. She doesn't look good at all."

She rattled off the address and hung up before the dispatcher could start asking questions. A passerby stopped to ask if she could help, but Ella shooed the Good Samaritan away, saying that she had things under control and that the medics were coming.

The medics arrived, and Ella said, "She's my friend, and I thought she was off the drugs but she, I don't know, fell off the wagon, I guess."

While one medic was taking Kathy's vital signs, the other one asked, "What did she take?"

"I have no idea," Ella said. "She used to do a lot of different shit."

The medics placed Kathy on a gurney and slid her into the ambulance, and Ella asked if she could accompany them to the hospital.

Sorry, they said, against company policy. They were taking her to Mount Sinai, and Ella would have to take a cab.

At the hospital, the doctors did whatever doctors do when someone is brought in unconscious and the medics have been told that the patient had a bad reaction to an unknown recreational drug. While all this was going on, Ella sat patiently in the ER waiting room reading magazines that were three years old. And like the good friend she was supposed to be, she held on to Kathy's purse, which contained her cell phone, making it unlikely that when she came to she'd make a phone call or leave the hospital before Ella had a chance to talk to her.

Five hours after being admitted, at approximately five-thirty in the morning, Kathy walked into the waiting area, white as a sheet, barely able to walk.

Ella stepped up to her and said, "Kathy, are you okay?"

"Who are you?"

"I'm the person who called the medics after you OD'd on whatever drug you took."

"I don't do drugs," Kathy said.

"Well, I kind of doubt that John and Helen's lawyer is going to buy that." John and Helen were the Petermans, grandparents to Kathy's child.

"What?" Kathy said. "How do you . . ."

"We need to talk," Ella said.

"Is that my purse?" Kathy said.

"Yes. I picked it up when they took you to the hospital. And like I said, we need to talk."

Kathy snatched her purse out of Ella's hand. "I don't know you from Adam. Get away from me."

"Kathy, listen to me. If we don't talk, your ex-husband is going to get custody of Maddy."

"What are you talking about? And how do you know my daughter's name? Goddamnit, who are you?"

"I know this is confusing, Kathy, particularly in the condition you're in right now, but you need to talk to me. For Maddy's sake."

Ella took her arm. Kathy resisted a bit, then went along as Ella led her over to a table in the nearly empty cafeteria.

"Now listen carefully. You're a witness against Toby Rosenthal, and if you don't say the right things when you testify at his trial, I'm going to have to tell the Petermans' lawyer about what happened tonight. I'm going to say you took too much coke or heroin and . . ."

"I didn't do any coke, and I've never taken heroin in my life."

". . . then had to be hauled off to the hospital and left Maddy stranded with your sitter, who expected you to pick up your daughter hours ago."

"I don't understand what you want."

"I know it's hard for you to concentrate right now, with the drugs and the trauma and all that, but what you need to realize is that I'm a witness to what happened tonight. The medics who picked you up off the street are witnesses, and I have their names. Most important, there's a record of your being treated at this hospital for a drug overdose. Now we're going to talk again, after you've had a chance to recover, but the thing you need to understand tonight—or I should say this morning—is if you don't do what I ask, your ex-husband is going to gain custody of your beautiful little girl. And neither of us wants that to happen."

Ella stood up and handed Kathy two twenties. "Take a cab home, not the subway. Your daughter needs you. But tomorrow we'll get together and talk, right after that NA meeting you usually go to."

The next day, as promised, Ella met with Kathy again. The woman was angry and at the same time frightened. Ella once again explained that if Kathy didn't cooperate she was going to let her daughter's grandparents know what had happened, which would almost certainly result in her ex-husband being given custody of her child.

"What do you want me to say at the trial?" she asked.

"Just the truth, Kathy. You say you saw Toby Rosenthal sitting at the bar; no one is denying Toby was at the bar having a drink. But you didn't see him shoot DiNunzio. That is, you saw DiNunzio get shot, and you initially thought it was Toby who shot him, but now you're not sure.

"You see, I've been to the bar, and you were seventy feet away from DiNunzio when he was shot. And it's dark in McGill's. Plus, you were busy getting drinks ready to take to another table, and you weren't really looking at DiNunzio's table. You understand, Kathy? You can verify Toby was in the bar, but you just can't say with certainty that he was the killer."

"I picked him out of the lineup," Kathy said.

"Kathy, that was a *terrible* lineup. The only person who looked like Toby Rosenthal in that lineup was Toby Rosenthal. None of the other people looked the least bit like him. If a man had been in the lineup who was Toby's height, and looked more like him, you might not have picked Toby. And the cops, they really sort of steered you into picking Toby. Didn't they?"

Kathy shook her head but didn't say anything.

"Don't worry. Before the trial, you and I are going to practice your testimony over the phone. I'm going to pretend to be the prosecutor and I'll ask you questions to make sure you've got your answers straight. We won't meet again. But Kathy, if you tell anyone about the discussion we had today, or if you don't do what I want, I'm going to be forced to talk to the Petermans' lawyer about how you started doing drugs again."

"Why are you doing this to me?"

"It's nothing personal, Kathy. You were just in the wrong place at the wrong time."

Ella took an envelope out of her pocket and slid it across the table. "There's ten thousand dollars in that envelope—I'll bet Maddy can use some new clothes when she starts kindergarten this year. This is just my way of showing how much I appreciate you helping me."

Kathy hesitated, didn't meet Ella's eyes, then took the envelope.

Ella rose from the table. "I'll call you again soon. Until then take care of yourself. And Maddy."

27

DeMarco had been expecting the temperature in Minneapolis to be tolerable, figuring a place that was arctic in the winter wouldn't be too bad in the summer. Turned out he was wrong. Both days he spent there, it was over ninety degrees, and so humid he felt as if he was in an outdoor sauna. It also turned out to be a wasted trip. The lawyer who'd prosecuted the Minneapolis case brushed him off, saying she didn't know anything that could help and was too busy to talk about a case that had been dismissed eight years ago and that the DA's office had no intention of retrying.

Of the six cases DeMarco was investigating, the Minneapolis case was unique. It was the only one where a witness had been killed; he had been run over while jogging. So DeMarco went to see the Minneapolis cops to ask if they had any new leads on the killer. They didn't. They figured it was just your garden-variety hit-and-run: A guy's jogging in the morning darkness, someone hits him by accident, then panics and flees the scene. To which DeMarco said: "Didn't it bother you that this man was a major witness in a murder trial?" The Minneapolis cops responded with: *"Hey! We don't need some smart-mouthed New York investigator telling us how to do our job."*

"Sarah," DeMarco said, "get me a ticket to fucking Phoenix."

"You don't have to be so crabby about it," Sarah said.

He couldn't help feeling crabby. The only thing he had, after all the time he'd spent, was that a tall, dark-haired, possibly handsome guy had been involved in the cases in Las Vegas and Houston. And that maybe he was working with a woman. But that's *all* he had. He felt he was wasting his time and the taxpayers' money—not that he cared about the taxpayers' money—and doubted that he'd have any better luck in Phoenix on a case that happened ten years ago.

In Phoenix, in 2006, a rapacious real estate developer named Caldwell Hudson got into a fight with his wife. Hudson stomped out of his mansion, drove to a bar, and had five or six or seven shots of tequila. He left the bar, drunk as a skunk, still boiling from the fight with his spouse, then ran a stop sign and T-boned a pickup driven by a man named Alfredo Gonzalez. In the back of the pickup were the lawn mowers and weed whackers Mr. Gonzalez used to take care of the yards of rich people like Caldwell Hudson.

Hudson and Gonzalez exchanged curses, Gonzalez gave Hudson a little shove when Hudson got in his face, so Hudson—who always went about armed for no good reason other than that he had the *right* to go about armed—pulled out his .45 and shot Gonzalez. When it occurred to him that he'd just killed a man, Hudson got back into his car and sped away. Hudson's Hummer was barely damaged in the accident.

Unfortunately for Caldwell Hudson, a married couple saw the accident and saw Hudson shoot Gonzalez. The woman got Hudson's license plate number. Another man—a Mexican trapped inside Gonzalez's T-boned truck—was also a witness. The only good news—from Hudson's perspective—was that the event occurred at one in the morning and the only light near the scene of the accident was a streetlight approximately forty yards away. Nonetheless, all the witnesses said that Hudson, and everything he did, was clearly visible.

———◆———

The lawyer who'd prosecuted the Hudson case was a cocky bantam-weight named Harry Taylor and he was now the Maricopa County attorney. When DeMarco was ushered into Taylor's office, he found him in a tuxedo, trying to tie his bow tie. Taylor explained that he had to leave in five minutes, as he was speaking at some event that evening. But after DeMarco told him the reason he was there, Taylor gave up on the tie, punched a button on his phone, and said, "Adele, call my wife and tell her I might be a few minutes late, but not to panic."

"Hudson's defense," Taylor said, "was that somebody who looked like him stole his car, which had his gun in the glove compartment, and it was this *other* guy the witnesses saw kill Gonzalez. He said he'd had a fight with his wife, drank a bunch of drinks, and figured he was too drunk to drive. Plus, he said, he didn't want to go home to his bitch of a wife, so he checked into a motel at least an hour before the shooting. His car, he said, was stolen from the motel parking lot; he'd been so drunk he'd left his keys in the ignition. And his car was later found at the airport, no gun in the glove compartment, and wiped clean of prints."

"How did he expect that alibi to hold up?" DeMarco said.

Taylor laughed. "Because the clerk at the motel backed up his story. He said Hudson checked in when he said he did and paid cash, so there was no credit card record. But I wasn't worried. I had three witnesses, and this clerk had about as much credibility as my teenage daughter does when she lies to me; I mean, he just *looked* like a sneaky, lying weasel. I figured no jury was going to believe him. Those twelve citizens, good and true, would conclude that rich Mr. Hudson had paid off the clerk, which I'm sure he did.

"Then the Mexican witness, a guy who mowed lawns with Gonzalez, disappears. He was an illegal, so we told him when we interviewed him that he didn't have to worry about being deported, but we figured he didn't believe us and took off. Or maybe he took off because he was paid to take off.

"But I'm still not worried, dummy that I am. I have two witnesses, the man and his wife, both upstanding citizens. Then Hudson's lawyer hands me pictures of two local guys who had prior convictions for grand theft auto, and says the cops should have investigated them for stealing Hudson's car. Well, these two guys both looked like they could have been Hudson's cousins, if not his brothers; it had to have taken *weeks* for Hudson's lawyer to find them. And neither of them had an alibi for where he was the night Gonzalez was killed, not even some half-assed I-was-drinking-with-my-buddy alibi. Somebody had obviously paid both of them to take the heat, telling them there was no way we could make a case against them, not after we'd arrested Hudson.

"So now, thanks to a lying motel clerk and two look-alike car thieves, the stench of reasonable doubt hangs in the air, and I offer Hudson manslaughter instead of murder two if he'll plead guilty. He tells me to go shit in my hat.

"Ten months later we finally go to trial, because Hudson's lawyer did everything he could to delay it. I've never seen a lawyer come up with more reasons why a trial couldn't start, but I can hardly wait to get the man and his wife on the stand."

"But they changed their testimony, didn't they?" DeMarco said, just to shorten the story, which Taylor seemed to enjoy telling.

"Yep. Got in the chair, swore on the Holy Bible, and lied like mother-fuckers. It was too dark, they said, and they couldn't be sure it was really Hudson they saw. Maybe it was one of the two car thieves but they couldn't say which one. Nope, they just couldn't, not in good conscience, say it was Hudson who shot Gonzalez. After Hudson walked, I told those two that I was going to nail their lying asses for perjury, and they looked scared after I got through screaming at them, but they didn't buckle."

Taylor paused—for the sake of drama, DeMarco assumed—before he said: "But one thing I noticed at the time was that the woman didn't look particularly healthy. She was real skinny and sort of a pale yellow color and had brown teabags under her eyes like she hadn't slept in a month."

"Is this relevant?" DeMarco asked.

Taylor smiled. "Yeah. It's relevant, because a month after the trial, the woman got a brand-spanking-new liver. She had been on the transplant list for over a year and would have died soon if that liver donor hadn't miraculously come along. I never even knew she was sick, but someone smarter than me found out."

"So who did it? Who orchestrated this thing?"

"I have no idea. Hudson's lawyer was obviously involved, but I suspect that he had help."

"You didn't come across anyone who met with the witnesses or—"

"I'm telling you, DeMarco, I have no idea who got to the witnesses. And I looked hard to find whoever it was. But you could be in luck."

"How's that?"

"Hudson's lawyer was a guy named Foreman, like the boxer. He works in a firm with two dozen other shysters and about three years ago, the firm cleaned house and got rid of all the deadwood. One of the guys they booted out was a senior partner named Katz who'd worked at the firm for twenty years. I know he hates Foreman's guts, and I suspect he'd be happy to dish out all the dirt he can about his old firm."

Taylor punched the button on his phone again and said, "Adele, come in here and help me tie this damn tie."

28

The next day DeMarco called Ben Katz and asked to see him regarding a case his old law firm had handled in 2006. Katz said he wasn't interested in talking; it was ten in the morning and he sounded as if he had just woken up. DeMarco, figuring this wasn't a time for subtlety, said, "I'm trying to find a way to screw your old partner, Foreman."

Well, come on over, Katz said.

Katz was a red-faced, overweight man with wispy blond hair and a boozer's nose. He was wearing Bermuda shorts, flip-flops, and a lime green T-shirt stretched over his big gut. He rented a small apartment in a large apartment complex with a pool the size of a bathtub. It was the kind of place where young people without much money would live, not a former partner in a prestigious law firm.

Katz asked if DeMarco wanted a screwdriver, a little eye-opener to begin the day. Sure, DeMarco said. He wasn't going to drink it; he just didn't want Katz thinking he disapproved of a guy who drank his breakfast. He also wondered if Katz's drinking was one of the reasons he was booted out of his firm.

He told Katz he wanted to talk about the Hudson case and about the possibility that Foreman could have hired someone to tamper with the witnesses—and then had to listen to Katz rant about Foreman and how he himself was now an ambulance chaser working out of his apartment because of that bastard. Finally, he got to Hudson.

"I remember the case," Katz said. "Foreman kept bragging about bagging a client like Caldwell Hudson and how he was going to bill him at three times his normal rate; he knew Hudson was so damn rich, he wouldn't care. And right after the trial, Foreman bought a Porsche Boxster. But I'd figured he was going to lose. I'd read what the papers said about the witnesses, and I thought the best Foreman would be able to do was get Hudson a plea deal for manslaughter.

"Anyway, one night I run into Foreman in a bar. We were never really friends, but he waves me over like I'm a long-lost buddy and offers to buy me a drink. I say something like, 'You're in a good mood tonight,' and he says, 'Why wouldn't I be. I got the world by the balls.' So I ask him, since I knew Hudson was his biggest case at the time, if he's managed to get a decent plea for him, and that's why he's celebrating. Well, he says, 'I ain't takin' no stinking plea bargain. My client's an innocent man.' I say, 'Come on, who are you kidding, you're never gonna get him off.' Well, he says . . ."

Katz polished off his screwdriver before completing the sentence, then looked into the glass as though he couldn't figure out where all the booze had gone. "I'm gonna get another drink. You want one?"

DeMarco said no thanks, he was still working on the one he had. Then he had to wait as Katz took his time mixing another drink, took a gulp, then went to the bathroom, leaving the door open so DeMarco could hear him piss. Finally, he came back to the living room.

"Foreman," Katz said, "is the kind of guy who always wants you to think he's got a secret, that he knows something you don't, but he'll never tell you exactly what he knows. You know what I mean?"

"Yeah," DeMarco said.

"So when I asked him how he expected to get Hudson off, he gives me a wink and says, 'I brought in the pros from Dover.'"

"The pros from Dover? Who was he talking about?"

"I don't know, and of course he wouldn't tell me."

"But he said 'pros,' plural?"

"Yeah, acting all cagey and sly, like the asshole he is, but that's all he said. So maybe he did hire someone to help with the witnesses, but that's all I know and I have no idea who it might have been."

"Well, hell," DeMarco said. He stood up, about to say, *Thanks for the drink and taking the time to talk to me,* when Katz said, "But I know someone who might be able to help you."

Elinore Rodgers lived in a small stucco house in a neighborhood that appeared to be trending downward. The yard was landscaped in typical Arizona fashion: gravel and cactus plants, no trees or grass. Elinore answered the door wearing a powder blue jogging suit, but even dressed casually she looked elegant. She was tall and graceful and her hair was the color of pale champagne. DeMarco thought she looked like the ideal executive secretary, the kind you might find sitting outside the Oval Office. She had been Foreman's secretary before Foreman fired her.

DeMarco explained why he was in Phoenix and recounted for her what Katz had told him about Foreman's bringing in "the pros from Dover" on the Hudson case. He said he was hoping that she might be able him identify the pros.

"They fired Katz," Elinore said, "because he was a drunk. But they also fired about ten other people, good people, who the senior partners felt weren't pulling their weight. I'd been with the firm for twenty-five years and I knew more about the law than ninety percent of the lawyers who worked there, including Wayne Foreman. But I wasn't versatile when it came to all the electronic computer stuff, even though I took classes on my own time and tried to learn."

Elinore looked away and sniffed, and DeMarco thought she was going to cry. But she didn't. She said, "I was fifty-seven years old and didn't have a chance of getting a job in another law firm, but Foreman didn't care. He tossed me out, and eventually I had to sell the beautiful home I'd lived in for twenty years and move into this god-awful place. But if you'd come to me even a year ago, Mr. DeMarco, while I was still trying to find a job, I wouldn't have talked to you. I wouldn't have wanted anyone in this town to think I was a person who couldn't be trusted with a law firm's secrets, even a law firm that had treated me so badly. But after three years of job hunting . . . Well, fuck 'em."

DeMarco could tell that Elinore Rodgers didn't normally—or ever—say things like "fuck 'em," but she'd clearly reached her limit.

"But about the Hudson case," DeMarco said to get her back on track. "Can you remember . . ."

"Five or six months before the Hudson trial, a man came to see Foreman," Elinore said.

"A tall, dark-haired, good-looking guy?" DeMarco said.

"I don't remember him being good-looking or tall. In fact, I can't really remember anything distinctive about him other than he had a ponytail and was wearing scrubs."

"Scrubs?"

"Hospital scrubs, like doctors wear during surgery, although I doubt this person was a surgeon. He was probably an aide who pushed patients around in wheelchairs. When he came to the office and asked to see Foreman, I asked his name but he wouldn't tell me. He said that Foreman was expecting him. I called Foreman, described the man, and Foreman said to send him right in.

"Two minutes later he leaves and Foreman tells me to come into his office. When I walked in, he was writing something on an index card—it turned out to be an address—and he said he wanted me to deliver an envelope to a house. He didn't want to wait for a messenger service or FedEx or anything like that; he wanted me to deliver it personally, and right away. But when he reached for the envelope he knocked his coffee cup over and spilled coffee all over the envelope and everything else on his desk. I started to get some paper towels to wipe off his desk, but he told me to get going.

"Well, I decided to put whatever was in the envelope into another envelope. It seemed unprofessional delivering something with a big coffee stain on it to anyone associated with the firm. So I opened the envelope—I knew Foreman wouldn't mind, since I handled all his correspondence—and saw it contained medical records."

"Medical records?" DeMarco asked. "Whose records were they?"

"I don't know—there was no name on them. Anyway, I delivered them to a house on Canyon Drive. After Hudson was acquitted, the DA made accusations about Foreman somehow engineering a liver transplant for a witness in return for her falsifying her testimony, which, of course, Foreman denied. He told the DA, 'How would I know anything about a witness's medical condition, medical records being confidential.' After he fired me, I thought about talking to someone in the bar association but never did. At the time, I still thought some law office might hire me."

"Who was the envelope addressed to?" DeMarco asked.

"It wasn't. It was blank."

"So who did you give it to?" *Please, please don't tell me you shoved it into the mail slot.*

"A young woman," Elinore said. "I remember she was very pretty. I told her I was delivering something for Foreman and she said she'd been expecting it. She took the envelope, thanked me, and I left."

"So you never got her name?"

"No."

"Did you see a man at the house, a dark-haired, handsome guy?"

"No, just the woman who came to the door."

"What did she look like, other than being pretty?"

"Oh, tall, good figure, short blond hair. That's all I can remember."

"Do you remember the address of the house?"

"No, but I could find it again. It was a spectacular house, and, like I said, on Canyon Drive."

An hour later—after DeMarco treated Elinore to lunch—they went for a drive. Elinore recognized the house as soon as she saw it. It was the last house on the street, sitting on a hill overlooking the city. Tall wrought-iron gates barred the driveway. DeMarco wrote down the address.

After DeMarco dropped Elinore off back at her sad little house, he called Sarah. For the first time since leaving New York, he finally had a solid lead. He told Sarah to find out who was living in the Canyon Drive house before the Hudson trial.

The intern was a bloodhound with a keyboard. She called him back the following day and said the house was owned by a Chinese investor who lived full-time in China.

"Aw, shit!" DeMarco said. Couldn't anything be easy?

"Calm down," Sarah said. "The Chinese guy rents the place out, and he uses a property management company there in Phoenix. It rents for twelve grand a month, by the way."

"Call the property management company," DeMarco said. "Say you work for the Manhattan DA and your boss needs to talk to whoever rented that house in 2006. Threaten them with subpoenas and warrants and lawsuits and anything else you can make up that sounds threatening."

"I can do that," Sarah said. DeMarco *really* liked this kid.

While waiting to hear back from Sarah, DeMarco decided to go for a swim in the motel pool, since it was about 110. How could people live in this part of the country in the summer?

Paddling around in the pool—the water hot enough to boil an egg— he thought about how he could find the guy who had delivered the medical records to Foreman. All he knew about the man was that he had a ponytail and probably worked in a hospital, and eventually concluded it was going to be impossible to find him. He then wondered if there was some way he could squeeze Foreman, although lawyers were notoriously hard to squeeze; squeezing a lawyer was like trying to squeeze Jell-O. Maybe if he told Foreman that Elinore Rodgers was willing to testify that she knew he'd been given copies of medical records . . .

His phone, which was on a poolside lounge chair, started ringing. He paddled over to the side of the pool, clambered out, banging his bad leg, but reached the phone before it went to voice mail. It was Sarah.

"I talked to the property management company. A lady there named Judy Gleeson will show you the rental records if you can prove you work for the Manhattan DA."

"Text me the address," DeMarco said. "Then go out and buy yourself a milk shake or something, and put it on my expense account."

"A milk shake? I was thinking more along the lines of an appletini."

"What's that?" DeMarco said.

"A martini made with an apple liqueur."

"Are you old enough to drink?"

"Yes. I'm over twenty-one. And I'm not a virgin, either."

"Aw, geez, you didn't have to tell me that."

———— ◆◆◆ ————

Judy Gleeson turned out to be a pleasant, talkative woman about DeMarco's age. Her office was in a shopping mall in Phoenix, and the windows were covered with photos of homes the company rented as well as those it was trying to sell.

DeMarco showed her the badge identifying him as a special investigator for the Manhattan DA. "Well, okay," Judy said, barely glancing at his credentials before handing them back. "The young lady in New York who spoke to me said this concerned a murder. This is so exciting!"

DeMarco said, "We have no evidence that the person who rented the house was involved in the murder, but he or she may have some information that's pertinent. So can you please give me the renter's name?"

Judy flipped open a buff-colored file folder that was sitting on her desk. "His name is William S. Cantwell. After your assistant called, I looked at the file, and I remembered him. He was very handsome and very nice. Polite, no trouble at all—not one of those tenants always calling to complain about something."

"Do you know if Cantwell was his real name?"

"Well, I guess I don't know for sure, but he showed me a driver's license with his picture on it. And we don't rent out homes like Mr. Wu's to anybody who walks in off the street. We're talking about a two-and-a-half-million-dollar home. So we require references and do credit checks. I also have Mr. Cantwell's social security number, a copy of his driver's license, the references he provided, and the policy number for his renter's insurance."

DeMarco almost rose from his chair, raised his hand toward the heavens, and shouted, *Thank you, Jesus!*

"Can I see the copy of his driver's license?" DeMarco asked.

"Sure," Judy said, passing an eight-by-eleven piece of paper over to him.

The copy of the driver's license showed a man with a full head of dark hair, looking relaxed as he smiled into the camera. DeMarco had to admit he was a good-looking guy. The license was from Washington State and had a Seattle address on it; the expiration date was 2009. Cantwell's date of birth was also on the license. He'd been born in 1966, which meant he'd currently be fifty years old, and was forty at the time of the Hudson case.

"Who provided the reference for him?" DeMarco asked.

"A company like ours in Seattle, one that manages top-of-the-line properties. Mr. Cantwell rented a penthouse apartment there in 2004."

This was getting better and better. It was in Seattle in 2004 that the former Microsoft executive had been acquitted of rape because a witness changed her mind.

"Can you tell me Cantwell's social security number, and can I have a copy of the reference letters and his driver's license?" DeMarco asked.

"You bet," Judy said.

"By the way, do you know if Cantwell was married?" DeMarco asked.

"I don't know if he was married or not—he didn't list a wife on any of the paperwork I have—but I think he lived with a woman."

"Why do you think that?"

"Because once a month I'm required to check on the properties we rent. Normally, Mr. Cantwell would be there when I dropped by, or sometimes he'd just tell me to use my own key to get in, but once a woman let me in."

"Did she give you a name?"

"Not that I recall. I knocked on the door and she said something like, 'Yeah, Bill told me you'd be dropping by.' But I don't remember her telling me her name."

"What did she look like?"

"Very pretty and very young. I mean she was *way* too young for him."

"How young was she?"

"Early twenties, I'd say."

Meaning she'd be in her early thirties now, DeMarco thought.

"What did she look like?" DeMarco asked. "Blond, brunette? Tall, short?"

"Oh, she was blond, but I don't know if that was her natural color. I remember she had a cute, short haircut and thinking if she'd been more approachable I would have asked her who cut it. And she was tall. I'm five six, and she was at least three or four inches taller than me."

So who was the woman? Was she just Cantwell's girlfriend or was she his partner? And could she have been the woman who visited Randy White's sister in the nursing home?

Well, he'd worry about the woman later. Right now what he needed to do was track down Cantwell, and having the guy's picture and social security number meant that it shouldn't be too hard. And if he was involved in the Toby Rosenthal case, he'd be in New York.

DeMarco called Sarah right after leaving Judy Gleeson's office and gave her everything he had on Cantwell.

"You got him!" Sarah said.

"No, Sarah, *we* got him. Now we just have to find him."

He called Justine next. He told her about Cantwell, how he'd identified him, and how he was fairly sure that he was the man involved in the cases in Houston and Las Vegas as well as Phoenix—although he didn't have proof, not stand-up-in-court proof. But at least he was no longer chasing a shadow.

"I told you there was a guy," Justine said, sounding smug.

"But I don't know if he's in New York," DeMarco said.

"He is," Justine said.

DeMarco started to pack, but then decided to head over to the hotel bar and have a martini. He figured he deserved a drink or two for having ID'd Cantwell.

Then Sarah called.

"William Cantwell's dead," Sarah said. "He died in 2014."

29

Two years earlier
Santa Barbara, California—2014

Bill's getting sick and dying was the worst experience of Ella's life.

They'd just finished a job in Las Vegas and were planning to take the year off. Bill, for whatever reason, had a hankering to go to New Zealand, and he wanted to take cruise ships to get there, stopping at a few islands in the South Pacific along the way.

Bill loved cruising. He liked the entertainment on board the ships; he liked going to the casino and playing craps with a crowd of cigar-smoking, boisterous men. He liked sitting on the deck sunbathing with Ella at his side, looking good in a small bikini. He liked sipping a drink on the balcony of their suite—and they always had a suite with a balcony—and looking out at the ocean, hoping to spot porpoises or dolphins or whales. He acted like a little kid every time he saw one.

What he really enjoyed were the dinners. On a cruise ship, unless you asked to sit alone, they'd seat you at a table with a bunch of strangers—or at least they were strangers at the start of the trip. By the end of the cruise, they were all Bill's best friends. Bill was the life of the party, got everyone talking, knew more jokes than anyone else; he'd buy the table bottles of champagne to celebrate virtually anything. Everybody loved Bill.

On the way to New Zealand, he started to feel tired all the time; the slightest activity would wear him out. And despite having always had a good appetite, he didn't seem to feel like eating. Then the abdominal pains started, the pain radiating to his back, and Ella started to get worried. The doctor on the cruise ship, who Ella suspected was a drunk, couldn't find the problem and didn't have the equipment he needed to do all the tests he'd have liked to. By the time they reached Australia, Bill's eyes had a yellowish tinge, which Ella knew was a bad sign and could indicate liver problems. Lord knows, Bill drank enough to have screwed up his liver.

Ella forced him to go see a doctor in Sydney, and that's when they found out what was wrong. It was pancreatic cancer, the really aggressive, always fatal kind. And the cancer had already started to metastasize. The doctor told them that Bill had maybe nine months to live, more likely six, and the last three were going to be bad. And they were.

They decided to go back to the States to get a second opinion even though they both knew it wasn't going to make any difference. They flew to Los Angeles, where another oncologist confirmed what the Aussie doc had told them. Bill was going to die.

The way Bill reacted surprised Ella. She thought he would have gotten angry and bitched about the unfairness of life. She thought he'd spend hours weeping and feeling sorry for himself, bemoaning the hand that Fate had dealt him. But he didn't. He said repeatedly, except at the very end, when the pain was unbearable, that he'd had a great life and had lived it to the hilt. Sure, he'd said, I'd expected to live to eighty or ninety, but when you think about all those poor bastards out there who've never had what I had . . . Well, I really can't complain, and I have no regrets. And the amazing thing was that he seemed to mean it. They talked it over and decided to spend his last few months in Santa Barbara, where Bill's mother lived. It was a gorgeous place to live—or die.

Ella had liked Bill's mom the first time they met, at their wedding, and in the next five months they became close as they cared for Bill together. Janet Kerns was a lot like Ella in many ways. She hadn't been raised dirt-poor in some backwater town, but she hadn't come from a rich family, either. And like Ella, she married the first time for love. Bill's dad had been fairly well-off, but he hadn't been superrich. Husbands two, three, and four—the ones who followed after Bill's dad died—*were* superrich. And none of them stayed married to Janet all that long. What did last was the money she got when the divorces were final, including her fully paid-off home in the hills of Santa Barbara.

After the initial shock wore off, Janet stopped crying and rolled up her sleeves and pitched in with Ella, doing what needed to be done. In the evenings when Bill was resting fitfully, they'd have a drink together and talk about everything under the sun. One thing they didn't talk about was what Bill had been doing for a living since he was disbarred. Janet was smart enough to know that she didn't want to know and Ella, of course, didn't volunteer a thing.

By the time the end finally came, when Bill was nothing more than skin and bones surrounding a sack of pain, Ella helped him on his way. The hospice nurse said the morphine should be used as needed to control his pain, adding, "At this point, you really can't overdose him." What the nurse meant was: *When the pain gets to be too much, it's okay to give him enough to kill him*—and Ella did.

Neither she nor Bill's mom cried much the day he died; they'd done all their crying a long time ago, and both were relieved that he was no longer suffering. He was cremated, then Bill's mom rented a sailboat— one of her ex-husbands had taught her to sail—and she and Ella spread Bill's ashes in the Pacific. When Ella saw a porpoise surface, she didn't think it was a sign from God or anything foolish like that—but she was pleased, and knew Bill would have been delighted.

***

After Bill died, Ella took stock—the way she took stock the day she graduated from high school in Calhoun Falls.

Most of the money Bill had made in his lifetime was gone. Most of it he'd spent simply *living*—on the homes he rented, on the cars and boats he leased, on living life to the fullest. Bill Cantwell had never traveled in anything but a first-class seat. Then there were the bad investments: the land deal in Florida and the software company disaster in San Diego. And the cancer, of course, ate up a good chunk of his money, as he and Ella didn't have health insurance. Ella figured that in the time she'd known him, Bill had made about eleven million dollars, and all that was left was about three million. How in the hell could he possibly have gone through eight million dollars in a fifteen-year period? Or to put it differently, how had she *allowed* him to blow through eight million?

While three million might sound like a lot of money, Ella was only thirty-one years old when Bill died, and you can't retire at the age of thirty-one with only three mil in the bank. For one thing, the money she and Bill had made couldn't be put into mutual funds or invested with Edward Jones and allowed to grow; that would leave a money trail for the IRS to follow, and she couldn't afford the risk. In other words, the three million she had was basically stuck in a coffee can, buried in the backyard, instead of generating income for Ella to live on. One of the things Ella needed to do was figure out how to launder the money so she could invest it in something safe—and not in get-rich-quick schemes involving people willing to take dirty cash. Like the people in the disastrous Florida land deal.

But say Ella lived to ninety, which was not an unrealistic possibility. That meant three million dollars would have to last about sixty years, and three million divided by sixty was fifty thousand per year. Who wanted to live on fifty a year? Ella certainly didn't. That was the very definition of middle class, and she had no intention of living in some tiny house, buying a gas-friendly car, agonizing over every purchase she made.

Ella had a fuzzy idea of the future she wanted. She wanted to be retired by the age of forty. She wanted oceanfront property in

California—Santa Barbara, Monterey, Carmel, someplace like that. She wanted to summer somewhere cool, yet civilized, like the San Juan Islands off the Washington coast or Whistler up in Canada. Maybe she'd start up a little business that might be fun, like an art gallery, or learn to sail like Bill's mom. And there might be a man in this hazy vision of the future, but if there was, the most important thing about him would be his net worth. Whatever the case, all she knew for sure was that three million bucks wasn't going to cut it.

So Ella decided that she was going to keep doing what she and Bill had been doing together. At least for a few more years. Bill had taught her all she needed to know—and the truth was, she was actually brighter than Bill. Maybe at some point she'd get a partner—a *junior* partner—but her initial inclination was to go it alone.

She thanked Bill's mom for all she'd done for Bill and her, left Santa Barbara, and drove to San Antonio. She could have flown, but she liked the idea of driving to the place where Bill had his start; it was sort of like a pilgrimage, and as the highway passed under the tires, she thought about Bill and the life they'd had, occasionally weeping but more often smiling.

The morning after she arrived in San Antonio, she walked into George Chavez's office as soon as the office opened. He had no idea who she was, as Bill had never introduced her to him or told him about her. She bluntly told George that Bill was dead and that she'd been working with him since she married him—and that things were going to continue the way they'd always been. George would still act as her agent/middleman, and when a defense lawyer needed an "exceptional jury consultant," he'd call Ella and he'd continue to get his 10 percent commission.

After George got over the shock of Bill's death, and after Ella convinced him she wasn't some sneaky undercover cop, it didn't take him long to make up his mind; going along with Ella's plan was better than losing 10 percent. Plus George really had nothing to lose. From his perspective, he didn't do anything illegal; he just put Bill—now Ella—in touch with other lawyers, and what happened after that didn't involve him at all.

Unfortunately, the first solo job that came her way was the Toby Rosenthal case—a job more complex than any she and Bill had ever handled together.

Part IV

30

—◆◆◆—

After DeMarco learned that he'd been chasing a dead man all over the country, he decided to return to New York and regroup.

He called for a meeting with Justine and Sarah; that it was a Sunday didn't matter to him. Sarah recommended they meet for breakfast at a place in the East Village, explaining that its brunches were the best.

Justine arrived on time, wearing jeans and a sunflower yellow blouse, her gray-streaked brown hair tied back in a sloppy ponytail. The bright morning light did not do her any favors.

Sarah was ten minutes late and wearing a short red dress and high heels, and DeMarco suspected she was wearing what she'd been wearing the night before. Her hair was in disarray—but then it usually was—and she looked . . . well, "sated" was the only word that came to mind. For a moment DeMarco had an impulse to give her some fatherly advice on the fickle nature of young men, but he decided to keep his mouth shut.

They ordered breakfast, and while they were eating DeMarco told them he now firmly believed that Bill Cantwell had been involved in undermining the trials of the men and women accused of murder and manslaughter in Phoenix, Houston, and Las Vegas. He concluded with, "I mean, I can't *prove* that this guy blackmailed and bribed and disappeared witnesses, but I think he did. Hell, I *know* he did.

"I also know that Cantwell had a woman working with him," DeMarco said. He went on to explain that the law firm secretary, Elinore Rodgers, who delivered the medical records to Cantwell's home in Phoenix, saw her. So did Judy Gleeson, the lady who worked for the property management company. Both Elinore and Judy had described her as young, blond, and pretty, and Judy said she was about five foot nine.

"But was the woman Cantwell's girlfriend or his accomplice?" Justine asked.

DeMarco said, "I think she was his accomplice. Most likely a woman, not a man, helped Randy White's sister commit suicide—and that means she's a serious player and not some gal who just collected Cantwell's mail and shared his bed."

"But you can't prove this," Justine said.

"No. I can't prove anything," DeMarco said. "And even if I could prove the woman was helping Cantwell, there's nothing to link her to the Rosenthal case."

"Well, there's one thing," Sarah said.

"What's that?" DeMarco said.

"San Diego."

DeMarco said, "What are you talking about? I didn't get any indication that Cantwell or the woman was involved in acquitting the heiress in the San Diego."

Sarah said, "The lawyer in the San Diego case went to law school with David Slade. They graduated the same year, and based on some comments on Slade's Facebook page, I know they're good pals."

"Why are you just telling me this now?" DeMarco said.

"I'm not. The file I gave you identified where the various lawyers went to school. Maybe I should have highlighted it for you."

"Maybe you shouldn't be a smart-ass," DeMarco said.

Turning to Justine, DeMarco said, "So where do we go from here?"

"Find the woman," Justine said. "See if she's in New York."

"How do I do that?" DeMarco said. "All I know about her is that she's blond."

"I've got some ideas," Sarah said.

Justine rose and said, "I gotta get to the office. I've got a trial that starts tomorrow."

"It's Sunday," DeMarco said.

"Tell me about it," Justine said.

"You need some help?" Sarah asked Justine.

"No, but thanks for offering. And good job, Sarah. You're going to make a great lawyer."

"I'm not sure I want to be a lawyer," Sarah said. "I mean, I'll get a law degree, but I'm thinking maybe I'll get a job with the FBI. I kind of like hunting criminals."

"FBI!" DeMarco said. "I've got boots taller than you."

"That's why they give you a gun," Sarah said.

———◆◆◆———

Sarah identified the woman—and it didn't take her long at all.

She used three different online companies who claimed they could provide information contained in public records, such as divorces, liens, and criminal convictions. One of the companies turned up the fact that Bill Cantwell married a woman named Ella Fields in Hawaii in 2003. The state of Hawaii had a record of the marriage. Now all DeMarco had to do was find the woman; how hard could that possibly be?

It turned out to be impossible.

DeMarco told Sarah to see if Ella Fields had ever obtained a driver's license in the states of Washington, Arizona, Minnesota, Texas, or Nevada—the states where DeMarco suspected Bill Cantwell had plied his trade. What DeMarco wanted was a photo of Fields and her social security number. But Sarah struck out; no pretty blonde named Ella

Fields or Ella Cantwell had a driver's license in *any* state. She checked with NCIC, the National Crime Information Center, to see if Fields had a criminal record. She did not.

So DeMarco called Justine and asked her to use her clout to see if anyone named Ella Fields or Ella Cantwell had ever obtained a passport. DeMarco needed her help, because if he and Sarah tried to penetrate the bureaucratic titanium shield surrounding the State Department they might not get what they needed until the next millennium.

He told Justine: "Have NYPD make the request and imply, or lie—I don't care which—that this is terrorist-related to speed things up."

It still took over a week to get a response from the State Department; maybe if Ella's name had been "Fatima" or "Jamala" they would have acted faster. At any rate, State had issued four passports to women named Fields, Ella who were in their early thirties, the age DeMarco figured his Ella Fields had to be. One of the women was pretty but black. The second was so homely that no one who wasn't legally blind would have called her pretty. The third was a teacher in Iowa, attractive, but not a knockout, and only five feet two inches tall.

The fourth Ella Fields was a five-foot-nine blond bombshell.

And DeMarco couldn't find a trace of her anywhere in these United States.

"Find this fuckin' woman," he growled at Sarah.

DeMarco wasn't a paperwork guy. He wasn't an Internet hunter. Looking at a computer monitor gave him a migraine or put him to sleep. So while Sarah was scouring the Net trying to locate Fields, DeMarco decided to see if he could prove she was in New York. Right now he *thought* she might be in the city, but he had no evidence. He also thought—again with no proof—that she might have been behind the busboy's skipping town and Esther's stroke. So what he was going to do was go talk to people and show them Fields' passport photo and—he hoped—get someone to confirm the woman was indeed messing with the Rosenthal witnesses. If he could prove she was in the city, maybe then Justine would be able to get NYPD to use a few of its thirty thousand cops to hunt her down.

DeMarco took a cab over to the Astoria Houses in Queens, where Edmundo Ortiz had lived before he vanished. He wondered who had come up with the name, making a public housing project sound like something just down the road from Downton Abbey. The Astoria Houses occupied thirty-two acres on the banks of the East River and consisted of twenty-two six- and seven-story brown brick buildings. Three thousand New Yorkers, mostly black and Hispanic, lived in the buildings—not members of the British aristocracy.

He located the building where Edmundo Ortiz had lived, brushed by a couple of teenagers who looked like predators, and went inside. The elevators weren't working, and he had to trudge up—or *limp* up—five floors on his cane. By the time he got to the apartment where Edmundo used to live, his leg was screaming for mercy.

DeMarco had decided to begin by asking the people who now occupied Edmundo's apartment if they'd heard from him, like maybe he'd called to have his mail forwarded or asked them to ship him something he'd left behind. He doubted he'd get that lucky, but if he could find Edmundo, then Justine could ask him directly if Ella Fields had anything to do with his leaving town.

He knocked on the door, and his knock was answered by a stout Hispanic woman in her twenties wearing flip-flops, shorts, and a white T-shirt spotted with what looked to DeMarco like Gerber baby food: squash, pumpkin, some gooey yellow vegetable. The woman was holding a chubby boy clad only in Pampers; behind the woman, clutching her knee, was another kid, maybe three, a cute-as-a-button little girl with ringlets of curly dark hair. The little girl smiled at DeMarco; the woman did not. When DeMarco showed his investigator's credentials, she somehow managed to look both frightened and defiant.

"I'm sorry to bother you," DeMarco said. "I just wanted to ask if the man who used to live in this apartment has contacted you since he left?"

"No hablo Inglés."

He had the impression she spoke English but didn't want to talk to him because she thought he was a cop. Or maybe she thought he was one of the storm troopers working for ICE. "Look, I'm not here to hassle you about anything. You haven't done anything wrong. I'm just trying to find Edmundo Ortiz."

"No hablo Inglés."

"How 'bout this woman?" DeMarco said, showing her Ella Fields' photo. "Have you ever seen her around this building?"

"No hablo Inglés."

At that moment the baby in her arms began to shriek, and DeMarco wondered if the woman might have pinched the kid to cause a distraction. Whatever the case, she muttered, *"Lo siento, lo siento,"* and closed the door in his face.

And that's pretty much the way it went for the two hours he knocked on doors showing people Ella Fields' photo and asking if anyone had heard from Edmundo. No one knew anything. No one wanted to talk to a white guy who represented the government. Ironically, the most cooperative people he talked to were the hard-looking teenagers standing on the stoop, who said they sure as hell would have noticed a chica who looked like her.

DeMarco had to wait almost twenty minutes for a cab to pick him up at the Astoria Houses—what a surprise—then he headed over to the assisted living facility where Esther Behrman still lived. He had learned that she was now bedridden and grouped with the Alzheimer's patients and folks with maladies that required round-the-clock nursing care.

He walked into the building and immediately noticed that the doors weren't locked, but as it was the middle of the day, maybe that wasn't so surprising. He supposed if he'd looked like some raggedy-ass street person, someone might have rushed over and asked him what he wanted—but he didn't look like a bum and was at an age that he could be visiting his mother if she lived in the place.

He proceeded across the lobby to a reception desk, where a woman in her sixties was talking on the phone. When DeMarco stopped in front of her, she put her hand over the phone and said, "Just sign in," and pointed to a clipboard with a sign-in sheet.

DeMarco looked at the sign-in sheet. Visitors were supposed to write down their name, who they were visiting, and, if they'd parked in the facility parking lot, the make and license plate number of their car. He wondered how long they kept the sheets. He didn't sign in, however; he just stood there impatiently waiting for the lady to get off the phone, which she eventually did.

"May I help you?" she said. Before he could answer, she said, "If you're here to see one of our residents, just sign in."

DeMarco imagined the doors were locked at night and there might even be a rent-a-cop patrolling, but during the day it was obvious you could just walk in, and nobody—certainly not the busy lady at the desk—would be likely to notice or stop you. And if you were stopped and required to sign in, all you'd have to do was write down a phony name and illegibly scrawl the name of the person you were supposedly coming to see.

"Do you ask to see people's IDs when they sign in to see somebody?" DeMarco asked.

"What?" the lady said. DeMarco noticed she was wearing a name tag that identified her as Nancy.

DeMarco pulled out his credentials. "Nancy," he said, "I'm an investigator for the Manhattan DA. I'm here to ask some questions pertaining to a crime."

"What kind of crime?"

"Murder."

"Oh, my God!" Nancy said. "Are our residents in danger?"

"Absolutely not," DeMarco said. "I'm just trying to find someone I need to talk to, and your residents may have encountered this person. Now, do you ask to see IDs when people sign in to see your residents?"

"No. Why would we?"

DeMarco almost said: *So if a person visiting the old folks here is a thief or a con man then the cops might have a chance to catch him.* But there was no point in saying that. "How long do you keep these sign-in sheets?"

"Oh, we throw them out at the end of the week."

Which made DeMarco wonder why the hell they even bothered with them. But it didn't really matter, because it was unlikely that Ella Fields, if she'd signed in at all, had used her own name.

"Does this place have surveillance cameras?" DeMarco asked.

"A few," Nancy said. "They're aimed at the entrances, so we can catch somebody if they try to break in."

"How long do you keep the tapes?" DeMarco said.

"They don't use tape. They're digital, and they record for a twenty-four-hour period and then start over."

Great.

DeMarco showed Nancy Ella Fields' passport photo. "Have you ever seen this woman?"

Nancy squinted at the picture. "No, I don't think so."

"I may need to show this photo to some of your residents and the staff. But first I need to speak to a lady named Leah Abramson."

"I think I should call the director," Nancy said. "My boss."

"You do that," DeMarco said, "but tell me where I can find Leah first."

———◆◆◆———

DeMarco knocked on Leah Abramson's apartment door, and a tiny woman with short gray hair and bright blue eyes answered. She was wearing a T-shirt with one of those pink breast cancer ribbons, blue jeans, and sugar white running shoes.

"Yes?" she said when she saw DeMarco standing there, looming over her.

"My name's DeMarco. I work for the Manhattan DA. I wanted to talk to you about what happened to your friend Esther."

"It's about damn time," Leah said. "Come in. Oh, you got ID? You could be a mad rapist for all I know, I should be so lucky. I'm just kidding, but let's see your ID."

DeMarco liked Leah immediately. She had to be close to ninety, but he got the impression that there wasn't anything wrong with her mind. He showed her his credentials, and she pointed him to a love seat in her living room. She took a seat on a floral-patterned couch; her legs were too short for her feet to touch the floor.

"So somebody finally believes that somebody tried to kill Esther."

"To tell you the truth, Leah, we're not sure but—"

"Well, I'm sure," Leah said. Then she had to go through the whole story again, which DeMarco had already heard from Coghill and Dent: how Leah had found pills in Esther's pillbox that didn't match the pills in the Coumadin and digoxin vials in Esther's medicine cabinet, and how the facility nurse had found diet and antihistamine pill bottles in the closet that contained pills that looked just like Esther's prescription meds.

"People think that everyone who gets old, their minds turn to mush," Leah said. "Well, Esther and me, we used to watch *Jeopardy!* together, and got the answers right more than half the time. We'd do the crossword puzzle, and usually get most of it without having to cheat and look at the answers. And they give us tests in this place to see if we're getting Alzheimer's. You know, they show you a ball and a horse and a car, and ask you five minutes later if you can remember what you saw. Well, I never failed the damn test and neither did Esther. So I'm telling you that Esther didn't mix up her pills, and she never took a diet pill in her life."

"I believe you, Leah."

"What I can't figure out is *why* somebody would want to do that to her. She has money, but she doesn't have any relatives who would want to bump her off so they could inherit. And Esther's will leaves almost all her money to a children's hospital."

"I'm going to tell you something in confidence, Leah, because I trust you. Do you promise not to repeat what I'm about to say?"

"Scout's honor," Leah said, holding up her right hand as if she was taking an oath in court.

"Someone may have tampered with Esther's medication because they didn't want her to testify at the Rosenthal trial."

"Is that true?"

"I don't know, but it's a possibility I'm looking into. Let me ask you something: How could somebody have gotten inside Esther's apartment to mess with her medications? The cops said there wasn't any indication that somebody had broken in."

"I've thought about that," bright-eyed Leah said. "I suppose it could be like in the movies, where somebody picked the lock, but Esther has a good lock on her door. Another possibility is all the residents have to give a copy of their apartment keys to Needleman in case we have a heart attack while we're locked inside, or in case maintenance needs to get in for whatever reason."

"Who's Needleman?" DeMarco asked.

"The director of this zoo. He's actually a lackey for a big corporation that has assisted living places all over the country, and he's in charge of this one."

"Where does Needleman keep the keys?" DeMarco asked.

"Beats me, you'd have to ask him. But I imagine it's like in the building where I used to live. There's probably a box somewhere that has all the keys for all the units."

"Okay, I'll ask Needleman about that."

"There's one other thing," Leah said. "About a month before Esther had her stroke, she had her purse stolen at the Manhattan Mall. They bus us over there once a week so we can stock up on Depends."

DeMarco laughed.

"Anyway, Esther had her purse stolen when she was in the ladies' room, and her keys were in her purse, but the security guys found her purse only half an hour later and the only thing missing was Esther's cash. I figured the thief was probably some junkie, but after what happened to Esther, I started thinking: What if the thief pressed her apartment key down into putty, like they do in the movies, and then had a copy made?"

What DeMarco was thinking was that if Esther's purse had been stolen from the ladies' room, it was most likely a lady who'd done the stealing. He took out the picture of Ella Fields and showed it to Leah.

"Have you ever seen this woman?"

Leah studied the picture. "Pretty girl," she mumbled. "No, I don't remember ever seeing her. You think she's the one who hurt Esther?"

"Maybe, but I can't even prove she was in New York when Esther had her stroke. So I was thinking that I'd show her picture to people here and see if anyone saw her."

"Do you have another copy of that photo?" Leah asked.

"Yeah."

"Then let me show it to residents," Leah said. "Half of them can't remember what they had for breakfast, and I'll know which ones to talk to. But you can talk to the staff. They won't take me seriously, but they'll pay attention to a cop."

"Can you show it to Esther?"

"I will, but it won't do any good. She can move her left arm a little, but she can't walk, and she can't really talk, just makes these strange squawky sounds, and the words get all jumbled. She sits in bed all day now watching the TV over her bed, but that's just because the TV's always on. I can't tell if she really wants to watch or if she understands what she's seeing. It makes me cry to see her that way. You look into her eyes and you can see she's still inside there somewhere, not all the time, but some of the time. What kind of monster would do something like that to Esther?"

DeMarco didn't have an answer for that.

———◆◆◆———

DeMarco spoke to Needleman, a hand-wringing toady who was mostly worried about his company being sued if somebody had broken into Esther's apartment. He had both feet planted firmly in the camp that Esther had mixed up her medications. He reluctantly agreed that DeMarco could show Ella Fields' photo to his staff—nurse's aides, housecleaners, cooks, security guards, and maintenance personnel. DeMarco spent two hours doing that—and nobody recalled seeing Ella Fields.

———◆◆◆———

When the guy with the cane showed Curtis the woman's picture, he stared at it for a long time, keeping his head down, forcing himself not to react, the way he did when he played poker and was dealt a full house. But he was thinking: *Holy shit, that's her!* When she'd paid him to keep tabs on Esther Behrman, her hair had been dark brown—but the blond woman in the picture was definitely her.

He still didn't think she had anything to do with Esther having a stroke. How could she possibly have made that happen? And all he did was call her each day and tell her that Esther had shown up in the dining room for lunch. But he remembered what she'd told him the last time he saw her, when she gave him the one-grand bonus. She'd said that *if* she had committed a crime, then he was an accomplice. He didn't know what he was an accomplice to, and he wasn't about to ask the investigator what the woman had done, so all he said was: "Nope, never seen her before. And I'd remember a woman who looks like her."

After the guy left, Curtis thought about calling her—he still had her phone number—then decided not to. He didn't know what was going on, but he did know that he didn't want to get in any deeper than he already was.

31

Ella spent three days following the eHarmony lady, Rachel Quinn. She was hoping she'd get lucky and find something about Quinn that she could use to blackmail, bribe, or otherwise coerce her.

But it appeared that all Quinn did was work. She'd leave for her office in the Financial District at six in the morning and she never got back home until after seven or eight. At lunch, she'd go to a gym near her office, put herself through a grueling workout, eat a salad afterward, and return to work. The lady was determined to keep her figure. In the evening when she got home, she'd walk her dog, this hyperactive little brown-and-white terrier.

Ella could never understand why people got pets: the hassle of feeding them, getting them shots, finding someone to care of them if you wanted to take a trip. Then there was the whole shit-and-a-bag thing: walking behind some mutt, standing around looking into the air while the dog took a crap—as if you didn't want to *embarrass* it—and then, the most disgusting part, picking up the poop in a bag. Yuck! At any rate, every evening when she got home from work, Quinn would take the terrier for a walk, and if it was nice outside, she'd walk about a mile to an ice cream place; have a small cone like a guilty pleasure; then walk back home with Fido, window-shopping on the way.

Ella had been hoping to learn that Quinn had desires for something more scintillating than pralines and cream; it would have been better if she'd enjoyed a little recreational coke, was a closet lesbian, or hung around with some shady character who'd been arrested for insider trading. It was not to be. The woman was boringly, annoyingly squeaky clean. Ella suspected that there was going to be only one way to deal with Quinn, and it wasn't a course of action she wanted to take.

She thought briefly about breaking into Quinn's apartment, where she might find something juicy, like maybe a diary in which she admitted to having a kinky sex life—not that it seemed likely—or some evidence that she'd committed some sort of financial crime, which also seemed unlikely. Eventually, she decided not to take the risk. Quinn's building had a doorman, there was a camera in the lobby, and she imagined a person in Quinn's income bracket would have multiple good locks on her doors. And then, of course, there'd be the fucking dog to deal with.

She finally decided that she'd get back to Quinn after she'd dealt with the major problem in ensuring a not-guilty verdict for Toby Rosenthal: finding the man who "really" murdered Dominic DiNunzio. She was running out of time. The trial was only six weeks away.

———◆———

Ella told David Slade that she needed information on all of Dominic DiNunzio's clients going back at least five years, so Slade asked the judge to issue a subpoena. He'd told the judge and the prosecutor up front that his defense was proving that someone other than Toby had shot DiNunzio, and that this person could very well be someone connected to the victim's accounting business. For example, maybe DiNunzio had been about to tell the IRS that one of his clients was guilty of income tax evasion, and the client decided to kill him to silence him.

Slade also maintained that the police had rushed to judgment, refusing to even *consider* that after Toby left the bar, someone who looked like him came into the bar and shot DiNunzio.

"'Rushed to judgment' my ass," Justine Porter said. "Five people saw him shoot the guy."

"That's not true," Slade said. "Five people saw *someone* shoot Mr. DiNunzio, and they incorrectly identified my client. As I stated at the arraignment, Your Honor, I can present case after case where innocent men have gone to jail because of faulty eyewitness testimony."

In the end, Judge Martinez granted Slade's request for a subpoena. Like the prosecutor, the judge thought Slade's argument was specious, but he didn't want to leave room for an appeal based on the fact that he hadn't allowed Slade the opportunity to develop a logical, if unlikely, defense.

Ella had a messenger service pick up the files on DiNunzio's clients from Slade. The files included not only the clients' names but also their addresses, phone numbers, dates of birth, and social security numbers; the birth dates and social security numbers were taken off the tax returns DiNunzio had prepared for his clients.

Ella put on comfortable, lounge-around-the-house clothes—a soft white jogging suit and slippers—and began the cumbersome task of going through the client list to identify the person she wanted. The first thing she did was to eliminate anyone who wasn't between the ages of twenty-two and thirty-two—and the result was not good at all. Almost all of DiNunzio's 250 clients were older than forty, and most were in their sixties and seventies. She ended up with only seven men who were approximately Toby Rosenthal's age.

Ella's next step was to obtain photos of the seven men. She found four of them online in places like Facebook and LinkedIn. None of the four looked the least bit like Toby Rosenthal. For the three men whose photos she hadn't been able to find online, she contacted an active-duty policeman she and Bill had worked with in Las Vegas, and in return for fifteen hundred dollars, he obtained DMV photos of the three. One of the men, to Ella's delight, looked *somewhat* like Toby—dark hair, handsome regular features—but then Ella saw on the man's driver's license that he was six foot three and weighed 190 pounds. Toby was five foot seven and weighed 135.

That was *really* going to be a problem, that Toby was such a shrimp.

Ella figured that many of DiNunzio's clients most likely had children and grandchildren, and it was possible that one of those people might look like Toby. But running down the male offspring of 250 people was going to be a horrendous task, and then, even if she found a man who matched Toby's description, she'd have to come up with a reason why the son or grandson of one of DiNunzio's clients had decided to kill him.

She knew that she was going down the wrong path and needed to do something different. She decided to take a break and made an appointment at a spa about two miles from where she lived. She'd picked the spa based on Yelp recommendations and its location; she wanted to walk there, hoping the exercise would also help clear her head.

At the spa, she signed up for the works: an hour in a steam room to sweat out the toxins, a deep massage, a wax job, a facial, and then a manicure and pedicure. She was absolutely *glowing* when she walked out. She always found it hard to believe that Ella Sue Fieldman of Calhoun Falls, South Carolina, was completely comfortable spending seven hundred bucks at an upscale Manhattan spa.

As she walked back to her apartment, an approach to finding DiNunzio's "real" killer that had nothing to do with his clients occurred to her. She figured if she took this approach she'd have a much better chance of locating the ideal candidate. Then, of course, she was going to have to find some way to link him to DiNunzio—and that wasn't going to be easy. But, one step at a time.

Ella started surfing the Net, the wonderful Net. She limited the search to articles posted in the last year, looking at stories related to organized crime in the greater New York area. Specifically, she looked at criminal cases and arrests that had photos accompanying the articles. At three in the morning, her eyes feeling as though they were coated with wet sand, she found what she wanted.

In a photo in New York's *Daily News*, five men were shown coming down the steps of the New York County Courthouse on Centre Street. In the background was the magnificent building, with its towering marble columns and the chiseled inscription: *The True Administration of Justice Is the Firmest Pillar of Good Government*. Yeah, you betcha, Ella thought.

In the center of the photo was a huge man in his sixties with kinky gray hair and big ears. He looked as if he weighed three hundred pounds, and he was scowling ferociously at whoever was taking the picture. The man was Vincent (Vinnie) Caniglia, a minor Mafia figure.

The media had had a field day with Vinnie, because he'd been arrested for having twenty thousand dollars' worth of stolen Viagra pills in a storage locker that had been traced to him. The headlines in the various papers read: *Hard Time for Caniglia*; *NYPD Busts Hardened Criminal*; *No Time to Be Soft on Crime*.

With Vinnie were four guys who worked for him, and one of them was pointing at the photographer and shouting. Ella figured he was saying something like, *You don't get dat fuckin' camera outta da boss's face, I'm gonna kick your ass*. Three of Vinnie's associates were large men, though not as large as Vinnie. But the fourth man was a little guy whose head barely came up to Vinnie's armpits.

And he was perfect.

The short man was identified in the photo as Dante Bello. It was a beautiful name, and Ella wondered if Dante's mother had thought her son was going to grow up to be an opera singer instead of a hood. Ella had her Vegas cop get her a copy of Bello's driver's license and his criminal record. The driver's license said Dante Bello was five foot six and weighed

140 pounds; Toby Rosenthal was five foot seven and weighed 135. Toby was twenty-six years old; Dante was twenty-nine. Both men had dark hair and regular features. Toby's eyes were brown; Dante's were blue—but that didn't matter. When Toby's and Dante's photos were placed side by side, the men didn't look like twins: Dante's lips were thinner, his eyes were set closer together than Toby's, and whereas Toby looked like a spoiled angel, Dante looked *hard*. The bottom line, however, was that in a dimly lighted bar Dante and Toby would look very, very much alike.

According to his criminal record Dante Bello had been convicted only twice. One conviction was for assault—beating a man senseless in a bar fight; he was sentenced to eighteen months and served ten. The second arrest was for being part of a crew that broke into a Best Buy in Yonkers and afterward attempted to sell a fifty-inch plasma TV to a cop for three hundred bucks. Dante did the whole eighteen months for that one.

The two convictions didn't tell the complete story, however. Although Dante had been convicted only once for assault, he'd been arrested four times for the same crime, and the pattern was obvious: Dante would get drunk, then take offense at some real or imagined slight and go berserk. Maybe his violent temper was because he was a little guy and felt the need to prove how tough he was. He reminded Ella of the Joe Pesci character in *Goodfellas*: a violent little psychopath, not intimidated by others no matter how big they were. The second notable thing about Dante's record was that although he was arrested for assault several times, he was never convicted again—and Ella could imagine Dante, accompanied by a couple of Vinnie Caniglia's bigger boys, discouraging the victim and witnesses from testifying.

But Ella had found her man, a violent, honest-to-God Mafia thug— the perfect person to frame for killing Dominic DiNunzio. Now the problem she had was to find some way to link Dante Bello to DiNunzio. In other words, she needed to find a motive for Dante's killing DiNunzio, because the beauty of Toby Rosenthal's defense was that Toby had no known motive.

32

DeMarco, having had no luck in getting anyone to admit they'd seen Ella Fields, headed over to Starbucks on Chambers Street—Sarah's office away from the office—hoping she'd been more successful than him. When he walked in, he saw her chatting with a good-looking young guy with longish hair and soulful eyes. DeMarco couldn't help wondering if *he* was the reason Sarah preferred to work at Starbucks.

He took a seat across from her, and Sarah said, "This woman has done everything she can to stay off the grid. I did a credit check on her—I got her social security number when we got the passport information—and her credit rating is worse than mine, and not because of student loans. Her problem is she's never borrowed any money, so she has *no* credit history. She's never had a mortgage or a car loan. She doesn't have credit card debt, because as near as I can tell she doesn't use credit cards, which is almost impossible not to do."

"Huh. What else?" DeMarco said.

"I've used four of those people-finder Internet sites, like the one that turned up her marriage to Cantwell. She has no past-address information."

"I can understand that," DeMarco said. "In Phoenix, Cantwell rented the house where they lived and everything was in his name. It's like the guy was trying to protect her by not listing her as being a tenant."

"Something else is weird," Sarah said. "I went to Justine's office and called the IRS and told them I was her."

"You little devil."

Sarah smiled. "Anyway, I told whoever I talked to to call the DA's public number so he'd know he was really talking to an ADA. When the guy called back, I said I wanted to know if Ella Fields had ever filed a tax return. He said no. I then asked him if Bill Cantwell had ever filed one and he said yes. When I asked him if I could get copies of Cantwell's returns, he said, Not without a subpoena. I said, The guy's dead! And he said, Not without a subpoena. So I asked him if he could tell me just one tiny thing: Did Cantwell file as single, married filing jointly, or married filing separately? He said Cantwell filed as single."

"Huh," DeMarco said again. "So he didn't want her on his tax returns so later, when he got busted for income tax evasion, she wouldn't go down with him."

"Maybe," Sarah said. "Or maybe she wouldn't let him put her on his tax return. She never took his last name after they married."

"So how do we find this woman, Sarah? We're running out of time here. The trial is only a few weeks away."

"Do you still think she's here in New York?"

"Yes." DeMarco had no evidence to support that conclusion, just his instincts, but he trusted his instincts.

"Well, in the past," Sarah said, "Cantwell always rented some swanky place—like the penthouse apartment in Seattle and the house in Phoenix where he was paying twelve grand a month. What I can do, I guess, is start calling property management companies that rent out high-end places and see if they've rented to a lady named Ella Fields."

DeMarco groaned, lowered his head, and rapped his forehead three times on the table. Sarah looked over at the young guy she'd been talking to and rolled her eyes, her expression saying: *Hey, what can I tell you? He's a nut.*

DeMarco worked with Sarah for the next four days, calling property management companies that leased expensive houses and apartments in New York—and he knew they weren't getting to all of them. Folks advertised on their own when they wanted to sublease; they stuck pieces of paper in coffee shops where you could rip off a slip with a phone number on it; they posted on fucking Craigslist. DeMarco was hung up on; placed on terminal hold; promised somebody would get back to him and no one ever did. He was told that client information was confidential, and, as his mood grew increasingly worse, he screamed that he'd get subpoenas and disrupt their fucking businesses for weeks if they didn't cooperate. Do what you gotta do, asshole, he was told. Most people, however, cooperated, but the answer was always the same: We have no client named Ella Fields.

After he couldn't take it anymore, he gave Sarah the sort of clear, precise directions a true executive gives a subordinate. He said, "Just do something, I don't know what, but find that goddamn woman."

"What are you going to do?" Sarah asked.

"I'm gonna go talk to people face-to-face so I can hit them if they give me any shit."

Actually, he didn't know what he was going to do.

33

Ella learned that Dante Bello lived in the East Village in a 1940s brownstone with his mother, Lena. She followed him for four days, just as she'd followed Rachel Quinn, hoping that by following him she'd somehow be inspired.

Each day he left his apartment about noon, and the first thing he did was walk *his* dog—a midsize black one that Ella thought was some kind of Labrador. Just as with Quinn, Ella couldn't imagine why New Yorkers, living in apartment buildings, would want dogs. Anyway, after the dog had taken a crap, Dante would return to his mother's place, change clothes, and then walk six blocks to a run-down bar called Frank's Lounge. While she was watching Dante, Ella saw two of the men who'd been in the courthouse photo with him and Vinnie Caniglia enter the bar. It appeared that Frank's Lounge was headquarters for Vinnie C's pathetic crew of thugs.

During the four days she watched him, three of those days Dante stayed inside Frank's Lounge until six and then returned to his apartment, where Ella imagined he had dinner with his mother. She had no idea what he could possibly be doing inside the bar all afternoon. One afternoon, he left the lounge and took a ride in a sedan with Vinnie and another man, and Ella followed them to a pawnshop in Queens.

Ella suspected the pawnshop owner might be someone who fenced whatever Vinnie's guys stole.

After Dante would dine with his mom, he and his friends would entertain themselves. One night it was a sports bar where they watched a Mets game and played pool; another night it was a shabby card place in Brooklyn where they played poker; two of the four nights they went to bars that attracted single women with big hair, tight skirts, and too much makeup. One night Dante left with a blonde who was two inches taller than him.

Ella never saw Dante or anyone else in Vinnie's crew doing anything that appeared to be illegal, and she couldn't help wondering how they made any money. Maybe they were lying low because of the Viagra bust, but whatever the case, Dante's life as a gangsta appeared incredibly monotonous.

Ella was stuck. She couldn't find any way to link Dante Bello to Dominic DiNunzio. As near as she could tell, Dominic and Dante had only two things in common: They were both wops and they both liked dogs. Yep, Dominic, too, owned a dog—she'd learned this from his obituary—but in Dominic's case that made some sense, as he owned a home and had three kids. But what good would it do her that Dominic and Dante both had dogs?

She could imagine one scenario: Dominic and Dante are both walking their dogs in one of those parks where they're allowed to unleash their mutts so they can run around and hump each other. And Dante, being the violent nut that he is, gets into a fight with another dog walker, pounds on him, and Dominic witnesses the encounter—and then Dante decides to kill Dominic because he's a witness.

No, that was just stupid. Although she had no problem at all imagining Dante beating someone half to death, it would be almost impossible to put him and DiNunzio in the same park, at the same time, and then build a credible backstory that would support such an event.

Another possibility, she supposed, was to build a paper trail showing that Dominic was laundering money for Vinnie Caniglia's low-rent Mafia operation. She would have to break into Dominic's office and, with the aid of a hacker, plant files in his computer that would provide evidence that he was in cahoots with Vinnie—and then create some scenario where there's a falling-out between thieves and Vinnie sends Dante to whack Dominic to keep him from talking. But Ella knew that the chances of making that work would be almost impossible. It was too complicated; there were just too many moving parts. She'd have to somehow establish that a respected member of the community, a man with no criminal record, had a secret life working with a minor Mafia don.

Shit.

Then Ella made what she considered to be a brilliant intellectual leap: Who said there had to be *any* link between Dante Bello and Dominic DiNunzio?

———◆◆◆———

Ella again dressed in comfortable lounge-around-the-house clothes, made a pot of coffee, and went on another Internet Easter egg hunt. This time she searched for articles mentioning Vinnie Caniglia or Dante Bello—and she found the golden egg.

One month before Dominic DiNunzio was killed, Vinnie Caniglia and his boys were involved in an altercation in Atlantic City, and the event made the papers because of the mayhem that ensued. Vinnie had been playing craps at the Borgata Casino—and into the same casino comes another hood, named Carmine Fratello, accompanied by his girlfriend and a couple of his pals.

According to the press, there was a history of bad blood between Carmine Fratello and Vinnie Caniglia, and the next thing you know, Vinnie and Carmine are chest-bumping and screaming at each other, their entourages get involved, a punch is tossed, and a brawl commences. Innocent bystanders are knocked to the floor, chairs are overturned, drinks are spilled, chips are scattered, and every security guy in the casino is needed to break up a fight involving six or seven beefy Italians. Naturally, after the fighters are pulled apart, Fratello and Caniglia threaten each other: "I'm gonna kill your fuckin' ass."

And Ella knew all this because, as is often the case these days, bystanders had videotaped the combatants on their cell phones. One guy posted a video of the fight on YouTube, showing blood pouring out of Vinnie Caniglia's nose. But it wasn't Vinnie's broken nose that interested Ella.

It was Carmine Fratello who caught her eye.

Carmine Fratello was a big, overweight man who looked Italian and had short dark hair. Dominic DiNunzio was a big overweight man who looked Italian and had short dark hair. Otherwise, Carmine didn't really look too much like Dominic. By comparison, Toby Rosenthal and Dante Bello looked enough alike that they could have been first cousins—whereas Carmine's face was rounder than Dominic's, his nose was longer, his chin was more blunt, and his hair was receding faster than Dominic's.

But it didn't matter. *Close enough* was all that Ella required.

Ella needed one crucial piece of information when it came to framing Dante Bello for Dominic DiNunzio's murder—and this could be a deal breaker if she didn't get the answer she wanted.

What she needed to know was where Dante had been the night Dominic DiNunzio was killed. If Dante had a credible alibi for his whereabouts that night, then Ella was screwed and would have to start all over. But based on what she'd seen during the four days she followed him, Dante was most likely eating dinner with his mom or was with his low-life friends at Frank's Lounge the night Dominic was shot—and if that was the case, he had no alibi at all. If one of Dante's goombah buddies swore that Dante was with him, no jury would believe the goombah. Ditto with Dante's mom. What mother wouldn't lie to protect her son?

On the other hand, if Dante was in jail or if there was a photo of him passing through a tollbooth or a date/time-stamped credit card receipt showing he was in Jersey on that fateful evening . . . well, then Ella was screwed. And to find out where he was, the only way she could think was to ask him.

Ella didn't want Dante to see her face, so she called his apartment at eleven a.m., figuring he would just be getting out of bed to take his dog out for its midday dump. His mother answered, and Ella asked to speak to her son.

"He's in bed," Lena said.

"Wake him up," Ella said. "My name is Detective Margret Ross, NYPD." There actually was a Detective Margret Ross who worked robbery/homicide at the 105th Precinct in Queens.

"A detective?" Lena Bello said.

"That's correct," Ella said, "and this involves a serious criminal matter and I need to speak to him."

"My boy didn't do anything."

Ella didn't bother to say, *Yeah, right.* She said, "I need to speak to him, Mrs. Bello. Immediately."

Five long minutes later, Dante picked up the phone and said, "Who the fuck is this?"

What a charmer. "As I told your mother, Mr. Bello, my name is Detective Margret Ross, NYPD."

"Yeah, so what?"

"On March fifteenth of this year, a man fitting your description killed a clerk named James Kim in a liquor store in Queens."

"What?" Dante said.

"Last week a witness came forward and provided us with a telephone video record of the man leaving the liquor store, and facial recognition software led us to you."

"Oh, bullshit," Dante said.

"No, Mr. Bello, it's not bullshit. I will tell you, however, as this will come out in court anyway, that the photo of the man's face in the video is somewhat blurred, and our facial recognition software also made possible matches with five other men who look similar to you. But only you and one other suspect have criminal records, which is the reason I'm investigating you."

"Hey, I didn't have anything to do with a goddamn liquor store. I'm telling you, this is bullshit."

"Calm down, Mr. Bello."

"Fuck you, 'Calm down.' You call me and tell me I killed someone and—"

"Mr. Bello, the reason I'm calling is to give you the opportunity to tell me where you were at approximately seven-thirty p.m. on the night of March fifteenth. If you have a credible alibi, I can eliminate you as a person of interest."

"March! That's over four fuckin' months ago. How the hell would I know where I was? Tell me where you were four months ago."

"I don't need an alibi, Mr. Bello, but unless you want to be arrested for Mr. Kim's murder, you do. Now, I can send a couple of cops over to pick you up and bring you to the precinct, or you can cooperate with me."

"How the hell can I cooperate? I don't know where the fuck I was!"

"Mr. Bello, I'm going to give you two days to do some research. If you have a calendar on your phone, take a look at it. Look at your credit card bills and see if you made a purchase at the time Mr. Kim was shot. Call your credit card company if you have to. See if you had an appointment with someone, an appointment that can be verified. If you can provide some documentation that proves you were not in Queens the night Mr. Kim was killed, I'll be satisfied. If not, well, I'll just have to proceed with my investigation, which probably means that I'll arrest you."

"You gotta be shittin' me."

"I'll call you the day after tomorrow at this time, Mr. Bello, and if you're not home when I call, I'm going to put out a warrant for your arrest. Have a good day."

Two days later, as promised, Ella called Dante Bello back.

"Well," she said. "Where were you on the night of March fifteenth?"

"I was at a Knicks game. I went with a couple of friends."

"Really," Ella said, making it clear she found that alibi a little too convenient.

"That's right. I did like you said and checked my, my calendar and it said 'Knicks game.' I should have remembered, cuz the fuckin' Knicks lost and it cost me fifty bucks."

What Bello had done was obvious. He couldn't prove where he'd been on March fifteenth and had checked the Knicks schedule and saw they played a game that night at the Garden. To make the story ring a bit truer, he noted that they'd lost and decided to embellish the story with the part about how he'd lost a fifty-dollar bet.

"Do you still have the ticket stub from the game, Mr. Bello?"

"Fuck, no. Who the hell keeps ticket stubs?"

"How did you pay for the ticket? Online? By credit card?"

"Nah, we bought 'em from a guy outside the Garden and paid cash. Going to the game was a last-minute thing, so we scalped the tickets. You gonna arrest me for that?"

"What are the names of the men who went to the game with you?"

"Joey Netti and his cousin, Jimmy."

"What's Jimmy's last name?"

"Netti, just like Joey. I told you, they're cousins."

"And where do they live?"

"Here. Manhattan."

Ella didn't say anything for a moment, letting the silence convey her doubt. "Mr. Bello, do you understand that if I learn that you've lied to me—"

"Hey! I never ripped off no liquor store. I'm not some fuckin' junkie punk. I don't do shit like that. I've never done shit like that. You asked where I was and I told you. So you can take your face recognition software and shove it up your ass."

Dante slammed down the phone—and Ella smiled. Dante had no alibi. No jury was going to buy his story—backed up by two hoods like himself—that he'd been at the Knicks game when Dominic DiNunzio was killed.

34

DeMarco sat in Justine's office, watching her eat her lunch in between court appearances. Lunch today was a hot dog purchased from a street vendor.

DeMarco said, "I'm spinning my wheels here. I can't find Ella Fields. I can't prove she had anything to do with Esther's stroke or the bus-boy splitting town. I can't prove she's had any contact with the other witnesses."

"What are you saying, you wanna give up?"

DeMarco shrugged. "Right now, as far as you know, the three wit-nesses you have are solid and they're going to testify against Rosenthal. So unless they change their testimony, you don't really have a problem."

"But I won't know that I have a problem until I get them on the stand and they suddenly can't remember what they saw that night. Do you want to take the chance that your cousin's killer may get away with what he's done?"

Goddamnit! DeMarco thought. It irritated the hell out of him, how this woman kept trying to make it *his* responsibility if the case went south on her. But rather than say that, he said, "The only thing I can think to do at this point is talk to the witnesses. I'll ask them if anyone has spoken to them about the case, but mainly I just want to see how they react."

"I don't know," Justine said around a mouthful of hot dog. "It gets tricky, interviewing witnesses. You can't say anything to them that might later be construed as trying to influence their testimony to better support the prosecution's case."

"I know that," DeMarco said.

"Yeah, all right, go ahead," Justine said once she'd finished chewing. "But be careful."

———◆———

DeMarco decided to start with Rachel Quinn. The barmaid and the bartender both worked the evening shift at McGill's, so he'd save them for later and catch them at the same time.

Quinn worked in the Financial District, on Water Street, just off Wall Street, in Lower Manhattan. DeMarco called her office and spoke to a secretary, saying he represented the Manhattan DA and needed to speak to her. The secretary told him he'd have to wait until four p.m., as Ms. Quinn was in meetings until then.

DeMarco found Rachel Quinn very attractive, and he couldn't imagine why a woman who looked like her would have to use eHarmony to find a man. He also wished he wasn't using the cane, and hoped she'd give him the chance to explain how'd he suffered an "athletic" injury and that the cane was only temporary.

"You told my secretary you're here regarding the Rosenthal case," Rachel said.

"That's right," DeMarco said. "I just have a couple of questions and I'll be out of your hair."

Instead of telling him that she had time for only a couple of questions because she was a Very Important Wall Street Person whose schedule was chockablock, she said, "Would you like a cup of coffee?"

"Sure," he said, and discreetly admired her backside as she walked over to a credenza and poured him a cup. He took a sip of the coffee and could tell it wasn't the Folgers he normally drank at home. It was probably made from some exotic Hawaiian bean that cost forty bucks a pound. And judging by the woman's corner office, which had a view, he realized that Rachel Quinn was in a whole different league financially than a GS-13 civil servant. He needed to tamp down the sexual fantasies and get to work.

"I can't give you a lot of the specifics, Ms. Quinn, but—"

"Call me Rachel."

"Thanks. As I was saying, Rachel, I'm afraid I can't share the specifics with you, but the district attorney is concerned that someone might tamper with the witnesses in the Rosenthal case and—"

"Tamper how?"

"By attempting to bribe or intimidate them into changing their testimony."

"Do you think someone could bribe me?" Rachel said—and now there was a spark of indignation in her kind brown eyes.

"No, I'm not saying that, and please don't take offense. I just want to know if anyone has approached you to discuss your testimony."

"No. No one has talked to me about the case, except for the ADA, what's her name, Potter."

"Porter. Justine Porter."

"Right. And all she did was go over the statement I'd made to the police to make sure I agreed with the statement the way the cops typed it up."

DeMarco hesitated, and Rachel asked, "Is there anything else?"

DeMarco wanted to show Rachel Ella Fields' photo but knew if he did he was taking a risk. If Fields had gotten to her in some way, Rachel would lie about knowing her, then might warn Fields that DeMarco was hunting for her. But DeMarco was convinced, based on the way she had responded to his questions—and based on his gut—that Rachel was honest.

"Yes," DeMarco said. "Have you ever seen this woman?" He passed her Ella Fields' passport photo.

Rachel didn't just glance at the photo; she studied it. "I don't believe I've ever seen her, and I think I would have remembered someone as striking as her. Who is she?"

"All I can tell you is that she's someone I need to talk to."

He could tell that his answer didn't satisfy her, but he didn't want to go into detail about Fields.

"Has anyone tried to discuss the case with you at all?" DeMarco said. "I'm not talking about someone asking directly about your testimony. I'm talking about someone you just met taking an interest in the fact that you're a witness expected to testify at the trial. This person would be subtle about it."

"No. I've talked to a lot of people about seeing that man getting killed; it was pretty traumatic. But the only people I've talked to are people I know, like my family and friends and people here at work."

"Good," DeMarco said. "But if a stranger does try to talk to you about the case, or if you see the woman whose photo I just showed you, could you let me know right away?"

"Am I in danger?" Rachel asked.

"No," DeMarco immediately said. "I have no reason whatsoever to believe you're in any danger."

He wasn't being totally honest with her. What he should have said was that he didn't *think* she was in any danger. In only one of the six cases he'd investigated had a witness been killed, and in all the other cases it appeared as if Cantwell had gone out of his way *not* to kill people. The damn guy had even arranged for one woman to get a new liver to keep her from dying. Regarding the mercy killing of Randy White's sister, she hadn't been killed because she was a witness.

On the other hand, DeMarco didn't really know how the busboy in the Rosenthal case had disappeared. Did he leave New York voluntarily or was he paid to leave—or was he buried in a strawberry field in New Jersey? Then there was old Esther Behrman and her stroke. If Esther's stroke wasn't an accident, then it was attempted murder.

Still, he didn't really think Rachel Quinn was in danger, because no way would anyone be crazy enough to murder a witness when two of five witnesses were already gone. That would trigger a manhunt for sure.

But Rachel Quinn wasn't a dummy. She asked, "Has someone attempted to get to the other witnesses?"

Fortunately for DeMarco, he could answer that question honestly. "Not that I know of," he said, which was the truth, since he didn't really know what had happened to Esther or Edmundo Ortiz. "And you're the first witness I've spoken to," DeMarco added, which was also true.

DeMarco decided it was time to leave, before Rachel asked more questions he didn't want to answer. He said, "Thanks for the coffee. It was very good." He placed a card on her desk that had his cell phone number on it and said: *Joseph DeMarco, Special Investigator for the Manhattan District Attorney.* He'd had Sarah make him fifty of the cards on her computer and print them out on heavy bond paper. "Please call me if anyone tries to discuss the case with you in a way that seems odd."

"I will," Rachel said.

DeMarco turned to leave, then stopped and faced her again. "Would you mind if I asked you a personal question?"

"I don't know," she said. "What's the question?"

"I saw from the police reports that you were on an eHarmony date the day Dominic DiNunzio was killed."

"Yes," Rachel said, now looking a bit defensive.

"Well, I'm single myself, and I've been thinking about looking into one of those computer dating sites." He wasn't, but he wanted Rachel to know he was available.

"I can't recommend it based on my experience," Rachel said, "but it's worked out very well for some friends of mine."

"I have to tell you that I'm surprised a woman as attractive as you wouldn't have all sorts of men trying to date her."

Instead of appearing to appreciate the compliment, Rachel looked annoyed. "I work a lot and really don't have many opportunities to meet single men. I don't hang out in bars and I don't date coworkers. So far the online dating thing hasn't worked out, but maybe it will for you. Now I have to get to a meeting."

As DeMarco was leaving he thought: *I'm an idiot.* He'd been thinking that maybe when the Rosenthal trial was over he'd give her a call, but the way she'd reacted, like he'd accused her of being an unmarriageable spinster . . . Sheesh.

———— ◆ ————

DeMarco decided to have dinner before heading over to McGill's. He wanted to get there about seven-thirty, the time Dominic had been killed. He ate at a Thai restaurant about six blocks from McGill's and decided to walk there afterward instead of taking a cab. That turned out to be a mistake, because by the time he reached the bar his leg was throbbing. He usually carried a couple of Motrin with him, but wouldn't you know it, he hadn't tonight. He was starting to think that the damn doctor had misread the X-rays that showed the bone was healed.

He took a seat at the bar and watched Jack Morris make a martini for a customer. DeMarco felt like having a martini himself—a little medication for the pain—but since he was supposed to be an investigator on duty, he decided not to.

This was the first time he'd visited the crime scene. Because of the lighting, it wasn't an ideal place for a witness to identify a suspect, but

DeMarco would have been able to identify Toby Rosenthal if he walked through the door. The bartender would certainly have had no problem identifying him, as Toby had been sitting two feet from Morris when Morris poured him a drink before Dominic was killed.

Morris finished making the martini, dropped in a lemon twist, and placed it in front of a heavyset, swarthy guy with a five o'clock shadow at the other end of the bar. DeMarco couldn't help noticing that the guy looked a bit like Dominic—but then a lot of guys looked like Dominic. Off the top of his head, DeMarco could name three people that he knew personally who looked like Dominic.

Morris appeared in front of him and said, "What can I get you?"

"Nothing," DeMarco said. He flipped open his badge case and showed Morris his credentials. "I work for the Manhattan DA. I need to talk to you about the Rosenthal case."

"You do?" Morris said, going wide-eyed.

DeMarco figured that Morris had assumed he was a cop, and most people tend to become alarmed when a cop says he wants to talk to them. So DeMarco wasn't surprised by Morris's initial reaction—but he quickly became suspicious of the man.

"I wanted to ask if anyone has spoken to you about the testimony you plan to give at Toby Rosenthal's trial. I mean, someone other than the detectives assigned to the case or the ADA." DeMarco had been about to say more, but Morris immediately said, "Nope."

Now that was *wrong*. Morris should have been surprised by the question. He should have said, *What do you mean, talked to me about my testimony? Who would talk to me and why would they talk to me?* He should have been curious, the way Rachel Quinn had been curious, but he wasn't. His immediate reaction was to deny—quickly and casually—that anyone had spoken to him.

"Are you sure, Mr. Morris? That you haven't spoken to anyone about the case?"

"Yep," Morris said. "I haven't said anything to anyone."

DeMarco stared at Morris for a long beat, his expression conveying his disbelief. "It would be a pretty serious situation if anyone has tried to make you change your testimony, Jack, and you withheld that information from me. What I'm saying is, you could be in deep shit, like go-to-jail deep shit."

Now Morris was offended—or pretended to be offended. "Hey, why would I lie about something like that? I'm telling you, no one's talked to me."

DeMarco had been thinking that he might show Morris Ella Fields' passport photo as he'd done with Rachel Quinn—but decided not to. His gut had told him that he could trust Rachel; that same gut was now telling him that Morris was lying to him.

"Okay," DeMarco said, sounding skeptical, which he was. "But if someone does talk to you, you need to contact me immediately." DeMarco placed his card on the bar and Morris, after a moment, picked it up and put it in a pocket.

"Yeah, sure," Morris said. "Now, if there's nothing else, I need to see if that guy over there needs another drink."

"Where's Ms. Tolliver?" DeMarco asked. "I need to speak to her, too."

Morris swiveled his head, searching the bar for Kathy. "She's around here somewhere. She might have gone back to the kitchen to get appetizers for one of the tables. Oh yeah, there she is."

DeMarco turned and saw a stunning young woman with long dark hair and wearing a short skirt enter the bar carrying a couple of plates. She took the plates over to where two young guys were seated. The guys tried to engage her in conversation and before she walked away Kathy smiled and said something that made them laugh. She knew her tips depended on being nice to the customers and that flirting was in her best interest.

When she reached the bar, she said to Morris, "Jack, two Heinekens for those jerks over there."

DeMarco walked over to her and said, "Ms. Tolliver, my name is DeMarco and I'm an investigator for the Manhattan DA. I need to speak to you about the Rosenthal case."

"What?" Kathy said. Like Morris, she looked shocked, and maybe DeMarco was reading too much into it, but she seemed even more shocked than Morris had. And she looked . . . Hell, "guilty" was the first word that came to mind.

"Can we sit down someplace to talk?" DeMarco said.

"Yeah, I guess, but can we go outside?" Kathy said. "I need a cigarette."

"Sure," DeMarco said, although the way his leg was aching, he would have preferred to sit at a table and ask his questions.

He waited while she told Morris to deliver the beers to the two guys who'd been hitting on her. Then he had to wait while she searched her purse for a pack of cigarettes and a lighter—and while she was searching, she was frowning, as if she was thinking hard about something.

Outside, she lit a menthol Marlboro and blew smoke over DeMarco's head. In the streetlight, she looked tired and older than twenty-four. DeMarco could see the lines starting to form next to her mouth: stress lines, disappointment lines, the sort of lines a woman gets when she can't ever seem to catch a break. He could imagine what Kathy Tolliver would look like when she was forty.

"So what's this all about?" she said.

DeMarco said the same thing he'd said to Morris, to see if he'd get the same reaction: "I want to know if anyone has spoken to you about the testimony you plan to give at Toby Rosenthal's trial. I mean, someone other than the ADA or the cops assigned to the case."

"I don't understand," Kathy said. "What do you mean?"

"I mean what I just said. Has anyone asked about the testimony you plan to give at Rosenthal's trial?"

Instead of answering his question, she said, "Why would anyone do that?"

"Please, Ms. Tolliver, just answer the question. Has anyone spoken to you?"

She took another drag off her cigarette and looked away from him as she did—which was one reason DeMarco hated questioning smokers. Taking a puff on a cigarette provided time for stalling and coming up with a lie. Finally, Kathy said, "No, no one's talked to me, just those two old cops and that tight-assed prosecutor."

"You're sure?" he said.

"Yeah, I'm sure. What does that mean, Am I sure?"

"It means you need to understand that if you lie to me you could end up in serious trouble. And if you lie in court . . . You do not, under any circumstances, want to commit perjury."

Kathy shook her head, as if she thought DeMarco was being an asshole. "I wish I'd never been here the night that guy got killed. I've got a kid to support, and I can't afford to miss work to testify at some trial. And now I've got you here hassling me."

"I'm not hassling you, Kathy. I'm just making sure that you understand the importance of telling me the truth."

"I *did* tell you the truth. Now, can I go back to work?"

Again he thought about showing her Ella Fields' passport photo—and again he decided not to.

"Sure," DeMarco said. As he waited for a cab, he called Justine, and left a message when she didn't answer. "I think somebody might have gotten to two of the Rosenthal witnesses."

◆◆◆

Justine called him back twenty minutes later. "Are you positive?" were the first words out of her mouth.

"Am I positive?" DeMarco answered. "No. I'm going off a guy being too quick with an answer and a gal taking a puff on a cigarette."

"What?" Justine said.

"Never mind. Look, I'm almost positive, based on the way the bartender acted, that somebody talked to him about his testimony. I'm not as sure about the barmaid, but my gut tells me that somebody *might* have talked to her."

"Well, shit," Justine said. "Do you think they're going to change their testimony?"

"I have no idea, but I wouldn't be surprised if they did."

Neither of them said anything for a moment, then Justine said, "Well, I gotta find out. I don't want to get blindsided at the trial. I'm going to reinterview them, and I want you to be there."

35

When Jack Morris was notified that the ADA was going to reinterview him, he called Ella to let her know. "What should I tell her?" Morris asked.

"I'll let you know," Ella said.

Ella sent David Slade a text message saying: *Meet me at the place we met the first time at 8. Text me when you arrive and I'll tell you which room I'm in.*

Slade responded by texting: *It's about damn time.*

Slade was upset because he'd texted her several times since their first meeting asking for another meeting so he could get an update on where she stood with the witnesses and each time she'd refused, telling him that a meeting was unnecessary.

Slade knocked on the door of Ella's room at the Mandarin Oriental at exactly eight p.m. It was as though he'd been standing outside the door waiting for the hour to strike. He was wearing a dark blue suit, a light blue shirt, no tie. He was, Ella had to admit, a good-looking man.

Before Ella could say anything, he said, "Your behavior is completely unacceptable. I don't have a clue what's going on with the witnesses and what you've been doing. I can't prepare a defense if I don't—"

"Would you like a drink?"

"No, I want to know . . ." He took a breath to calm himself. "Yeah, fine, a scotch would be good."

Ella took two airline-sized bottles of Glenfiddich from the minibar. "I don't have any ice," she said. "We'll have to drink 'em neat."

She handed Slade his drink. "Relax, David. We're in great shape. I told you when we first met that I wouldn't be meeting with you often. We just can't take the chance of anyone putting the two of us together. It's bad enough that there are a string of text messages between us, even if the phones we're using aren't registered to us. You can just never be sure these days when it comes to the privacy of telephones."

"Yeah, I understand that, but—"

"Here's where things stand right now," Ella said. "Mr. Ortiz, the bus-boy, is on a fishing boat in the Bering Sea. Nobody else knows where he is, and he won't be coming back to New York for the trial."

"Yeah, I'd heard he'd disappeared."

"Mrs. Behrman has had a stroke and will be unable to testify at Toby's trial."

"That was fortunate, but then considering her age, maybe not unexpected."

"Fortunate?" Ella said. "Do you really believe what happened to her was a matter of luck?"

"Oh," Slade said, and he looked stunned, as if it had never occurred to him that by hiring Ella he could become an accomplice to murder. "How did you—"

"I'm not going to discuss the details with you, David. All that matters is that Mrs. Behrman won't be testifying at Toby's trial. Now, regarding the bartender. Do you recall what Jack Morris said at Toby's lineup?" Before Slade could answer, Ella said, "He said 'I *think* it's number four', after which the detective said, 'You think?' and Jack said, 'No, it's him, number four.' Jack, in other words, wasn't sure that Toby was the man who shot Dominic until prompted by the detective. So at Toby's trial, Jack will say that he's sure Toby was the guy he served a drink to, but he can't be positive, not *really* positive, that Toby was the shooter. He wasn't positive at the lineup, and he won't be positive at the trial. Jack, you see, has a rather significant gambling addiction, and I'm enabling his bad habit by giving him cash periodically so that he can continue to gamble."

For the first time since entering the room, Slade smiled. "You're good."

"I had help," Ella said, wanting to maintain the illusion that she had a partner.

"What about the barmaid?"

"Kathy Tolliver has a child, a darling little girl," Ella said, "and she's involved in a custody battle with her ex-husband's parents. The basis for the custody battle is that Kathy has a history of substance abuse. Kathy has been clean the last nine months, attending NA meetings, but unfortunately she recently fell rather badly off the wagon. She OD'd on something, passed out on the street, the medics were called, and she had to be taken to a hospital. There's a record of her stay in the hospital, of course. And because Kathy was in the hospital, she didn't pick up her little girl from the babysitter's until six the following morning. The good news for Kathy is that the only one who knows about her falling into her prior bad ways is me. Her kid's grandparents won't learn of her slip, provided she testifies to what she *really* saw at Toby's trial."

"And what did she really see?" Slade asked, now looking amused.

"Kathy can definitely say it was Toby sitting at the bar. She has no doubt about that. She was standing only five or six feet from him. But was it Toby who shot DiNunzio? DiNunzio was seventy feet away from her, in a dimly lighted bar, and now, months later, she just can't be positive that he shot DiNunzio, although it was certainly someone who looked like him."

"I like it," Slade said. "What about the last witness, Quinn?"

"I haven't figured out what to do with her. You may just have to live with her testimony."

"That's not good," Slade said.

"David, right now there are two witnesses who are going to say that they can't identify Toby as the shooter. So the *only* witness who will be able to identify Toby is a woman who says he ran past her table after DiNunzio was shot."

Slade, being a lawyer, wanted to debate the issue—lawyers want to debate everything—but Ella kept going, "David, the killer was *running*. Do you recall what Rachel Quinn said to the detectives when they interviewed her in the bar?"

"No, not exactly. I'd have to look at her statement again."

"Well, I know what she said. She said she never saw Toby sitting at the bar; she was too busy flirting with her date. She said she saw Toby—or the man she thought was Toby—walk over to a table and shoot DiNunzio. But Toby's back was to her when she saw him shoot DiNunzio. Then she said she saw him run out of the bar. When the detective asked if she got a good look at the shooter's face, she said, 'A *good* look? Well, he ran past me, but I'm *pretty* sure I'd recognize him again.'"

"She picked Toby out of the lineup without hesitation," Slade said. "She said she was certain he was the shooter."

"Yes, but at this point, as I already said, she's the *only* witness who's certain, and she wasn't certain when the cops first interviewed her. And since the other two witnesses will testify that they can't be sure it was Toby, I'd say you have more than enough to create reasonable doubt."

Which made Ella think of Bill calling himself the Creator of Reasonable Doubt. Now *she* was the Creator.

"I don't know," Slade said. "I'd feel better if—"

"Let's move on," Ella said. "Let's talk about the man who really shot DiNunzio."

She opened the manila file folder that had been sitting on the coffee table between her and Slade, and placed an eight-by-ten photograph of Dante Bello on the table. Tapping the photo with one red fingernail, she said, "There's your killer. His name is Dante Bello."

Slade studied the picture and said, "He certainly looks like Toby. I mean, he's not an exact doppelgänger, but—"

"Dante Bello is five feet six inches tall. Toby is five seven. Dante weighs only five pounds more than Toby, and he's only three years older than Toby. He has Toby's dark hair and regular features, and I believe he could be mistaken for Toby running out of a dimly lit bar. Furthermore, Dante Bello is a low-life hood employed by a Mafia boss named Vinnie Caniglia."

"Caniglia? That name sounds familiar."

"It should. Vinnie stole twenty thousand dollars' worth of Viagra, and the press here had a ball with the story."

Slade laughed. "Oh, yeah, now I remember."

"Dante Bello," Ella said, "is a violent little thug, and a stupid one. He has one conviction for assault and multiple arrests for assault. There's a pattern of him getting drunk and beating up folks who offended him for one reason or another."

"But why would he shoot DiNunzio?" Slade asked. "How did DiNunzio offend him?"

"Before I answer that question, do you recall a shooting that happened in the Bronx at the Patterson housing project about two months ago?"

"No. Why would I?" Slade asked. People who lived in housing projects weren't the sort he represented—or paid attention to.

"Well," Ella said, "a young black man shot another young black man because the victim was wearing a gray hoodie and the shooter thought he was the guy in a gray hoodie who'd ripped him off in a drug deal. It was a case of mistaken identity. I did a very quick Internet search and easily found two other cases in the last year where men were killed by mistake. All three cases were gang-related. Two involved men connected to drugs, the one here in the Bronx and another on the south side of Chicago. The third case was in LA, involving a Hispanic gangbanger killing a student because the student looked like the guy who'd shot the gangbanger's brother. I'm willing to bet that if I did more research, I'd probably find a dozen other cases where men were killed because they were mistaken for the wrong person."

"And that's what you're saying happened with DiNunzio? That this Dante character mistook him for someone else?"

"Exactly."

"So who was he mistaken for?"

"About a month before Dominic DiNunzio was killed, Vinnie Caniglia and some of his crew got into a brawl with another gang of thugs in Atlantic City. The leader of the other gang was a man named Carmine Fratello. Punches were thrown, Vinnie's nose was broken, and witnesses heard Carmine and Vinnie threaten to kill each other. There's actually a YouTube video of the fight. Anyway, according to the *Daily News*, there was a history of bad blood between Vinnie and Carmine. I have no idea if this is true, but it doesn't matter, because the paper said it was so."

"Was Dante Bello at this donnybrook in Atlantic City?" Slade asked.

"I don't know," Ella said. "He wasn't named in the papers, and I didn't see him in the YouTube clip. But it doesn't matter."

"It doesn't matter?"

"No." Ella opened the manila folder again and took out another photo. "This is Carmine Fratello."

"He doesn't look *anything* like Dominic DiNunzio," Slade said.

"Sure he does. He's a heavyset, swarthy guy with short dark hair. I realize that he doesn't look like DiNunzio's twin brother, but on the street, on a dark, rainy night—and it was dark and raining the night DiNunzio was shot—or in a dimly lit bar, a man who has a history of getting drunk and hurting people might mistake Carmine for DiNunzio."

Slade started shaking his head, and Ella could see he wasn't convinced.

"Look, here's what I have in mind for Dante," Ella said, and laid out her plan for framing Dante Bello for Dominic DiNunzio's murder. When she was finished, Slade said, "I suppose it could work. I have to think about how I'd present all this to a jury."

"It *will* work," Ella said. She almost added: *If you do your damn job right.*

"After I've taken care of the details with Carmine Fratello," she said, "we'll get back together and talk again. What you need to do next is hire an expert; an engineer or a college professor would be best. You have this expert make a video that shows how well you can recognize a face in a brightly lit room and from the same distance the witnesses saw Toby. Then what you do is have the expert turn the lights down to match the lighting in McGill's. Your expert will be able to show how much less clear the face is and how easy it would be to mistake Dante Bello for Toby Rosenthal or to mistake Carmine Fratello for Dominic DiNunzio. Then what you do—because at this point the only witness that will identify Toby as the shooter is Rachel Quinn—is you have your expert demonstrate on the video how difficult it would have been for Quinn to see Toby or Dante as he *ran* past her table. Which is what Toby did, and Quinn couldn't have looked at Toby's face for even a tenth of a second."

"Huh," Slade said. "I like it. I mean about the video expert. We can do a little demonstration for the jury showing two different men who are very similar in appearance running past Quinn's table. With the right video, none of the jurors will be able to identify with certainty who they saw. I'll also introduce testimony about people who've gone to prison because of faulty witness identifications, and as you suggested, testimony giving examples of other mistaken-identity killings."

"Good," Ella said, but she was thinking: *Do I have to do all the fucking work here?*

Slade said, "But I'm still worried about Quinn testifying. It would really be best if she didn't."

"Well, like I said, arranging that might be difficult, and there's not much time left before the trial. If you'd been able to get a longer delay . . ." She didn't complete the sentence; she'd made her point. "Anyway, there's one other thing we have to discuss tonight. I've been informed that the ADA is going to reinterview the witnesses before the trial."

"I'm not surprised by that," Slade said. "So what's the problem?"

"We need to decide if we should have the barmaid and the bartender stick to their original statements when they're reinterviewed, or say what they're going to say at the trial. It would be best if they blindsided Porter by changing their testimony during the trial, but on the other hand, I don't want to confuse these people, and I don't think we want them on record too many times with the same story."

"What do you recommend?" Slade said.

Ella thought for a moment and said, "I think we tell them to tell Porter what they're going to say at the trial. I've been over their testimony with them several times on the phone, and I think they'll do okay. I know the bartender will be fine. The barmaid's a little shakier, but . . . well, you might as well find out now how she's going to do in the witness chair. The other thing is, when Porter finds out that she now has only one witness that can positively identify Toby, maybe she'll dismiss the charges against him."

"That's not going to happen," Slade said. "Not with Justine Porter."

Slade drained the scotch in his glass and said, "You and your partner have done a good job. I still don't like the fact that you haven't dealt with Quinn, but overall . . . Well, I'm impressed. Is there more scotch in the minibar?"

Ella knew it wouldn't take much to get Slade to spend the night with her. She could tell that he found her attractive; most men did. If she indicated that she was in the mood for having sex with him, she was sure he'd call his wife and tell her he wouldn't be home until the wee hours. The funny thing was, since Bill had died, she hadn't had much interest in sex. She didn't know why, but she just didn't feel the urge anymore. It was as if some part of her had died with Bill. She thought that maybe she should take Slade for a little spin around the block just to see if she could jump-start her libido. But not tonight.

"There's more scotch, and you can stay here and have another, but I'm afraid I need to get going. But maybe next time we meet, I'll have more time."

Or be in the mood.

36

ADA Justine Porter, with DeMarco in attendance, interviewed the Rosenthal witnesses in a small conference room down the hall from her cluttered office. The witnesses were interviewed separately and Justine started all three interviews the same way, casually saying she just wanted to go back over the statements they'd made to the police and ask the questions she was going to ask at the trial to make sure the witnesses weren't surprised by them—and to make sure that she wasn't surprised by their answers. Not a big deal, she said.

Rachel Quinn smiled at DeMarco when she sat down—which pleased DeMarco—and she was finished in less than five minutes. Her responses to Justine's questions were given without hesitation: She said that she clearly saw Toby Rosenthal shoot Dominic DiNunzio—that although Toby's back was to her, after the shooting he ran past her table. She had no doubt—as she'd told the detectives at the lineup—that Toby was the killer.

The bartender Jack Morris was a different story. When Justine asked him if he was sure that Toby Rosenthal had shot Dominic DiNunzio, Morris said, "Well, like I told the cops, I *think* it was him. I know Rosenthal was the guy I served a drink to, but I can't be a hundred percent certain he shot that man. What I'm sayin' is, I was busy making drinks and the guy who did the shooting was like fifty, sixty feet away and I'm just not sure I can swear it was Rosenthal, although it could have been."

Justine sat back in her chair as if she'd been slapped, then she launched into him, saying the last time she'd interviewed him he had been a hundred percent sure it was Toby who'd shot Dominic. Morris responded with: "Well, I don't remember it that way. And I'm telling you pretty much what I told the cops at the lineup, that I think it was him. But at the lineup, the only guy who looked like Rosenthal was Rosenthal."

The last question Justine asked was: "Has anyone talked to you about the testimony you plan to give at Mr. Rosenthal's trial?"

"Just one guy," Morris said.

"Who was that?" Justine said, ready to pounce.

"Him," Morris said, pointing at DeMarco.

When Morris left the interview room, Justine closed her eyes and muttered, "Fuck me." She'd forgotten the tape recorder was still running.

———◆———

Morris had been completely relaxed when Justine questioned him. He didn't get nervous even when Justine tried to squeeze the truth out of him. Kathy Tolliver was different. She was clearly on edge even before Justine asked a question, and her eyes kept darting about as though she was trapped in the room and looking for a way out. After Justine finished her introductory statement, Kathy said, "Is it okay to smoke in here?"

Justine was about to tell her no, but before she could, DeMarco said, "Sure, go ahead. Nobody's going to arrest you for smoking. Now perjury, that's a different story."

"What?" Kathy said.

DeMarco half-filled a drinking glass with water from a pitcher on the table and pushed it over to her. "Use that for an ashtray."

Kathy lit a cigarette—then started lying, just the way Jack Morris had. She said she was sure that the guy sitting at the bar was Rosenthal, but was she sure that he was the man who shot DiNunzio? Well, it was hard to be a hundred percent sure, she said. You know, the lighting in the room being what it was, how far away Dominic's table was from the bar, her being distracted, putting cherries and lemon slices in the drinks Morris made . . . Yes, she'd said at the lineup it was Rosenthal who shot Dominic, but now, you know, months later, it was just hard to be sure.

After Kathy left, Justine sat there silently for a moment with her eyes closed. Finally, she said, "You know, if anything happens to Quinn, or if she changes her testimony, Slade will ask for a dismissal, and the judge will grant him one."

"Quinn isn't going to change her testimony," DeMarco said. "I don't know how Slade—or Ella Fields—got to the other witnesses, but they won't get to her."

Justine sat there another minute—then shouted: "Son of a bitch!

DeMarco said, "We need a warrant to look at the witnesses' phone and financial records—especially their phone records. Their financial records might prove they've been bribed. But the phone records are the main thing. If they called Fields or she's called them, we can find her, and then go from there."

"What would be the basis for a warrant, DeMarco? We have no evidence that anyone has tampered with the witnesses—they just changed their testimony, which is their right. And you can't prove that Fields or anyone else has been in contact with the witnesses. If you could at least prove she's in New York—"

"Hey!" DeMarco said. "It's your damn job to come up with justification for a warrant. Quit trying to lay this whole thing on me."

The conversation went downhill from there, as DeMarco and Justine snarled at each other.

But Justine was right. He had to prove Ella Fields was in New York.

Part V

37

What Ella had to do next was turn a brute named Carmine Fratello into a victim.

Carmine lived in Hell's Kitchen, less than a mile from Ella's place in Chelsea, and Ella decided to walk there, as it was a lovely summer day. It occurred to her as she was walking that when it came to the Rosenthal case the beauty of Manhattan was that it was so small. Not only did Carmine live within walking distance of Ella's apartment; he was also less than a mile from McGill's Bar & Grill in Midtown South. And Dante Bello, who lived in the East Village, was also about a mile from McGill's—and when you thought about all these folks living so close to each other, that wasn't at all remarkable.

The island of Manhattan is only thirteen miles long and two and a half miles wide. It covers a mere twenty-three square miles. By comparison, Disney World in Orlando is about twice the area of Manhattan, covering forty-two square miles. Yet within Manhattan's small area one point six million people live, meaning there are about seventy thousand residents per square mile. So *everybody* in Manhattan lives or works near everybody else in the borough. And what all this meant was that Carmine Fratello could have some plausible reason to be near McGill's when Dominic DiNunzio was shot.

Carmine's apartment building was an older one, probably prewar, and the place was not impressive. There were black garbage bags on the landing near the front door, and the door itself looked as if someone had whipped the paint off it with a chain. Ella took a seat in a coffee shop across the street from the building and called him.

A woman answered, saying, "Hello?" Ella assumed it was Carmine's wife. Based on the research she'd done, she knew Carmine was married to a woman named Theresa and had three kids.

"I need to speak to Carmine," Ella said.

"He's sleeping. Who are you?"

It was ten in the morning, which reminded her of Dante Bello, not rising until almost noon to walk his dog. Didn't any of these people get up at a respectable hour? "A business associate," Ella said.

"Business associate, my ass," Theresa Fratello said. "All Carmine's business associates are guys."

The way Theresa sounded, Ella wondered if Carmine was the unfaithful type. Then she remembered the article about the brawl in Atlantic City saying that Carmine had been accompanied by his girlfriend, not his wife. "Mrs. Fratello, please put Carmine on the phone. This call could be worth a lot of money to him."

Theresa Fratello didn't say anything for a moment, but being a wife and a mother, if the call was about something that could make her husband money, she couldn't afford to let jealousy screw it up. "Hang on a minute," she said.

A minute turned out to be five minutes, but eventually Carmine came on the line. "Who the fuck is this?" Which, Ella recalled, was exactly the way Dante Bello had answered the phone the time she called him.

"I'm a lady who's willing to pay you twenty grand to tell a lie," Ella said.

"What?"

"I'm in the coffee shop across the street from your building. I'll give you ten minutes to get over here. If you're not here in ten minutes I'll find some other hood to do what I need."

"Twenty grand?" Carmine said.

"Ten minutes, then I'm gone."

"What do you look like?"

"Red hair," Ella said.

Five minutes later—enough time for Carmine to throw on a white wifebeater T-shirt and a pair of sweatpants and slip into flip-flops—he entered the coffee shop. He looked heavier than in the pictures Ella had seen of him in the papers. His dark hair was uncombed and he hadn't shaved for a couple of days; his big gut strained the wifebeater and he had more hair on his arms and shoulders than some apes.

He saw Ella immediately. There were only three other people in the coffee shop: a kid fiddling with an iPad, a man in his eighties reading the *Times*, and the barista, a girl in her twenties who probably had a master's degree in some subject that was useless in regard to getting a job.

Ella was wearing the long red wig she wore the day she met Jack Morris in Atlantic City, a green T-shirt that clung to her breasts, tight jeans, and high heels. She figured it wouldn't hurt to seduce Carmine a bit—and when Carmine arrived at her table the first words out of his mouth were: "Whoa! You're a babe." Ella could see that Carmine was not a sophisticate; she just hoped he was bright enough to do what she needed.

"Sit down," Ella said.

"Let me get a cup of coffee first. Can you wait that long, honey?" Carmine got his coffee and took a seat. "You said twenty g's."

"You know Vinnie Caniglia?" Ella said, already knowing the answer.

"Yeah, I know the fat fuck. This have to do with him?"

"How 'bout one of his guys, a man named Dante Bello?"

"Yeah, I know him, too, the little shit."

"Well, Carmine, I'm willing to pay you twenty thousand dollars to implicate Dante Bello in a murder he didn't commit."

Carmine laughed. "You're shittin' me."

"Nope. You're going to be subpoenaed to testify at the murder trial of a man named Toby Rosenthal. You're going to say—"

"How do I know you're not a cop wearing a wire?"

"I guess you don't, Carmine. And these days, cops don't wear wires. Communication equipment is so sophisticated that the old guy over there reading the *Times* could be recording this. This button on my jeans could be a listening device. But why don't you just listen to what I have to say and see if you think this is the sort of thing the cops would do to put a low-level hood like you in jail."

"Hey! Fuck you, 'low-level.'"

Ella reached into her purse and pulled out a white business envelope filled with twenties and hundreds. She opened the envelope and showed Carmine the money. "There's ten thousand in the envelope. Are you interested or not?"

"Maybe. Keep talking."

"As I was saying, you're going to be subpoenaed to testify at the trial of Toby Rosenthal, who's been accused of murdering a man named Dominic DiNunzio. You're going to say that you frequently go to a bar named McGill's on—"

"Never heard of the place."

"Quit interrupting, Carmine; just listen. As I was saying, you're going to say you go to McGill's all the time. You're also going to say, under questioning, that there's been bad blood between you and Vinnie Caniglia for a long time. You're going to talk about the incident in Atlantic City where you got into a fight with Vinnie and broke his nose."

"You know about that?" Carmine said.

"Yes, it was in the papers. You're going to say that Vinnie threatened to kill you."

"He did."

"And that you've seen Dante Bello following you."

"I ever saw that little shit following me, I woulda stomped him like a bug."

"You're not going to say that, Carmine. You're going to say that Dante has been following you—that he's been *stalking* you—and you know he's a vicious little prick who works for Vinnie . . ."

"Well, that part's true."

". . . and you'd heard that he might even be a button man for Vinnie and you were afraid he might kill you."

"I'd never be afraid of a mutt like him."

Ella shook her head. "I can see this is going to take some work."

"What's that mean?"

"Never mind. By the way, what is the story of the bad blood between you and Vinnie? The papers didn't say."

Carmine sipped his coffee as he thought about what to say. "Ten, fifteen years ago Vinnie and me both worked for a guy named Frank Vitale. Frank's dead now, but Vinnie ended up getting the bar Frank used to own. Anyway, Vinnie got busted for killing a guy over in Jersey and it looked like he was going to go away for a long time. So, Vinnie claimed that I, uh, *allegedly* killed a guy in a warehouse in Red Hook when Vinnie and I were, uh, allegedly robbing the place. I mean, I couldn't believe he would do that to me. In the end no one went to jail, but no thanks to fuckin' Vinnie."

"Did you attempt to retaliate against Vinnie for implicating you?"

"I would have killed him, but Frank wouldn't let me. Then, you know, time goes by and it's not worth it. But we never worked together again."

Ella thought about the story and concluded it didn't really matter other than in establishing that the papers were right about Vinnie and Carmine having a reason to dislike each other.

"Okay," Ella said. "There's one other thing." She took out of her pocket a glossy page that had come from a Macy's catalog and showed it to Carmine. On the page she'd circled a London Fog trench coat. "Send your wife to Macy's and have her buy that trench coat for you. That exact trench coat. I want her to buy it, not you, and tell her to use cash. After she buys it, tell her to drag it on the ground, spill a couple of drinks on it, wash it half a dozen times. You know, do whatever she has to do to make it look like you've owned the coat for a while. And that's basically it. That's all you have to do to make twenty thousand."

Carmine ran his fingernails over his cheek, the sound like a bastard file being dragged across a pipe as he scraped his beard. "I say I've had a beef with Vinnie, that I saw fuckin' Dante following me, say I was worried he might kill me, and I own a trench coat. That's it? For twenty g's?"

"Yep," Ella said. "But we're going to practice your testimony several times before the trial."

"And Dante ends up in jail for murder?" Carmine said.

"I doubt it," Ella said. "We—the people I work for—don't care about what happens to Dante. If he's arrested for murder and convicted, well, that's okay, but that's not our objective. Our objective is only to show that Dante might have seen you go into McGill's and tried to kill you. Do you understand?"

"Not really."

Ella sighed. Did everything have to be so hard? "Like I said, we're going to talk several times before the trial and you're going to practice your testimony with me. Now, can you think of a reason why you might go to McGill's frequently?"

"No. I told you, I don't even know where it is. I wanna drink, I go to my usual places around here."

Ella pulled out a tourist map of Manhattan and showed him the location of McGill's. "Do you know anyone who lives near the bar?"

Carmine squinted at the map. "Yeah," he said. "I got a cousin who lives about four blocks from there."

"Do you know this cousin well?"

"He works for me. And his mother, my aunt Lucy, she lives about two blocks from him. Oh, and there's a restaurant here," Carmine said, stabbing at the map. "I go there with my wife a couple of times a year because she knows the gal who owns it. She went to high school with her."

And Ella thought: *the little island of Manhattan*. She loved it.

Then Carmine grinned. "There's someone else who lives a few blocks from there, too."

"Who's that?" Ella said, seeing that Carmine was dying for her to ask. "My girlfriend."

"Now that would be perfect," Ella said. "That's the reason you go to McGill's. You go to see your girlfriend a couple of times a week, and you stop off in McGill's before or after you see her."

"I don't know," Carmine said. "Theresa wouldn't be too happy to hear me talking about Nadine. I mean, she knows I got a girlfriend, but as long as I don't rub her nose in it . . ."

"For twenty grand," Ella said, "your wife can live with the humiliation. And she doesn't have to be in court when you testify. I want to go with the girlfriend story. Now, show me on the map exactly where she lives."

Carmine did.

"Like I said, Carmine, we're going to practice your testimony, but the main thing you need to remember is you go see your girlfriend all the time, and when you do, you drop by McGill's. You also know that Dante Bello has been stalking you, and most likely because you broke Vinnie's nose in Atlantic City. Last, you have a London Fog trench coat that you wear when it rains. Are we on the same page here, Carmine?"

"You know, maybe this is such a big deal, it's worth more than twenty. I mean, I don't know how much time I could get for perjury, but—"

"Don't get greedy, Carmine. You probably can't remember the last time you made twenty thousand dollars for a single job. Now, I'm going to give you half the money today. I realize you could stiff me and take the money and not testify, but if you do that you won't get the other ten."

"Hey, I don't stiff people, honey, and it pisses me off you'd say that. I give my word . . . Well, it's my *word*."

Yeah, right, like a criminal's word was worth Carmine's considerable weight in gold.

"There's one other thing I need you to do. The trial starts in about three weeks, so until then I want you to stop by McGill's at least twice a week. And when you go there, chat with the bartender. His name is Jack. Do you understand? Jack is going to testify that you go to McGill's all the time."

"Okay. How do I get ahold of you?" Carmine asked.

"You don't. Give me your cell phone number."

Ella left a puzzled but pleased Carmine Fratello sitting in the coffee shop, counting the money she'd given him. Tomorrow, she'd call Jack Morris and tell him that if he was asked during cross-examination if a man named Carmine Fratello was a frequent patron at McGill's, he would say yes. She'd also mail Jack a couple of grand for him to lose in Atlantic City to keep him content.

38

Ella needed to meet with David Slade again, but before she did, she wanted to take one last look at Rachel Quinn. At five, she dressed in a T-shirt, shorts, and running shoes and walked to Rachel Quinn's office on Water Street. She didn't bother to disguise herself in any way, as she wasn't planning to approach Quinn. She was waiting when Quinn left her building, and when Quinn caught a cab, Ella caught one too and followed her back to her apartment. Half an hour later, Quinn left her apartment, did the poop-in-the-bag thing with her dog, walked a mile to the ice cream place, bought a cone, and returned home.

Ella thought about it for a long time, and came to a decision: David Slade was just going to have to live with Rachel Quinn as a witness.

Ella made a reservation at the Hilton in Midtown and texted Slade. *Meet me at the Hilton tomorrow at noon.*

Slade arrived dressed in jeans and a T-shirt. The first thing he said was, "I'm supposed to be at my son's baseball game. My wife is not happy."

Ella had forgotten it was Saturday, but Slade's domestic problems were the least of her concerns.

"Okay," she said. "This is the way Toby's trial is going to go. The prosecutor will call the detectives to the stand and maybe a crime scene tech, and she'll ask if they can prove Toby was in the bar. They'll say yes, that they have eyewitnesses who can put him there, as well as his fingerprints. On cross, you'll ask if they found any physical evidence that Toby murdered Dominic DiNunzio, like a gun or gunshot residue or a shell casing with Toby's fingerprints on it. They'll say no. Then you'll ask—you'll ask this as many times as you can—if they found any motive for Toby to kill Dominic.

"The prosecutor will then call the witnesses. She'll ask Jack Morris if Toby was in the bar that evening. He'll say that Toby was indeed in the bar—something you're willing to concede—but he'll also say that he can't be certain it was Toby who shot Dominic. On cross you'll show Morris—and the jury—a photo of Carmine Fratello. You'll ask Morris if Carmine is a frequent customer at McGill's, and Morris will say yes."

Slade said, "The prosecutor will object to me showing him Carmine's picture. She'll say it's irrelevant."

"That's your problem. Figure out how to deal with the objection. Next the prosecutor will call the barmaid, and her testimony and your cross-examination of her will be identical to the bartender's.

"Last, the prosecutor will call Rachel Quinn, and she'll say she saw Toby shoot Dominic, then run past her table. She'll say she's positive it was him. On cross, you'll make her admit that whoever killed Dominic had his back to her when the shooting happened and that she saw the killer only when he *ran* past her table. You'll ask her how she can be so sure that the man she saw *running* in the dim light of the bar was Toby. You'll hammer the word 'run.'

"Then it's your turn. You present your experts, who'll talk about men being sent to jail because eyewitnesses made mistakes. You show pictures of men who've been mistakenly convicted, and how the innocent man doesn't look anything like the man who committed the crime. Your video expert will show his video proving how difficult it would have been for Rachel Quinn to accurately identify Toby as he went sprinting past her.

"Next you call one of the detectives back to the stand. You ask the detective to confirm that the night Dominic was killed it was raining hard, that at approximately seven-thirty p.m. in March it was dark out, and that Dominic was wearing a trench coat and a hat. You show the jury pictures of dead Dominic sitting there at the table, still wearing his trench coat and his hat.

"Then you call Carmine Fratello to the stand. Carmine will tell about the bad blood between him and Vinnie Caniglia, how Carmine broke Vinnie's nose in Atlantic City, and how Vinnie threated to kill him and that Dante Bello has been stalking him. You then ask Carmine if he owns a trench coat like Dominic's, and he says no."

"No?" Slade said.

"That's right. Dominic had a Burberry trench coat with a belt. The trench coat owned by Carmine is the same tan color and the same length as Dominic's, but it's made by London Fog and doesn't have a belt. You don't want the trench coats to be identical. That might smell to the jury. But they don't have to be identical. On the dark, rainy night Dominic was killed, he was wearing a tan trench coat similar to the one Carmine has. And Dominic was wearing a hat, making it even harder for Dante Bello to be sure it was Carmine Fratello.

"At any rate," Ella continued, "what happened that night was Dante saw a man he thought was Carmine enter McGill's. He knew Carmine went to McGill's all the time, as the bartender testified. So Dante thought it was Carmine who went into McGill's, then Dante—this criminal, this violent moron who gets drunk and beats people up— decided to kill Carmine. It took him a while to screw up his courage, but he eventually walks into McGill's—into this dimly lit bar—and up to a man sitting there wearing a trench coat and a hat, shoots him three times, then runs out of the bar.

"Finally, you call Dante to the stand so everyone can see how much he looks like Toby. You put their pictures side by side so the jury can see them, then you have your video expert show their pictures again side by side in the exact lighting that was in the bar that night. You ask Dante about the bad blood between Vinnie and Carmine. You ask Dante if he shot Dominic. Dante will deny it, of course, but who's going to believe a hood like Dante? If Dante is asked to prove where he was that night, he's going to say—I know, because I already asked him—that he was at a Knicks game with two of his fellow hoods. But nobody is going to buy that story."

Slade walked over to a window and looked out, mulling over everything Ella had told him. He could see the top of the Manhattan Bridge from where he stood. Finally he said, "It could work, but I still don't want Quinn testifying."

"She's *going* to testify, David; get on board with that. I've given you enough that a lawyer with your experience and ability can create reasonable doubt when it comes to Toby. They have only one witness who was sure it was Toby. One! You have two witnesses who say they can't be sure, you have a defendant with no motive, and you have a credible alternative suspect who looks like Toby. And Dante Bello, unlike Toby Rosenthal, is a man with a criminal history."

"But . . ."

"David, I'm not going to kill Rachel Quinn, and the only way I can ensure she won't testify is if I kill her. I already took a significant risk with Esther Behrman, so you're just going to have to do your job and convince a jury that Dante Bello shot Dominic DiNunzio."

"I want to remind you," Slade said, "that our deal was you get the second half of your fee only if I'm satisfied you've given me an effective defense. Well, I'm not satisfied."

Ella had hoped it wouldn't come to this—but there was no way that Slade, or Henry Rosenthal, wasn't going to pay her the other million she was owed. She'd worked too hard, and she'd given Quinn a brilliant defense. A first-year law student could create reasonable doubt when it came to Toby Rosenthal.

"David, you *are* going to pay me. I told you when this all started that my partner and I are not the kind of people you want to renege on. And these witnesses who are now prepared to testify for Toby? Well, I can always make them change their minds."

Slade didn't say anything. He just looked at her, the look of a stubborn man used to getting his way—and not one who liked to be threatened.

Tough shit. Ella left him sitting there in the hotel room glowering. And it was a shame. Ella actually had been in the mood.

39

DeMarco woke up wanting to kick something. He needed proof that Ella Fields was in New York and had had contact with the witnesses. If he could find proof, then maybe Justine would be able to get the warrants he wanted so that he could look at the witnesses' phone and financial records. He called Sarah to see if she'd had any luck with the property management companies, knowing that if she had, she would have called him. He just called her because he couldn't think of anything else to do.

"Sorry," Sarah said.

He stopped to have breakfast at a greasy spoon near his hotel, and picked up a newspaper that was lying on the table next to his. One of the stories on the front page, given almost as much space as the latest news from the Middle East, was about a movie star who'd committed suicide. The guy was handsome, only thirty years old, made four or five million on every picture—and he goes and kills himself. What could he have possibly been depressed about? The article said he died at the home of his girlfriend, a gorgeous actress, who lived in Malibu.

And something clicked.

Why did Bill Cantwell die in Santa Barbara, California? Cantwell had been a gypsy, living all over the country. He'd been raised in

Colorado, practiced law briefly in San Antonio, married in Hawaii, and lived in at least six different cities that DeMarco knew about. So why did he die in Santa Barbara? He called Sarah back and asked her to see if she could figure out what was special about Santa Barbara.

"His mother lives there," Sarah told him forty-five minutes later.

"His mother?"

"Yeah. Maybe she has some idea where Ella Fields is. I mean, if Cantwell was married to Fields at the time of his death . . ."

"Email me everything you've got on Cantwell's mom and get me a ticket to California. And remind me to tell Justine to give you a raise."

"I'm an intern, remember. How can I get a raise?"

"Well, I'm going to make her give you something."

Janet Kerns, Bill Cantwell's mother, lived in a large and stunning Spanish-style home in Santa Barbara. The house, surrounded by a rose-colored stucco wall, had a view of the Pacific Ocean and the Channel Islands. Before visiting Janet, DeMarco had learned that she had been widowed once and divorced three times, "Kerns" being the name of her fourth husband. She was in her late sixties, slim and fit, and amazingly well preserved. DeMarco didn't know how much of Janet's appearance could be attributed to good genes and exercise and how much credit went to a California surgeon, but whatever the case, Janet Kerns was a lovely woman.

DeMarco never even got through the door. When he knocked and Janet asked what he wanted, he said, "Mrs. Kerns, my name's DeMarco. I'm an investigator for the Manhattan DA and I need to ask you—"

"Manhattan?"

"Yes, ma'am," DeMarco said, and presented his credentials. "My boss sent me out here to ask about your son and—"

"My son's dead."

When she said this, he could tell her son's death was still a painful memory, and always would be.

"I realize that, Mrs. Kerns, and I was sorry to hear that he'd passed away, but—"

"I'm not 'Mrs.' Kerns."

"Fine," DeMarco said. The damn woman wouldn't let him get two words out without interrupting. "As I started to say, *Ms.* Kerns, I want to ask about your son's wife, a woman named Ella Fields."

"Ella?" the woman said.

"Yes," DeMarco said. "Now may I come in?"

"Why are you asking about Ella?" she said, still blocking the doorway.

"It relates to a murder that occurred in New York and—"

"Are you saying Ella murdered someone?"

"No, ma'am. I know for a fact that she wasn't involved in the murder. But she may have information related to what happened, and I need to speak to her."

"Why?"

"I can't tell you that," DeMarco said. "Now can you tell me—"

"If you can't tell me why you're asking about Ella, I'm not going to tell you anything."

"Ms. Kerns, the Manhattan district attorney can subpoena you and force you to fly to New York for a deposition, where you'll be speaking under oath."

That was a lie, but how would Janet Kerns know otherwise?

"If you'd like to avoid the hassle of traveling to New York at your own expense and possibly spending several days waiting to be deposed . . ."

"What do you want to know?"

"The first thing I want to know is what your son did for a living."

"I really have no idea, and that's the truth. Bill got a law degree, then was disbarred due to a terrible misunderstanding in San Antonio, and then he started some sort of consulting business. But Bill and I weren't close, and I really have no idea what he did for a living."

DeMarco didn't believe her, at the least the part about her not being close to her son.

"And what can you tell me about Ella Fields?"

"Nothing, really. I barely knew the woman. I met her at Bill's wedding, then didn't see her again until Bill came here to . . . to die."

"Why did he come here to die if you weren't close to him?"

"He didn't have health insurance, so he came here so I could help him. He had pancreatic cancer and there wasn't anything they could do for him, other than make him comfortable. So he and Ella lived here with me until he passed, and after the funeral, Ella left, and I haven't seen her since."

"Do you know where she lives?"

"No. Bill didn't own any property, he rented, so as far as I know she didn't have a home to go back to."

"Do you have a phone number for her?"

"No. Ella and I never became friends. You would have thought that taking care of Bill while he was dying would have brought us together, but it didn't. I really didn't care for the woman at all."

"I see," DeMarco said. What he wanted to say was: *If you didn't care for her, why are you being so goddamn protective of her?*

"Do you have any of your son's possessions here, papers that might give me an idea where she might be? Maybe you kept his phone, and it would contain her number."

"No. The only thing I kept of Bill's was a watch I gave him when he graduated from law school."

She looked away, and DeMarco thought for a moment she might cry, but then she sniffed and said, "If there's nothing else, I'm late for my Pilates class. I'm sorry, but I have no idea why Bill married that woman or where she might be right now, and I'm sorry you wasted your time coming here."

DeMarco thanked her and gave her his card and asked her to call him if something occurred to her that would help. He was sure the card was going to end up in a trash can—or, this being California, in the recycle bin.

———◆———

DeMarco was certain that Kerns had lied to him. She cared about Ella Fields, and he bet she knew where Fields was. Or if she didn't know where she was, she probably had a phone number where she could reach her.

He thought for a moment, and called Justine Porter.

"We need to look at Janet Kerns' phone records," he said. Before he'd flown to California, he'd told her about Bill Cantwell's mother. "I think she might call Fields, and if she does, and if Fields is using a cell phone, we can locate her."

"How many times do I have to say it, DeMarco? We don't have justification to get a warrant to look at anyone's phone records, much less the phone records of some woman in California whose son died before Toby Rosenthal did anything."

"I wasn't thinking about a warrant. I know a guy in DC. He's basically a hacker. I think he could—"

"No! I will not do something illegal, nor will I allow you to do something illegal."

"Do you want to win this goddamn case or not, Justine?"

Justine hung up on him.

———◆———

Janet Kerns suspected that the investigator, detective, whatever he said he was, didn't believe her about not knowing what Bill did for a living and where Ella was. But she'd told him the truth.

Bill had told her that he was a jury consultant and provided other services to lawyers after he was disbarred. And she supposed that might have been the case—he had a law degree and he might have been able to assist practicing attorneys in some way—but she'd always suspected he was lying. Her son had been one of the most charming people she'd ever known—and one of the biggest liars she'd ever known.

She'd always believed—although she never said this to him—that Bill was some sort of flimflam man. The way he lived—the houses he rented, the wedding in Kauai, the cruises he took, the way he and Ella dressed—made it obvious that he lived high off the hog. She'd always been afraid that one day she'd hear on the news that her son had been arrested for swindling millions of dollars out of a bunch of gullible fools.

Whatever the case, she'd told DeMarco the truth: She didn't know what her son did for a living. She'd also told him the truth when it came to Ella: She didn't know where Ella was and didn't have a phone number for her. But she'd lied about their relationship: She'd become really close to Ella as Bill was dying, and she would be forever grateful for the way Ella took care of Bill in his last horrible months. After Bill's funeral, though, Ella hugged her and said good-bye, and they both knew that they would most likely never see each other again.

But now Ella was in danger; Janet was certain of that. She didn't know why DeMarco wanted to talk to her, but he was clearly hunting for her. If Ella and Bill had been engaged in something illegal, and if Ella was still doing something illegal . . . Well, she *owed* Ella. She owed her for bringing joy to her son's life and for being there at the end of his life, and that meant much more to her than whatever laws Ella and Bill might have broken.

And though she didn't know how to contact Ella directly, she thought there might be a way to get a message to her. Bill had told her, years ago, that if she ever had an emergency and needed to reach him urgently, she should call a lawyer named George Chavez in San Antonio. Bill had said that his job required him to move frequently, which meant he was constantly changing addresses and phone numbers, but Chavez would know how to reach him. What Janet didn't know was if Chavez would be able to get a message to Ella.

She called her Pilates instructor and canceled her session and went online. She found a number for a "George Chavez, Attorney-at-Law," in San Antonio. He appeared to be the only Chavez practicing law in San Antonio, which surprised her.

She called the number, and the phone was answered by a woman who said, "Law office."

"I need to speak to Mr. Chavez," Janet said.

"I'm sorry," the secretary said, "but Mr. Chavez isn't in the office today."

"This is urgent," Janet said.

"Well, I still can't help you. Mr. Chavez told me that he wasn't to be disturbed today for any reason. Would you like me to take a message? He'll probably be in tomorrow."

"Yes. My name is Janet Kerns, and I'm Bill Cantwell's mother."

"Okay," the secretary said, sounding like: *Is that supposed to mean something to me?*

"Tell Mr. Chavez he needs to call me as soon as possible, that this regards a very serious matter. My phone number is . . ."

The next morning, as Janet was about to walk out the door to have lunch with a girlfriend, her phone rang.

"This is George Chavez. You called my office yesterday."

"Yes. As I told your secretary, I'm Bill Cantwell's mother."

"Yes."

Just "Yes," which seemed odd to her. Why wouldn't he have said, *I'm so sorry that Bill died,* or something like that?

"Bill told me once that if I ever needed to get a message to him, like if I was sick or got into an accident, I should call you and you would be able to relay the message."

"I don't know why he would have done that. Bill worked for me years ago, but he left my employment, oh, gee, back in the '90s, like '93 or '95, and we didn't stay in touch after that."

Chavez was lying. Bill had told her about Chavez long after 1995. Was he worried that someone was monitoring the phone call? Or maybe he didn't really believe she was who she said she was.

"Listen," she said. "All I want you to do is pass on a message to Bill's wife, Ella Fields. Tell her to call me. It's urgent. She may be in some sort of danger."

"Some sort of danger? What does that mean?"

"I don't know you, Mr. Chavez, and you don't know me, and I'm not going to say anything more. But if you cared about my son and if you care about Ella, please have her call me."

"I'm sorry, but I don't know any Ella Fields. I have to go now."

"Wait." But he was gone. Goddamnit.

Well, there wasn't anything else she could do to warn Ella. She was sure Chavez was lying, or at least she was sure he was lying about not having had any contact with Bill since the 1990s. But was he lying about not knowing Ella? She had no way to be sure, nor did she have any other way to contact Ella. But she'd done her best; she'd tried.

Good luck to you, Ella dear. Now where the hell were her car keys?

40

Ella had been busy. She was like the guy in the circus act, the one who starts all the plates spinning at the top of a bunch of long poles and then runs from pole to pole, giving each pole another spin to keep the plates aloft.

One plate was Jack Morris, going over his testimony and making sure he understood he was to testify that Carmine Fratello was a frequent customer in McGill's.

A second plate was the barmaid; she'd called Kathy four times to go over her testimony. The waitress said all the right things, but, unlike Morris, she lacked conviction. She paused and hesitated, hemmed and hawed. At the conclusion of one phone call, Ella screamed that if she didn't get her fucking act together she was never going to see her fucking kid again. All that did was make Kathy cry, and it took five minutes to get her calmed down so Ella could make her repeat her testimony.

She called her old friend Shearson out in Seattle, and he confirmed that Edmundo Ortiz was still at sea and would remain at sea until after the trial. And as far as Shearson knew, no one had come around asking about him. By the way, Shearson said, Edmundo was doing a damn fine job as the ship cook.

She checked on Esther Behrman's condition by talking to Curtis, the maintenance man. According to Curtis, Esther just lay in bed all day, couldn't move much more than one arm, and sounded like a duck when she tried to talk. Curtis didn't think Esther was long for this world—which would be a blessing to everyone, including Esther, as far as Ella was concerned.

Ella's biggest problem at this point was Carmine Fratello. She'd met with him in a motel in Jersey to go over his testimony. She didn't like meeting with him, but they had too much to talk about to do it on the phone. One problem with Carmine was that he thought he might be able to get her into the sack, and she'd hurt his feelings when she told him there was a greater chance of Martians landing in Times Square than of him screwing her. The major issue with Carmine, however, was that he wasn't very bright.

"Do you go to McGill's Bar and Grill frequently?" Ella asked, pretending to be Slade cross-examining him.

"'Yeah, uh, I guess.'"

"No! Don't say 'I guess.' Why the hell would you say 'I guess'?"

"It's just an expression."

"Well, stop using it! When you're asked if you go there frequently, just say yes. In fact, don't say anything more than yes. Then the lawyer will ask 'How often do you go?' And what do you say?"

"Shit, I don't know. 'Frequently.'"

Jesus Christ. "You say you go there two, three times a week. 'And were you there on the night of March fifteenth?'"

"'I don't know. I don't remember.'"

"Good. That's good. How could you possibly remember where you were four or five months ago?" Ella said. "Now: 'Do you have a trench coat like Exhibit A?'"

"Exhibit A. What's Exhibit A?"

"You're killin' me, Carmine," Ella said. "The defense attorney is going to enter Dominic DiNunzio's coat into evidence. He'll call it Exhibit something or other. Exhibit A, Exhibit D, whatever. Haven't you ever been to court before?"

"Yeah, lots of times," Carmine said, sounding proud of himself.

And so it went, but in the end, Ella was confident—well, maybe not "confident" but pretty sure—Carmine would do okay on the stand.

Overall, Ella was feeling good about the Rosenthal case, and she decided to take a day off and treat herself to another afternoon at the spa, followed by an expensive dinner. There was nothing wrong with rewarding herself for a job well done.

Ella walked into the apartment in Chelsea a little tight from the wine she'd had with dinner, and just as she opened the door, her cell phone rang. But not one of the cell phones she used to communicate with David Slade and the witnesses—the one she used to talk to George Chavez and a few other folks.

She looked at the caller ID and, by God, it was George calling. Why was he calling? Had he lined up a new case for her already?

"Hello, George," she said.

"I got a call from Bill's mother."

"What? Why would she call you? How did she even know to call you?"

"She knew to call me because Bill told her one time that if she ever had an emergency and needed to reach him, I would know how to get a message to him. I'm a little pissed about that, but since Bill's dead . . ."

"So what did she want?"

"She wants you to call her. She said it was urgent and that you might be in danger."

"Danger?"

"That's what she said. I pretended not to know who you were or how to reach you, but I decided to pass on the message. You do what you want. How's the case going out there?"

"It's going fine," Ella said, distracted by what she'd just learned. "Thanks for calling, George."

———◆◆◆———

What on earth could Janet mean by saying that she was in danger? And how would Janet know?

She had to find out what was going on. She decided not to use a cell phone in case someone decided to look at Janet's phone records. She found a pay phone—it took her forty minutes to find one—and made the call.

"Janet, it's Ella."

"Thank God you called," Janet said. "A New York cop came to see me a couple of days ago. He said—"

"A cop?"

"Yeah. His card says he's a special investigator for the Manhattan DA, so I guess he's a cop. Anyway, he was looking for you."

"Why would he ask you?"

"He said he knew you'd been married to Bill. He also knew that Bill had died here in Santa Barbara. Maybe he looked at the death certificate. Anyway, that's why he came to see me, and he wanted to know if I knew where you were or how to get in touch with you."

"But why?"

"He said it was related to a murder in New York."

"A murder?"

"Yes. When I asked him if he was accusing you of murder, he said he knew for a fact—those were the words he used, that he knew for a fact—that you weren't involved in the murder. But he said you had information related to it."

"Well, I don't," Ella said. "I have no idea what he's talking about. So what else did he say?"

"Nothing else, really. He just wanted to know if I had a number for you or knew some way to reach you."

"What did you tell him?"

"I told him I had no idea how to get hold of you."

"I appreciate that, Janet. I don't know what he wants, but I don't want to have to deal with him."

Janet paused. "I like you, Ella, I really do. I'll always be grateful for the way you stuck by Bill when he was dying. So I don't know what's going on, and I don't want to know, but I thought you should know that this guy's hunting for you."

"What's his name?" Ella asked, but she was thinking: This cop could destroy everything I've worked so hard for.

"His name is Joseph DeMarco."

"DeMarco," Ella repeated. "What does he look like?"

"Like a thug. Dark hair, hard face, maybe six feet. Oh, and he uses a cane."

41

DeMarco returned to Manhattan, intending to break the law.

The problem he had was that one point six million people lived in Manhattan. During the workweek, people poured in from the other boroughs and New Jersey and Connecticut, and the population swelled to three million. And, for all DeMarco knew, Ella Fields wasn't living in Manhattan. She could be living anywhere in the five boroughs among the eight point six million people in the greater New York area. Finally, there was nothing to say that she was using her own name; in fact, at this point, and after the way Sarah had hunted for her, DeMarco was sure she wasn't.

While he'd been in California, Sarah had continued to beat the bushes, trying to find someone who had leased or rented an apartment to Fields. She'd contacted upscale hotels to see if Fields might be staying in one, living off room service. She'd continually checked to see if Fields had used a credit card in the New York area or anywhere else in the world. She'd checked with auto rental companies to see if Fields had rented a car. She'd checked with the NYPD traffic boys to see if Fields might have been issued a parking ticket, a speeding ticket, a DUI. Nada, nada, nada, and nada. Which made DeMarco more certain than ever that Fields had a fake ID and that Sarah was never going to find her.

He couldn't give up on the case, for one thing because he knew Mahoney wouldn't allow him to give up. Another reason was that he'd promised his aunt Connie that her son's killer would go to jail, and the way it looked at the moment, that might not happen. Justine was down to only one solid witness, Rachel Quinn. Rachel might be able to convince the jury that Toby did it, but with no motive and no physical evidence, the odds were dropping.

But there was also a third reason he wasn't going to give up: his ego. He hated to lose, and he refused to let Ella Fields beat him.

So his plan was to call Neil and break the law whether Justine liked it or not.

Neil lived in DC. He called himself an "information broker," but in reality he was a guy who, for a healthy fee, could get you data on just about anyone. The man slithered electronically through firewalls or called on contacts he'd developed over the years in places that stored records, places like banks and telephone companies. DeMarco figured that once he was able to identify people the witnesses had been talking to, he would have something to work with, regardless of whether the information was legally obtained or not. At this point, screw "legally obtained." He had to find Ella Fields.

Before calling Neil, DeMarco decided to meet with Sarah one last time to see if she'd made any progress, and if not, to tell her to go back to doing whatever it is that interns do. He'd also tell her that if she ever needed a recommendation, he would write one saying that she could walk on water without getting her shoes wet.

On the way toward the Starbucks near the courthouse, his cabdriver was forced to take a detour around one of the never-ending construction projects in Manhattan, and passed near the 9/11 Memorial—and DeMarco had one of those forehead-smacking moments.

The Ring of Steel. Why in the hell hadn't he thought of that earlier?

New York's Ring of Steel is modeled after a similar surveillance system in London with the same name, and was installed post-9/11 to prevent terrorist attacks. The ring consists of over eight thousand cameras, located mostly in Midtown and Lower Manhattan, that protect high-value or symbolic targets, such as the New York Stock Exchange, Grand Central Terminal, and the 9/11 monument. Sophisticated software could be programmed to look for individual faces or even shapes, like a backpack sitting on the federal courthouse steps.

That's about all DeMarco knew regarding the system, and everything he knew he'd read in the paper. The Ring was classified like a military program, and the guys in NYPD's Counter-Terrorism Bureau were as tight-lipped as the FBI and Homeland Security agents they worked with.

DeMarco called up Justine.

"I want to use the Ring of Steel to locate Ella Fields."

"You gotta be kidding," Justine said.

"No. You keep saying that the only way we might be able to get a warrant to look at the witnesses' phone records is if we can prove Fields is in New York and has approached them. Well, Rachel Quinn works in the Financial District, and there're a zillion cameras down there, so if Ella Fields has been anywhere near her office there's a good chance one of the cameras picked her up. I want the antiterrorist boys to stick Fields' passport photo into their fancy software and see if they can spot her."

"Oh, is that all," Justine said. "DeMarco, you do realize that those people don't work for me and . . ."

"Yeah, but—"

". . . and if the DA wasn't willing to push NYPD to give me the resources I needed to track down Cantwell and Ella Fields in the first place, what do you think he's going to say when I tell him I want to start hunting for Fields with surveillance cameras. On top of that, Jim Kelly . . ."

Kelly was the deputy commissioner who ran the NYPD Counter-Terrorist Bureau.

". . . is a prima donna who hobnobs with the FBI and CIA, and half the time he acts like he doesn't even work for the city of New York.

What I'm saying is, if the DA were to ask Kelly to use his cameras to hunt for Fields, he'd tell the DA to go shit in his hat, and maybe rightfully so. Toby Rosenthal killed *one* guy, Joe. The Ring is being used to prevent fanatics from killing thousands."

DeMarco didn't say anything for a moment, then said, "Well, I know a guy who can talk to Kelly."

"You mean Mahoney?"

"That's right. Mahoney can threaten to cut off some of those federal antiterrorism funds pouring into New York, and that will get Kelly's attention."

DeMarco called Mahoney and told him where things stood: that he'd identified a woman named Ella Fields who he was convinced had tampered with two of three remaining witnesses in the Rosenthal case. He told Mahoney, "The only way I can think to find this woman is to use the Ring of Steel. If I don't find her, the guy who killed Dominic has a very good chance of getting off. So can you light a fire under the asshole who controls the Ring and get him to help me?"

The next day, Mahoney called him back. "Kelly said he'd do it. You need to get Fields' picture to a guy named Dimitri. He's one of Kelly's technicians."

Dimitri? "Thanks, boss," DeMarco said.

DeMarco met Dimitri in a bar off Broadway that charged fifteen bucks for a martini. The guy looked like a gangster: ferret-faced, slicked-back hair, dressed in a tight, shiny suit. He also had a Russian accent.

DeMarco knew that Russia produced a lot of mathematicians and computer weenies, and if they weren't committing computer crimes back in Russia, they were employed all over Wall Street as quants and embedded in companies that needed tech-savvy folks. DeMarco, however, didn't care that Dimitri might be a Russian spy who had managed to penetrate the NYPD. All he cared about was that Dimitri might be able to prove Ella Fields was in New York.

DeMarco gave Dimitri Ella Fields' passport photo, and three days later Dimitri met DeMarco in the same bar and handed him a photo showing a clear image of her standing near the building where Rachel Quinn worked.

In the surveillance photo, Fields was wearing shorts and a T-shirt and running shoes. She wasn't disguised in any way. She was also one spectacular-looking woman; she had outstanding legs. She appeared to be staring at the entrance to Rachel Quinn's building, as if waiting for Rachel to appear. Or at least that was the way DeMarco intended to interpret the photo.

DeMarco called Justine. "I can prove Fields is in New York. I have a photo of her standing in front of the building where Rachel Quinn works. It looks like she might be waiting for Quinn to come out of the building. Now do you think we can maybe get a couple of warrants?"

The next day, DeMarco and a weary-looking Justine Porter were sitting in the chambers of Judge Walter Hoagland. Hoagland was seventy-four years old, six feet four inches tall, and rail-thin. He probably weighed 140 pounds. He had a chicken's beak for a nose and about six strands of yellowish white hair that he combed over his liver-spotted skull. It was well known that Hoagland carried a .32 automatic beneath his black robe when he was in court; he'd never drawn the weapon, but was secretly hoping that one day an opportunity would present itself.

Prosecutors loved Hoagland; his judicial peers did not. Hoagland was reversed more often on appeal than any other criminal court justice in Manhattan, and his fellow justices wanted him gone. The problem with Walter Hoagland was that he was simply tired of criminals getting away with crimes he knew they'd committed. Once, when he'd had a few too many drinks, he told a reporter that any system that relied on twelve idiots to determine guilt or innocence was doomed to fail.

The consequence of all this was that if Hoagland—the jury be damned—was convinced a defendant was guilty, he made no effort to hide his feelings and ruled against almost every objection and motion made by the defense. He also had a tendency to instruct juries in such a manner that if the jurors followed his instructions they would almost certainly find the defendant guilty. At this stage of his life, Hoagland didn't care if he was reversed on appeal. His attitude was that if some animal was turned loose to prey upon the public, it wasn't his fault, as he'd done his best.

Hoagland didn't bother to read the ten-page affidavit that Justine Porter had spent all night preparing. He said, "Just tell me what this is all about."

So DeMarco explained. He said that a couple named Bill Cantwell and Ella Fields had been running around the country for over ten years making witnesses change their testimony or disappear, and as a result rich folks were acquitted of murder and manslaughter. Hoagland was fascinated.

DeMarco explained how he'd come to his conclusions after looking at what had happened in cases in Phoenix, Las Vegas, and Houston, and surprisingly, Hoagland didn't rush him. DeMarco concluded by saying that Ella Fields was in New York—that he had a surveillance photo proving this—and that one of the witnesses in the Rosenthal case had disappeared and another had had a stroke that might not have been due to natural causes. On top of that, two other witnesses who had been willing to testify that Rosenthal killed Dominic DiNunzio had now changed their testimony.

"You really think this woman tried to kill an old lady?" Hoagland said.

"Yeah, but I can't prove it," DeMarco said.

"So what do you want?" Hoagland said.

"Your Honor," Justine said, "we want a warrant to look at the phone records of people who may have communicated with Ella Fields. That includes Rosenthal's lawyer and two of the witnesses."

"Why are you bringing this to me instead of Judge Martinez?" Hoagland asked.

Martinez was the judge who had presided at Toby's arraignment and would be presiding at his trial. And the answer to Hoagland's question was: *We're bringing this to you because you're more likely to give us a warrant.* But Porter couldn't say that. Instead she said, "Your Honor, this isn't about the Rosenthal murder case directly. This is about building a case to convict Ella Fields and David Slade of witness tampering and possibly attempted murder. If we presented this to Judge Martinez it might constitute a conflict of interest and could cause Judge Martinez to recuse himself, which wouldn't be fair. To Judge Martinez, I mean."

"Aw, bullshit," Hoagland said. "You came to me because Martinez is a pussy." He paused, then said, "I'll tell you what. I'll give you the warrant to look at the witnesses' records, but stay away from Slade. Looking at the records of a shark like Slade could cause everyone problems if he found out. If you get something from the witnesses' records, *then* maybe I'll let you look at Slade's."

"Thank you, Your Honor," DeMarco and Justine simultaneously said. Then they hustled out of Hoagland's chambers before he could change his mind.

42

Ella had never in her life been more terrified.

She couldn't understand how this guy, DeMarco, had identified her. It just didn't make any sense. Even if one of the witnesses—like the barmaid or the bartender—had told DeMarco that a woman had coerced them to change their testimony, they wouldn't have been able to identify her as Ella Fields.

Nobody in New York—not David Slade, not the witnesses, not Carmine Fratello—knew her name was Ella Fields. She'd never told any of those people her name. She'd even worn disguises when she met with them so they would have a harder time identifying her. And when she rented the apartment in Chelsea, rented a car, and paid for the hotel room where she met with Slade, she didn't use a credit card in her own name.

Bill had always been incredibly casual—*foolishly* casual, in Ella's opinion—about protecting his identify. He figured the way he would get caught was that one day a witness he thought he'd turned would turn on him, and Bill would show up for a meeting and the cops would nab him—and it wouldn't matter what ID he was carrying in his pocket. He also hadn't paid a whole lot of attention to phone security until Ella started working with him.

But there was one thing Bill did do that Ella really appreciated: He did everything he could to protect her by making sure she couldn't be tied to his activities financially. When he rented a house, he rented it in his name only. He filed a tax return every year based on a phony salary that he claimed he made as a consultant, but he filed as being single; he never asked Ella to take his last name after they were married. Ella was listed as a joint holder on his bank accounts, but Bill was the one who deposited the money. His objective was to make sure that Ella didn't wind up in jail for income tax evasion, wire fraud, or any other financial crime. And when Ella started working with him directly, one of the first things Bill did, at her insistence, was get her a bulletproof false identity.

Bill knew a man in San Antonio who made his living making IDs for Mexican illegals. The guy didn't spend a whole lot of time on the Mexicans, but for Ella, he went all out. The real Carol Owen was a runaway from El Paso, the same age as Ella, who had disappeared at the age of fourteen. She had most likely died, but then Carol's drug-addict mother died too, and Carol was never declared legally dead. So the guy in San Antonio obtained Owen's social security number and birth certificate, and using those documents he got Ella a passport, a driver's license, and credit cards. She even had an AAA card in case her car broke down.

When Ella was working and had to show an ID for anything—such as renting a car—she used the Owen ID. The only time Ella used her real ID was when she'd traveled with Bill on vacations and they were doing things that were totally legitimate, such as taking a cruise. But even then, Bill paid for things using his credit cards.

What all this meant was that if Ella slipped up, the cops might learn that there was a Carol Owen who was tampering with witnesses, but Ella Fields would be able to get on a plane and fly far away as Ella Fields. But somehow, this damn guy, DeMarco, had learned that she was married to Bill—he must have found a record of their marriage license. And then—and this was the part that made no sense—he'd concluded she was in New York and involved in the Rosenthal case. How in the hell could that have happened?

When it came to cell phones, which could be easily monitored and used to track people, Ella was particularly careful. She had one phone in the name of Carol Owen that she used for communicating with George Chavez, and she put down that phone number when she rented an apartment or made an airline reservation. But she used prepaid cell phones for everything else, and when she came to New York one of the first things she did was buy half a dozen burner phones; she used a different phone to communicate with Slade, each of the witnesses, Curtis, and Carmine Fratello.

She didn't see any way DeMarco would know about Carmine or Curtis, but if he got a warrant to look at the witnesses' phone records, he'd see that the witnesses were communicating with someone with an unregistered phone. And if he asked the witnesses who had called them, what story would the witnesses give? The other problem—the bigger problem—was that if the cops got the numbers of the phones she'd used to talk to the witnesses, they could locate her using them.

She needed to get rid of all the damn phones.

She also needed to find out if DeMarco had asked the barmaid and the bartender about her. So she called them, and was furious to learn that DeMarco had spoken to them and asked if anyone had tried to get them to change their testimony. They both said they lied to DeMarco and told him that no one had talked to them. Well, at least that was good.

She then called Curtis, the maintenance guy at Esther Behrman's assisted living place, and asked if a cop named DeMarco had asked about her—and that's when she learned that DeMarco had shown Curtis her picture.

"What!" she shrieked.

Curtis said, "In the picture you had short blond hair, not like the hair you had when we met, but I knew it was you."

"What did you tell him?" Ella said.

"I said I never saw you before. But he went all over the place showing everyone your picture. I don't know if anyone else said they saw you."

"Why in the hell didn't you call me when he asked you about me?" Ella said.

"I don't know what happened with Esther, but I do know I didn't do anything illegal. I just didn't want to, you know, get in any deeper."

Son of a bitch! DeMarco not only knew her name but had a photo of her. If the bartender admitted that she'd paid him off or if the barmaid said that Ella had forced her to change her testimony, she was screwed.

What she should do was get the hell out of New York. The trial started in two weeks, and there was really nothing more she needed to arrange when it came to Toby Rosenthal's case. All the witnesses and Carmine Fratello were prepared to testify and Slade was ready to present his defense, the one that would point to Dante Bello as the killer. And as she'd already told Slade, whether he liked it or not, she wasn't going to do anything to Rachel Quinn. So her work in New York was done and there was no reason to stay in the city any longer—other than to make sure Slade paid her the million he owed her.

She hunted through her rented apartment in vain for a hammer; apparently, the doctor who had subleased her the place had never had any use for one. So she took a brass candlestick, laid a thick towel on the doctor's hardwood floor, and used the candlestick to smash all her cell phones to smithereens—including her Carol Owen phone. She didn't think DeMarco could possibly know about her Carol Owen ID, but she couldn't take the chance. As upset as she was, she just whaled the shit out of those phones, plastic pieces flying all over the apartment. She was lucky she didn't end up with a splinter in her eye, not to mention that the doctor wasn't going to be too happy when he saw the condition of his candlestick.

She left the apartment and walked down the street and dumped the remnants of all the phones into several different trash cans just in case there was still some functioning electronic part she hadn't managed to kill, then stopped at a store and bought three more phones so she'd have clean, untraceable ones to use.

Returning to her apartment, she started toward the bedroom, planning to pack her clothes, but then saw her reflection in a mirror. She'd been running her hands through her hair as she paced the apartment, and her hair was sticking up in *spikes.* And her eyes. She had the eyes of an animal with its paw caught in a trap.

She stopped and looked directly into the mirror and said: "Ella Sue, get a fucking grip on yourself."

She sat down on the bed and asked herself: What did DeMarco really know?

He knew she'd been married to Bill. But so what? Being married to Bill wasn't a crime, and she doubted that DeMarco could prove that she'd worked with Bill. He knew what she looked like, but again, so what? If he could *prove* she'd tampered with the witnesses in the Rosenthal case, then he could arrest her—but the only way he'd be able to prove that was if Jack, Kathy, or Edmundo talked, and she knew these three wouldn't talk, as they'd all accepted money from her.

She needed to keep her eye on the big picture, and the big picture was that she wanted to keep on doing this kind of work until she'd made enough money to retire comfortably. She could, of course, do what she'd planned to do when she first left Calhoun Falls, and marry a rich guy; she knew she was attractive enough to snag one. But she liked doing what she did. She enjoyed the challenge and being her own boss and living the way she wanted without having to compromise to keep some man happy. And she'd proved with the Rosenthal case—a case more complicated than any she and Bill had ever dealt with in the past—that she could do the work on her own. After David Slade got an acquittal for Toby Rosenthal he would definitely refer her to other lawyers, and George Chavez could use her success in the Rosenthal case to get her other clients.

What she needed to do was not panic, and stay in New York until the trial started just in case Slade needed her help—and to make sure Slade paid her the final installment. In the meantime, and although she had no reason to believe her Carol Owen ID had been compromised, she'd find someplace else to live and whenever she ventured outside she'd wear a disguise.

The following day, Ella packed her bags and moved out of the apartment in Chelsea. She rented a room for two weeks at a cheap hotel in Chinatown, paying cash. The place was a god-awful dump; a Motel 6 looked like the Ritz-Carlton compared with it.

Next she called the forger in San Antonio and told him to make her another ID as good as the Carol Owen ID. He said it was going to take him at least a month—and she told him to speed it up. If she had to run, she wanted to be able to run under some name other than Ella Fields or Carol Owen.

She thought again about the calls she'd made to the witnesses and the possibility of the cops looking at the witnesses' phone records. How would the witnesses explain, if asked, who'd called them from an unregistered cell phone? She thought about that for a bit, then had to hunt for almost an hour to find a pay phone.

She called Jack Morris and Kathy Tolliver and told them what they would say if someone asked about the phone calls she'd made to them. Jack said he could use a little more cash—big surprise, he'd had another bad weekend in AC—but he was cool about what Ella wanted him to do.

Kathy was not so cool. The girl started shrieking about how Ella was going to land her in jail and how then her daughter would be taken from her no matter what happened at Toby's trial. So Ella had to calm her down, threaten her a bit more about what would happen to her daughter if she didn't testify correctly at the trial, and then made sure Kathy knew what to say if anyone asked about her phone records.

Yeah, everything was going to be all right.

43

DeMarco couldn't believe it.

They'd used the warrants granted by the Not-So-Honorable Walter Hoagland, contacted phone companies and banks, and examined the financial and telephone records of the bartender and the barmaid. They were both swimming in credit card debt, and the bartender appeared to be a degenerate gambler, based on his almost weekly trips to Atlantic City. But neither Jack Morris nor Kathy Tolliver had come into money since the Rosenthal case started—at least they hadn't deposited money in their bank accounts or paid down their credit card debt. If they'd been bribed, they'd been paid in cash—and he had no way to prove that.

Phone records showed that Morris and Tolliver had both received several calls from a prepaid cell phone—but not from the *same* prepaid cell phone. When Justine asked the service providers to locate the phones that had been used to call the witnesses, she was informed that the phones were no longer in service. Son of a bitch! DeMarco was certain that the person who had been calling Morris and Tolliver from the prepaid phones was Ella Fields—but again he couldn't prove it.

Livid, DeMarco went to McGill's and leaned on Jack Morris and Kathy Tolliver again—and they both lied to him again. Kathy claimed that the calls were from her Narcotics Anonymous sponsor, and when DeMarco demanded the sponsor's name, Kathy said, "They call it Narcotics *Anonymous* for a reason." DeMarco told her how much time she could serve for perjury—doubling the amount she'd probably get. He also said she could be sent to jail for obstruction of justice if she was lying. Hell, maybe the DA could even find some way to make her an accomplice to Dominic DiNunzio's murder, since she was obviously helping Toby Rosenthal avoid going to jail. Tolliver looked for a minute as though she might throw up—but she didn't buckle.

Morris, on the other hand, wasn't the least bit nervous. Jack had a lot more grit than DeMarco had expected. He said he gambled a bit, borrowed some money from a shark, and the shark called periodically to hound him for his money. He wasn't about to tell DeMarco the shark's name. "The guy might not break my legs for being a little late on a payment, but if I gave his name to the DA's office, I could be walking on crutches for a month."

The warrants that he and Justine had worked so hard to obtain hadn't accomplished anything.

He called Justine to tell her where things stood, and started ranting. He couldn't find Fields. He couldn't prove that she'd committed a crime. He couldn't prove that she'd tampered with the witnesses, or disappeared Edmundo Ortiz, or attempted to kill Esther Behrman. The whole time he was yelling, Justine kept trying to interrupt to tell him something. Finally, DeMarco said, "So I don't know what the fuck I'm gonna do now."

Justine said, "Well, if you'd shut up for two seconds and let me talk, I've got some good news for you."

44

Toby Rosenthal's trial was scheduled to start in a week, and Judge Martinez called for a pretrial meeting with Justine Porter and David Slade. Martinez just wanted to get an idea of how long the trial would last. The reason he wanted to know was that he was planning to take a vacation immediately after the trial and wanted to start booking reservations—although he didn't tell the lawyers this.

When Martinez asked Porter how many witnesses she intended to call, Slade wasn't really paying attention. He was thinking instead about his daughter, who had just turned thirteen. The girl had been an absolute angel growing up, the apple of his eye, a joy to be around. But as soon as she hit thirteen, she morphed into this sullen, belligerent airhead who spent all her time texting her girlfriends.

Last night at the dinner table she'd announced that she was getting a small tattoo on her lower back, just above the crack of her ass. The tattoo was a Chinese symbol that meant fate or destiny or some fucking thing. When his wife objected, saying she was going to do no such thing, his daughter said that she had a right to do what she wanted with her own body and called her mother a control freak. Things escalated from there. So when Porter started naming the witnesses, he really hadn't been paying any attention because for one thing, he already knew who her witnesses were going to be.

The detectives, Coghill and Dent, would be called, maybe one of them, maybe both. They would discuss how they had identified Toby and what had happened at Toby's lineup. Slade suspected that Porter would use the detectives' testimony as an opportunity to show the jury pictures of Dominic DiNunzio: Dominic sitting at the table where he'd been shot, his shirt soaked with blood, his eyes half-closed, looking convincingly dead. And Slade wouldn't object to showing the jury the gory photos because he wanted the jurors to see what DiNunzio looked like—and later be able to conclude that he'd been mistaken for Carmine Fratello by Dante Bello.

A CSI tech would be called to testify that Toby had been identified as being in the bar based on his fingerprints being on a glass—which Slade was willing to stipulate. Slade would ask the tech if they had found any physical evidence that Toby Rosenthal had shot Dominic, to which the tech would respond no.

Then Porter would call the witnesses.

"How many witnesses do you intend to call?" Judge Martinez asked.

"Four, Your Honor," Porter said.

Slade thought: What? Did she say four?

"Excuse me," Slade said. "I missed that. Did you say you were calling four witnesses?"

"Yes," Porter said, a slight smile on her face. "I'll be calling the bartender, Jack Morris; the barmaid, Kathy Tolliver; and one customer who was in the bar at the time of the shooting, a lady named Rachel Quinn." Then Porter paused dramatically before saying: "And a busboy named Edmundo Ortiz."

Slade couldn't believe what he'd just heard. "I was under the impression that Mr. Ortiz wasn't available to testify?"

"What gave you that impression?" Porter said.

"I don't know," Slade said, but he was thinking: *What the fuck is going on here?*

Still reeling from what he'd just been told, Slade told the judge that most of his defense would be based on cross-examination of the prosecution's witnesses. He would be calling a law professor from Columbia who would discuss several cases in which men were wrongly convicted based on faulty eyewitness testimony, and an engineer who would demonstrate, using a video, how the lighting in McGill's would have made a positive identification of Toby Rosenthal almost impossible. He concluded by saying, "But, Judge, I'm still trying to run down a couple of people."

"If you're about to ask for another delay, Mr. Slade," Martinez said, "it's not going to happen."

"No, Your Honor, I'm just saying that I'm still trying to locate two people who may have a significant bearing on Mr. Rosenthal's defense and may be called to testify."

The reason he told Martinez that he was trying to locate two witnesses was that he was going to spring Carmine Fratello and Dante Bello on Porter during the trial. He would say that they weren't on his original witness list because he hadn't been able to find them until the day before the trial started.

"Whatever," the judge said, ready to conclude the meeting. "The trial starts as scheduled next week, and I wouldn't expect it to last longer than two weeks. And I'll be moving things along to make sure that's the case. Thank you both for coming."

As soon as Slade left the judge's chambers, he sent a text message saying: *We need to meet. Urgently!!!*

But his phone informed him the message had not been delivered. He sent it again, and again was informed the message hadn't been delivered. Goddamnit! What the hell was going on?

When DeMarco had called Justine to complain that the warrant they'd obtained from Judge Hoagland hadn't done them any good, Justine had said, "If you'd shut up for two seconds and let me talk, I've got some good news for you."

"What good news?" DeMarco had said.

"Guess who called my office this morning."

"Who?"

"Edmundo Ortiz. He told me he's been in Alaska working on a fishing boat but if I send him an airline ticket, he'll fly back for the trial. When I asked him if he was planning to say that he could identify Toby Rosenthal as the killer, he said yes, indeed he was."

"You gotta be shittin' me," DeMarco said.

"Nope. When I asked Ortiz why he left New York and if anyone had tried to get him to change his testimony, he evaded my questions. All he would say was that he left because he got a good job out West and he just called me because he was trying to be a good citizen and knew it was his duty to testify. What I think happened is Fields forced him to leave town—or maybe she bribed him with the job he got—but the guy's conscience got the best of him. God Bless the new Americans," Justine said.

45

Ella called David Slade's office. She wanted to give Slade the number of the new burner phone she'd use to communicate with him in the future. She told Slade's secretary that she was Judge Martinez's clerk, and Martinez wanted to speak to him. She figured Slade would take a call from the judge.

Slade came on the line, sounding vexed. "Yes, Your Honor. What can I do for you?"

"It's not the judge, it's me," Ella said.

"Where the hell have you been?" Slade said. "I've sent you a dozen text messages."

Ella started to tell Slade to calm down but before she could, Slade said, "The case has fallen apart. We need to meet. Immediately."

"What do you mean it's fallen apart?" Ella said.

"Not on the phone," Slade said.

Ella hadn't told Slade that a DA investigator named DeMarco was hunting for her—and she decided not to tell him now; he didn't handle stress all that well. But she was afraid that DeMarco would follow Slade and Slade would lead him to her. She told him, "If we meet, you can't be followed to the meeting place."

"Why would anyone follow me?" Slade said.

"You just never know," Ella said.

"Well, I'll be careful," Slade said.

"Being careful won't be good enough," Ella said. "The cops could put a dozen people on you. They could use a helicopter to track you or stick a GPS device on your car."

"They'd never do that," Slade said. "I'm a lawyer."

Ella laughed, though it wasn't exactly a laugh.

Then Slade said, "Does it really matter if they follow me? The thing that's important is that they don't know we're meeting. My mother-in-law has a beach house on Long Island, and she's not using it now. If you're sure the cops aren't following you, you need to get to the beach place before me; the front door key is under this little lawn statue of a leprechaun. There's no way for the cops to know that you'll be inside. Then we'll talk and I'll leave first and you can leave after I do. Just don't park near her place."

"That'll work," Ella said. Slade gave her the address of the beach house, and Ella arrived there an hour before he did and parked a mile away.

"So what's going on?" she asked Slade as soon as he stepped into the house.

"There was a meeting yesterday with the judge who's presiding over Toby's trial."

"Why?" Ella asked.

"He just wanted to get a sense of how long the trial would last."

"So what's the problem?

"The judge asked about the number of people we'd both have testifying so he could get an idea how long it would take to present our cases. And that's when Porter said she had four witnesses."

"Four?" Ella said. "There should be only three."

"Yeah, well, that's when I heard that Edmundo Ortiz is planning to testify."

"Goddamnit!" Ella shrieked.

"For whatever reason, the damn guy decided to come back. Which means that now we'll have two people testifying that Toby did it, and two who will say they're unsure."

"Get another delay," Ella said. "I need time to deal with this."

This was the last thing she needed, with DeMarco hunting for her. She also knew there was no way Slade was going to pay her the million he owed if he had to walk into court facing two honest witnesses. He could still win; he might be able to create enough reasonable doubt with half the witnesses saying they couldn't identify Toby as the shooter. The problem now, though, was that the bartender and the barmaid had been a fair distance away from Toby when he shot DiNunzio, but Toby had run right past Quinn's table and almost ran into the busboy. So the prosecution was going to argue that the *best* witnesses had identified Toby and the jury should take that into account. She needed time to unravel all this, but then Slade said, "I can't get another delay. Martinez told me today he wouldn't give one. So what are you going to do?"

Not 'What are *we* going to do?' What are *you* going to do?

Ella walked over to one of the windows and looked out at the ocean. This was her dream: a place with an ocean view, her reward for becoming so much more than Ella Sue Fieldman from Calhoun Falls, South Carolina. Now everything she had worked for might go up in smoke.

"Which of the two witnesses is more important?" she asked Slade.

"What do you mean?" Slade said.

"I mean, if you had to pick between Rachel Quinn and Edmundo Ortiz, which of the two would you prefer to testify?"

"Ortiz, of course," Slade said. "He was shakier on his identification at the lineup, he never saw Toby shoot Dominic, and then there's the fact that Quinn will come across better than him. She's well educated and most likely articulate, and Ortiz . . . Well, you know what I mean."

"Yeah, I do," Ella said.

She had to do something about Rachel Quinn, and she had to do it quickly.

46

"When is Ortiz arriving in New York?" DeMarco asked.

"This evening," Justine said.

"We need to put him someplace where Fields can't find him."

"Yeah, I know. I've reserved a room for him at the Howard Johnson's in Soho. I'll have a cop meet him at the airport and—"

"I'll meet him," DeMarco said. "I want to talk to the guy. I want to see if he'll admit that Fields made him leave the city."

"I don't know," Justine said. "I don't want to lose this guy as a witness."

"Justine, we have no evidence that Ella Fields has done anything illegal. But if Ortiz will admit that she—"

"Joe, my priority is convicting Toby Rosenthal, not Ella Fields. If Ortiz admits that Fields bribed him to leave, then the judge might not allow him to testify."

"Only if you tell the judge," DeMarco said.

"Or if Ortiz is worried that he can go to jail for taking a bribe, then I don't know what he'll do. Maybe he'll split again. So I don't want to do anything that makes him change his mind about testifying against Rosenthal."

"Okay, I hear you," DeMarco said. "But I still think I'm the one who should pick him up. We want to minimize the number of people who know where he's staying before the trial. We can't take a chance that Fields might locate him and do something to him."

"Yeah, all right," Justine said, and she gave him Ortiz's flight information.

DeMarco hated to lie to Justine—well, maybe he didn't really *hate* it—but he was going to question Edmundo Ortiz. He wanted to know what Fields had done. He wanted proof that Fields had done *something*. And after the Rosenthal trial, if he could convince Ortiz to testify against Fields, he was going to find some way to track her down and have her arrested for witness tampering. Ella Fields had become his white whale—and he was going to bag that whale.

DeMarco met Edmundo Ortiz in baggage claim at JFK. He was a small guy—five five or so, with graying dark hair and a thick black and gray mustache—but one of those small guys who looked as if he could bench-press three times his weight. Edmundo Ortiz had done nothing but hard work all his life.

DeMarco explained that he worked for the DA's office, and started off by telling Edmundo that the state of New York was very grateful that he had come back to testify at Rosenthal's trial.

"I'm just doing my duty," Edmundo said, but he didn't sound proud. He sounded nervous—and maybe guilty.

DeMarco explained that he was taking him to a hotel and that Edmundo would stay in the hotel until the trial. He said that the ADA would meet with him before the trial and go over his testimony but that other than that, he could just relax.

"Think of this as a vacation," DeMarco said. "Eat room service, watch TV, swim in the pool. But you can't leave the hotel. Okay?"

Departing the airport terminal, DeMarco asked, keeping his tone casual, "What were you doing out in Alaska?" Edmundo had flown in from Anchorage.

"I'm a cook on a fishing boat, a crab-fishing boat. When the ship docked at Anchorage, I called the lady, the prosecutor, and told her I needed a ticket to fly back if she wanted me to testify."

"A crab-fishing boat. Wow. I've heard that can get pretty hairy sometimes. I mean if you have a storm or something."

"It wasn't too bad, at least not so far this year. It's a good job."

"How'd you get the job?"

Edmundo paused. "A friend told me about it. I applied."

DeMarco felt like making a buzzer sound. Lie!

DeMarco didn't ask anything else while they were in the cab. At the hotel, as Justine had told him, Edmundo had a reservation under the name "Manuel Rivera" and the bill was charged to a city credit card that Justine used. His room was nothing fancy: queen bed, no view, no mini-bar, small TV. DeMarco hoped he wouldn't go stir-crazy inside the room.

"Now," DeMarco said, "I gotta ask you something, Mr. Ortiz, and you need to be straight with me." He took a photo of Ella Fields from the inside pocket of his suit jacket and said, "Did this woman make you leave New York so you wouldn't testify at Toby Rosenthal's trial?"

Edmundo studied the photo for a long time—time he was most likely using to decide what he planned to say. "No. I have never seen her before," he said.

Lie! DeMarco hammered away at him for the next ten minutes, saying how it was good that he was willing to testify but it was important to know if someone was tampering with witnesses. DeMarco didn't threaten him and he didn't treat him like a criminal; he just kept saying how important it was to do the right thing, just like it was important that he tell the truth at Rosenthal's trial. He emphasized how much he admired him for being willing to take time off from his job, fly all the way from Alaska, but as good as all that was, he needed to say if the woman in the photo had coerced him in any way.

DeMarco couldn't budge him. Edmundo wouldn't look him in the eye; he just kept shaking his head and softly saying, "No, no, she never talked to me."

DeMarco finally gave up. He told him again that he needed to stay inside the hotel until the trial, and this time Edmundo asked him why.

"For your own protection," DeMarco said. "You're an important witness in a murder trial and, well . . . Just stay in the hotel." He could see that he was scaring him and he thought: *Good. Let him be scared.*

———◆◆◆———

DeMarco went to the hotel bar, ordered a beer, and spent a few minutes mulling over where things stood. Then he called Justine.

"I've been thinking about something," he said. "Who's the better witness, Rachel Quinn or Edmundo Ortiz?"

"Quinn, of course. For one thing, Quinn actually saw Rosenthal shoot DiNunzio. Then there's the fact that Quinn, being a lawyer herself and having a better command of English than Ortiz, will be better able to handle Slade's cross-examination. Plus, if you go back and look at statements they both made when they were first interviewed and at the lineup, Quinn was more positive about ID'ing Rosenthal."

"Yeah, that's what I thought," DeMarco said.

"Why are you asking this?"

"I think it would be smart to watch Quinn until the trial. As long as no one knows where Ortiz is except you and me, he should be safe enough. But Quinn . . ."

"Quinn lives in an apartment with a doorman and her office in the Financial District has more security than I do here at the courthouse."

"But when she's not in her office . . ."

"Do you think Fields will try to kill Quinn?" Justine said.

"I don't know," DeMarco said, and he reminded Justine of the witness in Minnesota who'd been killed in a so-called hit-and-run accident.

"Come on, DeMarco, we're not dealing with the Mafia here," Justine said.

"People like David Slade and Ella Fields are a lot brighter than the Mafia guys I've encountered, and Toby Rosenthal's father has money coming out of his ears. So I think they're a bigger threat than your average wiseguy. We need to keep Rachel Quinn under surveillance until the trial, and that means I'm going to need some help. I'll pick her up when she gets off work today and make sure she gets home okay, but I can't watch her twenty-four hours a day. On top of that, keep in mind that I'm not carrying a gun."

"Okay, you watch her today and put her to bed, and I'll get somebody to help you tomorrow."

"Good," DeMarco said.

47

———◆◆◆———

Ella set up a meeting with Carmine Fratello at a bar near his apartment, one of those dark, dingy places that would go out of business as soon as its regular clientele, all folks in their seventies and eighties, passed away. Fratello was dressed in a bright Hawaiian shirt and jeans that made his ass look wider than the bumper on a Greyhound bus. Ella was wearing the long red wig she'd worn every time she'd met with him. She was really nervous about being out in the open now that she knew the cops had her photo, and every time she went outside she wore different-colored wigs, sunglasses, and hats.

She was already at the bar when Carmine arrived, and when he sat down he said, "So what's up, doll? Don't tell me you wanna go over my testimony again."

"No. I need a couple of things from you. And I need them fast."

"Okay," Carmine said.

"First, I need a gun."

"Whoa!" Carmine said.

"I want a revolver, small enough to fit in a purse but with stopping power."

Ella didn't know anything about guns other than what she'd seen in movies or read in novels. She knew she wanted a revolver only because you didn't have to worry about shell casings being ejected and revolvers supposedly malfunctioned less often than automatics. But she and Bill had never owned a gun, and she'd never fired one.

"I got a thirty-eight with a three-inch barrel," Carmine said. "It's untraceable. I bought it from a guy who stole it from another guy."

"That'll be fine," Ella said. She didn't care if the gun was traceable or not. After she used it, she would immediately dump it someplace it would never be found.

"You can have it for, oh, let's say, eight hundred."

She figured Carmine was ripping her off and expected her to haggle over the price, but all she said was, "Fine."

"So what else you need?" Carmine said.

She told him.

"Jesus," Carmine said. "Are you serious?"

"Does it look like I'm serious, Carmine?"

"That's going to cost you. I mean, it's going to cost you a lot."

"I figured that. And I'm willing to pay you five to set this up. But I need everything ready to go by this evening."

"Then I better get going," Carmine said. "I'm going to have to make some calls."

Ella removed one of the newly purchased prepaid cell phones from her purse. "Use this phone when you make the calls. Don't use your own phone."

"Okay. I'll get back to you in a couple of hours. But don't be surprised if I can't line this up, not this fast." Carmine paused, the gears in his small brain clearly spinning. "I know this one guy, this Jamaican . . . Anyway, what number do I call you at?"

Ella told him, and handed him the five thousand.

Carmine rose from the table, then he laughed. "Never in a million years would I have ever expected all this when I first met you. You are one dangerous broad."

48

DeMarco was waiting outside Rachel Quinn's office building. He was dressed casually—jeans, a faded blue polo shirt, running shoes. He also had on sunglasses and a dark blue baseball cap. He wasn't trying to disguise himself; he was just dressed comfortably for following someone. As far as he knew Ella Fields had no idea who he was and what he looked like, but if Rachel saw him, she'd probably recognize him because of the damn cane. He was hoping she wouldn't see him, however, because if she did he'd have to explain why he was following her, which he didn't want to do. He didn't want to tell her that he was worried that Ella Fields might try to kill her.

Rachel came out of the building at six forty-five dressed in a sharp-looking dark blue suit, the skirt stopping just above her knees. She looked professional, yet at the same time sexy. She was able to wave down a cab five minutes after she stepped outside.

DeMarco now had to scramble to find his own taxi. Fortunately, he spotted a Wall Street big shot who was just about to get into a cab. The guy was dressed in a three-thousand-dollar suit, blabbing on a cell phone as he opened the rear door of the cab, and DeMarco pushed him out of the way. DeMarco held up his DA investigator's credentials and lied, "NYPD. Police business. I need this cab."

"Hey!" the big shot said. "You can't—"

DeMarco slammed the door shut and told the cabbie, "Follow that cab, the one that just pulled out. Go!"

Rachel's cab dropped her off at her apartment building, and she chatted briefly with the doorman before she went inside. DeMarco paid his cabbie and took up a position on the street half a block from the entrance to her building. There was no place else for him to go; there weren't any bars or coffee shops or restaurants nearby where he could sit and see the entrance.

He wondered how long he would have to stand there. Most likely Rachel was in for the night and wouldn't go out again, but he'd have to wait at least until dark, maybe nine-thirty or ten. He noticed it was a nice evening, a good evening for taking a stroll, and he thought: Dear Lord, please don't let the woman be a jogger. If she went for a run he'd never be able to keep up with her.

DeMarco thought briefly about what he would do if he saw Fields. If Fields walked into Rachel's building, he was going to have to follow her in and stop her. He couldn't let her knock on Rachel's door and shoot her when she opened it. And if he stopped her, he'd search her whether she liked it or not, and if she had a gun, he'd detain her and call the cops. If the gun wasn't registered or if she wasn't licensed to carry, she could be arrested, and that would maybe get her out of the way until after the trial.

If Rachel came out of the building, and if he saw Fields following her, then he'd call the cops and he'd stick with Rachel until the cops arrived. If Fields didn't go near Rachel, he probably wouldn't do anything. But if Fields approached Rachel, then he'd stop her and search her to see if she was carrying a weapon. It occurred to him a second time that it would be good if *he* were carrying a weapon.

But he didn't see Ella Fields. There were a lot of people on the street at seven-thirty at night—folks bustling home from work, people walking their mutts, domestics trudging home after a day of tending to the kings and queens of Manhattan—but he didn't see any tall, gorgeous blondes with short hair.

Then he noticed a car parked halfway up the block. A woman was sitting in the car, but the car was too far away for him to make out the woman's features. Whoever it was had long red hair and was wearing sunglasses. DeMarco also noticed that the woman's parking spot allowed her a good view of the entrance to Rachel's building.

Ten minutes passed and she was still sitting there. Maybe she was just waiting for someone—but DeMarco decided to take a closer look.

———◆◆◆———

Ella was focused on the entrance to Quinn's apartment building, and she barely noticed the guy with a cane walking down the sidewalk in the direction of her car. Then she thought: Cane! Shit, could that be DeMarco? When Janet had given her DeMarco's name, she'd done a quick Google search for a photo of him, but "Joe DeMarco" was too common a name. But the guy met the general description Janet had given her, the big thing being the cane. So was it DeMarco, and was he here for her?

But then the guy limped by without even glancing in her direction, and she watched in the mirror as he continued down the street and turned a corner.

Thank God.

———◆◆◆———

When DeMarco had been about twenty yards from the parked car, he thought: It's her! It's Fields! She had red hair that came down to her shoulders—probably a wig—and big sunglasses that covered a good part of her face, but it was her. He was sure. DeMarco hadn't slowed down or looked directly at her; he'd just kept walking. But as he'd walked, he'd noted the license plate number on Fields' car.

He'd walked to the end of the block, turned the corner, and immediately punched the plate number into his phone so he wouldn't forget it.

Then he called Justine. She didn't answer. Goddamnit! He left a voice mail saying: "Ella Fields is sitting in a car outside Quinn's apartment. I need a cop down here right now."

Ella smiled. Rachel Quinn had just stepped out of her apartment building. She was wearing a sleeveless white blouse, shorts, and running shoes. Her dumb little dog was on its leash.

Ella looked in the rearview mirror and didn't see the guy with the cane. Good.

When Rachel started walking in the direction of her favorite ice cream shop, Ella started the car.

DeMarco peeked around the corner after he called Justine—and saw Rachel come out of her building with a small dog on a leash.

Aw, shit!

She started walking north. He glanced over at the car where Ella Fields was sitting, and she was still sitting there, following Rachel with her eyes. DeMarco started walking fast to catch up to Rachel, and at that moment Fields' car pulled away from the curb.

DeMarco started running, holding the cane in his hand. He needed to catch up with Rachel in case Fields tried something.

He was about to call out to Rachel, but Fields drove past her without even slowing down. DeMarco stopped running and bent over and placed his hands on his knees. His right leg felt as if it was on fire. He'd been afraid that Fields was going to pull out a gun and shoot Rachel as she drove by, but she hadn't. She'd just continued down the street in the same direction Rachel was headed and was soon out of sight.

DeMarco called Justine again. He wanted a cop—Fields could still be somewhere in the neighborhood—but again Justine didn't answer. He sent her a text: *Call me!*

———◆◆◆———

DeMarco fell in behind Rachel. Because of the dog, she wasn't walking that fast, and he eventually caught up with her and fell in about thirty yards behind her. He had the passing thought that she looked great in shorts.

He hadn't known that she had a dog—but he was willing to bet that Fields knew. And maybe that was why Fields had been parked near Rachel's apartment, because she knew that Rachel was going to take her pet for its evening walk. But why did she take off as soon as Rachel started walking?

For all he knew, Fields could have driven to some spot where it would be easier for her to take a shot at Rachel. Or maybe she'd driven toward some intersection where she could run Rachel down, although Fields would have to be madder than a hatter to attempt a hit-and-run with all the people on the street, all of them with cell phone cameras.

DeMarco looked down the street, ahead of Rachel, but he didn't see any sign of the gray Camry that Fields had been driving. Maybe Fields had taken off, but still: Why had she been sitting outside Rachel's apartment?

As he walked—his leg hurting like a motherfucker—he thought about telling Rachel that Fields had been outside her apartment, but decided not to. There was no point in alarming her, and by tomorrow, if Justine kept her word, there would be guys with guns looking after her.

DeMarco wondered how far she was going to walk—he hoped not far—and wished she'd slow down. He also wished that Justine would return his call. An unarmed man with a bad leg wasn't an ideal bodyguard.

A mile later—DeMarco still about thirty yards behind her—Rachel went into an ice cream shop.

And less than three seconds after she stepped inside the shop, a car door opened. The car was parked right in front of the ice cream place.

DeMarco didn't notice if it was the gray car Fields had been driving—and the reason he didn't notice was that he was completely focused on the person who stepped out of the car. It was a tall, slender woman, and she was holding a gun down by the side of her leg—but he couldn't see her face because she was wearing a black ski mask.

The masked woman pushed open the door to the ice cream shop, raising the gun as she walked in—and DeMarco sprinted toward the shop. He crashed through the door less than a second after the woman entered, and when he did, she swung around fast, most likely intending to shoot him—but by then his cane was already in motion, and smashing into the side of her head.

Rachel and the girl behind the counter screamed and Rachel's dog started barking like crazy, but DeMarco ignored them as he kicked the gun from Fields' hand. He noticed she was wearing gloves and a long-sleeve jersey and jeans. He knelt down and pulled the mask off her head.

It wasn't Ella Fields. It was a young black woman in her twenties.

Five minutes later the cops arrived.

49

Ella was running for her life.

She drove toward the Lincoln Tunnel, and after she passed through the tunnel, she was just going to keep going. Out of Manhattan, out of the state of New York, maybe out of the country. She was driving the car she'd rented under the name of Carol Owen and as soon as she could, she'd stop someplace and buy a used car with cash, and then just keep driving. She had no idea where she was going to go. All she knew was that she needed to stay out of sight and off the grid until she could figure out what to do next.

She was now sure the guy with the cane she'd seen walking by her car was DeMarco—and he'd fucked up everything. She'd been parked across the street from the ice cream shop in a place where she could see the interior through a picture window. She'd known that Rachel Quinn had been headed toward the shop when she took her mutt for a walk, so she'd driven past Quinn and arrived at the shop before her. The Jamaican girl was already waiting in front of the shop in her car when Quinn arrived, and Ella saw her get out of her car wearing a ski mask—and then that fucking DeMarco came out of nowhere, burst into the shop, and hit the Jamaican in the head with his cane.

And now her life, as she'd known it, was over.

Ella had decided that the only way she could ensure an acquittal for Toby Rosenthal—and make sure she collected the million Slade owed her—was if Quinn didn't appear as a witness. If Slade had done his job and gotten another delay, she might have been able to find another way to deal with Quinn, but since he'd failed and she'd run out of time, killing Quinn was the only solution.

She'd asked Carmine Fratello to do two things. One of those things was to get her a gun—the snub-nosed .38 in her purse on the passenger seat. The other thing she'd asked Fratello to do, figuring a Mafia thug like him would know somebody, was to put her in contact with a professional killer, one brave enough or dumb enough or greedy enough to kill a person in broad daylight in the ice cream store. She was hoping the cops would think that Quinn and the clerk in the ice cream store had been killed in a robbery and not conclude that Quinn had been killed because she was a witness. But regardless of what the cops thought, Quinn would be dead, and the only witness left to testify against Toby Rosenthal would be the busboy.

She'd met with the Jamaican girl in the Bronx earlier in the day. She'd expected that the killer would be a man and was surprised when a young woman in her twenties walked up to her in Denny's. The girl scared the shit out of her: slim muscular arms, a thin scar on the left side of her face, eyes so cold that Ella doubted she had a soul. The deal was that she'd pay the Jamaican forty thousand to take the risk of killing Quinn, twenty up front and the other twenty after the job was done.

Her real plan, however, had been to kill the Jamaican when they met the second time—which was the reason she'd bought a gun from Carmine. The last thing she wanted was to have some professional killer able to identify her and testify that she'd paid to have Quinn killed; she knew if the Jamaican was ever caught for some other crime she'd give up Ella in a heartbeat. But after Ella met the Jamaican in Denny's, she began to wonder if she'd be able to kill her. Her conscience wouldn't have bothered her—the woman was a killer, after all—but she was afraid the Jamaican would be too hard to kill.

Now she didn't have that problem. She had a much bigger one.

The Jamaican didn't know Ella's name, but DeMarco did, and DeMarco would show the Jamaican Ella's photo, and without a doubt—to get a reduced sentence—the Jamaican would testify that Ella had paid her to kill Rachel Quinn. Ella was willing to bet that within an hour—as soon as the Jamaican got over being cane-whipped by DeMarco—there would be a warrant out to arrest her for attempted murder.

Ella felt her eyes well up with tears. It just wasn't fair. She'd worked so hard to become who she was today. She'd escaped the fate of being raised by shitty, apathetic parents, overcome a lousy education, and become a skilled professional in something she excelled at. If she'd been able to keep working just a few more years, she would have been able to retire in style. But now that wasn't going to happen. Thanks to DeMarco, the cops knew who she was and what she did for a living and they would be hunting for her. It was going to be impossible to line up another job helping some slimeball lawyer get his rich guilty client off for murder.

Then she thought: Quit feeling sorry for yourself. It's not the end of the world. It wasn't like she was penniless. She had over four million bucks—the three million she'd had before the Rosenthal case and the million Slade paid her at the beginning of the case. Not as much as she wanted to have before she retired, but certainly enough to get by. She'd get a new ID, sneak across the border into Mexico, and from there head to someplace cheap but civilized—maybe Panama or some city in South America. Yeah, she'd be just fine.

And that's when she saw the cop car behind her, its light bar flashing. That damn DeMarco. He must have gotten her license plate number and put out an APB on her, and then the cameras in the tunnel must have captured the license plate.

"Ella Sue," she said out loud, "you are fucked."

Epilogue

The Jamaican girl, whose name turned out to be Abrianna Clarke, gave up Ella Fields to get a reduced sentence.

Justine Porter told Abrianna that she knew Fields had hired her to kill Rachel Quinn and that if she didn't agree to testify against Fields, Abrianna—who was on parole for an armed robbery conviction—would go back to Bedford Hills to serve out the remaining seven years of a ten-year sentence. On top of that, Justine promised that Abrianna would also be convicted for gun possession and attempted murder.

Abrianna agreed to testify against Fields in return for a four-year sentence.

Four years was a bargain for attempted murder—but Justine wanted Ella Fields more than she wanted Abrianna.

Now, with Abrianna willing to testify that Fields had paid her to kill a witness, Justine sat down with Edmundo Ortiz, Kathy Tolliver, and Jack Morris and did her best to scare the bejesus out of them. She said if they agreed to testify that Fields had bribed or blackmailed them to change their testimony against Toby Rosenthal, she'd give them immunity for any crimes they may have committed—such as lying to her when she questioned them. Lying to a police officer or an officer of the court is a felony called "obstruction of justice," Justine explained, and if they committed perjury during the Rosenthal trial, she was going to nail them for that as well.

She also told them she had subpoenaed their phone records—which she had—and would use them to make the case that they'd conspired with Fields. She said this even though she knew the phone records didn't really prove anything. It may have been illegal to lie to a prosecutor, but it was acceptable for a prosecutor to lie to a criminal.

Edmundo Ortiz and Kathy Tolliver eventually told Justine what Fields had done and agreed to testify against her. Edmundo said that Fields had threatened to turn his family over to immigration and then essentially bribed him with a new job. Kathy told how Fields had drugged her, then threatened to tell her ex-husband's parents that Kathy had overdosed on drugs, which could have resulted in Kathy losing her daughter. Neither Edmundo nor Kathy said anything about the cash Fields had given them.

Jack Morris, however, stuck to his story, saying no one bribed him or threatened him and that he was going to testify that he still wasn't sure Toby shot Dominic DiNunzio. Jack had grit.

***

Toby Rosenthal's first trial ended with a hung jury.

David Slade did a brilliant job convincing some of the jurors that even though three witnesses—Rachel Quinn, Kathy Tolliver, and Edmundo Ortiz—had identified Toby as the killer, they were mistaken. The lighting was bad, Slade said. The killer ran by the witnesses too fast, Slade said. And see, Slade said, how one witnesses, Jack Morris, was honest enough to admit that he couldn't be sure that Toby was the one. And some of the jurors bought the possibility that Dante Bello—who came across as a complete punk at the trial—could have been gunning for Carmine Fratello and shot Dominic DiNunzio by mistake. Carmine, in spite of all of Ella's worries, did a wonderful job testifying for the defense, pointing the finger at an outraged Dante Bello.

Toby's second trial, held six months after the first one, didn't go so well, because Dante Bello was dead and Carmine Fratello was in jail for killing him.

Carmine claimed killing Dante was a case of self-defense.

He said he came out of a bar one night—this was after Toby's first trial—and Dante took a couple of shots at him, but fortunately missed. Dante's motive was that Carmine had tried to frame him. Well, Carmine said, he couldn't live the rest of his life waiting around for that deranged little shit to kill him, so he killed Dante when the opportunity presented itself.

The police—and Carmine's lawyer—explained that self-defense didn't work that way. They said Carmine couldn't lie in wait for a guy walking his dog and come up behind him and shoot him in the back of the head because the guy had taken a shot at him two weeks earlier.

Faced with a first-degree murder charge, Carmine told the cops everything he knew about Ella Fields: how she'd paid him to lie at Toby's first trial and how she came to him later to find a professional— the Jamaican girl—to kill Rachel Quinn. In return for his cooperation, he was allowed to plead guilty to murder two.

So Carmine wasn't a witness at Toby's second trial—but he would be one at Ella Fields' trial.

Edmundo Ortiz flew back to his home port, Seattle, after the first trial and went out to sea again as a cook on one of Shearson's fishing boats, but he returned for Toby's second trial. As far as Edmundo was concerned, he couldn't have asked for anything more. His daughter and her two kids were happy in Seattle, his daughter had been reunited with her husband thanks to the help of a coyote that Edmundo paid, and Edmundo had a job he loved and that paid very well. America was a wonderful country.

After he was found guilty at his second trial, Toby Rosenthal was sentenced to fifteen years in prison for the second-degree murder of Dominic DiNunzio. He would be eligible for parole in seven years. And it looked as if Toby would survive until he was paroled. He'd been taken under the protective wings of his new boyfriend, a very large Albanian doing twenty-five to life for a couple of murders he'd committed. The one thing Toby refused to do was give a reason for why he killed Dominic DiNunzio. Toby's new lawyer was appealing the verdict, and he didn't want Toby making a confession.

David Slade was convinced that he had an ulcer even though several doctors told him otherwise. All Slade knew was that he was in constant pain—stomach pains, chest pains—and suffered rashes of an indeterminate origin, all caused by the never-ending stress of not knowing if he'd be arrested. Everyone in the legal community in New York was certain that he had conspired with Ella Fields to suborn the witnesses in the Rosenthal case—but so far Fields hadn't pointed the finger at him. Fields had said only two words since she'd been arrested, and those two words were spoken at her arraignment: "Not guilty."

But in spite of the fact that Fields didn't give Slade up as an accomplice to everything she'd done, Slade's law firm gave him the boot. A vigorous defense was one thing, but colluding with a woman to kill a witness . . . Well, that just wouldn't do.

And Henry Rosenthal refused to pay Slade's fee.

Leah Abramson called DeMarco to tell him that her best friend had died.

Leah said, "Are they going to get that bitch for what she did to Esther?"

"No, Leah, they won't," DeMarco said. "But she's going to be convicted of a bunch of other crimes and spend a long, long time in jail."

John Mahoney met Connie DiNunzio at their son's grave at Mount St. Mary Cemetery in Queens, where Connie knelt and placed a bouquet of flowers near the headstone. Mahoney had to help her to feet, and then they took a seat on a stone bench that had an engraving of an angel and the name of a little girl who'd died when she was only six months old.

Connie looked terrible, Mahoney thought. Grief had bent her back and added a decade to her face. He knew she'd never get over the loss of her son.

"He was a good man," Connie said. "It's a shame that you never got to know him."

"I know," Mahoney said, "and I'll go to my grave regretting that."

Mahoney asked if Dominic's wife and kids were going to be okay financially, and Connie said they would be. Dominic had a big life insurance policy—he'd always been worried about having a heart attack because he was overweight—and his family would be fine. Plus Connie had money, and she planned to leave it all to her grandchildren when she passed.

They didn't really have much else to say to each other, and Connie said she had to go; she was having dinner that night with her grandsons. She rose from the bench with a grunt and started to walk slowly toward her car on her swollen ankles, then turned and said, "I look back on my life, and the only thing I was ever truly ashamed of was having that fling with you, knowing that you were a married man. I don't regret having Dominic—I'll never regret that—but I do regret ever having met you. I don't ever want to see you again, John."

Mahoney watched her walk away, then took a flask out of his jacket pocket and sat there on the angel bench and sipped Jameson whiskey until the light faded from the sky.

—◆◆◆—

Ella Fields was at the Rose M. Singer Center at Rikers Island awaiting her trial.

When the cops pulled Ella over in the Lincoln Tunnel, Justine had told them to hold her as a material witness in the attempted killing of Rachel Quinn until she could figure out another charge. Then the cops found the .38 in Ella's purse and she was charged with possessing an unlicensed firearm. Then they found identity documents, including a passport, in the name of Carol Owen and she was charged with carrying a fake ID.

After Justine got the Jamaican girl to agree to testify against Ella, an attempted-murder charge was added to Ella's indictment. And after Kathy Tolliver and Edmundo Ortiz agreed to testify that she'd attempted to get them to change their testimony through coercion, witness tampering charges were added.

At Ella's arraignment, Justine was like an avenging angel, and Ella was not granted bail. Justine argued that the court couldn't grant bail to a woman with no fixed address and potential access to an unknown quantity of money. Justine also pointed out that a woman with false-identity documents clearly had the resources to flee the country if so inclined. The judge agreed with her.

So off to Rikers Island Ella went to await her trial—but Ella wasn't finished.

Ella had a plan.

DeMarco was worried, really worried.

He'd just sliced the ball so badly it ended up in the adjacent fairway.

His hip was fine now. The bone had healed completely, he didn't need the cane, and his leg didn't ache a bit. But ever since the injury, he'd been slicing the ball on almost every drive. He was convinced that his mended hip had something to do with his problem, although he couldn't understand why or how. He desperately needed professional help.

As he walked over to try to find his ball, he thought briefly about Ella Fields, wondering when they were ever going to get around to trying her. He wanted to be there when they sentenced her to years in prison. DeMarco didn't know her backstory, but the woman was clearly a sociopath and she belonged in a cage. He was proud that he'd been instrumental in making sure she ended up in one.

The first thing Ella did after she was arraigned was call George Chavez from a monitored phone in Rikers. She said, "I want to see you. Get your ass out here now."

George was bright enough to know that he didn't want to piss Ella off, so he flew to New York.

Without any preamble, Ella told George that what he was going to do was find somebody that could do what she and Bill used to do. "If you don't," she said, "I'm going to rat you out."

Two months later, Ella met with a young guy in his thirties named Michael. He was good-looking, very confident, very smooth—and she liked him immediately. He didn't look at all like Bill, but he reminded her of him. She explained to Michael that she couldn't do anything about the weapons charge and the false-ID charge, and she'd have to serve time for those crimes. But she wasn't going to serve time for attempted murder or for witness tampering, which provided the motive for the attempted murder.

"There are four witnesses who can testify against me," Ella said. "Kathy Tolliver and Edmundo Ortiz, for bribery and blackmail and God knows what else. Then there's the Jamaican girl and Carmine Fratello, who are serving time in two separate prisons."

"Bad things can happen to people in prison," Michael said.

Ella smiled. "Exactly," she said. "So do what you gotta do, and after I'm out of this mess, well, maybe you and I can work together."

Regarding Ella's lawyer, another smart young guy, Ella had met with him only a couple of times. During their first meeting, she'd said, "Your primary job at this point is to delay my trial as long as possible."

There was one other loose end that Ella would deal with once she was out of prison. She hadn't decided yet what she'd do—but she'd definitely do something.

The loose end was DeMarco.

Acknowledgments

The idea for this book came when I was listening to the radio one day, probably on my way to the golf course, and heard about some case where a guy was being tried for killing someone four years after he was arrested. Four years! A little research showed that two or three years between the arrest and the trial wasn't at all unusual. My first thought was: *Why should it take so long?* My second thought was: *Man, I'll bet all kinds of things can go wrong if it takes that long before the trial is held.* Well, my third thought was: *What if somebody made it his—or her—job to make sure things go wrong before the trial?* And thus *House Witness.*

I particularly want to thank attorney Stephen Bean and judge James Donohue for taking the time to answer a host of legal questions I had when writing this novel. When it comes to matters of law, however, any errors in this book are mine alone—and in some cases I decided to take a wee bit of literary license when it came to the law for the sake of the plot.

I also want to thank Grove Atlantic for being willing to publish the twelfth Joe DeMarco book. In particular, I want to thank Morgan Entrekin, publisher of Grove Atlantic, for taking the time to personally read and comment on this book; and my editor, Allison Malecha. This is the first time Allison and I have worked on a book together and it was a pleasure. Also, I want to thank copyeditor Tom Cherwin and Managing Editor Julia Berner-Tobin for their excellent work on this book.

Read on for an excerpt from Mike Lawson's next Joe DeMarco thriller, *House Arrest*.

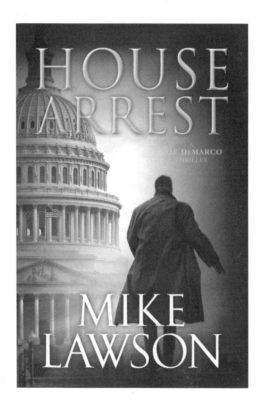

Available in hardcover and ebook.

1

The killer knew the location of every surveillance camera in the Capitol.

He was dressed in a dark blue uniform: a blue baseball cap, a dark blue short-sleeved shirt, and matching pants with cargo pockets. An equipment belt held a holstered .40-caliber Glock, zip ties that could be used as handcuffs, an extendable metal baton, and a canister of pepper spray. On his feet were black combat boots. On his hands were thin, black leather gloves.

The rotunda was dimly lit because of the hour, and as the killer walked he followed a route he'd practiced many times, staying against the walls, taking advantage of shadows. Nonetheless, three cameras captured his image, but as he passed into camera range he would turn his head, placing his big hands over his face, the bill of the baseball cap further obscuring his features. The cameras, however, did record a blue-and-white insignia patch on his right sleeve.

He ascended a marble staircase, and on the third floor he again kept his head lowered, so the bill of the cap and his hands blocked his face from a hallway camera. Once he was past the camera, he quickened his pace until he reached the main door to the politician's suite of offices. Before he opened the door, he unholstered the Glock, pulled a silencer from a pocket, and screwed the silencer into the barrel of the weapon.

The door was not locked. The politician most likely locked it when he left for the day, but there was no reason to lock it when he was there. What did he have to fear? He was in one of the most well-protected buildings in the United States.

The killer walked into the suite, holding the gun down at the side of his leg. He passed several small offices and desks in open areas where secretaries, aides, and interns usually sat. Because of the hour, he'd been hoping the politician's staff had left for the day; most of them usually left by seven or eight, unless there was something extraordinary going on. If any of them hadn't left, he'd have been forced to kill them too, which he really didn't want to do.

The politician he'd come to kill was seated behind the desk in his office. There were a Virginia state flag and an American flag in floor stands behind the desk, photographs of party leaders on the wall, and on his desk, a photo of his late wife. A smiling portrait of the fool who was now president was prominently displayed.

The politician wore a white shirt, the sleeves rolled up, and a blue-and-red-striped tie loosened at the collar. He was holding a phone to his right ear, and the killer heard him say, "Kathy, if you don't get on board with this—"

At that moment the politician saw the killer standing in the doorway but didn't see the gun he was holding next to one leg. He was puzzled by the appearance of the killer, wondering why he had come to his office, but he wasn't concerned or alarmed. Why would he be concerned? The U.S. Capitol Police were there to protect him.

He said into the phone, "Kathy, hang on a minute." Cupping his hand over the phone, he said, "Can I help you, Officer?"

The killer raised his weapon, pointed it at the man's chest, and whispered, "Tell her you'll have to call her back."

"What?"

"You heard me. Do it, or I'll shoot you."

Eyes expanding with fear, the politician said into the phone, "Kathy, I'll have to call you back," and disconnected the call—and the killer shot him in the heart.

The politician slumped back in his chair, dropping the phone on the carpeted floor, and the killer shot him a second time, in the forehead. Blood splattered the wall behind the desk, creating an interesting Rorschach pattern. The politician fell forward after the second shot and ended up, still seated, with his head resting on the blotter on his desk. The blotter slowly turned from green to dark red as the pooling blood from the forehead wound formed a halo around the dead man's head.

The killer didn't bother to pick up the two shell casings ejected from the Glock. He could have, but he didn't. He wasn't worried about leaving evidence behind. He removed the silencer from the gun, put it back in his pocket, and holstered the Glock. He then made his way back through the maze of staff offices, and when he left the suite, he locked the door behind him. If anyone came to see the politician tonight— though it was unlikely, considering the hour—they'd think that he had gone home for the day. His body shouldn't be discovered until the next morning, when his secretary, who was always the first to arrive, came to work. In fact, given that this was a Friday night, it might not be discovered until Monday.

The killer walked down the stairs to the rotunda level, again always mindful of the cameras, then took another staircase to reach the subbasement of the Capitol. In the subbasement, he unlocked a door marked with the letter E and a series of numbers. The room he entered was a small closet, and inside it was a gray metal cabinet containing electrical equipment. On the floor of the closet was a gym bag he'd placed there hours ago.

Now he would wait an hour and hope that was enough time.

The waiting didn't bother the killer; he'd spent a lifetime standing around waiting.

The hour passed, and he took out his cell phone and made a call. He let the phone he was calling ring five times but hung up before an answering machine could pick up.

He left the electrical equipment closet, taking the gym bag with him, and walked down the hall to an office that had the words *Counsel Pro Tem for Liaison Affairs* written in flaking gold paint on the frosted-glass window of the mahogany-stained door. The phone the killer had called before he left the closet belonged to the man who occupied the office, and he'd called to verify that the man was no longer there.

He unlocked the door with a key he'd had made a month ago. The office was small and practically barren. There was an old and battered wooden desk, a wooden chair behind the desk that could swivel and tilt backward, and another, plain wooden chair—a visitor's chair—in front of the desk. On the desk was a phone connected to an answering machine and a laptop computer. The only other items in the room were a four-drawer gray metal file cabinet and a coatrack near the door. Hanging on the coatrack were a tan London Fog trench coat and a battered L. L. Bean Scottish-tweed rain hat.

The killer didn't turn on the lights in the office. Moving quickly, he removed his equipment belt and stripped down to his underwear; he didn't remove the gloves he was wearing or the ball cap. He took his cell phone out of a pocket and placed it in the gym bag. He left the silencer in the pocket of the pants he'd been wearing. Now, attired in only his ball cap, his underwear, black socks, and thin black gloves, he removed a flashlight from the gym bag, one small enough to hold between his teeth. He also removed a screwdriver.

The killer took the visitor's chair and placed it beneath a ventilation grille in the ceiling. He unscrewed the four screws holding the grille in place, set the grille on the floor, and put the pants, shirt, boots, and equipment belt holding the Glock he'd used inside the ventilation duct. Before he placed the boots in the duct, he removed inserts that

4

had made him an inch taller. He didn't, however, put in the ball cap he was wearing. He left the cap on his head.

Next, he removed the black leather gloves and put them on the desk, and from the gym bag he took latex gloves, the kind surgeons wear. He donned the latex gloves and pulled from the gym bag a baseball cap identical to the one he was wearing. He made sure the two long, dark hairs he'd placed inside the cap were still there, and then put the ball cap and the leather gloves inside the ventilation duct and screwed the grille back into place. After he finished inserting the screws, he used the screwdriver to scratch the ventilation grille, making bright white marks in the metal, as if the screwdriver had slipped several times while he was threading in the fasteners.

He put the visitor's chair back where it had been originally and placed the screwdriver inside the center drawer of the desk. He removed his own clothes and boots from the gym bag next—clothes that appeared to be identical to those he'd been wearing—and got dressed. He also put on an equipment belt that was in the gym bag; the belt too appeared to be identical to the one he'd placed in the ventilation duct and included a holstered .40-caliber Glock. After he was dressed, he stood without moving for about sixty seconds, mentally reviewing everything he'd done, trying to think of anything he'd forgotten. He decided he was good; the entire operation had gone precisely as planned. He was pleased—and frankly somewhat surprised—that he was so calm.

The killer had never killed before.

He opened the office door and peeked down the hall. It was empty, as he'd expected at eleven thirty at night. He walked back to the electrical closet, holding the now mostly empty gym bag, and stepped back inside. Then he realized he *had* forgotten something and laughed out loud. He took off his cap, removed the wig from his bald head, and placed the wig in the gym bag. That would have been a hell of a mistake, if someone had spotted him with a full head of hair.

Now he had hours to wait, but that was okay. It'd give him plenty of time to think of the things he could do with the money he'd earned.

———◆———

The dead politician was discovered by his secretary at seven o'clock the following morning.

The politician's name was Lyle Canton. He was the House majority whip.

His killer was arrested thirty-eight hours later.

2

The J. Edgar Hoover Building, headquarters for the Federal Bureau of Investigation, is less than a mile from the U.S. Capitol. Ten minutes after the body of Congressman Lyle Canton was found, six FBI agents arrived in a black Chevy Suburban SUV, blue and red grille lights flashing. While the agent in charge went to look at the body and take over control of the crime scene from the Capitol Police, another agent commandeered a conference room that would be used as a temporary command center.

The Capitol had been locked down by the Capitol Police before the FBI arrived, but now an announcement was made telling everyone who wasn't law enforcement to gather in the rotunda. It was still early morning, and a Saturday, but there were about twenty civilians in the building. The Capitol Police checked each person's credentials, patted him or her down for weapons, and searched all backpacks and purses. Then all twenty people were moved into a conference room and told they'd have to remain there until they were interviewed by the FBI. One of the people turned out to be the chief of staff of the Senate majority leader. He was dressed in casual clothes and had stopped by the Capitol only to pick up something from his office on the way to his daughter's soccer game. He told the Capitol cops who his boss was and demanded to be released immediately. An unimpressed cop, not adequately trained on how to address his betters, told him to sit down and shut up.

More Capitol Police were called in—over a hundred of them—to assist the FBI in searching the building and to make sure no one was lurking in a closet with an AR-15. As the Capitol has about six hundred rooms, it took several hours to complete the search.

At the time, it never occurred to the FBI that the killer could be a Capitol cop.

By noon there were over forty FBI agents and crime-scene technicians at the Capitol, all of them wearing blue windbreakers with *FBI* on the back in yellow letters. The Speaker of the House and the Senate majority leader had been informed that no business would be conducted in the Capitol for the rest of the weekend—not that much business was ever conducted there anyway, even during the workweek.

The agent in charge of the investigation was a man named Russell Peyton, a twenty-five-year veteran of the bureau. J. Edgar Hoover may have been a pudgy cross-dresser, but Peyton was the type of agent Hoover had almost always hired: tall, slim, white, male, Protestant, and married. At the age of fifty-two, Peyton was in better shape than most men half his age because, unless a case prevented him from doing so, he jogged five miles every day. He suspected that with this case he wouldn't be jogging—or for that matter sleeping much—until the killer was apprehended.

The director of the FBI had told Peyton, "I'll need updates every four hours because the president told me he wants updates every four hours."

The FBI director was a man named Ronald Erby. He'd been in charge of the bureau for only a few months, since the president had fired his predecessor for reasons that people were now writing books about.

Erby was a lawyer who had spent some time in law enforcement prior to his appointment, but he was best known for his political acumen and his unwavering loyalty to the president—which was the main reason he was now the director.

Erby and Peyton both knew that the president had liked Lyle Canton—Canton had been a lapdog for the president during his campaign—but a lot of Republicans didn't care for Canton because of his abrasive personality. As for the Democrats, it would be literally impossible to find a Democrat inside the Beltway who didn't despise the man. Nonetheless, and regardless of Canton's popularity—or lack thereof—it was unacceptable to have one of the leaders of the Republican Party assassinated. At noon the president was going to stand in the Rose Garden and make a speech praising Canton for his service to the nation and promise that everything that could be done would be done to bring his killer to justice—and Director Erby wanted some answers by then.

Based on the last call Canton had made—to Texas congresswoman Kathy Thomas—and the time of death as estimated by the FBI's pathologist, Peyton knew the congressman had been killed sometime between 10:13 p.m. on Friday and approximately 4:00 the following morning. Peyton's agents went to work compiling a list of everyone who had been in the Capitol during those hours. They interviewed the Capitol cops who'd been on duty and started looking at video footage obtained from the many cameras in and around the building. An elite team of crime-scene technicians dusted Canton's office for fingerprints, took photos, and vacuumed carpets for trace evidence. The two shell casings found in Canton's office were the first pieces of evidence they bagged.

Peyton learned Lyle Canton had a reputation for working long hours, but the specific reason he'd been in his office at ten o'clock on a Friday night was that he'd been doing his job: whipping up support for a bill that would go to the floor for a vote in a week—a bill that many Republicans didn't like. In other words, Canton had been twisting the arms of reluctant Republicans like Congresswoman Thomas to make sure they didn't stray from the herd.

About four hours after the body had been found, Peyton held a meeting in the commandeered conference room with four of his senior agents. Peyton had been getting periodic updates, but he wanted his senior people to have the whole picture and to make sure he had the latest news, so he could brief his boss and his boss could brief the president.

"Jack, you go first," Peyton said to one of the agents.

Jack said, "The big thing is, we're ninety-nine percent certain we've got the killer on video. He's either a Capitol cop or somebody disguised as one. But we don't have a clear image of his face."

One of the other agents said, "You're shittin' me. That means the shooter could still be in the building. He could have—"

Peyton held up a hand for silence and said, "Go on, Jack."

Jack went on. "This guy knew where every camera was, and he kept his head turned away or placed his hands over his face when he was in camera range. And he was wearing gloves, which is another reason we're pretty sure he's the killer. Why would a guy be wearing gloves this time of year?" It was late June. "Anyway, we can see him on a camera walking up the stairs leading to Canton's office. About two minutes before Canton made his last phone call, which he made at ten thirteen p.m., we got him walking down the hall toward Canton's office. Three minutes after Canton's last call, he walked back up the hall. This means that Canton was most likely killed at about ten fifteen. We can tell from the video footage that the killer is white, about five eleven, and weighs around one eighty. The techs will get us more precise measurements. He's wearing one of those ball caps the guards here wear, but you can see he has dark hair. He doesn't have a limp or anything else that's distinctive about the way he moves."

"How many people were in the building when Canton was killed?" Peyton asked.

"Forty-three," Jack said.

"That's all?" Peyton said.

"It was a Friday night, and with the weekend coming there just weren't that many folks working late. At the time of the killing there were twenty-four cops guarding the entrances and patrolling the grounds. There were four aides in various offices researching sh-, stuff for their bosses. There was an IT guy trying to fix a computer, eight janitors who were on the Senate side vacuuming and cleaning toilets, two gals making copies of some bill that was about five thousand pages long, and one guy trying to fix the sound system in one of the hearing rooms."

Jack paused and smiled slightly. "In addition to all those folks, the House minority whip, Conrad English, was in his office with a twenty-two-year-old intern who works for a congresswoman. They were just a few doors away from Canton's office but didn't see or hear anything. One of the Capitol cops said there's a rumor going around that English, who's married, and the intern spend a *lot* of late nights together and probably didn't hear anything because—"

Peyton said, "I don't want to hear any nonsense like that unless it bears on the murder."

"Yes, sir," Jack said. "Last, there was a lawyer down in the subbasement, some guy named DeMarco. He got here at nine forty-five and left about fifty minutes later. So that's a total of forty-three people. And even though we now know the killing happened about ten fifteen, we're interviewing everyone who was in the building between eight p.m. and seven this morning. So far no one has reported seeing anything useful, like a Capitol cop walking around wearing gloves."

"How do you know who was here during those hours?" Peyton asked.

"During normal working hours, people who have the right badge can just walk in and out of the building. They have to pass through the metal detectors and go past the guards, of course, but they're not logged in and out. For some reason—maybe just to keep the guards awake—after eight p.m. everybody going in and out, even if they have the right ID, is logged. We haven't finished looking at the cameras near the entrances yet, but we will, then we'll confirm that everybody who entered after eight is on the log."

Peyton said, "We need to know exactly where every security guard was at about ten."

Jack said, "I realize that, boss. We're building a matrix showing everyone's location at that time, then confirming their locations through interviews and video footage."

Two hours later, Jack came back to Peyton and said, "We've got something interesting. As you know, the shooter was wearing what appears to be a Capitol cop's uniform, but we took a close look at the patch on his right sleeve. It's not an exact duplicate of the insignia patch the Capitol Police wear. I mean, it's the correct colors—blue and white—shows the Capitol building, and has 1828 on it, but—"

"What's the 1828 mean?" Peyton asked.

"That's the year the Capitol Police were founded. Anyway, the image of the Capitol and the oak-leaf cluster on the patch are slightly different in a number of small ways. What I'm saying is, the patch appears to be a fake the shooter had made, but it's not an exact duplicate of a real insignia patch. We're getting the names of companies that could have made the patch, but it's going to be a long list and will include companies in China, Vietnam, and Bangladesh. As for the uniform the guy was wearing—blue shirt, dark blue cargo pants—you can buy those clothes anywhere. Same with the stuff on the equipment belt, the zip ties, the baton, the Mace. You can buy all that commercially and online. But if we can find the shirt with the patch on it, that'll be a significant piece of evidence."

Peyton called Ronald Erby and gave the director another update.

"I've told the head of the Capitol Police that I want all his people polygraphed," Peyton said.

"Can he do that?" Erby asked. "I mean, without his cops raising a stink and getting union reps and lawyers involved?"

"Yeah. His people agree to periodic polygraph testing as well as drug testing when they sign on. And naturally anyone who refuses becomes an instant suspect. I've also told him I want to see the personnel files on all his cops, including ID photos."

"How many people does he have?" the director asked.

"About thirteen hundred, but we'll immediately weed out anyone who's not white or male or who doesn't meet the physical description of the killer. But I seriously doubt it was a Capitol cop who killed Canton. For one thing, a cop wouldn't have to make a fake insignia patch for his shirt.

"I also don't think this was terrorist-related, and we should tell this to the media at the next press conference, just to calm everyone down. A terrorist most likely would have killed several people, not just one guy, and some organization would have taken credit for the killing. It's also hard to imagine that some politician did this. I mean, the Democrats hated Canton, but I can't imagine a politician actually murdering him."

"Yeah, but the man went out of his way to make enemies," the director said.

What the director meant was that Canton was the designated hatchet man for the Republican majority in the House. The Republican Speaker of the House wished to be viewed as a reasonable man who could work with those on the other side of the aisle and he tried his best not to poke the Democrats too rudely in the eye with a sharp stick. He left that job to Lyle Canton. Canton was the one who made brash statements to the media castigating the Democrats for their opposition to every Republican-sponsored bill. And Canton didn't choose his words carefully when he accused Democratic Party leaders of being responsible for every malady affecting the country. So the Democrats hated the man, particularly the Democratic minority leader, John Mahoney, who was usually Canton's primary target.

"The last time I can think of that one American politician shot another," Peyton told the director, "was when Burr killed Hamilton. These guys assassinate people with money and lies, not bullets. A more likely possibility is that some nut could have taken offense at something Canton was doing—like maybe this bill he was working on last night—but this doesn't feel like a nut to me. A nut would have walked up to Canton at some event and started spraying bullets, like the guy who shot Giffords."

He meant Congresswoman Gabrielle Giffords, who had been shot in the head in an assassination attempt near Tucson in 2011. In addition to Giffords, twelve other people had been wounded, and six were killed.

"This was planned well in advance," Peyton told Erby. "The shooter got a uniform, made up his own Capitol Police insignia patch, and he knew where every camera was on the route to Canton's office. He had to have spent days, if not weeks, planning this, so this was done by someone who spent a lot of time in the building."

"Like a Capitol cop," Erby said.

"But if it was a Capitol cop," Peyton countered, "why make a fake patch?"

Peyton continued. "I think this was personal, and not politically motivated. Canton was an abrasive asshole, and I suspect he stepped on a lot of people to get to where he is today. Maybe he destroyed someone's reputation. Maybe he crushed someone's career. We're going to have to take a hard look at his personal life and his past to find people who had some reason to kill him."

"I assume you're going through all his hate mail," the director said.

"Yeah, everything he got in the last year," Peyton said. "The Secret Service had already investigated the people who sent them before he was killed, and they didn't see any serious threats, but we're going back over everything. So far no one has popped out that looks promising, but we're still digging."

"You seem to be ignoring the most obvious suspect, Russ," the director said.

"I'm not ignoring him, boss," Peyton said. "I just haven't figured out what I'm going to do about him."

"Do you know where Sebastian Spear was when this happened?"

"Yeah. He was in China, and he's still there. According to his PR person, he's been there almost a week at a conference that was scheduled two months ago. But that means nothing. With his money, Spear could have hired the best pro in the business, and if everything that's been written about him and Canton is true, he had a better motive than anyone I can think of for killing Canton."

"You're going to have to tread carefully with Spear," the director said. "The guy's a politically connected billionaire."

"I know," Peyton said. "And right now I don't have anything to justify getting a warrant to look at his finances or his phone records or anything else. I could go to China to question to him but I think that would be a complete waste of time unless I can find something that actually ties him to Canton's death."

"So what are you going to do?" the director asked.

"I'm going to talk to the reporter who broke the story about Spear's affair with Canton's wife. She seems to know more about it than anyone else."